Romance • Adventure • History • War
ALBERT ZYGIER
Not for Women Only
Short Stories for a Lazy Day
I0847082

ALBERT ZYGIER

Not for Women Only

Short Stories for a Lazy Day

ARPress
45 Dan Road Suite 15
Canton, MA 02021
Hotline: 1(888) 821-0229
Fax: 1(508) 545-7580

Ordering Information:
Quantity sales. Special discounts are available on quantity purchases by corporations,associations, and others. For details, contact the publisher at the address above.

Printed in the United States of America.

ISBN-13:   Softcover   979-8-89676-415-1
               eBook   979-8-89676-416-8

Library of Congress Control Number: 2025909592

This book is dedicated to my parents Rubin and Phillis Zygier, my wife Ellen, my daughter Roni, my granddaughter Annie- who one day will be a Broadway Star, and to all the rest of my family. I want to thank my teachers that encouraged me to get to where I am today: Diana Shaman, Diane O'Connell, Leslie Shipman, and Marty Correia, and of course, my many writing group friends that read my stories and gave me their support.

TABLE OF CONTENTS

One: I, Miranda

Sandy, a good friend of mine that works as a producer in one of the TV networks that I am associated with, invited me to a Fourth of July party in East Hampton at the home of her aunt and uncle, a mogul in the real estate business. Everybody who is anybody will be there. She said. As it happened, I had just come back from an assignment in the Middle East, and after weeks of traveling from one country to another, I was worn out. So, I accepted. Who knows, perhaps I might find an interesting story just waiting for me there.

My name is Miranda Hathaway, I'm a correspondent, author, and contributor to many TV Networks. I'm about as tough and opinionated as anyone can be. I'm the youngest sibling out of six and also the only female. Growing up with five brothers made me tough and unlike Sandy's family, mine comes from the blue-collar side, but I don't hold that against her.

I don't dislike rich people; I want to be rich myself. Who doesn't? It's the way they became rich that bothers me. I'm thirty-six years old and have been married once, about ten years ago. I try to forget that part. I was young and silly. Don't think I hate men because of that. I date on occasion when I have the time and there is somewhere interesting to go or see, but in general men are the least important part of my life. At least for now. I'm just too busy.

There's more of course, but I don't want to bore you with my accomplishments except for one more. I truly am a pretty good-looking woman and yes, it's true that because of that, and I hate to admit it, I probably got ahead faster than many others, but I don't want anyone ever to call me out on that. One way or the other I would have wound up on top!

So, the Friday before, I stayed at Sandy's apartment, for she had a car and lived in Queens, closer toward the Hamptons. We had fun staying up late and drinking wine while watching one of our favorite movies on TV. Casablanca. We've seen this movie so many times we mimicked the dialog along with the characters from memory. How can anyone forget, "Play it again Sam…"

We drove early to miss the Hamptons traffic and checked into our B&B, unpacked and went shopping. We certainly didn't bring some old beach clothes with us, this was after all, a ritzy party so after a bowl of cereal and a cup of decaf, off we went to Main Street to check out their boutiques. Well, if you can't get some nice vacation outfits there, where can you?

I got myself a little champaign colored, Vera Wang dress that is just barely legal, even in South Hampton, and Sandy followed me with a different color. We didn't want to stand out too much. It would be a "visually impaired" person that wouldn't give us a second look. We arrived a bit late, partly because it took us some time to shower, makeup and dress and partly because it was the thing to do.

It wasn't too large a party, maybe forty-fifty people, the glitterati of the summer social season, artists, writers, bankers, ambulance chasers, real east agents, etc. I knew many of them by name. Many I knew didn't like me because of my exposés, but they were polite, at least to my face, including her aunt and uncle. Her uncle I really plastered a few years ago about his real estate dealings. I had no idea he was her uncle or I wouldn't have come but now that I was there I wasn't going to run and miss all the fun. I didn't think Sandy even knew about my articles, I met her afterward and didn't connect that she was related to him.

Their home would match anything the old robber barons had in Newport, Rhode Island. Well, what would you expects from a real estate mogul? We said hello to Sandy's parents. Nice people. Her father and mother, both lawyers working in a sidewalk office helping the poor. They seemed a bit out of place here. It was her mother's sister that made it big marrying the grand fromage.

In any case, I came to enjoy myself and maybe pick up something newsworthy along the way. It's true, I take a more liberal point of view of politics and business, but not enough to lean too far to the left. Like Socrates, I am the gadfly of the mighty and powerful. Anyway, it was a beautiful sunny day. A few cumulus clouds floating lazily under an azure sky. Contrails from planes on the way to Europe from JFK pointed eastward, like some giant white plumes of smoke.

Crystal glasses filled with French wine and champagne were passed around like water. Martinis and gin and tonics floated on waiters' trays like well-drilled military teams. Hors d'oeuvre like you would only see at upper class social affairs brought by young waitresses to the crowd that ate them up as if they hadn't been fed since last Sunday. They tasted as delicious as they looked. I helped myself to as many as fit on my napkin. No fool I.

Peace was in the air. Sandy left me for a while to be with her parents, so I went about greeting people that still liked me, there were a few. Even the ones that didn't, pretended they did. I was a star after all. Well, I respected that. I don't mind people that stand up for themselves no matter how wrong they are.

I mean, I didn't arbitrarily insult them, I just pointed out what I thought were their deficiencies, like overcharging rents from the working classes. All in all, I was enjoying myself. I saw men, and women give me look overs in my little dress. It helps to be well dressed and hold yourself up as if you were important as long as you don't make an ass of yourself. Be kind to dogs and children and the impecunious, (look that up), was my motto.

It was then that I saw him. A tall man. Probably six feet or so. Well-dressed in a pale blue Italian suit with an open collar and a blue ascot around his neck. He held a glass with a clear liquid that could be gin or water or even vodka but I didn't see him drink anything in the past few minutes that I observed him.

He was talking to two men, one a senator from New York, the other a publisher I knew quite well. I stood about ten feet away and occasionally I saw that man looking my way and give me that smoky smile. I am not that kind of woman that is fascinated only by a handsome face, so I turned a bit to the right and just looked at him from the reflection on my glass. I didn't want to be obvious.

I was surprised that I didn't think I ever met him though for some reason I thought that I have seen him before somewhere. It certainly couldn't have been recently for a face like that I don't think I would have forgotten. Maybe he had some small role in a film or video. Anyway, what did I care?

I finally turned to leave and as I turned, there he was, standing right in my way. He quickly apologized for startling me. "I'm terribly sorry," he said, "but I thought I recognized you. We actually never met in person but I know who you are. Miranda Hathaway. Right?"

Well, thought I, who wouldn't recognize Miranda Hathaway? He then introduced himself as Richard Porter, which at first didn't strike me at all. But as long as he introduced himself I might as well be polite.

"So, nice to meet you, Mr. Richard Porter," I said, what else would I do? And then it hit me, Richard Porter once wrote me a scalding letter in answer to one of my major articles on Defense Department spending. He

took me point by point and insinuated I had no idea what I was talking about and that I either do my research or perhaps devote my writing to fairy tales.

It was the most scathing and well-written letter I have ever received from a reader. I didn't answer off course because I had no real comeback then, so I just filed it and then forgot about it. That was, what? A few years ago? "Well, what are you two up to?" Sandy's voice suddenly popped in. "So you've met Richard, I see."

She added. "Richard and I actually slept together once…" and then stopped with a pregnant pause, "…when we were, what, four years old?" Her eyes twinkled as she said that. "We're distant cousins that used to be close but his was from a military family, so they never stayed in one place for long. We haven't seen each other in quite a while. Right Richy?" This she asked Richard as he still stared at me. "Isn't he one handsome man? If we weren't related I wouldn't let any other woman touch him."

It was obvious they were close at some point in time or, or she wouldn't be so familiar with him and then Richard bent down, as he was at least a head taller and kissed Sandy on her cheek while starring again, straight at me. Well, if he wants to make me jealous he is barking up the wrong tree.

"Oh, I see my mother calling me again. Excuse me…" Sandy said as she quickly turned and ran away leaving me with her dear ol' cousin. I turned and followed her with my eyes and didn't see a hair of her mother. Some friend she turned out to be. Did she think to set me up with this handsome man? Good luck!

"Why don't we have a drink?" Mister cousin said to me. I think my last drink was spiked because I answered, sure, instead of buzz off. A waiter passed, and he grabbed two glasses of something and prod me away from the crowd. "I wrote you a comment on an article you wrote some years ago and I never heard from you since. It was a bit harsh but you really should have done your research before you wrote it."

"Really," I said rather stiffly. "Really," he mimicked. "You should have gotten the figures from the DOD. By the way, where did you get them? Some opposition congressman I bet." "And where do you get your figures? You have an in from some congressional committee?" I retorted. He ignored me and went to complain about some other of my articles.

"You know, you're a bitchy person. All you do is complain about everything. You see no light anywhere. We shouldn't be doing this. We shouldn't be doing that. So what should we be doing? You never give us the benefit of your great expertise. You think the world should be holding hands and sing Kumbaya and then all will be well. Things just don't work that way. There was strife since we started to walk on two feet and there always will be..."

"Okay, I had enough of your bitching about my bitching. Who the hell are you anyway? All I know about you is that you slept with my friend when you both were four years old. This doesn't give you permission to..." And then I just had to laugh. Why am I arguing with a man I just met? What do I care what he thinks anyway?

I said goodbye or something like that and started to walk away. "I don't need this..."

"Oh," he said, "you can dish it out, but you can't take it?" Okay, that got my hackles up. "Do you work for the government or something? Because I know a lot of people who work for the government and..."

"...and what? You'll get me fired? You know that most people are afraid of you. Most of the people at this gathering are afraid of you. Afraid that you'll write something about them that will get them in hot water..." "They have nothing to fear if they are honest with..." "Oh..., so you are the arbiter of honesty. Your columns are the epitome of truth in this world. You are the messenger from..."

I was thinking of slapping him right there and then, but I stopped myself just in time. "I guess no one has ever spoken to you like that. Have they?"

"Who are you? Who are you really, some reporter out of the blue? I have never heard of you before. Did someone send you to harass me?" Honestly, I was a bit shaken. At first, I thought he was going to give me some line? So how did we get to this? Sure, I gave these people a hard time but I did it for a good cause. I want to expose them for what they are…

I was going to slap him again as I saw he was smiling that devilish smile of his. "What? Really, who are you? Mr. smarty pants? Have I been set up for a candid camera or something? Are you setting me up for a prank? It certainly isn't April Fools' Day yet."

"You are really beautiful when you're angry…" He started to say and at that comment, I did raise my hand to slap him. No one calls me beautiful and gets away with that. But Mister Porter reacted like a flash of lightning and caught my hand a few inches from his face.

He let it go and stepped back. "I'm sorry, I should not have said that. You are definitely not beautiful. In fact, far from it and I apologize." There was an old tree a few feet away, and he guided me behind it. At first, I thought he was going to hit me but then his eyes turned to mush.

"I admit, at first I was angry when I saw you. That article was not called for the way you wrote it. Let me finish. I just want to know; did you research it yourself or did you get this from some member of Congress?"

I didn't answer at first… "It's a simple question," he said. It was a simple question without a simple answer. It was also many years ago. But I did remember. It was Congressman Norman Sullivan that came to me with a large envelope and asked me to look it over and see if there was a story to it. With what I had there, it certainly was. Never in my thoughts did I think a congressman would put something over me. If, he actually did.

"I will review the story when I get back. Mr. Porter. How can I reach you?"

"Alright Ms. Hathaway, I will take your word for it." He handed me a card which I put away in my little cocktail bag. I haven't been so intimidated by anyone since a foreign correspondent had me trapped in an elevator at my first job.

After this encounter, I wasn't in the mood to stay at the party anymore. I saw Porter say goodbye to Sandy's parents and leave. I wonder if Porter knew I was coming and set me up. I'll have a little talk later with Sandy. When I found her, I told her I drank a bit too much and had a headache and was leaving, but she could stay as long as she wanted. The B&B wasn't too far away. I got to Main Street and found a coffee shop. I was overdressed for sure but I didn't care. Just let anyone start with me. Except for a couple of hors d'oeuvres, I haven't eaten anything since the cornflakes this morning, so I asked for an egg and cheese omelet and a cup of decaf when I heard a voice behind me.

"I hope you're not following me, Ms. Hathaway?"The line that struck me immediately was from Casablanca where Rick tells Sam, "Of all the gin joints in all the towns in all the world…" "Amazing that we should meet like that by chance and so soon… How did you find me?" I had to take a big breath because I didn't know what to answer. He wouldn't believe me anyway. "I followed your footprints." What else could I say?

We had a divider between us, so he asked if I would join him as his food was already on his table. I picked up my coffee cup and sat across from him and feeling like a fool. He smiled at me and I smiled at him till the waitress came with my eggs. "So, shall we call a truce while we eat?" "We can if you tell me honestly our little meeting wasn't a setup."

"Actually, it wasn't. I was here in South Hampton to rest up. I had just come back from a long tour outside the country and some friends invited me over for a week of sun and sand. Now that might sound strange as I just left a country full of sun and sand, but here at least no one was shooting at me. In any case, I met Sandy's parents, which by the way I haven't seen in at least ten-fifteen years, in a supermarket, and they invited me to the party."

"Now, I wouldn't have known you if we bumped each other in a dark alley at midnight but they pointed you out to me at the party by name as Sandy's friend. I have totally forgotten about that article as I had more important things on my mind the past few years, but then it hit me that you were the culprit that I was so pissed off at."

"Before that, though I usually don't do that, speaking to strange women I was not introduced to and you were so good looking in that cute little dress, ugh, I'm terribly sorry, I meant that you were so terribly looking in that ugly outfit.." How could you help to not at least smile…

"So, I said to myself, Rich, don't blow it. Ask her out and if you don't like her give her the business about that article later, but I did blow it. Didn't I? How are your eggs?" "You wanted to ask me out?" Yes, I asked that. He looked like a dream. "By the way, who are you really?" Richard had ordered pancakes and now he sliced a big piece off and smudged it in enough syrup to worry his doctor. "I guess you didn't look at my card."

I hadn't of course, so I said. "Do you want to tell me or do I need to stop eating and dig it out of my bag?"

"I am Lieutenant General Richard Porter, that's a three-star general which I'm sure you know. I commanded forces in a little mountain resort called Afghanistan, and I am back here for a tour in the Pentagon as, well, I shouldn't tell you, you might print it all over town."

"A three-star general you say?" I asked. Yes., three shiny little stars on my shoulders. Have you ever met a three star general in person?"

"Only once, but he was an old decrepit little man." If he thought he's going to impress me with those stars he has another thing coming. "You know, you really are an even more beautiful woman when you're sarcastic."

I kicked him under the table and thought of another line from Casablanca. "Louie, I think this is the beginning of a beautiful friendship."

Two: Sunglasses

Harry Baker was returning from his run through Central Park in New York. Still dressed in his running suit, he crossed Central Park West into 64th Street towards Broadway when he spotted a very attractive woman sitting by herself in an outdoor cafe. She was dressed in a yellow sundress and a large straw hat, and she wore a pair of large designer sunglasses he knew must have cost a week's pay of an executive secretary. He knew that because he was with his wife when she bought the same pair.

The woman must be an actress or model the way she carried herself, sitting so elegantly in that chair holding a drink with an umbrella in it. Harry himself was close to forty-five with an eighteen-year-old daughter that attended a prestigious school in Switzerland. Does he have the nerve to approach this woman? He asked himself. What would he say to her? He hadn't done anything like that since his marriage twenty-two years ago.

As he approached her closer, he saw her turn towards him and give him a sort of look over. Harry was tall, still slim with a stomach as flat as a washboard. He still had a full head of black hair that he had done only two days ago which cost him a hundred and twenty-five dollars with a tip.

While he was thinking what he should do, another man went over to the woman with apparently the same idea as he had in mind, but the woman turned him away and gave Harry a thin smile which gave him the confidence to walk over, but he wanted to impress her and so he stopped a few feet away and made a fake business call on his cell.

"All right then, make the deal for 38 million, and that's the final offer." He then hung up and removed his own sunglasses and gave her his practiced smile. "Ah, money, what would we do without it?" he said trying to impress her. "By the way, I couldn't help but notice your sunglasses, may I ask you where you bought them? I want to buy those for someone, but I have never seen this style anywhere around here."

The woman took her time while she took a sip of her drink. She then took off her glasses slowly, almost seductively, and looked at him with her auburn eyes that surprisingly had little make up on them, as if she didn't think she needed any, which in fact was true! "These glasses?" she asked lazily as she turned them in her hand. "I bought them in Rome this spring." "Rome?" Harry looked puzzled. "Oh, they don't sell them in New York?" He was now standing across what was a plastic separation of the cafe and the sidewalk. The woman looked Harry up and down as if he was some hick from Appalachia, "Well, I haven't seen them here either, but perhaps,

Tiffany would carry them. They carry very fashionable items."

Jack smiled, he saw the woman also smile and he guessed she was teasing him. "You realize that I can have you arrested right now…" he said solemnly. "Really, for what?" Still with that lazy look. "New York City Ordinance, CO-453-58."

"And that is?" she asked chewing on the earpiece of her expensive sunglasses. "Fabricating a story to a pedestrian on a sidewalk.""Oh, and you are a knowledgeable pedestrian? Perhaps a lawyer?" Harry didn't answer but came around the artificial separation and stood across from her. "May I join you and buy you another of what you're having, or are you waiting for an Arabian Prince to buy you another pair of those sunglasses?

She folded her glasses away and pointed to the empty chair with them. "You may if you like. It's expensive; I bought this drink …" "Yes,

I know, in Rome…" She had a great laugh, thought Harry, sort of like sparkling champaign. "I'm Harry…" Harry extended his hand.

"Natalia," she said shaking it. A waiter came by with a menu.

"Would you care to order, Sir?" "Bring the Lady another of those umbrella drinks, and I'll have a Gin and Tonic." The waiter left, and they stared intently at each other for a few minutes. "So, Harry, are you really interested in knowing where to purchase a pair of my glasses, or were you secretly admiring me from over there, while faking a phone conversation?" she pointed to the spot where she first saw him.

Harry's eyes crinkled into a smile while turning and looking in that direction. "Was I that transparent?" "I have you rather at a disadvantage. I am a novelist, and for my books, I sit here at this cafe once or twice a week for a few hours appraising people. I sometimes wonder who would dare to come over to a character like I am impersonating and you were the most interesting one, so far," she said.

"Oh? What about that man I saw coming over to you, just before I came by?" Natalia considered the question for a moment. "He wanted to see the color of my eyes. Not a bad come-on I suppose, but he did smell a bit of beer, so I told him I was waiting for my husband." Harry suddenly put on a concerned look on his face." Do you have a husband?" he asked.

"You mean in real life?" Harry shook his head, yes. "In real life…" Natalia grinned… "Do you care?"The waiter brought their drinks and asked if there was anything else they needed. They didn't. Natalia lowered her head but kept looking at Harry.

"If it's less complicated for you Harry, no, I am not married, at this time. Does that make it easier for you then?" Harry returned her look. What a gorgeous creature she was, he thought laughingly, he could hardly wait to bring her home to his pad.

"Okay. So, have you written anything I know? I don't recall an author named Natalia …" he asked playfully. "Well, I write under a pen name."

"A pen name, so what name would that be…" he asked.

She looked at him silently for a moment as if she was contemplating what to say. "Felicia Waldorf." She finally came out with. There was a pause. "Felicia Waldorf ? Where in heaven's did you come up with a name like that?" Harry asked chuckling. "That's a pretty clever name… Felicia…"

Natalia couldn't help herself and started to giggle but was cut off as she heard Harry's pone ring with a familiar sound. "Isn't that…?" Harry took out his phone from a side pocket, it was his daughter's unique ring, and she would be calling from Switzerland, and it was midnight there, and she wouldn't call so late unless something was wrong. He answered the phone apprehensively.

"Hello sweetheart, are you all right? Did something happen…?" he asked his daughter uneasily. Natalia now leaned forward with a worried look in her face, "What is it, Harry?" then grabbed the phone from him, "Darling, its mom, what's the matter? Were you in an accident?"

"Oh mother, I'm fine, I just flew in from Zurich wanting to surprise you, but no one's at home. Where are you?"

"She's at our apartment here," she whispered to Harry, "she just flew in, isn't it marvelous?" Then back to the phone, she said. "Dad and I are not far away dear. We'll be right there. It is such a lovely surprise…" Then again to Harry. "Can you believe that? She came home to surprise us. Pay for the drinks dear and let's go home." Their previous charade forgotten as they stood up to leave.

Both smiled at each other and then Harry leaned over and kissed his wife, Mabel, on the cheek. "Our daughter always had perfect timing…" he said as they laughed mischievously and walked out towards their apartment two blocks away holding hands. "So what do you think? Would you have fallen for my act?" Mabel asked.

"For Felicia Waldorf ? Any time! When did you come up with that name?"

"Never mind that. Your fake phone conversation... that's a first, and a $65 million deal, not bad..." "Don't overdo it, it was only 38 million..." Harry whispered as he put his arm around his wife's bare shoulders and pulled her lovingly to himself.

15

Three: Liz's B-Day

Okay girls, let's not make too much of it. Don't tell the maître d' it's my birthday, please... I don't want the waiters, handsome as they are, ladies, singing Happy Birthday to me in public. Let's just have a quiet dinner and enjoy our drinks. Do not make a fuss. Okay?" Liz Browning appealed quietly to her three friends, as they sat down around the table in one of the best restaurants in Manhattan.

There were four of them, all lawyers, working together at Haverston, Grant and Goldsmith, an international law firm downtown. It was Liz's thirty-fifth birthday and they were going to celebrate it in style and not planning to be too quiet about it either. She was the youngest of this group who called themselves the Four Musketeers, because they were close and because they won all their cases.

The other three were pushing forty and married, still, as befitting attorneys, they were all elegantly dressed in designer suits and stylish hairdos. All were slender due to their gym in the building's lower floor and watching their diet. Liz, however stood out a bit more, not so much because she was younger, what's a year or two, but she was taller than the others and there was something special about her too. She had a certain presence, that was just there.

As they sat down, they ordered drinks and chatted, mostly about men, especially the few that had recently joined the firm. It was all for fun of course and they tore some apart for being too short, too fat, to bald and such. Only one or two of them seemed to make a mark on the ladies, but, and a big but, they all were married.

"Too bad there's no one there for you, Liz," they teased her. More drinks were ordered and by the third they were quite happily light headed. It was Emma the oldest, sitting next to Liz, that sat facing the entrance, who saw a man enter alone to the restaurant.

"WOW! I think here comes Liz's Birthday Present." They all turned and followed the maître d' as he led the man to his seat which was two tables away. The man sat, and immediately took out his phone and seemed to write something on it. In a minute a waiter brought him a drink which he didn't even look at, still concentrating on whatever he was staring at his phone.

"He must have some important business there..." Emma, the second oldest, said in a cynical way. "God is he good-looking." Anne, two years older than Liz, murmured quietly. She was married with three children. "I'd sell my children for a week with him in the Bahamas..." slurred Emma, who obviously had a bit too much to drink.

"God, I'd sell my husband just for the night..." sighted Betsy. Liz hadn't said a word. She had looked at the man, and she certainly found him compelling. But what's the point, she didn't know him and she wasn't about to go over and ask him if he was married, engaged or with her luck, gay. It was easy for the others to quip; they weren't going to do anything about it except talk. Still, it was nice to have a peek at him on occasion.

He was tall of course. Dressed in a gray custom-made suit, for sure. He had an adventurer's face with a roman nose above a mouth that gave a hint of a smile, as if he shared a secret with someone he cared for and, he seemed just the right age for her. She had to shake herself out of it on occasion because at times she thought he had glanced at her also. Their food arrived a minute later and the waiter was passing it around. "Finally," Emma said, "I am starved."

"That does look good. Mind if I have a taste?" Anne asked of Emma's dish as the waiter passed it almost under her nose. And so, the ladies found another topic to comment on. The man forgotten for a moment as they practically demolished their dishes for the only thing they had for lunch was, either a yogurt or a plain salad. No woman in the company ever dared gaining an ounce.

Only Liz still concentrated on the man on occasion, shutting out her friends. He too had ordered a dish, though she couldn't see what, and yet, and her heart fluttered a bit, when she saw him look at her so nonchalantly while talking on his infernal phone. Probably to a woman.

About half an hour into the meal, Liz excused herself to go to the powder room. She did feel a bit woozy from the drinks she had and seemingly the food turned out a bit too rich for her. The moment she was out of the way Emma whispered conspiratorially to the group. "I have an idea. What if I go over to the guy and..." She explained her plan to the other two and they all thought it was hilarious. She then stood up and walked over shakily to the man's table.

"Hi," she murmured hoarsely, "I'm Emma, I am an attorney from a very, very large firm and I have a proposition for you, hic... Could you do us a big flavor... uh, hic... favor?"

"Hi Emma. It depends. What kind of, uh, favor are you proposing?" His voice was nonchalant. Emma felt a bit wobbly so she just sat herself down opposite him. "May I sit down, please, hic?" She was always polite with clients and in a way this man was a potential client.

"Of course," said the man. She leaned closer to him and he met her all ears. "It's my friend's Elisabeth's, hic, we call her Liz, birthday, and, and, I... I mean we, the girls and me, thought we'd have some fun with her."

"That's very nice of you Emma..."

"Yes. But, but, we need you to help us, hic..."

"And how can I help you ladies, Emma?"

"Well, first we'll make it worth your while. We'll pay for your dinner of course..."

"Of course..." Mimicked the man. "That's very kind of you. Then?" "Yes, then... there is more, hic,... We would like to make you a present for Liz. You see she is single and it's hard for her to meet a man, sooo... you'd come over like to our table and we would say Happy Birthday Lizabeth, this is your gift from us." Then she added, "Of course we'd make it worth your while. I think the girls would agree to perhaps five-hundred dollars?"

"Five-hundred dollars you say? Well, I don't know..."

Emma shook her hand. "Maybe a few dollars more if, hic..."

"Oh, no, I think that's fair. I mean for how long though..." The man asked with a facetious smile on his face.

"How, how long?" she asked puzzled.

"Yes, how long a time. An hour? Two? The night?" Emma was perplexed. By now her head hurt and she didn't really know what she was doing. "Dear Emma, have you any idea what you're asking me to do?"

Emma stared blankly at him. "I know you're a bit under the influence, so I'll overlook this, but I'm sure you don't really mean to ask me to do what you're asking me to do. Don't you think?"

"I'm sorry, hic..." Emma started to mumble.

"Come," the man stood up and took her by the waist and brought her to her friends table. "I think your friend is a bit under the weather... should I just sit her down here?"

"Of course. Right here. We must apologize, she's really not like that at all. We're just celebrating our friend's birthday..." Anne said as she helped the man put Emma in her seat.

"Well ladies, it was a pleasure to meet you all. Have a good time and don't drive, whatever you do." He gave them a half smile then went back to his table, then he asked the waiter for his check.

By then Liz had come back and wondered why everyone close by was looking at their table. "What's going on?" she whispered to her friends.

"Oh, nothing really, Emma just had a bit of a to do with that man yonder." She pointed her head towards him. "What do you mean?"

"We don't know, she hasn't come up for air yet." Liz looked towards the man as he paid his bill and walk towards the door but then he stopped at the reception desk and pointed towards her table. He did something else but she couldn't make out what. A moment later it looked like he held an envelope which he gave to a waiter and said something to him as he pointer at Liz's table again.

The waiter shook his head and walked over to her. 'Oh God, he probably wrote something nasty about Emma but blamed me for it,' she thought. When the waiter handed her the envelope, she glanced toward the door once more. The man smiled, threw her a salute and left. Just like that.

Liz held the envelope in her hand and was afraid to look inside. This will be the worst birthday she ever had. "Well, open it up, for Pete's Sake." All three said in unison." What's in there?" Elizabeth's hands were jittery as she opened the envelope and saw a note inside.

"There's a note? What's in the note Liz?" Betsy asked anxiously. Liz unfolded the note with a slight tremor in her hands and read it to herself.

Happy Birthday Elizabeth!

I'm off to the airport for a business trip overseas to a country that doesn't serve food like this, so at least I will have a good memory of a fine meal and some lovely ladies, especially one. I'll be back in two weeks, on the 14th. I would like to meet you here for dinner at 8 that evening if you can make it. If possible, leave your friends at home... Martin

"So come on, what does the note say?" Elizabeth smiled the biggest smile she could. "Oh, nothing much, he just wrote that he enjoyed meeting us all."

Four: The Painting of Martin Cooper

A friend of Martin Cooper mentioned to him that a new art gallery opening up on Madison Avenue and 68th Street in New York. During lunch he walked over to take a look. Either his friend got it wrong or he misunderstood him, but the gallery was closed, and will open this coming Saturday at three with an invitation only, gala. As a sign in the window so indicated.

Martin wasn't particularly a collector but if he saw something that interested him, he would buy it, if the price was right. As long as he was here he looked into the window which displayed some abstract art of a new artist, a D. Turner, of whom he has never heard off. To Martin this wasn't the kind of art he was interested in anyway.

But just as he was about to walk away, a young lady opened the curtain in the window and put in another painting on an easel in the front. She saw him looking at her and smiled then left back behind the curtain. The painting was on a medium sized canvas in a simple gold frame. It was a dark scene with an outcrop of rocks protruding from the surf. On top of the rock sat a man looking out to sea and next to him was a dog, a golden retriever, with its paw on the man's back as if he was consoling him. There was even a pitiful expression on the dog's face. The whole painting had a dark sad look to it.

How the artist captured that look Martin couldn't imagine but it was uncanny the way he did it. Martin stared at it in astonishment. Of course, he recognized who the man was and he knew the dog's name. Max. It was his wife's Golden Retriever.

His blood ran cold as he kept staring at the painting. He knew the place too. It was on Tablet Rock near Gloucester, Massachusetts, and he was the man sitting on that rock staring vacantly into the ocean like a lost soul. Which, in a way, he was, then. He was sad, mourning the loss of his wife a few weeks earlier. That was about two years ago.

He remembered he had just walked for miles on the beach with Max and sat down only to give him a rest and some water. He had sat there for at least two hours before he returned to the cabin he and his wife bought a few years after their marriage, not far from there.

* * *

When he left, he had seen no one. No person with an easel or pad, at least he hadn't noticed anyone. The way he felt then, he probably wouldn't have noticed an elephant staring him in his face. He had to have this painting and he also wanted to meet the Artist. The name was hard to read on the small canvas, but it looked almost the same as on the larger color scribbles. So, he went back and looked through the glass door but there didn't seem to be anyone around. There must be someone there, he had just seen a young woman put the painting out in the window. Maybe she's in the back.

After a few heavy knocks on the glass door she come out and mouthed silently that the gallery was closed. Martin hand signaled for her to come to the window. When her face appeared through the curtain he pointed to the painting and pointed to himself and mouthed that he wanted to buy it. But he wasn't convinced that she understood him. This time he pointed to the door and motioned for her to open it.

Finally, whether she understood him or not, she opened the door slightly on a chain lock. "Look," she said, "the gallery doesn't open till Saturday…"

"I know, I'm sorry. I wish to purchase that painting now."

"Now? But I can't sell anything now. The store isn't going to open till…" Martin was exasperated. "Look, give me a number of the owner or someone in charge. Please, that's me in the painting and I want to buy it before anyone else does. Just a telephone number is all I want." He said in an imploring tone.

"You're the guy in the painting." Are you sure?" she asked. "Yes!

Please, a number is all I want for now." "Alright hold on. I'll get you a card."

* * *

When he got back to his office he called the number on the card. The phone was answered by a secretary and he had to go through the usual rigmarole till he finally got a hold of the man in charge, he hoped, a Monsieur Arman Blanchard. He had a French Accent. After a hello, Martin explained his interest in the painting and knew that if he showed too much enthusiasm the price would probably go up. "I see," Monsieur Blanchard said. "Let mee check this out and I weeell call you back." It took about an hour till Monsieur Blanchard returned the call.

"Ah, Monsieur Cooper. I'm afraid there has been some misunderstanding. That painting was not supposed to be shown in the window, you see, apparently my assistant put it in by meestake. We were only showing Debra Turner's work at the opening; however we do have the painting that you are interested in and it is for sale. We seem to have some other interested parties in eet…" "I see," said Martin. "I bet," he thought to himself. "Well, can we get together…?"

"I veel tell you what. Geeve me your address and I veel zend you an invitation to the opening and vee can talk then." Apparently there was no other choice. He gave his office address but would have wanted to wring this guy's neck for being so bullheaded. They could have made a deal on the phone and Martin could have had the painting this afternoon. He certainly didn't believe someone else was already interested in it, they just put it out… Saturday couldn't come soon enough. Martin was there before three but it seemed the gallery was already open with a large group of well healed people.

Abstract art of colorful squares or blotches were apparently quite in vogue now. He entered the already crowded gallery wondering what they were giving away free then noticed the line for the wine and cheese. Ah, free food and drink, a sure enticement for a rich crowd. He wasn't interested in the food so he asked someone for the gallery owner, Monsieur Blanchard. He was pointed out talking with a few people in front of a large painting of what looked like a Rorschach test chart.

He waited patiently while a check was written and papers signed then went over and introduced himself to Monsieur Blanchard as Martin Cooper with whom he talked only a few days ago about... "Ah, Monsieur Cooper, yes I remember our call, please let us go to my office and discuss the painting you wish to buy." To Martin he seemed like a smart nosed yuppie that probably used his parent's money to open up this gallery. He didn't think he was even French nor spoke the language but he wasn't about to challenge him till the painting was in his hands.

"Ere we are. Please seet down. Would you care for some wine and cheese?" Martin indicated a no. "You still have the painting?" he asked anxiously wanting to get this over with. "By the way, who is the artist? I couldn't read the name on the canvas." "Ah... with deese we have a slight problem. You see, the artist right now wants to be anonymous do to some other..."

"Monsieur Blanchard," Martin interrupted him, "we are not making an international trade agreement here, I'm just interested in purchasing a small painting and not getting involved with affairs of state. Do you know the artists name or not?" Monsieur Blanchard was about to say something when there was a knock on the door and then it opened and a smart looking young woman dressed in a black cocktail suit walked in.

"Oh, I'm sorry Abe, I didn't know you were busy. People are asking for you to make some sales..." And then she stopped and looked at Martin. There was a pregnant pause and then her mouth opened in total disbelief. She seemed speechless for a moment then said. "I think I know you, you're the man in one of my paintings? How did you ever find me? My God, I wanted to meet you hoping you'd come back the next day but you never did and I had to get back to New York. This is truly incredible."

Just then Monsieur Blanchard stepped in interrupting what could be a disruption to a sale. "Ah oui, theere ees no time now. We have to get back to the gallery. Monsieur Cooper, we'll discuss your painting a little later. Come Debra let's get back before we lose some customers."

Martin didn't know what to make of this. The artist that painted him was a woman? He never thought about that. For no particular reason he thought it would be a man. This Debra certainly didn't look like an artist though how should an artist look like anyway? Monsieur Blanchard and Debra left the office and Martin had to follow, there was nothing else to be done. The whole thing was beginning to feel like some black market deal and Monsieur Blanchard certainly wasn't a Monsieur.

When he stepped back into the gallery he saw the two making another sale and then another. It was like selling hot cakes. Within half an hour they sold most of the paintings hanging on the wall. During a lull in sales Blanchard went to meet some other potential customers or suckers that just walked in and the artist came over to Martin.

"I'm sorry, it's like a madhouse here. I never thought I'd sell even one piece. Blanchard really has the knack. He could probably sell, what's the saying? Like selling..." "Coals to Newcastle?' Martin completed her line. "That's it!" She said with a wicked smile. "He's that good."

"So you're the artist that painted me? D. Turner?" "Yes, Debra Turner. Nice to meet you at last. I never thought I'd see you again. How did you ever find me?" "Just by chance, it a long story. You seem to be racking it in." "To be honest I wasn't selling much of my other works, like your painting and Abe there, thought I should try something else. We went to art school together, he's my second cousin, but the only talent he had was selling other people's work. Otherwise he's quite harmless. Actually his name is Abe Berger.

"Did you like my painting of you? You looked so sad and your poor dog seemed to be trying to cheer you up. I felt so sorry for you."

"Well, it was a bad time. I think it's a wonderful painting." Martin said. "I want to buy it but it seems, Arman? Or whoever," he looked at her in a funny way. "Abe? Seriously?" He shook his head. "Actually I don't know what he wanted to do. He didn't want to give me your name..."

Debra smiled. "I think I know why. He didn't want you to associate the old artist with the new. I am supposed to be a starving homeless artist who paints abstract art and if they thought I can paint realistically, like your painting, maybe they wouldn't be so interested. Do you really want to buy it, that painting, that is?"

"Yes I do."

"I'll tell you what. Buy me dinner tomorrow and we'll talk about it. You'll have to tell me why you looked so downcast." She wrote down her number in the back of a gallery business card. "Call me after two. Now I better get back and sell some more of my paintings." She left him with a wink.

Martin left the gallery. No point to speak to Abe or Arman again. The artist really intrigued him. Certainly not what he expected. He thought more likely an older man with long hair and a beard wearing torn jeans and sandals, not this trim young woman in a black cocktail suit. She certainly wasn't bashful, in a way she reminded him of his wife. She had been a strong woman too, a bit forward and certainly tenacious in character.

The next day a few minutes after two he called the number Debra gave him. "You're two minutes late Mr. Cooper," she answered with a laugh. Martin was a quick thinker and also had a good sense of humor himself.

"I don't know a Mr. Cooper but this is the Art Police and we have a complaint about one of your paintings…"

There was silence for a moment then more laughter. "You are a card Mr. Cooper. I like you. So where are you taking me?" "Don't you ever say hello first, Miss Turner?"

"You're too funny, Mr. Cooper. Hello…" Martin had to laugh inwardly. "Call me Martin, after all we've already known each other for what? Almost 24 hours?"

"Actually Martin, I've thought about you much longer. By the way, what ever happened to that retriever? I would like to meet him too." There was a momentary pause on the phone. "I'm sorry to say I lost him last year. He was fourteen and a half years old."

Another pause. "I'm so sorry. I thought about him often too. Look Martin, I'm in the middle of something, why don't you come by around four, I'm sure I won't be ready but if you're in good health come up to my studio, the elevator is broken, I'm on the 4th floor." She gave him her address and hung up. Martin didn't know what to make off her. He dated a few women after his wife's passing but none with that kind of gumption. None really interesting him like this one.

She treated him as a long-lost friend and he sort of liked it. She had a wry sense of humor. She was forward. She obviously was single but you never know with these artsy people. Is he somehow getting involved with some nut job? Well, he'll see.

Martin was a former Green Beret; he certainly could take care of himself against a trim woman in a cocktail suit, he thought. She lived on Broome Street off Broadway in what used to be some sweat shop now converted, he supposed, to a place for artists. He rang the bell which sounded like a bicycle bell for giants. "Come up," she said over the intercom, "I'm almost ready."

Martin walked up the wide staircase which was lit by a single incandescent bulb. If there were ghosts here this is the place they would be, he thought. By the time he got to her floor he almost felt winded.

"It's open," she shouted through the door over some loud wind machine. The studio was a huge loft. It had an open space with paintings of sea scape's and still life all over the place and a walled off area where he saw a bed through a partially opened door. Debra was dressed in jeans and a loose blue T-shirt. She was drying her hair with a hair dryer connected to a wall socked by at least three extension cords that snaked around the canvases. "Be right with you. I just came out of the shower." Then she pointed to an easel by a huge window. "Take a look."

Martin walked over and was surprised that it was a portrait of him. "If you don't like it you'll have to sit for me then. I painted it this morning from a small photograph I took that day." The canvas was about eight by ten inches and it was a profile of him but very recognizable. It wasn't a tight rendering of his features; it was painted with loose brushwork but be loved it. It was him to a T.

"I'll take it for another dinner date," he said while she was putting the dryer away. "Oh, you won't get away that easily Mr. Cooper," she teased him. "It will cost you more than a dinner." Martin didn't know what to say.

He had never met such a forward woman. What was she trying to say? He could verbalize with her all day of course, but what did it mean?

On the other hand, Debra was intrigued with him from the beginning when she saw him sitting on that rock with that sad dog next to him, what was that? About 2 years ago? It was such a sad scene and she felt something tragic must have happened to him. She always carried a camera with her besides a pad and charcoal pencils. She had felt a little guilty taking his picture without asking permission but she was an artist and she wanted to capture this moment for a painting. She also made some sketches so she could paint it when she got home to her studio in New York.

She even thought of going over to him but then the dog gave her a look that she could have sworn said, not now, I'm taking care of him. It was silly of course but he was a large dog so she stepped away. She came back the next day to see if the man returned but he didn't nor did he return the day after. By then she had to go back to her studio. It took her months to paint this man and his sorrowful dog the way she wanted it. After at least a dozen tries she thought she got it right. The rejects she had laid around the studio with all the other paintings.

Up till now she hadn't been too successful selling her seascapes and still life. People seemingly didn't go much for realism anymore and she didn't know what she was going to do till by chance she met her cousin Abe at a family function. They went to art school together but he opened up a gallery selling modern art. She dabbled in that and showed him some pictures she had on her phone and he convinced her to drop the realism and continue the abstract

"People love this, especially if it sold right and I can do this for you.

You'll see, by next year you'll be known in the art circles all over town." "So, where would you like to go..." asked Martin again, ."..To eat?"

He was still looking at his portrait and wondered in amazement the talent in this woman. She should have her canvases in museums. And he told her so.

"Sure. These kind of paintings..." she threw her arms about the studio, "are a dime a dozen. I have to compete with artists who paint this for a meal. Most are from Europe and they work like an assembly line. Most people wouldn't know a piece of good art if it hit them in the face. This kind of flowery art is for the hoi polloi, its cheap. But give them colorful splashes or circles and heavy brush strokes and the high brows think its art. That's what I'm doing now. Would you like to guess what I made last night?"

Martin of course had no idea; he just threw out a number. "Fifty K," he said. "Oh you poor uneducated soul," she said. "Not even close." That's how she left it and let him wonder. "You know what? Take me to Katz's, You know, the delicatessen on Houston Street. I'm in the mood for a large corn beef and pastrami sandwich. I haven't eaten in days from nervousness. My dad used to take me there. I love that stuff. Is that okay with you?"

Martin would have gone to Coney Island for a hot dog with her. She truly fascinated him by now. "Sure..." They took a cab to Houston and Ludlow and went in to Katz's, took their tickets and sat at a waiters table. Debra ordered her mix of pastrami and corn beef and Martin the same. He hadn't even heard of this place before.

While waiting for the sandwiches to come, Debra asked him, if she's not prying, what happened that day that he sat so sadly on that rock. Martin didn't want to go over all the details but told her that his wife was ill but never mentioned it to him. He was in the Army at that time serving in Iraq. She died in her sleep while he was chasing terrorist in the mountains. When he came back she was already buried by her family.

He then retired from the army and opened a security business. There was nothing much to say after that. She put her hand over his and that was enough. Their sandwiches came and she changed the talk to a happier subject. She pointed out to a table where Meg Ryan and Billy Crystal sat for the movie When Harry Met Sally and where Rob Reiner's mother said, 'I'll have what she's having' after Meg faked a sex act.

Martin just looked at her with a puzzled face. When she told him when the movie came out he said was a young lieutenant doing some undercover work in the Balkans then and hadn't seen the movie. "Well, it was a pretty funny scene, maybe I'll rent a DVD one day and we can watch it." She gave him a wink.

Martin wished it was tonight. He couldn't explain it to himself how much he was beginning to like this woman. Martin looked at the sandwiches that were piled practically to the ceiling with sliced meat. Debra had ordered Russian dressing on the side with French fries and cream soda. "My dad told me that's the only way to eat this meal. None of those new soda fads for him but if you want you can order a beer." Martin drank the cream soda and made believe he liked it but the sandwiches were delicious. They couldn't finish their sandwiches of course. Martin could but didn't want to look like a hog so they packed it up to go."

They came out of the deli and walked west towards the Village. Debra put her hand around his arm. Martin felt a tingle run down his spine. He hasn't felt like that in a long time. When he first saw that painting of his, never in a million years, did he ever think he would be dating the artist. It felt odd and very good.

On the next block they saw a homeless man and they gave up their sandwiches to him. At first, they just walked silently for a few blocks enjoying the cool air with a slight breeze coming from the Hudson River a few blocks away, then as they passed Lafayette street Debra told Martin a little about herself.

"I was married for a few months. A guy I met in art school. He was a very good artist. He wanted to go to Paris to study but I couldn't go. My mother was sick at that time and I couldn't leave her. It was an amiable divorce. Neither of us had any money or property, just a few canvases and paints so it was easy. I never heard from him again."

She continued. "I did odd things to make a sort of a living. I waited on tables during the night at a 24-hour diner and painted during the day. I needed the daylight for painting. Occasionally I actually sold some landscapes and a still life here and there. I even gave art lessons in a senior citizens center and then, I met 'Arman' at a family gathering," she laughed when she mentioned her cousin. "I never made much money before him."

Then she suddenly stopped. "By the way, How much would you have paid me for my painting of you?" she asked teasingly.

"I don't know, maybe a million..." "A million what? Oreos?"

They both laughed. They stopped for a light at McDougall Street and their eyes met. The light changed but they didn't move. They just stared at each other till Debra came closer to him. Then Martin bent down and kissed her lightly. She put her hand around his neck and kissed him back till they heard applause from people around them. Embarrassed, they ran laughing towards Bleeker Street then up to 6th Avenue.

They walked quietly hand in hand up a few blocks as if they had known each other for years. It was still light in the early evening. The streets were crowded as usual with locals and tourists, heavy traffic up sixth avenue with horns blaring. Another homeless person asking for a quarter for coffee. A typical Village scene.

They had no idea how far they walked till Martin saw a small music store in the middle of the block. Martin took her by the elbow and steered her towards the entrance. Inside, the store smelled musty and stuffed with rows of milk cases filled with old LPs and 45s, tapes from the 70s and 80s and something that looked like a gramophone from Thomas Edison's time. An old white bearded man came from the back, dressed in bell bottoms and a psychedelic T-shirt holding a paper cup of coffee.

"Hi folks, is there something special you are looking for" He asked taking a sip from the cup.

"Yes," said Martin, squeezing Debra's hand. "Would you have a copy of *When Harry met Sally?*"

Five: The Art Teacher

At the age of 70, Milton Hersh and his wife retired to a senior community in Miami Beach. Six months after his 75 birthday he became a widower. As with many others who lost their loved ones, Milton was devastated.

It took many more months for him to get his life back together again. Milton was a commercial artist and illustrator and he loved to paint in oils. One spring day, when he had enough of rainy days he decided to set up a still life of fruits and flowers and paint again in the spare bedroom that he converted into a studio.

Soon many of his paintings were hung in the community clubhouse which he again started to visit. Then one day the president of the club suggested he start an art class for the members. "Milton," he said, "why don't you volunteer and create an art class, I'm sure you'll get many people interested in it."

And so, Milton became an art teacher. The club purchased some sketchbooks at an art supply store with pencils and some pastel colors as a start. The class was advertised in the club, cafeteria, elevators, and on the swimming pool bulletin board. It was to start next week on a Wednesday afternoon in the library.

Milton was a bit anxious about it as he didn't think there was much artistic talent in the whole community. But, what the hell, what does he have to lose. It will get him out of the apartment for a while and get him around people. He didn't think anyone would show up anyway. Surprisingly, that Wednesday when he came into the library carrying his supplies, there were five women and two men sitting around a table chatting away.

"Hi, Are you all here for the art lessons?" he asked looking around the table a bit surprised. The students all shook their heads in the affirmative. Milton then passed a sheet of paper around for them to sign their names. Of course, he realized that it would probably be easier to go to Mars than to teach these people how to draw, or paint, however, he started this and he'll take it to the end. He'll begin with squares and circles then perhaps draw a flower. A daisy would probably be the easiest. Anyway, first things first. "Let's get to know each other," he said.

Milton called out the first name on the list. "Linda?" "That's me," Linda answered raising her arm. Linda was in her eighties as sure as the sun rose in the east, maybe even more but she had a happy face and Milton was sure that if she could hold a pencil she would be able to draw a square or a circle. He called three others and they seem to be in the same category as Linda. Nice ladies for sure.

Then he called Rose. No one answered so he called her name again hoping that Rose hadn't demised in the meantime but when he looked up he saw this petite woman with just a raised finger and a smile on her face that could send men to prison for thinking what Milton was thinking just now.

Rose couldn't have been older than around sixty. She had that face of an innocent child that you knew had the devil in her and yet it seemed so innocent. "Here..." she finally said as if he asked a silly question. Why haven't I seen her around before? Milton asked himself. Where has she been all the time I lived here. "I guess I'm the last then," a voice from the side interrupted Milton's trance. He looked to his right to see where that voice came from. He assumed it was Zelda.

"The zees always come last," she twittered. "Even in school I was always last. Zelda Zilnik. But my friends call me ZeZe." Zelda or ZeZe was also a pleasant-looking woman, at least mid-seventies with fire red hair and a smile as big as her face. The two men were husbands of two of the women who acted as if they were kidnapped for this class.

Milton thought this is going to be a fine crowd. He looked back at Rose and he saw her still smiling that coquettish smile at him which made him a bit uncomfortable. By the time the introductions were done, there wasn't much time left to start the lesson so Milton showed them what to expect the next time they met with a few parting words.

"It was very nice to meet you ladies and gentlemen and I hope we can draw something interesting by the time this class is over. Thank you for coming." Milton was putting his stuff away when Rose came over. "Do you need any help?" she asked in a husky voice that belied her size. Rose was probably five feet and a couple of hairs tall. She most likely weighted ninety pounds wet. But she had this bearing that made her seem much taller. Maybe it was her high heels but he thought there was more to her. If she wasn't a dancer or an actress I will eat my hat, he thought.

There was nothing else to pack. Milton had everything in a couple of Publix plastic bags, except for a pencil that rolled away from him to the other side of the table and so he pointed to it as he couldn't bring himself to say a word. Rose stretched over the table to get the pencil, exposing a fine set of legs. "Here you are teacher," she said so coyly that Marilyn Monroe couldn't have said it better.

Though the library was air-conditioned, Milton was beginning to break out in a sweat.

"Thank you," he barely got out. "I'll see you, next class, then," he said as he picked up the bags and forced himself to leave as he felt Rose's eyes follow him through the door.

Later that evening he met his friend, Harvey, on the club's patio for supper and told him what happened. "Rose is in your class?" Harvey asked a bit louder than necessary. A man at the next table turned and asked what class that was. And so, when Milton came into the classroom next Wednesday the student body seemed to have more than doubled. Now there were more men than women. All sat as close to Rose as they could. Including his friend Harvey.

Milton decided to hell with the men's names, he would start the class with art. He tore out blank pages from the sketchbook and passed them out with a pencil. There was a moving blackboard on the side used by the board of directors so he brought it over and slowly began to draw a daisy. Might as well give them something challenging and see where it goes. "First you draw a small circle," he said. Then draw these elongated ellipses around it. And then a long stem to which we'll add some leaves."

He drew it slowly so they all could follow it easily. He stopped at a point and walked around the room looking at the student's work. The men, of course, he knew, weren't here to draw flowers or anything else. They were here to sit next to Rose. So, the drawings they made wouldn't win a contest in a kindergarten class.

The ladies at least tried. Then he looked over Rose's shoulder, which by the way was as perfect as a Michelangelo's sculpture. No matter what she drew he'd give her an A+. At the end of the session, he collected all the papers and thanked the class again for coming. The men left the room but congregated outside the door. Waiting for Rose no doubt.

Milton looked at the men's papers which were filled with tasteless little comments, so he threw them into the wastebasket as he was sure they wouldn't come back. The ladies, his true students, he put away so he could write some comments later and encourage them on. Rose he put on top. Actually, hers wasn't bad at all. The middle circle was almost round and the petals were almost elliptical but the stem was perfectly straight as if she used a ruler. She didn't get to the leaves yet, but there will be time at the next session.

Milton was satisfied as he put the drawings away in a manila envelope. "So how did I do, teacher?" that seductive voice came from behind. Milton thought everyone left but Rose, he guessed, was waiting there behind him. Though his throat was as dry as a Matzo six months after Passover, he managed to say. "Very good for your first time, Rose"

"Thank you, Mr. Hersh. Is there anything I can do for extra credit?" Milton didn't know whether she was serious or making a joke so he just smiled sheepishly. Apparently Rose wasn't going to let this go. "Maybe we can discuss it over lunch or dinner, Mr. Hersh."

Milton wasn't made of steel. If he was some other man he was certain something would have come to mind to say to her but Milton truly was a nice gentlemanly person and didn't know how to handle a woman that talked in double entendre. His wife had been a very good woman and he truly loved her and their romance went as far as making out in his car but nothing like what he thought Rose was proposing. If she even was proposing.

He happened to look up and most of the men still hung around the door supposedly waiting for the Siren of Miami Beach to come out. Rose saw him look and shook her head. She had never made eyes with any one of them nor said anything remotely similar to what she said to Milton.

It was something about Milton that struck a note and she wanted him to come to her. In a way, she was a bit embarrassed playing this Femme Fatale role with Milton which she hoped was all in jest but he seemed to have taken it very seriously. She thought she'd back up a bit. "Okay, then, I'll see you next time. Thanks," and she headed towards the ladies' room, at least till the men get tired of waiting.

When she came in, she looked at herself in the mirror. Yes, she still had it. She was always small, almost like a grown-up doll and men flocked around her till she met her future husband, Thomas. He was as shy as Milton and for her then, it was love at first sight. And then, two years ago, Thomas had a heart attack. He just worked too hard and it finally got to him. One day he was working on a huge case, the next he was in a hospital emergency ward, and the day after, in an expensive box.

They were living in New York at that time, in a big house that was useless to her without Thomas. She had a sister, also widowed, who lived in Miami and she wanted Rose to come and live with her. That was about three weeks ago. She hadn't been out much but wanted to do something with her time besides laying by the pool being ogled by these old farts. And then she saw Milton. He so reminded her of her late husband and when she found out he would be teaching an art class, she joined in.

She thought she'd woo Milton but apparently, he didn't fall for her flirtations. Now she might have lost him altogether. After a while, when she thought the guys got tired of waiting, she came out and went home to her sister's apartment feeling melancholy.

For the next few days, she hardly left the apartment. The days were very hot and humid so it was a good excuse to sit home in a nice air-conditioned room and read a magazine though she just kept turning pages without interest. She tried some daytime TV but that didn't interest her either. A blanket of depression overwhelmed her.

A day later the temperature and humidity dropped down and after supper, her sister convinced her to take a walk with her on the beach which was a stone's throw away from the condo. The sun hadn't set yet and the sky was a pale orange with a cool salty breeze flowing from the ocean.

Rose wore a white sarong type of dress with bare shoulders and the cool breeze made her feel lighthearted. She took her sandals off and it felt good to saunter on the bare sand. As they walked down the beach they saw a man standing in the surf with his pant legs rolled up letting the foam coil around his feet. His sandals were strewn haphazardly on the sand behind him.

When they got closer, Rose recognized that it was Milton. It was almost sad to see him standing there alone staring at the darkening horizon. "Poor Milton," her sister said. "I guess he still misses his wife."

Rose turned to her sister and told her to wait a moment as she went over to him. Milton hadn't heard Rose's footsteps in the sand and so he was surprised to see her by his side.

"Sorry to disturb you, Milton." She almost whispered the words. "You looked like you were waiting for someone to come out from the sea." Milton looked down at Rose with a half-hearted smile. She was at least a head shorter than him. Her face had a melancholy look but was still as beautiful as her namesake. Rose.

In the fading light, she still had a presence. It would be a lucky man that could have her as a partner, he thought. "I guess I sort of was..." he said in a whimper, turning back to the sea. "Waiting for someone. I'm here most nights looking out there but of course, no one ever comes..." Rose took a step closer to him. "Maybe I could be that someone, Milton?"

Milton turned away from Rose because there was a tear in his eye. Did he just win the lottery? He thought... Rose's sister looked towards them for a few minutes and saw Rose take Milton's hand and lean against him and then she saw Milton put his arm around her shoulder. After a few moments, she turned and went back to her apartment with a smile on her face.

Six: The Unexpected Passenger

It was raining hard this Friday when David Alexander left his office in Mid-Town Manhattan. It was about ten-thirty in the morning on this dreary day and since he was the boss he decided to go home and work from there and give everyone in the office the day off. Usually, he walked home as he lived only about a mile away, but because of the rain, he decided to take a cab. David was in his mid-forties, a widower, tall, well built, a handsome face, retired from a ten-year stint in the army. Since then, he developed a research firm that made him a rich man in a few years.

Once outside he quickly grabbed a cab when some passengers got off in front of his building and gave his address to the driver thinking he would be home in about fifteen to twenty minutes. Sitting down, he took out some reports from his briefcase and started to read them. After perhaps ten minutes or so, when looking out the cab's window he found he had only traveled a few blocks and was just on the corner of Radio City Music Hall, waiting for a red light.

"What's happening up there?" he asked the Sikh driver. "It look like big accident ahead, Sir..." the driver answered in his melodic Indian accent. David thought maybe he would just get out and walk but the rain came down even heavier at that moment and as he was contemplating what to do, suddenly the cab's right door opened and a woman tried to enter then stopped and looked at him.

"Oh, I am terribly sorry, I thought the cab was empty, I've been waiting, God knows how long for one. Anyway, do you mind sharing it if you're going uptown on the east side, it's cats and dogs out there?" She didn't wait for an answer and just let herself in with her clothes all wet and hair dangling down her face.

"I can't believe this weather. Just what I needed today among my other troubles," she said, trying to dry her hair with a Prada scarf. David told her yes, that was where he was heading and he said he didn't mind sharing a ride. "Of course, I'll pay my share..." she added. She certainly could afford it, David thought to himself. She was well dressed and certainly looked as if she could afford anything. "Not necessary" he said. "Glad to help..."

"Well, thanks, you're a gentleman, we'll see..." she said, still drying her hair. While they were talking the cab had moved three more blocks and the driver decided to get off Sixth Avenue and turn east on 54th. But apparently, other drivers had the same idea and the crosstown street was just as jammed and they had to stop right on the corner by the Warwick Hotel.

"This is impossible, by the time I get home I'll be totally soaked and probably catch a cold, I need to get out of these clothes now. Oh, there's The Warwick, there's a boutique inside, perhaps I'll get out here after all." She then looked at David, "Look, I'm in a bit of a funk. Are you in some sort of a hurry?"

David looked at her closely for the first time. Even with her hair dangling wet over her face she was a stunning woman who, if she wasn't, should have been a movie star. "I guess not. May I help you with something?" "I need someone to talk to and not some sycophant that will just shake their heads at anything I say. A stranger is what I could use, I just need to talk to someone and yes, buy a change of clothes."

David paid the cab driver leaving him a big tip for abandoning him and they entered the lobby. "There's a bar," the woman said pointing, "would you mind waiting about fifteen minutes while I change? I promise, not much longer," she begged. David had to smile to himself as he actually agreed to do this and it might just be fun. Otherwise, it's just leftover Chinese food at home.

David was familiar with the bar in this hotel, he had brought clients many times for lunches and dinners here. He was met by Samuel, the maître d' but he told him he was with a lady and he didn't want her to know that he is known here. "Of course Mr. Alexander, we'll be discreet," said the maître d.'

He got a seat in a booth facing the entrance and ordered himself a drink. As he waited he shook his head again as he thought of how he got himself into this. No one would believe it in a million years. A beautiful woman comes out of the rain soaking wet and practically into his lap and asks him to listen to some sort of a story. Unbelievable!

Well, after twenty-five minutes, because he timed it just for fun, she walked in with two bags, which immediately the maître d' took over, and in a new outfit walked towards his table. To say she was jaw-dropping would not be an overstatement despite her lack of makeup. He was surprised that it didn't take her much longer. His wife, he remembered nostalgically, would have taken another hour.

Her hair was dry, apparently, someone lent her a dryer, and the new outfit she wore, looked like a cover shot from Vanity Fair. She sat down while the maître d' put her bags on the seat next to her. "Thanks for waiting. I suppose I took a bit longer. I'm sorry. I could use a drink..."

Before she could say another word, a waiter put down a Cosmopolitan with its pink fluid sparkling from the overhead lights. "Good day, Ms. Bennett, nice to see you again. Pretty bad out there..." "It is, Michael, could you be a dear and bring me a shawl please, I'm still a little chilly from the rain." "Right away, Ms. Bennett."

David ordered a refill for himself enjoying the repartee. He supposed this Ms. Bennett might be someone famous though he couldn't place her.

After the waiter left, the woman looked at him with red-rimmed eyes which he just noticed. Apparently, she'd been crying. "I'm sorry," she said, "I don't know your name..." And then surprisingly she stopped looking at him. "You don't know who I am either, do you?"

"I'm sorry, I don't. You seem a little familiar but I don't know from where and believe me, had I ever met you, I would not have forgotten..." She smiled at what seemed like a compliment. At that moment their drinks came and they gave a toast. David said to, "an interesting time," and she said looking down, "yes..." They took a few sips as they gazed at each other. "You still have no idea who I am, do you?" she repeated.

"I have a feeling you are well known by the way people look at you though I'm sure they would anyway and the service you seem to get from management is obvious that you are known here also." David put his drink down and sort of shoved it back and forth between his hands. The woman, Ms. Bennett, shook her head almost unbelievably. "You don't watch much television then, do you?"

"Well, the news mostly..." he answered looking at her, wondering if he should be embarrassed. "I'm Nicole Bennett." She extended her hand with a warm smile. "Does that sound familiar?" David took her hand. It was warm and strong not like some cold fish people shake hands with. Then somewhere in his deep consciousness, the name sounded familiar. She did seem like someone he should have heard off but it just didn't ring a bell.

"Still nothing?" she teased. David was beginning to turn red. "You are the Vice President of the United States..." he finally blurted out... Now she laughed out loud. "Well, I suppose that put me in my place. And I thought I was world- renowned." "Okay, so tell me. Who are you and why I should have heard of you?" asked David

Nicole looked at him for a few moments. Her eyes became moist again and David thought he had hurt her feelings somehow and was about to say something but she started to talk. "Maybe it's better that way, for the moment anyway. Maybe if you don't know me it might be easier for me to open up to you but tell me your name first. He did and she started to sob.

(three years before)

"Where have you been Michael, you were supposed to get ready for the Morgan's party. You didn't even answer your phone..." Nicole asked, as her husband walked into their apartment looking gloomy. "I'm not going," he said pouting. "I don't want to go anymore to your elitist friends parties anymore. The only friends we have are your show business friends and I'm tired of them. Parties, dinners, museums, art galleries, whatever, almost every night."

"I want a normal life. I want guys I can have a meaningful discussion with, rather than who's doing what show. I want children. I want a house in the suburbs, not a concrete cube. I want a white fence around the house. I want grass in the front yard. I want trees in the backyard and not to have to look across the street into the park to see any. I'm just tired of this pretentious life I lead, Nicole... I'm a simple engineer and I can't stand this any longer."

Michael slumped down into his easy chair and put his face into his hands. Nicole had stopped in the middle of putting on her Tiffany diamond earrings she bought for herself after her second Emmy when Michael started his rant. This wasn't the first time he expressed those feelings but it was the first time she actually took him seriously.

Nicole, that was Nicole Bennett, one of the most prominent dramatic stars on TV, with a show already in its ninth season, a show that made millions for her, a show she had dreamed about since she was twelve, and here he was bitching that it was too much for him. And kids? Who in blazes had time for kids at a time like this. It's been said she could run this show forever if she wanted to, and he wants kids?

"Don't be silly Mike, get ready, or we'll be late. I'm getting an award, you know..." "Screw your award! I'm leaving you!" He waved his arms around the decorated apartment. ."... And you can have all this crap to yourself…" "And so he left. Just like that…" Nicole said to David, snapping her fingers with tears flowing down her cheeks.

David took one of the restaurant's fine linen napkins and handed it to her. He didn't know what else to do. "I'm sorry…" Nicole said wiping her eyes. "I thought it would be easier to tell a stranger but really, it's not…" "Where is he now?" David asked quietly.

"Mike? Well, till now I really wasn't sure, we didn't correspond. For a long time, I hated him but I was busy with my show, and eventually, I just stopped thinking of him too. I threw all his pictures away and it was like he hadn't existed. But I don't hate him anymore.

It wasn't till about a year ago that she heard from him again. She told David. "He wanted to marry a girl he worked with in his office so he asked me for a divorce. He wanted nothing from me except my signature on the divorce papers. I supposed he lived happily ever after in some mid-western state like Iowa or Wisconsin. I didn't bother to find out. I was a Star!"

It was at this moment that David realized who she was. It was true, she was one of the biggest stars on TV. Nicole Bennett of the show, The Family Tree. His wife used to watch it; it was her favorite show. She watched it while he worked creating his business in their spare bedroom. She tried to tell him about it but he wasn't interested. Nicole Bennett of all people is sitting right across from him. He wondered what his wife would have said about that.

"You know David, I could use another drink, what about you?" She raised her hand and within a second there was the waiter as if he had sprung up from the floor. "Yes, Ms. Bennett, another drink? Of course. You too, Sir?" David shook his head, "Sure…"

Nicole looked up. "You're probably wondering why I am telling you all that, a perfect stranger?" She took a long sigh and smiled half-heartedly. "I guess you were such a good Samaritan when you took me into the cab, I thought maybe you'd… Well, to be honest, most of the people I know are just hangers-on. They're nice but all they want to do is please me. Not that I normally don't like that, you know how we Stars are, I suppose. 'Yes Ms. Bennett, no Ms. Bennett, oh, it's so sad Ms. Bennett,' and such. I have a few good friends but just my luck they're in Europe on vacation somewhere..."

It's sad but David imagined it was true, a least that's what he heard about these people. His wife always read those silly show business magazines and tried to tell him about it. Now she's gone and he can never hear her voice again. The drinks came, each took a few swallows and Nicole wiped a tear and continued.

"Well, this morning as I was getting made up for my next shoot, I get a copy of today's headlines, which was quite unusual, I hardly watch the news, it's always so dreary..." She stopped and choked up for a moment. ".. But apparently someone at the news desk, that I know, thought that I should see it first before it gets on the air...

At this point, she couldn't hold it any longer and tears began to flow like the rain outside. She couldn't stop and David again, grabbed a clean napkin, this time from another table, and handed it to her. "I'm sorry..." She sniffled again. "It was about Michael and his wife and their newborn child..." That began a new wave of crying as she took out a yellow note from her bag and handed it over to David to read.

David took the paper cautiously, read through it slowly, and looked up at Nicole whose eyes were down as she fumbled with the napkin back and forth between her shaking hands. He reached over and did something he never thought he would do. He took her chin and brought it up to face him.

"I'm so sorry..." he said, for what was written on the paper was devastating news. A single-engine plane crashed near an airport in Milwaukee and killed the pilot, Michael Hudson, the previous husband of the TV Star, Nicole Bennett. Also killed, his present wife, Martha Hudson. Their one-year-old daughter, Nicole, had survived with little injury.

"I didn't even know he was a pilot. I didn't know he had a child and named it after me." Cried Nicole, "I didn't even know he lived there. Milwaukee? Who lives in Milwaukee of all places? They say they were flying north somewhere for their vacation and were caught in a freak wind or something." She cried again for a few minutes. "I was angry at him again. He wanted a simple life and look what it got him." She stopped and swallowed hard. "I'm sorry, that was a stupid thing to say."

David got another napkin and handed it to her. She smiled at him and squeezed his hand. "He was my high school sweetheart but I left for New York, we lived in Philly, and we met by chance years later when he got a job here and we fell in love again and married while I was looking for jobs on Broadway. He supported me then..." She sniffled now and David had nothing to say. What could he say anyway?

Finally, Nicole said, "I'm sorry David, I'm keeping you away. I don't even know if you're married... or keeping you from your family. How selfish of me..." "No, I'm a widower and my children are away at school in Connecticut." "Oh my God, I'm so sorry..." and she started to cry again.

Just then the maître d' came over. "Is everything all right, Ms. Bennett? Is there something we can do? We just heard the news..." Nicole turned to him. "Oh Samuel, I'll be all right. Thank you... This is an old friend of mine, Mr. David Alexander..." She pointed to David as if she had known him for years.

'How do you do, Sir." The maître d' played his part. "Well, if there is anything the management can do for you, you'll let us know." With that said, he left. "So what will you do now?" David asked when they were alone again. "I... I don't know. Suddenly my carrier doesn't seem so important to me. I have five Emmys, I probably should have six but that actress in that fantasy drama won one year..." She looked up at David and grinned.

"Silly, isn't it? They sit on my mantle in my expensively decorated apartment, my lonely decorated apartment, with all my other awards and do nothing, and if I think about it, I am as lonely as they are." She picked up her glass and put it down again without drinking.

Nicole Bennett was an actress, an award-winning actress, so as much as David empathized with her tragedy, how much was real and how much was drama he wasn't sure but he was certain it was not a made-up story. Even the staff here had just heard about it on the news. "I was thinking of quitting my show, it suddenly feels meaningless." Nicole continued. "I play a widow, of all things, and run my family as if they were slaves and people watch this? What's wrong with them? Don't they have a life?" She looked down again and kept on twirling that napkin.

"What do you think, Mr. Alexander?" She then looked at him with her sad eyes. After a minute David said, "I really don't know. Did you think about what you would do after?" Her lips curved up on one side. "A good question. I don't know, I never gave it a thought till now..."

"Well, I'm sure you could retire. A house in Malibu or the French Riviera. You certainly could afford it, as you say. You could of course travel. You can go back to school and become a brain surgeon." He smiled.

Nicole guffawed. David leaned forward and spoke in a serious tone now. "Of course, if you retired suddenly, what would become of all the other actors in your show? As you just told me, you're the Star, and if you go, they'll have to cancel the show and not only the actors but the producers, directors, sound men, cameramen and a gaggle of others will lose their jobs so in a way you are doing good. People do need you. You practically support a hundred people or more and give pleasure probably to millions out there..."

"Are you a psychologist Mr. Alexander?" David chuckled. "Heavens no! I think I saw a movie once..." "Okay, okay, I get your point and I'm happy you talked me into it. Of course, it would be silly to quit. Acting is my life and it keeps me alive but I feel I must do something for the memory of my husband. I mean my ex-husband..." She took out her phone and dialed a number. "I'm calling my lawyer," she said. David tried to stand and leave her some privacy but she stopped him. "Oh, please don't go, this will only take a moment."

Someone answered the call. "Oh hi Emily, is John there, I need a few moments... Oh, you heard? Thanks, what can you do, yes, I'll hold." A moment later another voice came on. "Hi, John I need to... I didn't realize news traveled that fast, yes a terrible tragedy, thanks, I want to talk about..." By then David tuned the conversation out. It was none of his business. He was now wondering what the outcome between him and this woman will be? The Star part doesn't impress him that much but she is damn good-looking and does he dare ask her out or is that Star thing going to be in his way. After all, she must know quite a lot of male stars herself so why should she have anything to do with him.

On the other hand, what does he have to lose by asking? If she says no, he'll never see her again anyway. Okay, maybe he'll tune in to that show, at least once and have some bragging rights with his friends. And then he heard Nicole close the conversation. "...Thanks John, call me as soon as you know something."

After hanging up she looked at her watch. "Wow! It's only one-thirty. In that case, everyone is still probably waiting for me to get back to the studio so I better go. You know David, I don't know what I would have done if we hadn't met up so unexpectedly. I probably would have just gone home and cried. I think you saved me from making a big mistake, you should send me a large bill," she said smiling. Then she looked at her watch again.

"Well, I think I should go. I need to finish this shoot to make the deadline." They walked out of the restaurant into a perfectly sunny day. David thought he better ask her now or lose the opportunity. But it was Nicole that spoke up first. "It cleared up so I think I'll walk to the studio, it's only a couple of blocks from here." They shook hands but Nicole suddenly didn't let go as she looked up at David.

"You know, you're not a bad-looking fella, David. You attached to anyone?" David shook his head negatively. "Here, give me your phone."

David handed her his phone wondering what for, but all she did was put her phone number in it. "Now remember David, that's Nicole Bennett, the famous TV Star. Right?" she said with mock seriousness. "I put that in with my phone number. Under TV Star..."

"No way will I forget you or this day..." commented David.

"I would very much like to see you again, perhaps this weekend? Can you do that?" Nicole asked suddenly.

David shook his head in the affirmative as if he was five and someone asked him if he wanted to go to the zoo.

"Good, please call me tonight." She was about to turn and then stopped. "By the way, I told my lawyer that I would like to adopt that child." Then she turned and practically skipped away. David watched till she was lost among the crowd, smiled to himself, turned, and shook his head in amazement. "WOW!!" he yelled out loud turning pedestrian heads.

Seven: Alice

The last time I saw Alice was at her wedding, about fifteen or more years ago. We lived next door to each other in Forest Hills, a suburb of New York City. We've known each other all our lives and went to the same schools until high school. I, to The School of Art and Design in Manhattan, and she, to Forest Hills High.

Of course, we still saw each other practically every day, as our houses were attached, but suddenly we had separate interests. She found boys and I still played with model trains in my basement. Alice was a very pretty girl; she was a couple of inches shorter than me but dressed in what then was considered cool. I still dressed in jeans and T- shirts with famous railroad names on them. I was definitely not cool.

However, by the end of my first semester in high school, my parents sold our house and bought a co-op in Manhattan as my father became a partner in his law firm. There were no smartphones then. No way to communicate like kids do today. The Internet was a science fiction dream. It was by land-line that people interacted with each other. Our mothers were in touch occasionally by a Princes' phone and at the end of their gossiping about the old neighborhood handed over the receiver to us. It was a stilted conversation. We hadn't seen each other or talked to each other for a long time.

Me. "Eh, hi Alice, what's going on?" Alice. "Nothing much. How's life in the big city?" Me. "It's okay." Really exciting conversation.

When we were still young we occasionally went to a movie together, not just Alice and me but with friends. However, when I moved we just lost contact with each other. She most likely found all new friends in high school and so did I. But my parents, as I said, still kept in touch so that a few years later, actually five or six years later, we were invited to Alice's wedding. She was twenty and pregnant. I was twenty-one and didn't even have a girlfriend.

I haven't seen her in all that time so when we came to the wedding reception, I was totally bowled over when I saw her. Alice had just started to show but now I really appreciated how beautiful she was. She hadn't recognized me at all. I was a bit taller. I dressed differently. It was probably the first time she ever saw me in a suit. I wasn't a Burt Reynolds or a Robert Redford but I was okay. I didn't have a steady girl but I asked one of my female artist friends to come with me.

I met her fiancée, a tall good looking guy, he wasn't from our neighborhood. He was a basketball player from St. John's University where she also went. He seemed like a nice guy, and I don't want to demean basketball players, but I thought he had the brain of a gnat. Oh well, I wasn't marrying him so what did I care. And that was it. I haven't seen or heard from Alice again. I suppose even our parents eventually lost contact or I would have heard something. That's how it was when you move away.

After college, I was hired by a top advertising company and years later worked myself up to creative director. I never married. I don't know why. I went out with very nice women but something always kept me back.

And so, the years passed. I was in my late thirties by now. One day I went to see a new client in Great Neck and on my way back to Manhattan I just wanted to see what my old neighborhood looked like. I haven't been there since we moved. It wasn't that much out of my way, and just my bad luck I got a flat tire. Fortunately, it was near a diner we used to go to in my younger days, the Shalimar.

I pulled slowly into their lot and called Triple A. They said it would take at least fifteen to twenty minutes to come over so I went in for a cup of coffee and maybe some pancakes. I used to come to this diner many times with my parents on Sunday mornings for breakfast and I always had their pancakes. I even came here a few times with Alice and some friends after a movie for cokes and ice cream and it seemed nothing has changed. I thought it would be nice to see the place again.

They sat me by a window booth that I remembered sitting at, with Alice actually. Once we came by ourselves, it was after a movie we went to see where we held hands. It was some kind of Hitchcock horror film and Alice was pretty frightened and to be honest, so was I. I think we shared a banana split after. Sounds funny now. It was sort of nice but by the next day, it was as if nothing happened. I bought myself a new locomotive for my model railroad, so Alice was forgotten. Oh, we must have been about fourteen then.

"Are you ready to order, Sir, or do you need some more time?" asked the waitress standing suddenly beside me.

I hadn't even opened the menu; I was so into reminiscing the past.

I was about to order my coffee and pancakes as I looked up at her. She of course didn't recognize me but I knew who she was right away. Yes, it was Alice.

"Hi," I said but couldn't continue. There was a lump in my throat. Why would Alice be working as a waitress after marrying that basketball player? So I said, "Give me a minute please," then turned my head towards the parking lot so I could compose myself. She turned to go then stopped and looked back at me.

"You look familiar," she said as if also remembering something from the past, and then in a hoarse voice, she continued. "Why, you're Ted from next door, aren't you? I haven't seen you in a long time. I think not since my wedding."

In novels, we would have embraced and cried and retold our life stories right there, but it didn't happen that way. At that moment, the repair truck entered the parking lot looking for my car. Just my luck, they came early. I knew from experience that if you're not standing next to it they'll just leave, so I excused myself and said goodbye. I think I even said, "Nice to have seen you again," or something stupid like that and ran out.

I made it just in time as they were ready to leave. It would take them about fifteen minutes to fix the tire so I gave them a twenty-dollar tip and I went back inside. I felt awful. I don't know why. I certainly didn't do anything to Alice, but still, I felt bad for just bolting away so suddenly. Almost like a dog with his tail between his legs.

When we were young, I didn't think anything else about Alice except as a friend. Now, for some reason, I felt something much deeper. She must have been standing there watching me through the window and when I came back in, she had a reminiscent smile on her face and wiped some moisture away from her cheek with a napkin.

The diner was slow so we both sat down in the old booth we once had that banana split in and looked at each other. I held her hand in mine but now it was different than that time during that scary movie. I also noticed there was no wedding band on her finger. She looked older, of course, well, so did I. There was a bit of sadness around her mouth but she was still beautiful and I was willing to listen to any story she had to tell me.

Eight: The Escalator Affair

It's silly I know, but I fell in love with a man on an escalator in Macy's Department Store, the problem was, I was going up, and he was coming down. As we passed, our eyes met, and the Hallelujah Chorus rang in my ears. When I got upstairs, I watched as he got off thinking he would follow me, but all he did was look up with a smile and walk away in a hurry. That was about fifteen years ago, and of course, I never saw him again. I was eighteen and just starting college.

But my life had to go on. I went to graduate school and majored in journalism then found a great job at a major TV news station where about several years later I found the man I married. He was much older than I, but I was enchanted with him. He was a foreign correspondent who traveled the world and was always somewhere else a few thousand miles away. I saw him mostly on TV standing in front of some earth-shaking news event and sometimes ducking bullets on a front line. Our relationship existed of texting with an occasional call if he was close to a network.

I suppose I'm proud of him, but that is one reason we don't have children. On occasion, probably a seldom occasion, I sit home alone on my window sill after work and look down over Central Park with a cup of coffee in my hand and I reflect on that man I saw going down that escalator. It's then that I muse about how my life would have been with him. Though of course, it's a moot point as I didn't know him except for that look in the eye we, or perhaps just me, gave each other.

I could have had plenty of affairs, but that's not really me. Oh, I have male friends that escort me to dinners, and award shows where I pick up awards for Howard, like four Edward R. Murrow Awards, a Peabody, a Pulitzer, and such. All hanging on the wall or standing like little statues on a shelf in his office.

But that's as far as it goes with my escorts and I am fortunate that no rumors follow me around unless of course they're hidden in someone's closet. However, the news is a busy twenty-four-hour business, there is never a lack of it. Then one day at work while watching Howard streaming live on the monitors in the control room reporting a riot in Baghdad, a bomb goes off right in front of my eyes, and Howard disappeared in a cloud of smoke.

In the end, there was nothing left of Howard to bury but the funeral was large with many people in the business attending. The funeral itself became the news. It wasn't so much that I lost someone that I loved, I mean, I loved my husband, but in the end, I really didn't know much about him except he was a great newscaster. The awards on his office wall didn't do anything to warm my soul. It was like seeing something belonging to a distant relation.

It was about a year after on the 4th of July, some close friends of mine, a vice president and her husband from my TV station, invited me out to their summer house in the Hamptons. "You really need to get away for a few days, dear, take some days off and relax. Hear the ocean instead of cabs honking horns. Stay with us as long as you like…"

They were right of course. I needed to get away for a while, and they said I could stay for a week or more. I would be by myself after they leave Sunday afternoon, but they have some lovely friends next door, a retired couple who live there all year round if I needed some company. I had no use for strangers for now, but I was polite and thanked them, and I took up their offer.

It wasn't like going to jail. If I didn't like it, I could always leave and go home. Actually, I thought I'd write a biography about Howard. Howard was a great personality, and he was known all over the world. Yes, that's what I would do, maybe even stay there a few weeks which was coming to me.

Their house was set on the beach overlooking the Atlantic, and for the first time, I slept well. The weekend went fast, we saw a show in East Hampton's theater and had a barbecue on the beach where I met their neighbors, the Williamsons with whom I had an immediate rapport even though they were older than myself.

Midday Sunday, my friends went back to the City, and I was left alone. I was used to it, so I didn't mind, anyway it was time I started my book. By the end of the week I wrote at least twenty-thousand words, they just flew out of me like water into a glass. I was happy, and at the end of the day, Betty Williamson, the neighbor, came over and invited me to a small party the next evening for just a few dear friends.

"We have a friendly community here, and we get together often in the evenings, especially if there isn't much going on in town. I won't take no for an answer so please come about seven. I don't want to send my husband over to get you..." She smiled. "Sure, I'd love to," I said.

Saturday morning, I went shopping for a new dress, and some matching sandals then took a nap. I overslept, so I showered quickly then changed into my new dress and sandals. I also took a shawl as I knew the night breeze from the ocean was cool after sunset. I also brought a bottle of wine my friends had in their wine cooler as I didn't have a chance to get one in town and walked over about a hundred steps towards the Williamsons' house which already was bustling with guests. Small party indeed. They were mostly couples of course but there was a loose woman or so and seemingly a few local men who I hoped weren't set up for me, but at a closer look, they seemed old enough to be my fathers.

The talk was mostly highbrow; they all seemed a pretty moneyed crowd. New York, Boston, Philadelphia, and such. What museum or hospital they should support. What new art galleries opened up locally. Real estate prices in the Hamptons, were they up or down? Who divorced whom. Who married whom and such.

Since I work in an office at my TV station and am not on the air, nobody really knew me, but because I called the Williamsons' my friends, they assumed I was one of them. In any case, they seemed a nice and harmless bunch of opulent folks.

Nevertheless, it was a pleasant evening, the sky was cloudless, and of course, filled with stars one never sees in New York. You could see lights flickering from a cruise ship in the distance heading out to sea. Soft music from an older era played from some electronic device. People were talking now in a more mellow tone and sitting on beach chairs. Someone build a bonfire in the sand, and some couples sat by it. If I were with someone, it would have been a romantic evening.

I was just walked around in an observant mood, with a drink in my hand taking in the atmosphere, when I saw a lonely figure standing by the surf. I don't know what possessed me to walk over to him, perhaps he seemed as lonely as I. Nevertheless, I stopped a few feet beside him. "A delightful evening..." I said looking up at the starlit sky.

Without turning, he said. "For some people I guess..." Just what I needed, a party pooper. "I'm sorry, I shouldn't have interrupted you..." I said and started backing away when he turned towards me.

"Oh, please, I'm sorry," he said. "I thought you were someone else... yes, it is a pleasant evening." He smiled. It looked friendly. "I thought you were Betty and she sometimes gets a bit under my skin but please don't say anything to her. She's my sister-in-law, and I love her but..." He stopped, raising his shoulders. "Brenton is my oldest brother I just came in from Bel- Air for the weekend..." he gave me his hand. "I'm David Williamson."

Somehow his face looked familiar, but I didn't know from where. Maybe it was from a TV movie or a Broadway play. I knew he wasn't an anchorman from anywhere. I would have known our station's competitors, that was part of my job.

So, we both stood there by the water's edge looking up at the sky. The milky way was as bright as Macy's fireworks on the 4th of July. He pointed out some constellations to me and explained how they got their names. He had a marvelous voice. Maybe he did voice-overs, he certainly had the resonance for it.

Still, there was an undertone of sadness in all he said as if he suffered some distress lately. However, for some reason, I was attracted to this man despite my new widowhood. In the meantime, we just sort of started walking along the water's edge, nowhere particular, but away from the crowd. We had no reason for doing it, but it just seemed like a natural thing to do.

We were quiet for a while just enjoying the mood. We could see lights twinkling in the far distance along the shore, probably from Montauk. A cool breeze swept in from the ocean, and it gave me a chill despite my shawl. David saw it and added his sweater across my back. I said a thank you, and he just smiled, and we went onward.

Some small distance away, people who lived in a house opposite, left some beach chairs by the surf and so we sat down facing the swell hugging the shore. I haven't felt such peace in a long time. We weren't really that far away from the party and a soft tune floated across to us, it was a dance tune I hadn't heard in a long time, but the name escaped me. It was very touching. I could just visualize an old movie with an American Pilot dancing with his British sweetheart just before he goes off on a mission in World War II, maybe not to return.

"It's an old Glen Miller song from the 40s, The Nearness of You," he said suddenly as if he had read my mind. "Perhaps we should make it our song," he said looking straight at me. "Everyone should have a song that reminds them of good times." He added pensively. "And are these good times?" I asked reflecting his look. "You seemed to be somewhere else when I first saw you."

David smiled bitterly. "I was. Before..."Then he stopped, leaned back, and looked up to the stars. "Ah, it doesn't matter. I just arrived from California, I'm a scriptwriter, and... perhaps I shouldn't bother you with my problems, Betty told me a little about you losing your husband recently..." "That was about a year ago; I hope yours isn't that bad."

"Well, if I were writing a script I'd probably say it's worse. Sorry, I shouldn't have said that, I'm just a bit upset. Perhaps we should get back, Betty will probably have something to say about us. It's a small community, and by tomorrow she'll have us married with a dozen children."

When we got back, we separated. David was taken away by his brother and Betty took me by the hand. "So, what do you think of David." "You tell me about him first," I said. "Who is he and where did he come from?" "You like him?" "He seems nice."

"His wife divorced him a few months ago. Found herself a Hollywood producer who promised her a starring role in a movie. Probably some sullied porn flick..." That's as far as she got, for now, as a cake was brought out with candles burning.

As it happens, it was David's Birthday, and by then I couldn't get back to him without being obvious or pushy. I really didn't know anyone well, not even Betty so I just stood back and watched the event. I saw David looking at me once, in a sort of familiar way, but it was quick, and his brother started to talk to him again.

By chance, there was someone from our TV station there and she started to talk to me. I couldn't lose her. We talked about how nice it was out here and then about the station, and I really wasn't in the mood. I excused myself to go to the ladies' room and didn't see her afterward. In any case, she had a bit too much to drink, so maybe someone took her home.

As I walked out of the house, I saw David on his cell phone getting a bit annoyed by whoever he was talking to. I didn't want to look like I'm nosy so I went outside. By now people were leaving so I also left after saying goodnight to the Williamsons. In the morning I thought I'd come back and talk to David.

In my house, I had another glass of wine and fell asleep on the couch. I woke up in the middle of the night after some silly dream about David though I couldn't really remember what. Then I went upstairs to bed and slept almost till noon. After a quick breakfast of cereal, I decided to walk over to Betty and thank her for inviting me to the party. Of course, if David were there, I wouldn't be unhappy. But he wasn't, she told me. He had to take an early flight back to California this morning, but she didn't elaborate.

Well, thought I, that was that. No point in getting David's story if he's three thousand miles away. So, we talked about the weather and how long I'd be staying and what kind of shopping there is on the Island and who's my favorite shoe designer and such. After about half an hour and some coffee, I went back to the house and wondered what I was doing here.

I tried to start writing again but couldn't concentrate with David on my mind. I got angry and shut the stupid laptop down. I was here only a few days, and I already wanted to go back home. I was lonely. Betty didn't even have a goodbye from David for me. Was I just a five minute distraction for him? I thought I made some impression, but apparently, I didn't. I guess he had plenty of young starlets who he promised to write into his scripts, waiting for him.

The next day I packed my things and put the laptop deep into my suitcase, there was no point in keeping it out. I thanked Betty and her husband again and left the Hamptons for the City, at least there is much more to do there, and I had some friends whose shoulders I could cry on. By the afternoon I was back looking out on Central Park. I called a Chinese place down the block and ordered a steamed vegetable dish with brown rice and ate staring at Columbus' statue when my cell phone rang. I had left it on the kitchen table and by the time I got to it, whoever called, had hung up with no message and when I looked at the number, I didn't recognize it. Probably a sales call I thought.

I left half of my dinner uneaten and wondered about my apartment. I wonder why this guy, David, bothered me so much. Something kept nagging me that I remembered him from somewhere, but it just stayed hidden. I thought of calling my mother but changed my mind. She would ask too many questions that I had no answers for. Nor did I feel like calling any of my friends anymore for the same reason.

I turned the TV on to my news channel and watched that for a while. I never realized how boring news could be sometimes. Every day it's the same old stuff. The Republicans and the Democrats fighting each other. The North Koreans put up another missile that could reach America, they said. The Mayor still can't get any money for the MTA from the Governor, crime is up 8% ... It's as if I never left.

I shut the TV off just as a Macy's commercial came on and then, suddenly, it all came together. Macy's! Macy's! How stupid of me not to have recognized him before. Now I remembered the look he gave me when he blew out the candles at the party, it was the same look he gave me from the bottom of the escalator. Is this possible? I mean, it was so long ago I really had forgotten what he looked like.

About fifteen minutes later the phone rang again. It was the same number, and I really didn't want to answer it, but then I suddenly recognized 213, the Los Angeles area code, and my heart began to beat faster. Could it really be David? "Hello..." I said nervously.

"Hi, it's David Williamson, we met at my brother's house the other night in the Hamptons? I called before, but I guess you weren't in and I didn't want to just leave a message. I'm sorry I had to go away so suddenly, I had a problem at home I had to resolve quickly, and now all's well. It occurred to me only about an hour ago, but you probably don't remember that we actually met some years past, on an escalator, you were going up and I was coming down... and I was late for some meeting and..."

Nine: How I Met My Wife

It's obvious by the title what this story is about. But I have never thought about marriage, it seemed like an anchor to me, as I was in the army and stationed in hot spots all over the world. Why in heaven's name would I need a wife to worry about or her to worry about me?

I am 42 years old. I hold the rank of Brigadier General. I have, or rather had, a command of a special brigade I cannot talk about but it was in the thick of most actions we were in and then suddenly, to my chagrin. All at once, they want me at the Pentagon. They gave me a star to make me feel better and a command that at least will pique my interest.

I've taken a 30-day leave, the first in years before I am to report to the Pentagon in Washington and the desk Job. Though I am not a vacation person, I decided to spend some time with my parents who live in New York City, and which I haven't seen in person for quite a while. I did not forewarn them I was coming as I wanted it to be a surprise.

Well, it was a surprise, but a surprise for me, as they weren't home when I arrived. Fortunately, there was the next-door neighbor, Thelma, an elderly woman, a widow, a friend of my parents whom I have met some years ago that asked me to wait for them in her house. She was very nice and made me a cup of tea. I don't drink tea but it was a gracious gesture and so I drank it with a smile. She lived in a one-family house next door, so it had a backyard with a patio where I sat down and we had a nice little chat about our families.

My parents, she said, went to dinner with some friends in Westchester and probably won't be home till late and that I could make myself at home here. She also said her daughter and grandchild were coming over but I shouldn't worry, she will make sure I'm not disturbed if I want to take a nap. They'll just stay in the house.

Well, it was a perfectly cloudless afternoon. No humidity and the temperature one would wish to have all year round. I began feeling guilty thinking that they couldn't go out in the back because of me.

"Maybe I could just leave my bags and I would go out for a walk," I said to Thelma. We were close to everything a few blocks away, so it was no problem. She wouldn't hear of it, and what would my parents say if she didn't make their son welcome? To be honest, I felt tired. I've been out in the field in Afghanistan for months, so I agreed to just sit there. I had a book with me and thought I'd read it.

The surprise was that I actually fell asleep, something I don't remember ever doing, probably because no one was shooting at me and when I opened my eyes, a young girl of about twelve was staring at me. "Hi," she said as I sat up. "I'm Peggy." Well, the last time I spoke to a twelve- year-old was when I was twelve, so I smiled and wondered what to do. Now, I have a master's in psychology among others, and though it took me a few seconds to recover, I said, "Hi Peggy, I'm David."

It probably wasn't the brightest recovery I ever made, but she was twelve after all, so she just accepted my answer and we shook hands. "Grandma says you're coming to see your parents and they're not home..." Before Peggy had a chance to finish her sentence, another voice came from the house. "Peggy, what are you doing out there? Let the man sleep," the voice said, apparently from her mother who came out into the backyard.

Normally I don't get too animated when I see women. After all, I see them all the time. In the military there are plenty of them, handsome, pretty, engaging, even glamorous, I hardly give them a second look. I'm just not interested. I know what you're probably thinking and the answer is, I'm not. But Peggy's mother somehow was different. Oh, she was a looker alright. Well-dressed, surprisingly, in jeans without holes. She would have looked good in a potato sack. She had that aura of a well-accomplished person that is a little above the normal and yet she seemed touchable. Of course, I don't mean physically, though that too. But she was not aloof and

had a warm smile. These are the women I tried to avoid.

"Hi," she said, "I'm sorry Peggy disturbed you. You were napping so peacefully. I'm Dora, her mom." What can I say? I am an officer and a gentleman, so I got off my butt and said rather unconcerned. "A pleasure to meet you, Dora."

Could I have said anything more? Probably, but as I said before, I don't want to get involved with any women. Then Thelma came out also apologizing, but I poo-poohed her and I said it's okay, and then what I prayed for happened. Peggy had to go to a birthday party that afternoon and so they had to leave quickly. Thank goodness. I'll probably don't have to see them again.

Thelma asked me to stay for a quick supper until my parents came home. Thelma wasn't a threat, so I stayed. After a while, I forgot about the surprise guests and grandma didn't pursue any comments about her children and I certainly didn't ask, though I should have made a comment on how nice her children were but I am a prig sometimes and just let it go. However, Thelma was an intelligent woman, she had a Ph. D. in Economics and though it wasn't my field I found her comments quite interesting and so time went by quickly till my parents arrived and were quite happily surprised to see me, as I was with them.

My parents are also very educated, my father is an international attorney and my mother worked for him for a few years before he realized that she was a great catch and he better move fast before someone else finds this out. As far as I know, they are very happy together. I have another sibling, a sister who works for my father as an attorney.

We stayed up for a while in spite of my parents being exhausted from the dinner and the long drive, but I was glad to have a chance to talk to them. At about eleven, we went to bed. I can sleep anytime, anywhere but somehow couldn't this night. Something was on my mind, but I couldn't put a finger on it. Finally, when I did fall asleep, I dreamed that little girl, Peggy, was my daughter. I woke up with a start but as it was now past 5:00 AM, I decided to do what I always do at this time. I went out for a run.

The area we lived in is Forest Hills, next to it, about ten or so blocks away, is Kew Gardens which has a wooded park. Once you're in there you'd think you'd be in the country, that is if you didn't see the crap people throw all over the place. If this was in the Army I'd have the troops around there police it up till you could eat off the dirt. Nevertheless, it's quiet and solitary, especially so early. I ran for about two hours and came back to my parent's home. My dad was already up reading the New York Times and shaking his head.

"How can anyone believe this crap is beyond me..." he said about an article on our Congress. Discussing politics with dad would be an unending process so I just shook my head and grabbed a cup of coffee from the table. "You want me to make you something?" he asked politely. I knew my father well; he couldn't boil water so I politely I said would make something myself. However, soon my mother came down and took over and made me an egg and cheese omelet with a toasted bagel. A bit better fare than I was used to.

"So, what did you do all afternoon while you were waiting for us?" my mother asked. "Thelma was very nice to take you in and feed you. You should have let us know you were coming we'd have stayed home."

And then she said. "Usually she has her daughter and granddaughter on a Saturday afternoon. Did you have a chance to meet them?" She asked so matter-of-factly that the hairs on my neck stood up. Something I get before a battle when I know the intel isn't all there. We could walk into an ambush or the opposition had a larger force than we thought. It didn't happen too often because of my sensitive hair. I could smell something was up and took precautions.

This time I thought I would say as little as possible. "I took a nap when they came and they left soon after." This should have stopped my mother, but it didn't because now she started to ask questions I didn't want to answer.

"Isn't her daughter a lovely woman? She's divorced, but it was her that divorced her husband. He was some tree hugger in Guatemala or somewhere down there. I really don't know why she married him in the first place. By now I think Thelma said he remarried some woman he met in the jungle. They're divorced for almost 5 years. Isn't that so, Harry?" she asked my father, who looked up from the Times and murmured a guttural yes.

"And Peggy, her granddaughter, a real angel. I wish I had a granddaughter like that. You apparently don't ever want to get married and your sister is waiting for the Prince of Whales to ask her. What is wrong with you kids today?" "Mom, we're not kids," I said. "I guess I don't marry because I would have to leave her for months at a time and Jess, well, I'm not going to make excuses for her. Didn't she have someone steady last time she wrote?"

You'll notice my father was still reading the Times. "Your sister is much younger than you. I don't like it but she still has some time, but you're getting up there. If you have a child now, by the time college comes around, you'll be an old man."

Thanks, Mom, I thought. For this, I had to come home. We, I should say my mother, bugged me for another hour, and then she gave up. We talked about what I did and why I hadn't come sooner. In spite of it all, I loved my parents and I thought to myself that if I was in their shoes, I'd probably worry about my kids too. Parenthood was not an easy occupation.

We went out to dinner that evening with a cousin of mine that lived close by and had a good time. It was an early evening and everyone needed a good rest. My sister called and said she'll see me tomorrow. Unlike me, she had her own apartment on Columbus Circle across Central Park and unlike me, she's filthy rich.

By 10, we all went to bed, me and the seniors. As I said, I can sleep anywhere, anytime, it's from being out in the field where people shoot at you and when they don't, you better take that rest. So, I fell asleep in a soft bed. No, it wasn't the bed I slept in when I was a teen. My parents moved when money started to flow in. Now they live in the Gardens, a posh area in Forest Hills. The bedroom is for guests. It's really the first time I slept here in a long time.

Anyway, I slept pretty well till about 3:00 A.M. this time. I don't remember if I dreamed about something or anyone and it certainly wasn't about Peggy being my daughter, or about her mother, but something woke me up. I went to the kitchen and poured myself an orange juice. My father had a great library, and I went there and searched for a book, I didn't feel like going up for mine. There were at least a thousand books on a variety of subjects, even the three I wrote about infantry tactics, something on the type Rommel, The Desert Fox, who wrote after WWI. They weren't great hits with the general public, but I did sell a lot to the people I thought mattered.

Finally, I found something, though I don't know why I picked it. It was Jane Austen's Pride and Prejudice. Please, don't ask me why. I guess it was light reading and I loved the character of Mr. Darcy. In a way, I always thought I was a little bit like him. A bit of a dandy and a bit of a snub. Well, I'm overstating it a little. I'm not a dandy nor am I a snob it's just that sometimes I thought myself of that just for fun. I haven't read this book since I was a kid but I did see those movies as they played for the troops at USO shows. They're amusing and it's fun to watch old British gentry.

It was a pleasant night. The temperature was in the 70s, the humidity in the 50s. I put on the outside lights and laid in a hammock and started to read. "It is a truth universally acknowledged, that a single man in possession of a good fortune, must be in want of a wife."

I have forgotten that first line but as I read it, for some reason the hairs on my neck stood up once again and I started to laugh. I had to put my hand over my mouth so I wouldn't wake anyone up. Is that supposed to be a coincidence? My God, am I really looking for a wife? I put the book down on the grass and looked up at the sky. Most of the yard was covered by maple trees but there was a clear spot right above me and sure enough, I saw the wide "W" of the Cassiopeia Constellation. A woman.

Not far away another woman sparkled in the sky. Andromeda. This was too much. I turned over and tried to sleep. I awoke early from a dream about Peggy's mother, whose name for some reason I forgot. We were running away from home but were chased by the police. By now I thought I was going bananas and vowed not to sleep till I'm safely affixed to a chair in the Pentagon. There were times that I hadn't slept for 36 hours. It was in a firefight with rebels near Kandahar, Afghanistan. I probably could have stayed up longer but a bullet grazed my temple and when I next awoke, it was in surgery in a hospital in Germany.

There was no point in going back to sleep now, so I returned the book to where it was and went out for a walk. When I returned, my sister waited for me at the door. I love my sister. She is a beautiful woman about 15 years younger than me. She is smart and clever and just a joy to behold. I'd be jealous of any man that married her, but of course, I wished her all the best.

We embraced as if we hadn't seen each other for years, which in fact was true. I truly missed her. We got back to the garden and had some coffee and talked till our parents got up. Of course, she asked me if I had anyone who I was interested in but I didn't ask her about her boyfriends. I really didn't want to know about her boyfriends though I knew, from my mother, that she did date constantly.

We talked about little things a brother and sister normally would. "Oh, David, you know we constantly worry about you but are very happy about you being in DC. At least now we can see you often," she said. Then my parents came down and we talked some more. They asked me about what I was doing but what could I tell them that was not in the news.

Any way you put it, we were fighting a war and people were being killed. Good people and bad. I tried not to dwell on it and we finally changed the subject. "Let's have a barbecue," my dad suggested and my mom and sis thought it a great idea. We'll invite some friends and neighbors and have a great time.

Just what I need, I thought, but I couldn't let my parents down. They wanted to show off their son as hardly anyone has ever seen me. Dad and I went shopping at a nearby supermarket and bought probably more stuff than we needed. By the time we came back we were told we were going to have at least more than a dozen people. That's how it goes. My parents were known in the area and contributed to many charities and knew almost everyone which, thank goodness, they didn't invite.

I helped my father and some neighbors that came early to set up the barbecue and tables and chairs they kept folded in the basement. This was going to be a bigger party than we planned but what the heck?

Many people that came were surprised to see me and some knew me only from photographs. By one in the afternoon, things started to hop. A few neighbors were musicians and they brought their instruments with them, mostly guitars, one neighbor from Russia brought his accordion. My dad is a terrible cook, as I mentioned before, and usually burns much of the meat but except for my mother, no one cared. There was much food of all sorts as many also brought homemade goodies. I haven't been to such a party in years. Many years.

Around three, the next-door neighbor, Thelma, that took me in yesterday arrived with her grandchild, Peggy. Her daughter was nowhere in sight. Well, what did I care anyway, I told myself. And I didn't. Truly, I didn't. No, really why should I have. I only saw her for a few minutes. I forgot even what she looked like. Oh, God. I didn't.

And then little Peggy came over and said hello to me and that it was nice to see me again. Of course, I said, "It's nice to see you too Peg. May I call you Peg? And where is your mother?" A question that just slipped out of my mouth like catchup from a bottle. But young children, fortunately, don't grasp the nuances and she just said she was called to her office for a job that needed to be done today for a big meeting tomorrow.

I can't say I was disappointed because I certainly didn't want to meet her again. I really didn't want to complicate my life now. A new job waited for me at the Pentagon so I didn't need to muddle my head. I didn't even know why I even thought about her.

Soon the musicians played some old dance music and my sister asked me to dance. My sister was a great dancer after taking all those expensive lessons as a child. I too am a good dancer and danced with my mother and some other brave ladies at the party. After a while, I had enough and moved to a corner where my father was in a dialog with some men. It was politics of course.

As an officer I didn't want to get involved so I just stood there with a bottle of beer and half-listened in, till a bit later I saw Peggy's mother talking to my sister at the far end. How she got there I had no idea because I just wasn't paying attention. She could have been here for hours and I didn't see her. But she and my sister seemed to be having a great time, laughing and having some animated discourse. I still couldn't have cared less.

Eventually, I thought it might be ill-tempered not to at least say hello as she was talking to my sister but I didn't want to just walk over and butt in so I just moseyed by as if I didn't notice them. My eagle-eyed sister, after an agonizing moment, finally saw me and asked me to come over. "Eh David, I guess you met Dora yesterday, she just arrived." "Nice to see you again," I said diplomatically. To which she replied the same.

Now, my sister could have told me about her some time ago in a letter but probably had the good sense not to because she knew I didn't care. So, here we were with me staring like a schoolboy at this handsome woman dressed all in white, her eyes as blue as the afternoon sky, staring right at me like a queen looking down at one of her subjects. She certainly was not the least perturbed because she didn't have to be. It was I that had lost common sense.

"Dora was just telling me about her work," my sister said. "Dora is a civil engineer and is building a new bridge over the Hudson River past West Point. You can't imagine how many changes the politicians are making to the project. She had to prepare an official response today that it will cost a heck of a lot more money if they continue like that. We're talking millions, right Dora?"

Dora looked right through me and knew right away I couldn't have cared less but being a tactful person and somewhat intrigued with me, I supposed, she said yes, with those blue eyes staring at me and a token smile on her face. How can this happen to me, a general? At that moment my mother came over and asked my sister for some help in the kitchen.

"Can I help too..." Dora asked. "No, no, too many cooks and all that," answered my mother with a wink in my direction. What am I to do? Dora was still looking at me with that I know all about you and am not going to let you off easy, look. "What do you do, David?" she finally asked me. "Your sister tells me you're in the army?"

I could not believe that she rattled me so much or why I was so upset about it. I was a grown man who couldn't give a rat's ass about what women thought about me. I wanted to rattle her a bit too. She seemed so confident in herself. I wanted to choke her. I wanted to wipe that self-assured smile off her beautiful face.

I was so angry, mostly at myself. I don't need her. I'm a devoted bachelor. I shoot people. I wanted to say. But of course, I didn't. It would have been boorish of me. Instead, I held my breath for a moment, looked straight into those piercing blue eyes of hers, and said, "Dora, will you marry me?"

(Background on the Indian Mutiny)

The Indian Mutiny, or Sepoy Mutiny also know by many other names is a complex set of circumstances. One can look up on line if one is interested. The mutiny described in this story started on a Sunday, May 10th 1857 in a garrison town in Northern India named Meerut,

The are many factors, political and religious that lit its fire. On this particular day, the British introduced ammunition for a new Enfield rifle to a native cavalry regiment. The older rifles, flintlocks, were loaded through the barrel, simply put, powder was shoved into the muzzle following a patch then a lead ball which had to be rammed all the way down the barrel with a ramrod, then a finer powder had to put in a pan, cocked and fired. A very slow motion to load a musket. This was a rather tedious operation.

With this new rifle, a new cartridge was introduced and distributed to all British and Native soldiers. To make loading simpler, both powder and bullet was rolled into a cigar shaped cartridge. The powder end had to be bitten off by the soldier and the whole cartridge was shoves down the barrel in one motion which saved time, especially during a battle.

This cartridge had to be greased to go into the barrel easier. A rumor went about the Native Soldier or Sepoys, as they were called, who were both Hindu and Muslim, that these cartridges were greased with pigs' and cows' lard; thus, offending both religious beliefs.

The soldiers that refused to load these cartridges were imprisoned that day. The rest of the regiment later mutinied and released their fellow Sepoys who went about killing all English soldiers and their families. By the time Henrietta and her father came back to their cantonments, almost everyone had been killed. A simple explanation.

Ten: Henrietta Ashwood

(homeward-bound September 1857)

My father, James Ashwood, died of a broken heart on the 100th day of our voyage from Calcutta to London. It has not been a pleasant voyage due to the sadness in our hearts.

My father and I had been despondent by the massacre of my mother at the start of the Sepoy mutiny in May of 1857 in Meerut, a military post in northern India, and he singularly had not recovered since.

Standing by the rail with a shipboard acquaintance, a Mrs. Blackstone, a widow, whose husband had the misfortune of being killed by a Sepoy on the same day, we watched as my father's body, wrapped in a canvas shroud and weighted down with ballast, was waiting to be cast into the sea somewhere of the coast of Cape of Good Hope on the tip of Africa.

The ceremony was a simple one, as all funerals at sea are, a few of the crew with the captain performing the last rights. The captain reciting from memory though he held an old prayer book in his hands. Doubtless, from many burials at sea.

"...And so, in the name of our Lord, Jesus Christ, we commit the body of James Ashwood to the sea and may the Lord have mercy on his soul. Amen." "Amen," we all repeated. Prayers done, he nodded to the two sailors holding my father's body on a plank. They tilted it across the rail and it disappeared into the waves as if it was never there.

The rights done, the captain donned his cap and ordered his first mate to make as much sail as possible. He then turned to me and brought his knuckled fingers to a salute. "Begging your pardon Miss Ashwood, could you be so kind as to come to my cabin at your earliest convenience for I have a letter for you from the deceased, er... your father."

He saluted again and went towards the quarter deck to see the running of his ship. When he left, I stood there with Mrs. Blackstone, looking down at the waves, trying to find where the body of my father sank into the sea, but of course, that was impossible, as the sea seemed the same at every turn. I tried to shed a tear for him but none would come. I had cried myself out many times at the death of my mother all those months ago. Now, no more tears were left for my poor father to cry.

Mrs. Blackstone and I watched the swells till the sailors set all sail and the captain went down to his quarters. "I suppose my dear that you must see him now," she said pointing her chin towards the ladder. "I suppose I must. I imagine my father left some instructions for me to do when we arrive home. I feel so alone now that I cannot function. What am I to do? I have no relations back in England to take me in. I have no notion of my father's means. He has never taken the time to explain to me what we are to do when we arrive. Nothing..."

"Do not stress yourself, my dear, all shall be well. You must stay with me till you settle all your affairs. I have a large house in London that my husband owned and I sent a notice with the last packet ship to have it prepared for when I arrive. So you see, you will have somewhere to stay for as long as you need."

"I do not know what to say to your most kind offer Mrs. Blackstone..." "Psh, my dear. Do not distress yourself at all, are we not companions. After all, have we not shared the same misfortune? I have been away many years myself and do not remember most of the acquaintances I had, so I shall have a most welcome sister. Now go see the captain."

"Please come in Miss Ashwood," the captain responded to my knocking at the door to his cabin. "Would you care for some brandy or port?" he said standing and pointing to a chair. "Perhaps a glass of cherry, if you have it..." "Certainly, a glass of cherry it shall be." He motioned to his servant who poured a glass for me and put it on the captain's desk.

"Miss Ashwood," he continued as he scratched his stubbed chin. "A bad business this, a bad business indeed, a death at sea. Very, very tragic, I must say.""Yes. Thank you, Captain Culver. I thank you for your kindness..." "Yes, yes, quite alright. Well, that's over and done with now, over and

done with. Hmmph, all and proper. I have made a notation in the log of your father's, dear Mr. Ashwood's demise. Now Miss Ashwood, before your dear father passed, while you had gone to your cabin for a well-deserved rest, I am sure, he called me in, you see. He has given me a note addressed to you in case of his, hmmph, passing. Just in case you see..."

He reached into his desk drawer and withdrew a sealed letter and handed it to me. "He asked me to tell you, and I wrote that into my log as well, that all property of his is to be given to you to do with as you please. I have witnessed his last testament and it is so recorded." He pointed to the open log book again. "Of course, it is all yours but I suppose he wanted it to be all recorded officially, don't you know?"

I took the proffered letter and stared at it for a moment, thanked the captain for his service, and walked out of his cabin, leaving the glass of cherry, untouched, on his desk. I have always been an independent child. I have never stuck to conventions of the times. My father had a position as director in the Honorable East India Company in London. But when I was five he received a promotion and was sent to Calcutta, in India.

Though I don't remember much of my life in London, I was told that in Calcutta it was completely different. I do remember in London we had a house with perhaps a staff of 3 or 4 servants including a governess for me but she did not wish to travel so far. When we settled in Calcutta, my parents engaged a French woman for me, who came from an old family that colonized India even before the British.

Here we had perhaps a dozen servants, each one with a small task to do. There was the cook, the sweeper, the punkah walla, a man who worked the ceiling fan, a gardener, a butler, and much more as was the English custom. All English houses had these for less than a twopence.

In the beginning, it was only the governess that schooled me in French and mathematics and history and geography. As there was not much else to do I took to absorbing knowledge, unlike some of my friends who wished to only play with dolls.

In addition, my father hired a pensioned Sikh soldier, his name was Bazir, a Risildar-Major from a famous Company regiment, the 5th Bengal Lancers, who was a great teacher to me, instructing me in horsemanship and much more. When I was older, he taught me to shoot and hold a lance. He taught me soldiering and told me stories of his service for the Raj. In the end, I was almost closer to him than to my own father who was extremely busy with company business. Bazir also taught me to speak Hindi. And it was he who told me I could be whatever I wished to be.

I went to my father's cabin to read the letter. It was a small cabin much like mine, just enough for a bunk that hung from the ceiling, a locker, a small table or desk, some shelves with books my father never read, and a small portrait of my mother which hung from the bulkhead next to his bed. It smelled of sweat and purge from the long voyage and the smell of death permeated the air that soda ash could not relinquish. I left the door open and I lit the lamp and sat on the hard stool.

I took my father's letter and tore the seal open. What could he say to me I wondered. Well, I must read the letter and get on with it... It was dated three days before his passing, it was a day he had come to some awareness. It read:

My Dearest, Sweetest Child,

I am at a loss for words as I write this letter to you. If your sainted mother and I have not told you, you must know that we have been the proudest of parents in all the world.

Now I feel that I am at my last resort. I feel I cannot go on. Your mother was my life and when she died, may she rest in peace, I felt that part of me died also. I cannot live without her. My heart is broken without mend.

I hoped that I can be well until we arrive in London and I can settle my affairs and give you a proper home but I cannot be certain of that. Therefore, I am writing this whilst I am still in charge of my faculties.

In my baggage, there are papers explaining where to go and whom to see when you arrive in London. It is all done properly and you must see a Mr. Lawton, my solicitor, his address is in the papers in my locker and he will go over all the documents I drew up including a banker whom I knew from Calcutta, also an agent for the purchase of a house in London.

All is made clear in a separate packet. I wished I could do it all in person but I do not have the constitution at my disposal so you must do it on your own if I leave you. There is a list of mine, I mean our investments and bank holdings, that you can see very plainly and not be bothered by solicitor's confabulations. I know you are a very clever young lady and you shall overcome all these obstacles.

Your loving father... Etc. Etc.
James Ashwood

I reread the letter again. I knew of course how much my parents loved each other and understood the hurt my father must have had and the guilt he must have felt in the way she was massacred but what about me? I too felt the guilt. It was I that wanted to take the ride. I saw my father so seldom as he was always involved with company matters. He should have been strong for me too and not left me to fend for myself. After all, I know nothing about these affairs he left me to resolve. See solicitors and bankers and agents for houses? If I was a man, perhaps he would have taught me but now it's too late. He is gone. Now I was angry...

There was many a night my father had nightmares and called for my mother. To sleep he drank many glasses of wine or took laudanum. He hardly ate anything and I too hardly had a full night's sleep on the voyage. I decided not to go through his effects for now. What if I find a treasure, it will not do me good regardless now. I was tired but Mrs. Blackstone invite me for dinner so I went to her cabin. "Please come in my dear," she responded.

"I'm sorry I'm so late Mrs. Blackstone, I've just been over some of my father's effects and time just passed me by..." "Do not concern yourself at all my dear. I understand. However, the food has chilled and the ship's cook has doused the ship's ovens not that it tasted much better warm." Mrs. Blackstone smiled. "But we did manage some bread and cheeses and the captain sent over some port."

We sat in silence as we ate. I sat on the stool and Mrs. Blackstone sat on the cot with a small table between us hanging from the ceiling that swung back and forth as we sailed through the waves. After this dinner, we talked for a while about my father and what I should do when we arrive in London. I did not mention anything at this time about what I found. I had only known Mrs. Blackstone for the short while we were at sea, not that I did not trust her but I felt it was not the right time. She was still a stranger after all. But I did tell her what had happened to us and how we escaped at the last moment and how we couldn't even bury my mother.

"My poor dear," she said, "so young and gone through so much." And so we sailed on. We arrived at Cape Town for supplies three days later. We certainly needed fresh water and fresh food. I asked the captain to have a sailor move my father's Box to my room and put it under my bunk. It was my father's personal belongings I told him and there was no reason to think otherwise. In this small boat, I was never far away from it so there was no fear of it being stolen.

In two days when all was loaded, we sailed on the morning tide. Within forty days we passed the equator celebrating with the crew with King Neptune presiding over the Polliwogs. As we had none, for all the crew and we as passengers had crossed the equator before and so we were Shellbacks, there was no mischief to give anyone. But still, there was singing and dancing the jig and much rum passing about.

"At least it has taken some monotony from the voyage." Mrs. Blackstone said as we watched the sailors dancing the hornpipe. "That it has Mrs. Blackstone. The first time I remember very little but my mother told me the sailors sprayed me with saltwater christening me Princes of the Atlantic. I believe I was terribly afraid with all the humdrum about me and cried so much my mother had to take me below to the cabin."

After that, there wasn't much to do aboard. The Bombay Queen was a small ship used primarily for mail and special cargo and had room for only 4 passengers, Mrs. Blackstone and her maid, my father, and myself. So if it wasn't for Mrs. Blackstone I should have gone mad. Seeing each other day after day in the small space of the deck with nothing to see except water all around, the talk became scarce. But it was on one of those days when the sun shone strongly and barely a breath of air, the caption had the ships carpenter make us two canvas chairs and a canvas roof to give us shade that Mrs. Blackstone asked me lazily what I was to do with myself once we entered port.

"I am to see my father's solicitor and show him some papers that will settle where I am to stay, I suppose." "You must be very careful my dear Miss Ashwood, it is not that I distrust the men of the law but as a woman, a still very young woman you must be very careful how you will do business with them," said Mrs. Blackstone.

"I have wondered that myself. It frightens me a little too as I have never even spoken to a solicitor before. Have you Mrs. Blackwood?" "Well, in Calcutta after my husband was killed. I had to settle his affairs. The man thought me totally incapable of understanding anything. Repeating everything twice as if I were a child. I gave him a piece of my mind I tell you. If I were a man, they certainly would treat me in a more respectable manner."

"You know Mrs. Blackstone, I used to impersonate a boy in India. A native boy. I dressed in native garb, a puggaree on my head, no one knew the difference. I went with Bazir, the daffadar my father hired to be my riding instructor, and sometimes even on my own. We went to the bazaars and haggled with the vendors..."

"You mean your Bazir haggled..." "Oh no Mrs. Blackstone, I spoke Hindi, the native tongue, don't you know." My dear Miss Ashwood, you mean to tell me you spoke Indian?" "Well Mrs. Blackwood it's Hindi really, I spoke it very well and in fact still do. "You are truly a wonder Miss Ashwood; I have seldom met a European that spoke the native tongue. You amaze me truly..."

Mrs. Blackstone told me all she knew was how to tell the help to sweep the floor or make tea or get some water and some other housekeeping tasks but to speak the language truly fascinated her. I probably had a better education than most young ladies of the day. I am not saying that to sing my own praises it is just that there wasn't much else to do. Calcutta or Meerut is nothing like London or what I heard of Paris or Rome where a girl has friends and goes to swank houses or fetes or theaters to occupy her time. I had no friends my age but I did have a curious mind.

So, as the days went on Mrs. Blackstone told me of her brother and where she will stay. He owned five thousand acres in the country with a large house and a large income, also two children who were born years after she left for India. A widower now, his wife having died at childbirth with their third child and so he wanted her to stay with him till she settles herself. "You see, I too have to see a solicitor." She smiled.

In all the days at sea, she has never spoken of Mr. Blackstone, her husband. She was still a young woman, very pretty indeed, and I wondered that at no time did she mention him, and then suddenly without thought it just came out of me. "Do you miss your husband very much, Mrs. Blackstone?"

We were sitting by the mainmast trying to avoid the sailors working about us. It was late afternoon. The captain had just called for the lead man to throw the chip's log off the stern. I heard him say we were traveling at 4 knots in the peculiar sing-song manner of these sailors. Being versed in mathematics I worked out the simple equation that we shall make about 94 knots per day. I wished it was faster but we needed more wind. In that time I also watched Mrs. Blackstone trying to decide if she would answer me.

Her mouth turned into a snicker. "Ah yes, poor Mr. Blackstone. Do I miss him?" she answered dryly. "I hated the earth he stepped on." She stood and walked towards her cabin. "If you'll excuse me, my dear, I am very tired." With that, she disappeared down the gangway.

It rained the next few days and I did not see Mrs. Blackstone. I tried to knock on her door but she insisted she was well even though I heard some muffled sounds, like crying on occasion. But once the rain stopped she was on deck as if nothing has happened. It was as if those few days did not exist.

"What a wonderful day it is," she said. "Don't you agree Miss Ashwood? The captain says this should last a few days anyway." We spoke little in those few days. There was no mention of her husband. I suppose we were both thinking of what will happen once we land. London for me will be a strange and lonely place. As I mentioned, I have no relations left. My uncle and a cousin have died. They had no relations either, both being bachelors, and my father had to pay for their funeral, I remember my parent talking about it, so they do not find themselves in a pauper's grave.

Once we passed the Canary Islands on our starboard side, at least that's what the captain told us, for we did not see them, the weather started to cool down. It would now be at least 24 more days till we're laying off Cornwall, to signal London that we have arrived. "So, Miss Ashwood, have you made a decision where to stay in London? I do wish you would accompany me; I promise we shall have a grand time. We shall take to the theater and walk on the Strand and see London which I missed so much. It will be much easier for us two than be alone. What do you say?"

I did not need any more encouragement. It was a capital idea and she was right, women together can go places more so than a woman alone. Unlike men who can do anything and go anywhere without any comments from the nabobs. Oh, how I wished at that moment I was a man. "It will be my pleasure to accept your kind offer"

"It's all settled then. When we arrive at Cornwall, I shall include in my letter to my brother to have a room prepared for you so there will be no time wasted. I would also like to ask you to call me by my Christian name, Cora if it will please you." "Only if you will call me Henrietta." "Settled again... Henrietta." We giggled and embraced like two little girls.

Still with a while to go, we passed between the Azores Island on our port side and Madeira on our starboard again all without seeing them. A few days later the captain pointed straight east. "That was where Admiral Lord Nelson pummeled the French and Spanish Fleet at Trafalgar. Then up the Portuguese coast into the Bay of Biscay towards the Channel all without seeing a blade of grass.

One fateful morning, almost 140 days at sea, we approached our homeland at Foulmouth where the captain hoisted signal flags for the mail launch to approach. Cora and I sent letters to our solicitors that we shall arrive in port within days. Cora also sent a letter to her brother. That mail should arrive many days before us on a mail coach to London. The captain also informed us that the company will watch our ship as she sails through the coast along the Channel and up the Thames so that they will know exactly when we arrive. What wonderful news after this long, long, voyage!

London

Finally, we arrived in East London on the morning tide, at the Isle of Dogs, where the Company has her docks. It was a dreary cloudy day. Smoke from the chimney fires blackened the sky into a thick and smelly fog. At times it was almost impossible to see your hand in front of your face. It was a miracle we found the docks without piling our ship against the banks of the Thames. At the dock, we were met by a gaggle of solicitors, bankers and renters, and a few members of the board of the HEIC. Apparently, the captain wrote to the Company about the demise of two of their directors and so they came to pay their respect. It was much sorry for the loss, many regrets, such a young fellow, your poor mother too, all compassionate and remorseful and you must stop at our offices for tea at your convenience. Clear up some business, don't you know. Papers to sign and such and such all while my solicitor and his bankers and estate agents stood by. It was the same with Cora as her husband was a Peer. At least there was an inn where they made us comfortable. All in all, nothing was settled and we must see them all again. And so appointments were made.

In the meantime, Cora's poor brother stood by patiently waiting for the commotion to be done with, and then off we went with all our baggage in a carriage to Cora's London house. Cora's brother Mr. Hampton, Esq., seemed to have come out of one of Mr. Dickens novels that my mother used to read to me. A true Mr. Pickwick in real life. Such a jolly "hail fellow, well met." So glad to have seen his sister so well and her dear friend Miss Ashwood. We must do this and we must do that, anything at all to make a welcome home.

The home that we came to was, for me, as a royal palace after the bungalow that we used to live in India. Each room is larger than our own home. My room had a bed the size of perhaps 10 times the ship's cabin I have just spent almost half a year, at least that's what it seemed to me. It was marvelous. The food was outrageous. Meats, vegetables, fruits, cakes, soups. I thought I had died and gone to heaven. How I did without these things I could not imagine. Well, I shall never have to. Not anymore. No ships, well perhaps to cross the channel to go to Paris or Rome or Vienna but never again to India.

I did not get up till the afternoon of the next day once I went to bed after supper. How could anyone ever leave a bed so comfortable, so clean, so soft, so wonderful? But alas, I had to. There was the matter of my father's will, the bank, and the solicitor for the estate. I needed new clothes for mine certainly were not meant for London weather.

I also had to purchase or rent a house. I needed staff and perhaps a horse and gig to go about London. There was so much to do that I did not know where to start. It was a Godsend that I had Mrs. Blackstone, Cora, my new best friend. My only real friend. She took me everywhere, that is after my appointments at the Company offices, the solicitors, and the bankers. I found out I was an heiress. I was rich beyond my expectations. My father made certain of this. How happy would my mother have been having lived long enough to see this? How happy indeed!

The precious stones, I did not show at this time. I had no need. I purchased a vault and put them there to be safe and sound. At this moment I had no need for more. I had an allowance of 10,000 Guinness per annum and that will be more than I shall need. The other money was put in the bank and certain investments that my father had thought off while still in his senses. He had inquired about purchasing land but I did not think I would be able, at this time, to trust myself to run it, and to depend on someone else would be very foolish indeed.

For now, I did not purchase or rent a house. Cora was kind enough to have me stay for as long as I wished. Her husband's house was large enough to barrack a company of grenadiers. There was almost more staff than we had in Calcutta. Lord Blackstone, whoever he was, was certainly a rich man and it all belongs to Cora. I hired my own Lady's Maid, a young Irish girl, with a happy disposition as it was more a custom in society rather than a necessity for really, I certainly could comb my own hair.

At the first opportunity, we went to Bond street to purchase new garments for ourselves. Winter was in its midst and most of ours were from the tropic summers of India. We went around leaving cards for Cora's old friends to let them know she was back. The gentlemen from Parliament were coming back to London from their country estates to sit in Westminster and so the London Season will start soon. Dresses for that had to be ordered. It was all a whirlwind of activity.

I almost wish I was not rich but not quite, for I have seen the poor in the streets, and bless the Lord for my father's thoughtfulness, I do not wish it called larceny but perhaps misappropriation. What can I say, I believe it runs in the family now. In any event, there was nothing I could do. There was no way to pay it back to the rightful owners and if I tried, I'd look the fool. So I might as well keep it and enjoy life which will also give me the opportunity to do things I wish to do. Travel and of course give alms to the poor.

And so as a few weeks passed by, Cora was making plans to go to her brother near Redhill, where he owned property and a large house. She has as yet not seen her niece and nephew. I was beginning to feel guilty keeping her from it. But I had not had time to make new friends as most of Cora's friends and acquaintances were much older than myself. Their daughters were just the opposite, much younger than I, and I had not found my place in society as yet. Normally a mother or her sister or aunts or cousins would show her about it. I could not expect Cora to do all that for me, she needed her own life to fulfill.

It was now February of 1858. It was a hard winter for us. It had been a long time since I have seen snow on the ground or felt as cold. I did not fare well the last few weeks. I caught a Catarrh and wished I was dead. I was in bed succored by poor Cora who nursed me like a sister. How she did not catch it from me is a monument to her constitution.

But now I am done and it was a beautiful clear day at the end of February. We lived in Mayfair across from Hyde Park and decided to take the air. I put on a new coat made from lamb wool with ornate frogs across my chest and a large lamb hat making me look like a Russian Cossack. Cora and I walked along the frozen Serpentine in Hyde Park with other Londoners enjoying the midday sun. There was still snow on the ground with children and young people throwing snowballs at each other. Gentleman Riders pranced their horses on Rotten Row. Officers, some in mufti and some in uniforms doffed their hats or saluted. All was in fun and joyfulness was all around.

"What a wonderful day to be alive," said Cora. "Truly." Of course, I agreed with her. We walked arm in arm and I began to notice a strange circumstance as we passed people around us. I probably would not comment on it, it is just that I have thought about it many times in my mind.

It is that there were no single women walking alone. Well, there were single women but they had children with them, certainly not by themselves. It just wasn't a proper thing for a woman to walk by herself. She must be escorted, if not by a gentleman then by another woman be it a friend or relation or certainly be gossiped about. One of society's many rules I remembered my mother taught me. But, a gentleman, well, he could do anything.

I mentioned that to Cora as we walked and asked for her to see if what I thought was true. After a few minutes, she laughed and thought it was the most amusing thing. "I have never thought about it but it seems so true," she said.

"The men have no concerns such as we women," I observed, "they can do as they please, go where they want, and have no one to answer to. A woman has no such choices. I wish to go everywhere and see things. The world is so large and there are so many things to do in it and so many places to go. I would love to travel to all the great cities I have heard about. Paris, Rome, Venice, Vienna. Now I shall be expected to sit at home waiting for some matron to call on me or in turn wait until invited at some great house, and God help me if I had offended some society Nabob, then I shall have to sit at home knitting doilies for my furniture. It's not fair I tell you, Cora. Oh, how I wish I was a man sometimes!"

Cora didn't seem to be put off at my outburst, she too had an itch to do these things I alluded to, but of course, she couldn't have done them while her husband was alive, there she had to conform to the Company's propriety. Teas, cricket, horses, talk with the most boring people in the world. In India, especially if you are a wife to a high-position husband it was almost as if you were in prison. You are watched every moment. If you are seen with the wrong person, tongues will wag. You were never alone except in bed.

"Yes if you were a gentleman, then you would be free of conventions set to muzzle us, women. Too bad," she said. We made a few more turns around the park, then Cora declared. "We must get back I believe my friend is expected for tea."

Cora's friend was a grand lady, although not much older than Cora she seemed to have much influence in London society. Well, after all, her Husband is Lord Castleridge, a distant relative of the Queen. Lady Castleridge and Cora had been friends as children before she married a man twice her age. With really nothing in common with her husband except to give him two sons, she was quite on her own while he busied himself with affairs of state. They were extremely rich with an income of 120,000 per annum. At least those were the rumors that Cora told me.

It certainly did not matter to me or Cora. Lady Castleridge or as she wanted to be known to us as Flo from Florentine, a name she totally disliked. She was a frequent visitor at Cora's since we arrived and they were as close as sisters. By the time Lady Castleridge, as she was addressed in company or Flo by us, settled in and tea was served,

I totally forgot about any talk of being a man. I must admit I was a little in awe of Flo as she knew everyone and everything in London. She knew the right places to go, the right people to see, and the most amusing places for, yes, amusement. She was also a great gossip but not in any mean-spirited way. She had a charming way of telling us about Duke so and so and his mistress Lady so and so, or Mrs. X habit of this and that, etc, etc...

She never had a bad word for anyone even though the stories were very personal. I really liked her as much as I liked Cora. Once gossip was over, tea drunk, what were we to do on these fine evenings. There were some splendid plays in the West End and there was a new opening of Mozart's Marriage of Figaro at the opera, Flo said. She has heard that it was grandly staged with some new French Mezzo-Soprano playing a boy's part. Her name was Alicia Bonnaire. If the reader did not think I caught that part they are terribly mistaken.

"Shall we go see it then?" I asked anxiously. Now you might say what fun these ladies have, there seems nothing they cannot do. All so rich they might have the right ear of God. But money isn't everything, which of course any rich person can tell you. But imagine dear reader if all you have to do is wake late, eat a large breakfast, wait to read the Carte de visite dropped at the door to see who you will entertain for the day, or go visit. Then tea, perhaps a rest then a ball or two, truly hard work.

There were times I could scream from boredom. Just to get a lady to dress took over an hour if you rushed and ladies had to change clothes perhaps two or three times a day. I needed to be riding in the country with Bazir, camping by a river or stream or on top of mountains, and speaking Hindi with natives carrying their Jezils and Khyber knives by their side planning marauding parties against other tribes. Well, I would not exactly do that, but there was adventure there, there was danger, unlike riding in the park and avoiding children or dogs who ran between the horse's hoofs. The rich ladies did nothing, not even comb their own hair.

Well, I shan't bore the reader anymore with my pensiveness. Life is what it is. It was impossible to get tickets for Figaro except of course, for Lady Castleridge. It was the best seat for the three of us un-escorted ladies. The Three Musketeers is what they called us. Behind our backs of course.

I will also not explain the opera, it is complex, with many roles for men, and women and I'm certain a dog or horse somewhere. It is about marriage, jealousy, long-lost relatives, unexpected arrivals, men dressed as women, and of course, a man's role acted by a woman. Cora looked at me and I looked at Cora and winked. She of course grasped my thought. By the way, the music was delightful. It is Mozart after all.

Alicia Bonnaire was splendid in the role of Cherubino. It was truly the reason I came to see the opera. Though I cannot say I did not enjoy the rest. There was never a reason to tell Flo of my torment of impersonating a man. It was, after all, a silly notion but after this night an idea formed in my mind. "Somehow or other," I said to my companions, "I must meet that soprano." Cora nodded to me with understanding.

"Well, whatever for?" asked Flo. "I certainly would understand if you were a man, my dear Henrietta. Alicia is certainly pretty in a sort of way and men do like this kind of lady. But she certainly is not society my dear." "My dearest Flo," said Cora. "I did not take you for a snob..."

"Oh, poo." Flo waved her hand. "I was just thinking if my husband saw me with that company. Why he would have a convulsion." "Do not concern yourself, my dear, Henrietta has not as yet come out in society and is not known around. She would like to see her on a personal nature.

What Cora was trying to say is I have not been introduced to society. Though I am certain everyone who is anyone must know who I am. Rumors of a young woman who comes from India who must be filthy rich have spread through the London Nabobs. They just haven't met me in person as I had been ill and did not receive.

Usually, a young woman below the age of 16 is thought of as a giggling ninny. She is silent in company and in general, does not make a nuisance of herself. As the age of 18 comes along, a young woman is introduced to society in the season of balls which generally comes when the hunting season is over in the country. Again, it is not for me to explain this here. I had no knowledge of that myself till Cora explained it all to me.

London is a very large city with perhaps a few million people. Most are poor, some actually work for a living. There are the servants, the millers, the butcher, the bar keeps, etc. These of course are the lower classes. Nice people I suppose but the group, the socially acceptable people, of which I had become, are very few in comparison, perhaps nine or ten thousand families in all of England which if you count children, fathers, and mothers it might come to a figure of eighty to ninety thousand. I do not know exactly; I did not count them. Nevertheless, it is those people that make up the ruling classes. They make the season. If any poor do that it is not known. So, back to my "libretto" as they would say in the opera. I may associate with the lower classes because no one really knows me personally. This would be very difficult to explain to our dear friend Flo, though I must say she truly is a very nice soul and I'm sure gives alms to the poor. I did not try. However, she did have enough influence to have made an appointment with the mezzo-soprano for me. After all who would not do anything for Lady Castleridge.

The opera is closed on a Monday and so my appointment was made for tea at the hotel nearby where Miss Alicia Bonnaire was staying. Since the whole purpose was mine, it was decided I should go alone. I cannot tell you how fretful I was; after all, who was I to see a renowned opera singer. But I brought flowers and chocolates, I was told she loved, and a letter of introduction with a monogrammed coat of arms of the esteemed Castleridge family. Now, who could dismiss that?

Miss Alicia Bonnaire was, as it happened, an extremely approachable young lady not much older than I. An impish smile showed on her face when I spoke to her in French, though I must say perhaps a bit broken as I hadn't spoken it in years.

"Il est si agréable d'entendre ma langue maternelle parlée ici dans votre ville Mlle Ashwood, je pensais que seul l'anglais serait parlé ici .." She I saidn her melodic voice. "Ensuite, je dois présenter des excuses pour avoir parlé aussi sûrement Mlle Bonnaire.""Ah, think nothink off eet." She I saidn English, "but pleeese speak to me in Engleesh as I need ze practicee."

Well, it was as two old friends have met after a long absence. There were many cups of tea and sandwiches eaten as we told our stories to each other. The hours seemed like minutes as we gossiped in English and French, I have never felt time go by so fast. Soon it was time to say goodbye. I totally forgot why I came to see her. "Ve must meet a again, Mon Cher," she said to me. " I vuud very much lik to see you again..."

Of course, I said oui and it was arranged again for next week at the same time. I do not think I can wait that long. By the time I got out of the carriage, I nearly flew to the door where Cora awaited me. I could not even have time to remove my hat and coat before she asked me how it went. "I see you are smiling my dear so it must have gone off well," said Cora.

"Oh, it went brilliantly Cora. Alicia is such a wonderful person. So obliging. We were like old friends." Then we went up to the drawing-room and I told her all about it, including my forgetfulness as to why I really wanted to see her.

The week went by slowly but we were busy. The season will start soon and we needed dresses. It had to be the latest fashions from Paris. It was to Bond Street and Madam Mulier's shop where of course Lady Castleridge purchases her clothes. Shoes for dancing were needed. Cora was also going to the country to stay with her brother who does not come down for the season and so she needed country clothes and as I was to come too I must order for myself. There's also riding attire, church attire for teas and visiting. A Lady has never enough or tongues will start wagging.

So my day has come for my visit with Alicia. Now I shall remember why I came to ask her the first time. I left early as the weather looked like rain which is most afternoons. I called for a closed cab as it was also chilly towards the end of February. When I arrived at the hotel, the manager advised me that Miss Alicia will be a few moments late and if I don't mind he will seat me at her table where a waiter will bring a pot of tea while I wait.

He put me at a small private table facing the room. When I came last time I was too excited to look around me but now while I was waiting I turned from right to left and was amazed at the sight. It was of course the Victoria Hotel so I shouldn't have wondered that the room was brilliantly decorated with crystal chandeliers lit brightly with the new gas lamps. The ceiling was decorated with murals of heroic Greek figures. Exotic flower pots everywhere to block off a table. Mirrors, drapes, marble.

Then, when I turned to my left behind a large potted plant of a fern, there sat a most handsome man with fashionable cavalry whiskers and a magnificent head of dark brown hair. His dress was impeccable with a dark cravat in which sparkled a large diamond pin. A walking cane lay beside him with a silver head of a hunting dog. In his hand, he held a fluted glass of champagne. On his face, he held a slight smile that could break a young woman's heart. I have never seen a more handsome man.

I did not know what to do. I certainly couldn't stare at him all day, well, perhaps I could, but I didn't. A waiter saved the day by bringing tea and I looked around hoping Alicia would arrive at this moment. She didn't. And when I turned again, there stood the young man right in front of me. "I beg your pardon, Miss, I believe you dropped this..." he said in a

voice that would put an angel to shame. Of course, I did not drop anything but I was too nervous to say so. "I, I, I..." Was about all I could muster. And before you know it he sat down across from me. "May I?" he asked as he took the teapot and poured a cupful for me. His voice resounded in my ear, "Sugar?"

Is this going to go on forever, I asked myself. I hoped so, for even as I had a closer look at his face I saw a scar run across his cheek from the right eye down to his mouth. It must have been a saber cut for certain. He must have read my mind for he ran his fingers across it.

"May I introduce myself." He said in what now appeared a rather Germanic accent. "Heinrich Von Torten at your service." He said as he stood up and clicked his heels and bend down to kiss my hand. "Und you are...?"

"I, I, I..." I stammered. You might think I have never met a young man before. Well, in India there were many balls and fétes and such and I certainly was introduced to young men but I was in company. My mother was always there. Here I was alone.

I must say I was uncomfortable. I kept looking in the direction Alicia might come. Where the devil was she? Then I looked back at Heinrich Von whatever, and he had a mischievous smile on his face. With his right hand, he picked at his scar and just ripped it off his face, then he grabbed one of his whiskers and took that off all the while his smile became larger. He was sitting facing me so no one else could see it. If anyone looked this way they would just see my horrified look as he continued to disrobe his face, last of all his hair.

I did not know what to make of it. Am I being ridiculed in a pantomime of sorts? And then all came to light and a heaviness released itself from my chest and a large smile came over my own face. It was Alicia dressed as a man. "You should zee the look on your face," she said gloating at me. "Is it not much fun?"

What could I say. Either she was a mind reader and somehow knew why I came to see her or was it purely just a coincidence that she was having fun at my expense. "Ah, please forgeeve me my dearest friend. I hav displeased you, Mio caro."

I told her at first I was a little disconcerted, after all, one does not see things like that every day. But in the end, I was quite delighted. She quickly took out a mirror and put herself together as the man though without the whiskers as they required more glue she told me. The mustache apparently had enough, all that before a waiter came by. We had more tea and sandwiches brought to us and then it was I that told her why I had come to see her in the first place.

Well, one can imagine, that she took to this like a fish to water. She had impersonated a boy or young man for a long time. "It is the best way to see a place, is it not? I am recognized in the street many times and I have to stop and talk to people and so I disguise myself like this and now I can go anywhere. I can walk in all towns I play in the opera. It is much fun. Is it not?"

Of course, I agreed with her. It was what I wanted to do myself. And then I realized she spoke without an accent, well almost. "I am sorry Henrietta; I work very hard at the opera. Many days of rehearsals and performances. Yes? So I make many, how you say it? Pranks? Yes? Everyone knows I do that. I wanted to see how you make out. I hope you are not offended. I also speak many languages. We perform all over Europe so I speak their language if I don't they speak French, Like in Russia or Sweden. "So, can you teach me how to fool anyone as a man?" I asked her.

"Oh, that is very easy all you have to do is have the confidence. You must think like a man and act like a man and dress like a man of course, and people will think you are a man but it is up to you. I will show you."

She stood up. "I am dressed now as a man. A Prussian, an officer in a guard regiment perhaps but dressed in mufti. You see. They are very arrogant in the guard's Regiments. They know they are the best." She picked the walking stick. "So I will walk there." She pointed to a column about 10 paces away. "From there I will change my walk back and you tell me what you think."

She drew her shoulders back. Adjusted her coat and walked as if the place belong to her. Stiff and formal. A waiter that was coming toward her stepped away quickly to let her pass. She didn't even give him a glance. Once at the column she stopped and turned and winked at me. Then started to walk like a true aristocratic lady, perhaps even Flo. It was still stiff, without care but now there was a swing of the hips. The walking sticks and an umbrella. It was as if she was two different people and in fact, she was. When she came to the table she sat down ever so daintily unlike when she sat down as a Von.

I could not help but smile. "That was wonderful," I said. We will be playing here till mid-season, another 6 weeks. When I leave you shall become a man." She said with a twinkle in her eye. On the way back to Cora's, I already thought of the places I would like to go in Europe, perhaps even America, well if they build better ships for I will never travel in a vessel like the Bombay Queen again! This is my story of how I learned to masquerade as a man so I shall not dwell on all other matters. The invitations, the anxiety of preparations for the opening of the season. etc. etc.

The next time I met Alicia, she asked me to come early, and we practiced the walk-in in her hotel room. I was a quick student as I have practically acted like a boy most of my life in India. But eating, drinking, how to hold utensils, how to drink and hold a cigar, how men stand that smell I cannot imagine. How to wear a hat, how to sit, how to stand, and how to cross your legs. Men do it much differently than women, not that women can even cross their legs with all the silks they put on. One might think it simple but if there is a watchful eye a mistake can give it all away.

My biggest problem of course was my voice. Though a soprano, Alicia, also could have a lower range when she wanted to. It did not have to be perfect. I wasn't applying to go to politics or make speeches. I just needed to get by at a hotel or train station where everyone is in a hurry. She taught me to dress in a way that gave me a certain character and if I said the right things I could get away with almost anything. The character to portray should be a foreigner on a visit. If in London, act like a Hungarian for example. In Paris, a German. In Vienna, an English dandy. Even perhaps, as I spoke the language of a Maharajah. She taught me some accents to use and told me not to worry about perfection.

"The people will believe you because if you act like a snob and that you belong, they will accept you. Show them some money if necessary and you can be the King of Belgium for all they know. Because of Alicia, we were able also to use the opera costume department. Oh, how much simpler it is to dress a man!"

Needless to say, it took a few weeks to arrange everything including a new wardrobe for me in Regent Street. I had two suits, evening attire, an overcoat as it was still cold, socks, undergarments, cravats, hats, handkerchiefs, etc, etc. I must say it cost me many rupees.

In the meantime, the season started. I came out at some soirées and balls and met some young and middle-aged gentlemen who fell in love with me instantly. Or the money I was rumored to have. All society gentleman, some with grand names some not but of course no one in trade. I smiled and danced and I cannot say it was not fun however at this time I was not ready to be engaged. I was going to travel till I am an old maid.

By the second month all my apparel was ready and also Cora made plans to see her brother in the country who had no inclination to come up to London for, as he said, "all that nonsense." Now I was ready to try out my pantomime, but how and where? We started our little experiment, Alicia and I, one cloudless day in March, a rarity in London this time of year, we had a turn in the park. I dressed as "Henry" now, a nom de guerre Alicia devised for me as perhaps a pun on my own name.

We borrowed, through Alicia's good offices, from the costume department of the opera, something more mid-European. We dressed as two young gentlemen who had come to London to see its sights with an old tour guide in our hands. We had mutton chops and mustachios covering our faces so as to hinder recognition.

Our first consultation, after sneaking out of Cora's house was with a local constable that had seen me a few times, of whom we asked for directions to Hide Park. It was I who had the honor of asking. "Ah, my dear constable," that, in as low a voice as I could muster that sounded continental, "please to tell me the vay (a little Germanic) to the, how to say, Hide, qui, Park"

Well, just our luck we were presented with a garrulous copper. "Well, my young fellow and where might you be from. From across the Channel are ye? Come for a visit to old Blighty? Bless my soul, yer not from France are ye? My dear old dad fought the Frogs at Waterloo, shot his leg off, don't ye know..." And on. And on and on.

We sneaked away while a carriage was speeding on the street and he waved at it to stop. We looked at each other and laughed so hard we were beginning to draw a crowd. We quieted down and drew away. "Well, that was a good start," I said. "A really good start. Of course, we knew the way to the park so we just went there. No more asking directions.

We walked down Park Lane towards Apsley House where the old Duke of Wellington lived. Crossed the street into Serpentine Road along its narrow lake. We doffed our hats to the ladies and brought our canes to our brows for the gents. Alicia took out a cheroot and we smoked it as true gentlemen would. Since we did not know anyone, no one stopped us but we did notice some ladies give us the eye. At first, I thought I would die from freight but everything went well. For now. Our next feat would be to go to a restaurant for dinner where we would need to actually converse with someone.

I slept well that night but not before I dropped a letter to Cora on how things went and promised to come to visit her soon. My true test would be, and I thought it over in my head, to introduce myself to Lady Castleridge. If I can get through that, I shall be ready for anything.

In the meantime, I practice changing the appearance of my face. Different muttonchops and hairstyles. Different mustaches and eyebrows. The lady's maid that I hired was a young girl eager for mischief herself and helped me along. I warned her not to gossip to anyone outside the house about this masquerade on the punishment of instant dismissal.

A few days later we went to a restaurant where we again sat as foreigners trying to read the menu upside down and not pronouncing anything correct but very serious. We made certain the establishment knew we had money so we were treated like gentlemen. The food was good, the wine excellent, at least according to Alicia, who after all, is a world traveler and knew of these things. And so I was ready for my final test and then off to visit Cora as the newly arrived brother of Henrietta. Leftenant Henry Ashwood of the Bengal Lancers, wounded in India fighting the rebels, was on leave. Well, why not. Good as any...

I received a letter from Flo that she will be coming back to London in 3 days and wishes to come and see me and Cora. I needed to come up with a plan and it so happened that Lord Cardigan has made the Tines headline that he had a fight with some officer in the Horse Guards. He is an arrogant pompous old codger who practically killed all of his men in the Crimea not many years ago charging with the Light Brigade into Russian guns.

I met him by chance at a soirée some weeks ago all poshed up in his 11th Light Dragoon's uniform. No one really liked him but he had land and money and came from a long line of aristocrats so he had no small list of toadies at his side 'Haw Hawing' like trained monkeys.

When I was introduced to him he was very charming though a little honeyed. After I left I heard him whisper to his cronies that, "fow a twadesman's daughtew she could do for a nightcap." Well, he could wait till man goes to the moon. If it wasn't for Cora or Flo who was with me I would have given him a piece of my mind. The fool. However, he spoke in a peculiar irritating manner which I also remembered from India where a certain type of officer, primarily from the upper classes spoke by preferring to pronounce their 'r's at times as 'w's.

Instead of saying "May I introduce myself, I am Mr. Robert from Rochester." They would say, "May I intwoduce myself I am Mr. Wobewts from Wostecheh." Most annoying I must say but if you have money and influence one can do anything. And so when Flo comes for a visit I shall be one of those arrogant officers waiting in Cora's parlor for Henrietta. She shall be so attentive to my character that she should not notice my facade. I certainly hoped so.

So, the day has come, Flo is to visit at 2 in the afternoon. She arrived ten minutes past and asked for Cora and me. The butler informed her that Cora had gone to the country two weeks before but I am here to welcome her. "However, Miss Ashwood has a previous caller, unexpectedly," he said, "and so went to her room to change. Will Lady Castleridge be so kind as to await her in the parlor?"

When Flo came in, I stood up immediately and clicked my heels together with a snap. Flo ran her eyes over me and smiled but before she had anything to say I bowed and said, "Leftenant Hawy Winchestew of his Majesty's twelve Dwagoons. At youw sewwise." And kissed her hand. It is really not that simple to talk as a half-wit even with some practice, unlike Lord Cardigan who had practiced all his life. Nevertheless, Lady Castleridge took it in stride as she was used to talking to buffoons.

"Well," she said taking her hand back rather quickly, "and where do you come from, Sir?" Right to the point Flo was. "Well Madam, I come fwom India don't you know." "Hmm, have we ever met socially sir?" "I beweve we had Madam, at the Lowd Wichawd's Ball. But we wewe not intwoduced. I had the honow of dancing with Miss Ashwood but had to weve eawly."

"I see. Do you know Miss Ashwood well, Leftanant Winchester?" "Not well, I'm afwaid. But hope to wectify this in time..." "I see. Which

Winchesters are you fwom, I mean from Sir, the Marquis of Palister or the Duke of Dalrymple?" I am sowy neithew, I'm afwaid. My fathew was the Honowable Wevewant Wichawads fwom..." and then I burst out laughing...

Well, at first Flo didn't know what to make of it. She seemed nonplussed and confused. Then a bit of anger showed on her face but before it became unmanageable I picked the wig off my head and pulled the mustache off my lip. It was then she stood amazed." Henrietta?" she asked dumbfounded. "Henrietta, is that you?"

It took a moment after I sat her down and poured her a glass of cherry to put things right. Another few minutes to explain to her why I have done what I have done and a small apology if I frightened her. "I do not know what to say, my dear, your deception worked very well on me." She said other things but I snookered her and that was the important thing. Come summer, Mr. Henry Ashwood will be traveling to the Capitols of the world. In the next few days, I planned to go to see Cora at her brother's estate in Redhill, at Hampton House. Flo was very understanding. She is a good heart for a snob and I promised to see her when I return. I had another tea with Alicia and also promised to see her before she and the opera leave for their next engagement.

The Train

On the morning of my trip, my maid packed my valises with my new men's clothes. I tied a few turns of a large silk cloth about my chest to flatten my young bosom, a small sock in the right place as Alicia suggested, which gave me that manly look, though I wasn't certain why, as I put on man's trousers. I had by this time cut my hair stylishly short, something a woman would wear but that on a man would not look out of fashion. Gluing on a cavalry mustache and whiskers finished the look. I wore black half-boots and to top everything off with a silk hat.

I decided I would be an Englishman, an officer of the East India Company, home on leave due to a wound. I know England and its history, its kings and queens though not much of politics. Therefore, if I'm in a chance conversation I would not look like a fool as if I said, I was from Italy and was asked about Milan of which I know nothing. If I can pull it off, that will be delicious and if not, I shall lose nothing except the face. In any case, I won't be with too many strangers at Hampton Hall.

Looking at myself in the full mirror again, I looked at what I saw, a well-to-do young military gentleman, or a dandy. Even my maid commented that she would not recognize me in the street. "I hope you are right, Fanny, for it would be quite embarrassing otherwise." My regret was that I could not take my maid with me for it would not be proper for a young man to be traveling with a young female. But as I only brought my man's attire I would need no help.

I took a carriage to Waterloo Station. There it was the Brighton line till Redhill Station about 20 miles away from where I should be picked up by one of Mr. Hampton's drivers. The house was only a few miles further on.

I bought a 1st class ticket and entered the coach. I have never ridden on a train so I was excited as I sat in a compartment fit for 6 passengers. I was of course also slightly nervous to be alone with 5 men in such close proximity almost shoulder to shoulder. But they were either reading the Times or smoking their cigars and two conversed with each other. I had a window seat facing forward and there sat a man across from me.

I heard the conductor shout, 'All Aboard!" and soon, with a pull and chug, the train started to move out of the station. It seemed so different from a carriage ride, a little smother as there were no cobblestones or ruts in the road but still, the carriage shook a bit from left to right. As the train turned slightly my way I could see the locomotive billowing black clouds of smoke come right into the coach. I stifled a cough.

"It will never replace the horse, mind you," said the man facing me. I was obliged to answer or seem rude. "Hmmph," I said noncommittally, "True enough certainly not for the cavalry." "I say," the man kept on,

"You seem like a cavalryman. Are you a serving officer?" So it is in for a penny, in for a pound. This occasion will come up quite often and if I was to carry it off, I might, after all, start now.

"1st Bengal Lancers," I said rather aloofly as if I expected a superior talk to a tradesman. "Wounded in Cawnpore, returned home only recently. At your service, Leftenant Henry Ashwood, sir." "Ah, I thought as much, by Jove I can spot a soldier a mile away, not having served myself, don't you know, but I can certainly tell a soldier by his carriage. Ha!

You must tell me all about your adventures, sir, I insist." He then removed a flask and offered it to me. "The best French Cognac, sir. My name is William Cortney, from Sussex, sir, glad to make your acquaintance." He extended his hand.

I shook his hand and tried to squeeze as tight as I could, just like Alicia told me, and took the offered flask. I put the flask in my mouth and stuck my tongue in to the opening and made believe I took a hearty swallow, it was disgusting, I coughed slightly as it burned my tongue like fire. "My compliments sir, quite good, you can appreciate we never received such in India," I said with disguised delight.

"Ha, ha, right you are sir. It's Napoleon Brandy don't you know. The only good thing that name stands for." "Hear, hear," another passenger concurred. "And now sir, please tell me of your service to our Queen, we have heard so little of India here. Is it as exciting as they say?"

"Ah, India, you say Sir," I started. I remember I hadn't even thought about my voice. I just started to speak and watched the eagerness in their eyes. I told them what kind of people lived there, and some of their customs. Of a sect that strangles people in the name of their religion. And then I told them the stories that Bazir told me of his experiences in the Lancers. Even then, the Bengal Lancers were known in England. They were a fearless lot that defended the North West Territories of Bengal.

I also told them about the mutiny and how it started. "The cartridge, you say. The Sepoys thought it was greased with pig or cow fat, eh," said one of the cigar smokers. "Those buggers," another man answered. "I know we did no such thing. They were greased with beeswax. I know, I manufactured those cartridges. Well, well, do go on Sir." I told them of the massacres and why they hated the British.

"My God!" they all exclaimed. Everyone was still for a moment and the Sussex man passed his flask again to everyone. "Redhill, Redhill!" the conductor announced and I had to get off, in a way almost reluctantly for I had enjoyed the center of attention. None even commented or had taken notice of my higher-pitched voice. I suppose if you play as you belong, they will accept you. Just as Alicia said.

Everyone waved goodbye and I doffed my hat magnanimously. My, that was interesting, I thought. And now for more. The trap from Hampton House was waiting for me and the driver loaded my baggage and off we went as black smoke belched and the whistle blew and my passengers shouted a great 'Huzzah' from the coach's window at me from the receding train.

And now the real test begins, again. Till now I have talked with strangers mostly, but hence I shall be with my family, Cora's family. There will be the brother, that I have met as myself when the boat docked and then there were the children. Will I be able to keep my disguise complete with everyone watching? I shall need to be on guard at all times. How I walk, how I stand, how I cross my legs, how I cut my beef.

Hampton Hall

When I arrived, the whole household, it seemed, was outside awaiting my arrival. Cora embraced me lovingly before she realized that she shouldn't act like that to a male visitor. But she recovered quickly. "Ah my dear, dear Henry, it has been so long since I have seen you, It was in Calcutta I believe, you look quite grand... Much better than

I remember." She gave me a wink. "Allow me to introduce you to my dearest brother, George Hampton. George this is Mr. Henry Ashwood.

"A pleasure to meet you finally sir, my sister had told me so much about you.""Most of it true, I hope," I retorted trying to make light of Cora's compliments. "And these," Cora pointed to the anxious youngsters, "are my brother's children. The oldest is Jane, she's ten, and this young man is Jim, 8." The girl curtsied and the boy bowed his head like an aristocrat, then shook hands. "So delighted to make your acquaintance sir. You must tell me all about..."

"Please children, let us at least welcome Mr. Ashwood into the house before you pester him to destruction. Partridge, take Mr. Ashwood's things to her... his room. Henry, come in for some refreshments, and then if you wish you can go upstairs to freshen up, or perhaps you wish to go now?" said Cora, trying to get me to go up so she could have a word with me in private. Cora was quite surprised at the way I looked, I thought. When she first saw me in London I still looked amateurish. Now she marveled at the transformation.

"I shall just have some lemonade please and then I need to take a moment with my bags," I said. The children didn't want to let me go but I promised to return quickly. Cora followed me upstairs. "My goodness," she whispered. "I truly did not recognize you at first, dear. What a metamorphosis you have made."

I beamed. "Do you truly think so? It is all done with Alicia's help. I shall tell you all about it later" Cora just smiled with astonishment. She wanted to follow me to my room and continue talking but of course, realized that she couldn't. "Oh bugger, I can't come in," she said blushing. "Go freshen up, we shall talk later."

The first day passed quickly. When I came down I of course had to repeat again the stories I told on the train. Cora's brother was amazed and the children were enthralled. I certainly wouldn't tell them details of the massacres but told them about India itself, its strange customs and its bazaars and colorful people, to their wholehearted delight and with promises of more to come. Soon they went with their tutor for their lessons. Mr. Hampton being busy with his property, I was alone at last with

Cora. We went for a walk in the garden where behind some hedges, I finally broke down with laughter. Cora soon joined me. With tears in our eyes, we congratulated ourselves on pulling off a fine masquerade, though toward the end we felt guilty for beguiling at least the children.

"They are such a delight, I feel rather devilish for what I have done," I said. "Perhaps it was a mistake." "I know, I know, it is terrible but so enjoyable, is it not?" said Cora. "They shall be alright and when we decide to tell them, I am certain they shall come to love the prank we played. And do not worry about George, he's quite harmless and loves an amusing pantomime himself. And besides, I know the stories are true, they just aren't yours"

I went to bed early, I was exhausted after this day, more so mentally than physically. I slept well and woke up early. It was arranged if I so desired, that a horse would be available for me to go riding whenever I wished. I washed quickly and dresses carefully in a new riding fig and went to the stables. The stable boy had my horse saddled and off I went into the countryside. There was no fear of getting lost for the house, being built on a rise, could be seen for miles around.

The property was quite beautiful and I felt exhilarated after London's narrow and crowded streets and the country air was almost delicious. By the time I returned, all the family was having breakfast in the garden. It almost made me homesick for the veranda in India but not quite. The gardens here were lovely and the table was set under the shadow of an old elm and yes, there was green grass all around.

"Good morning," said Mr. Hampton. "Hope you had a pleasant ride." "Yes, thank you, you have a wonderful estate, I shall enjoy my morning rides here very much." "Come and have some breakfast." On the table were spread out smoked hams, eggs, butter, bread, cakes, and tea. The children were anxious for more stories but Cora told them there would be time enough later. "Mr. Ashwood," she said, "must have some peace, after all, that is why she... he had been invited here. For rest." She looked at me and shook her shoulders. "I'll get it right soon enough," she whispered to me under a napkin.

Though the children were disappointed, they consented to wait. Cora winked at me and passed me some toast. And so, later on, I told of more experiences. Cora had some of the neighbors for tea with young children to whom I told the exotic places I visited and later when they went to play to the adults I was more forthcoming about what I saw when the mutiny started. It was not a pleasant experience for me because what I saw was nothing compared to what actually happened after we ran from Meerut. Discounting of course the massacre of my mother which I didn't mention at all. Of course, everyone knew Cora was there too but she was in Calcutta and just a woman, at least that's what I thought at the time, and had no contact with the mutineers.

Samuel

It was the morning of the fifth day. The sun shone brightly through the branches of the trees in the small woods I loved to ride. There was a small creek that meandered through a little gorge where I let the horse have a drink after a hard ride. I dismounted and sat by a tree very content on watching the fine animal take water. The sun was warm and I felt lazy and so without consciousness, I fell into a light sleep, when someone kicked my boot slightly.

"I say old boy, are you Lieutenant Henry Ashwood from Hampton Hall, Mr. Hampton, and Mrs. Blackwell's friend?' At first couldn't see who it was that had spoken to me, all I saw was a man, who stood blocking the light. I stood up quickly and seemed speechless for a moment. "Why yes," I said awkwardly. "Hen... Er... Henry Ashwood at your service. Sir," I mumbled.

"By Jove, I'm glad to meet you, Sir, I thought it might be you. Mrs. Blackwell said you go riding here in the mornings. I have heard so much about you that I feel I know you already." "And you are...?" "Ha! Most unpardonable, Sir. Why I am Samuel Dunlop. My father owns the property next door. We are neighbors. That is the Hamptons and us." He extended his hand. It had a strong grip and it was all I could do to return the shake. "I had just come back from London when I heard there's a man from

India who fought in the mutiny and I thought I have to see you right away. I saw Mrs. Blackwell and she said you might be here by the creek." "Did she indeed?" I said, standing rather awkwardly for a moment.

Samuel Dunlop was half a head taller than I and not too much older, perhaps 2 or 3 years. He didn't have a face one might imagine some Greek God to have. He did though, have a grand head of curly sandy hair and somewhat short mutton chops around his ears but his face and eyes gave him a look of a sad basset hound one loves to tussle up and hold on your knees in the winter by the fire. There was no pretense there just an honest look of curiosity. I don't know why but suddenly I took to him. But I had to be careful I realized, and watch myself, lest I give myself away.

"I am terribly sorry to have come on like that, waking you up and all that. Mrs. Blackwell has also told me a little of your service with the Lancers and I was rather keen to make your acquaintance. I have always admired a soldier though I am sorry I never had the inclination. I say, would you come for tea? Do come, I will not take no for an answer." Cora had invited some people one night and I recalled she wanted to invite their neighbors, but the Dunlops were in London.

"I'm sorry, who are you again?" I asked. "Why Samuel Dunlop, a neighbor of Mrs. Blackwell's brother. I'm sorry, did she not mention me at all...? "Well, Mr. Dunlop, she did not." Samuel Dunlop seemed a bit let down. His eagerness melted away like a snowflake on a warm tongue. He backed off a little and his eyes looked dejected. I thought I embarrassing him.

"I, I, I am so sorry. I, I presumed she did," he said crestfallen. "Please accept my apologies for startling you so, I suppose it was just my eagerness..." I at once felt terrible to see this young man embarrassed so, after all, he was just trying to be friendly.

"Well, no harm done, I suppose you just woke me up from a disagreeable dream," I lied. I'm beginning to be too good at these lies I thought. "Sorry to be so gruff. Here old man let us shake hands to friendship. What do you say..." Samuel's basset eyes lit up like candles and his smile beamed. "Of course, old boy. To friendship."

He invited me again for tea and I graciously accepted. For tomorrow, but really do not want to go. And yet I did. We spend some time together, mostly talking about my assumed regiment, the Bengal Lancers, and how dashing he heard they were but I wanted to get back to Hampton House as I needed to get away from those eyes of Samuel's. I made false excuses, as I was starting to get very good at lying and rode off. I felt sorry I let him down but it all felt rather strange.

Cora knew something has happened when she saw me riding back. As I headed to the stables she followed me. "Henrietta... er... Henry, what is the matter?" She greeted me nervously. "Cora, my dear, I think things have gone too far. Why in heaven didn't you not tell me about Samuel Dunlop?" I said getting off my horse.

"Ah, you must have met him..." "Yes! I met Samuel, you shouldn't have..." "Oh, dear, what did he do? He just came riding here asking for you. I just mentioned a few words about your regiment. I suppose he found you." "Yes he did and he didn't do anything and it is not my regiment. I

don't belong to any regiment! And he invited me for tea to retell my stories again I'm sure. Do you know how many times I have to recite these lies? I do not think I can keep doing this. Strangers on a train or in the street I can do but now it's family and friends. This I didn't see forthcoming. I won't go on deluding the Dunlops, whoever they are! I must leave immediately" But by the afternoon Cora convinced me to stay. They were not committing a crime, she said. There's not much to do in the country, except teas or riding and shooting grouse, this will add a little spice to our mundane

life. "Why, it will be such amusing conversation for months."

Finally, I acquiesced but decided to leave shortly after back to London to be myself again. The next day Cora and I rode to the Dunlop's manor house for tea. There I was introduced to Samuel's parents. To my delight and in a way disquietude I really liked them all. It was hard for me to exploit their trustworthiness in me. I felt like I was taking too much advantage of people who were kind.

Samuel especially sat with admiration for my supposed achievements. By now I also started to mix my stories up and hoped no one noticed. Samuel's eyes disquieted me. I had never felt like that with any other man I ever met. What is wrong with me? Didn't I promise myself not to get involved with anyone till I'm an old maid, so why is this happening now.

Fortunately, Cora realized what was happening and tried to get me out of the situation. "I think," she said, "that Mr. Ashwood must be quite tired. He has really had no rest since he arrived. Everyone is so eager to hear first- hand news of India ..."

"Quite understandable," Mr. Dunlap agreed. "It is all your fault Samuel, your tiring poor Mr. Ashwood out. Let us have some tea. Mrs.

Dunlap, would you care to pour Mr. Ashwood a cup." "With the greatest of pleasure Mr. Dunlap. How do you take your tea, Sir, Russian or English?" The topic changed to local matters and Samuel asked me for a walk promising no talk of India. I wanted to refuse but couldn't from politeness. I also wanted to refuse because I was getting quite nervous being close to him, I was afraid my womanly side would emerge somehow and spoil the masquerade. But I went, we walked the gardens talking about London and theater. During the walk, I almost tripped on a tree root and Samuel just caught me before I fell. Something in him suddenly changed as he held me for an instant but at that moment Cora and Mrs. Dunlop came up and broke the spell.

"Will you be staying long, Mr. Ashwood, with the Hamptons?" asked Mrs. Dunlop. We made more small talk for a while as we walked back to the house. As Cora was saying her goodbyes to Mr. and Mrs. Dunlop, Samuel turned to me. "Have you ridden to Crawley yet Mr. Ashwood? It's a small village about 8 miles to the south, it has quite a decent inn, we could lunch there and you can further enlighten me on your travels, in peaceful surroundings if that would be agreeable to you."

What could I say to those puppy eyes? "Of course Mr. Dunlop; it would be my pleasure." We agreed that Samuel would come for me in the morning and ride to Crawley. Though I felt deep inside that I should not surrender to my feelings.

On the ride back in the carriage when I had Cora alone I told her of my suspicions of her duplicity, wanting me to meet Mr. Dunlop and somehow develop a close friendship. "My dear child, don't be ridiculous. Make it a challenge and see what becomes of it. Wouldn't it be wonderful to spend some time with such a handsome young man? Think of the irony." She smiled. "Come dear, where's the adventurous spirit I met on the Bombay Queen?" I gave her a lopsided smile. "You madam are a very, very wicket woman and when I can, I shall exert my revenge, you wait." Cora just patted my knee and smiled back. "We shall see."

Mr. Dunlop picked me up in the morning and we rode off to the village of Crawley. He took me to a quaint inn overlooking a slowly running brook. We took an outside table under an old Willow and ordered bread and cheese and some wine. We sat quietly until the food arrived just taking in the day. Mr. Dunlop made me feel as if I had known him all my life. It was so comfortable just sitting here with a friend.

Realizing this, I thought to myself that I really never had a close friend except for the few I only recently made. It was mostly Bazir and the servants that I was close to who taught me about life itself. My parents, though loving, did what all parents do, have the governess take care of me. She did but only with lessons.

I did study hard. I was interested in almost anything she taught. French of course. History of France and England and as her family came to India almost a century ago, it was Indian history as well. That especially was interesting what with the Maharajahs and Mogul Empires and Alexander the Great who conquered northern Afghanistan and Northern India, it was all like a fairy tale.

But I spend a lot of time with Bazir. We went everywhere. Mostly we sneaked out of the cantonments dressed as natives. It was my favorite part. I put on pajamas and a puggaree and smeared my face darker. It was interesting sometimes how the British treated even me when they thought I was Indian. Some of those events were not pleasant and I felt very wretched for Bazir and the natives.

I once asked Bazir how he felt about this but he just shook his shoulders and with his rich booming voice said. "One day my little princes, our day will come..." We didn't know at that time how prophetic his words were to be. I did not tell Mr. Dunlop about this observation. I don't think he would understand.

"A penny for your thoughts," said Samuel looking at my melancholy face. I took a bite of bread and cheese and took a swallow of wine. I had never drank much wine but I made the best of it. Smiling I said, "Just thinking of times past, old ghosts, you know."

"It must have been horrible to have been there during the mutiny. No one here knows much about it. All the newspapers can tell us are the beginnings as you know how long it takes for news to come home. Sometimes I wonder how I would do there if I was a soldier." I smiled again. "It is a hard life on the frontier, of that you may be certain. The climate is harsh, the temperatures can melt a rock and many people want to shoot at you," I said acerbically.

Samuel gave a wry smile. "Tell me, I wish to know more." We sat a few hours there as the sun made its way towards the western horizon. Samuel ordered supper and would not accept any money from me to pay for it. I in turn talked for hours about India. Mostly, well, practical all I told him, were Bazir's adventures that he used to tell me while we were sitting in the shade of a temple after a ride. There was no end to the stories. Bazir was with me for most of my life. Oh, how I missed him but he found a woman in Calcutta and married her settling in a small town north of the city, called Dum Dum.

Samuel just listened and listened without a word and I loved him for it. He was completely bowled over my so-called life. "I truly envy you, my friend," he said when I finally stopped. There was so much more to tell but it was getting late and we must be off if we are to get back before darkness set in.

In the next few days, Samuel and I spend time together. He for the adventure stories, I because I became acutely aware that I had unusual feelings for him. It was something I had not known before. It was a nagging of the heartstrings and I found it hard to fall asleep these past few nights. One night I thought of an idea that I discussed with Cora after breakfast. I would return to London and come back as myself, Henrietta Ashwood. We would say, though we felt terrible for the lie, that I was Henry's twin sister, after all, we can't make Henry disappear so suddenly. Even Cora had not planned on the complications this turned out to be.

I went back to London that day and changed into women's clothing. What a relief to be out of britches and jackets but not much better than being in layers of corsets, bustles, and crinolines which needed the assistance of my maid, to get dressed. Nevertheless in those, I didn't have to fool anyone and I could be myself. Alicia was still at the opera singing but in the afternoons she was free and we spend a lot of time together. Alicia wanted every detail of how the masquerade went by at Hampton House.

"It is the most fun to do these things," she said to me. "But what will you do now?" A fortnight later I and my maid boarded the same train I took before. It was filled with men that immediately stood and offered us their seats. No cigars were smoked and no brandy was passed around but it was the same type of tradesmen mostly. I again took the window seat facing the locomotive. All the men sat quietly reading the latest papers that finally we were getting some news from India.

My station soon came up and a porter helped us get our bags into the trap from Hampton House. When I stepped off the trap Cora embraced me like a long-lost sister. Again introductions were followed, Mr. Hampton remembered me from the docks and asked about my welfare but the excitement that greeted Henry wasn't there. After all, I was just a young woman and not a Bengal Lancer fighting off mutineers. But the children took to me as I brought them presents, a doll for the girl and a small wooden sword for the little gentleman. Cora told them I was Henry's twin and they inquired about him also and were sorry he could not come.

This time it was a more relaxing atmosphere as I wasn't pestered to tell any of my adventures I might have had in India and so left alone to prattle with Cora. We took walks in the garden and had tee. Took a turn in the nearby village. Life was simple but in the back of my mind, there seemed to be a query about a certain young man.

I was a little surprised that Cora did not bring him up but I played it to the hilt myself. I did not ask as if it did not matter to me. However I suspected Cora knew what I was thinking and after I was there a few days announced a dinner party in my honor for some friends, including the Dunlops, this coming Saturday.

Of course, I was a bit excited, anxious, and nervous. Would I feel something for Samuel when I saw him and would Samuel somehow see something in Henry's 'sister?' What will he say when he first lays eyes on me? Will he recognize me and give the jig away?

The next few days were all in a flurry as preparations were made. There was the dusting, sweeping, and rug beating. Silver polished and festive China taken out. Chandeliers dusted. There were the wines and flowers to be ordered and arranged. The choosing of the right guests, including of course the Dunlops, and then where to seat them and not make a faux pas. There is, of course, an order of precedence of who is more important than another and who will promenade who to the dining room. Cora relished it all.

The day finally came. The guests arrived in the evening in their carriages, fashionably late, and were ushered into the drawing-room. Cora introduced me to everyone and as they passed I heard the whispered gossip that must have come from London. "Did you hear, she has an income of 50,000 per year." Or, "She's an heiress you know, 70 thousand for certain." And, "I must introduce her to my nephew George he..." and so forth.

I was quite amused at how gossip travels so fast. It was the same in India. The Dunlops, being the highest-ranking Nabobs in the County came only half an hour late. My heart was beating quickly when I heard the Dunlops announced by the butler. Lord and Lady Dunlop came in and were greeted by Mr. Hampton and Cora. As the guest of honor, I stood next to them and was introduced again of course, as Henry's sister, Miss Henrietta Ashwood. The Dunlops greeted me without any recognition, thank goodness, and they inquired about the health of my brother. I was inwardly embarrassed that I had to lie again but as I said before, in for a penny, in for a pound.

It was then that I saw Samuel come in and my heart fluttered a little. He was so handsome in his tails and oh, that bushy head of hair. Cora was right, you just want to get your hands into it and mess it up. "Ah," said Cora, "It's young Mr. Dunlop, so nice to see you. May I introduce Miss Ashwood, Henry's twin sister?"

Samuel came over and took my gloved hand and kissed it and when he looked up I thought I saw a sign of recognition in his surprised face and thought the jig was up and my heart skipped a beat. "I say, Miss Ashwood. I knew I have seen you before. I believe it was at Lady Sinclair's Ball some weeks ago. Where you not there?"

"I, I believe I was Mr. Dunlop but I don't recall you there," I managed to reply. "No, I don't believe you might. I had come late and I saw you dancing at the other end then someone I knew stopped me and then the dance ended and I didn't see you again, I am sorry to say."

"Well Mr. Dunlop, I believe I left after that too. The room was very hot and I was very tired." "So this explains it and I am terribly glad to meet you here then," he said. And so, the butler called us in for dinner. I being the guest of honor and Lord Dunlop the ranking nabob, had the pleasure to escort me to the dining room. Mr. Hampton had the honor of escorting Lady Dunlop and Mr. Samuel escorted Cora. The rest in order of importance marched in behind us. We were a jolly little group.

At the table, Mr. Hampton, being the host, sat at the head of the table and Lord Dunlop at his right, and myself next to him. Cora is at the other end with Samuel on her right and the rest distributed alternately, male and female. The table was richly set with bouquets of flowers in monstrous epergnes and enough silver plate to pay for a small war. Next to Lord Dunlop, Mr. Hampton was one of the richest men in the county and so the proof was on the table.

As we waited for the first course, a fine light soup, Lord Dunlop enveloped me with polite conversation. He was worried if the mutiny had interrupted any cricket matches for that would just not do. Fortunately, the soup was served and saved me from a witless conversation.

Dinner was a large affair. Cora wanted to have a good showing for her brother's sake so that nothing was spared. Dinner was served a la Russe with the footmen serving each dish silently after each course was eaten. There was fish and foul, a roast and veal. Lobster and oysters. Vegetables and fruit. Each dish had its own cutlery to be eaten with and of course no lack of wines. After dinner, there were deserts of cakes and pastries and liqueurs. In my eyes, it was a meal fit for a king. In the end, Mr. Hampton asked for the cook to come in and we all applauded as she bowed, her cheeks red with embarrassment.

Occasionally during the meal, I would look down the table and catch Samuel peeking at me but quickly look away in embarrassment. Finally, dinner was over, and as custom dictated the ladies retired to the drawing- room for tea and chatter and the gentlemen stayed to talk and drink their port and smoke their cigars. For a moment I thought I was Henry and did not get up but a footman saved the day by pulling the chair almost from under me. I joined the ladies for the tea and gossip. As I passes Samuel, he gave me a wink which made me blush.

So the evening passed and it was time for guests to call for their carriages. Everyone complimented Cora and Mr. Hampton for a fine dinner as they said their goodnights. On the way out Samuel stopped by Cora and asked her if he could call on me tomorrow. "Yes, I'm sure Henrietta would be delighted," she smiled as she looked at me. "Of course," I said.

"Do you ride, Miss Ashwood...?" asked Mr. Dunlop. "Yes I do, Mr. Dunlop, as a matter of fact, Mr. Hampton gave me a horse to use. I do like to ride early in the morning," I said. "Then may I accompany you on your ride and show you our countryside, Miss Ashwood?" He said. "Thank you, I would be much obliged for your company, Mr. Dunlop," I said with a gentle smile.

"Would eight o'clock be convenient then, Miss Ashwood," he said. As soon as they all left Cora pocked my elbow. "Well," she whispered. "Is he not the most agreeable of fellows?" "Cora, did I not see him a few weeks ago?" I answered. "Yes, but then it was different, was it not? I saw your face..." "You, Mrs. Blackwood, are incorrigible."

I knew Mr. Dunlop and I could not go out riding ourselves as last time. Now, of course, I needed a chaperon, and Cora of course wouldn't miss this for the world. She was up early all feverish to see us together. Mr. Dunlop was early too as he met us by the stables. "Good morning Mrs. Blackstone, Miss Henrietta." He doffed his hat high.

"Good morning, Mr. Dunlop, I see you're an early riser." "So are you Miss Ashwood, Mrs. Blackstone?" he asked. "Is there somewhere special you would like to ride?" "I believe the North Meadow; my brother told me that would be a pleasant place to go." What an accomplished liar I am turning out to be.

Unlike before when I rode with him, I and Cora wore dresses in a riding habit to ride side saddle as was fashionable for a woman, though I would have preferred jodhpurs that would be quite indecent, and besides, it might be too close to my 'brother's look.' We mounted and rode off. After the ride through the meadow, Mr. Dunlop steered us towards the creek where he met "Henry." Once there, dismounted and let the horses cool off. "This is where I met your brother," Samuel said. "Now that I see you

in the daytime I see the similarity between you." "Of course, since we are twins only born ten minutes apart, Henry being the first." I had to look away as the lie slid out too easily.

"He certainly is a fine chap. He was telling me some exciting adventures he had with the Lancers. I know some of it was tragic but at the same time, he had lived a fuller life than I. I have no accomplishment to speak of. I can't even play cards well; I always seem to lose. I wanted to join the army, you know, but I'm an heir and papa won't let me go." He smiled sheepishly

"Well, Mr. Dunlop, the military is not for everyone. It is not just regimental dinners or dress-up for balls or fêtes. It is, at least in India much marching on dusty plains, and believe it or not, natives shooting at you." I said that humorously.

But Mr. Dunlop was quite serious. "I know all that. My uncle was a coronet at Waterloo and he told me many stories but still... Oh, if I could only be like your brother..." How utterly devastated I felt at that moment. A lie that started as a lark is truly becoming awkward. I just didn't know what to say. I felt terrible for Samuel. All this time Cora just walked behind us not saying a word.

"But I'm getting you melancholy," said Mr. Dunlop. "Forgive me. The horses are done, Let me show you something else." We mounted again and Mr. Dunlop showed me some of the same places he showed 'Henry' but of course, I made believe I saw them for the first time and commented on how lovely they were. I looked back to Cora occasionally and saw that wicket smile on her face. When we get back I shall have a little talk with her.

We returned to Hampton's house by noon. I was tired and gloomy and hungry but without an appetite. Cora left me with Mr. Dunlop as we said goodbye. We invited him for luncheon but he declined as he said his father needed him for something. I think he was just a little nervous having Cora with us.

I was too tired to eat so I went up to rest. My Lucy helped me out of my clothes and asked me about Mr. Dunlop. We have become somewhat close as she was just my age and someone to confide in. But after I had at least a small glass of cherry I went to bed. Of course, I could not sleep. It bothered me that I had to tell so many lies to someone I was so fond of if not with more serious feelings.

With that, I awoke to a knock at my door that it was time for tea. Again as Lucy helped me into the multi-layered garments I thought of how easily a man can dress. Tea was served in the gazebo where Cora was ready to pour. She handed me a cup and just waited for me to say something. Since I didn't, Cora asked what I thought of young Samuel now.

"A charming young man," I said. I wasn't going to fall into Cora's trap. "I shall have to see him again, I suppose, before I leave. It would be the polite thing to do.""The polite thing to do, you say. My goodness Henrietta- isn't he the most handsome of man. I would just like to put my hands into those sandy curls of his and hold him to my bosom. Oh, if only I was your age. Wouldn't you?"

My cheeks flushed red. I wasn't prepared for such a talk. This is the first time this has happened to me and I wasn't even certain what it was. I wanted to strike back at Cora for embarrassing me so openly. "Weren't you in love once and then look what happened," I said cuttingly.

"Well, touché my dear," answered Cora without taking offense. "I told you something of my husband before but there is more, much more. May I tell you of my love affair?" She suddenly became serious.

Cora poured herself a cup of tea but did not drink it. She looked at me soulfully as if deciding, then in a low voice, she started to talk. "When I first met my husband-to-be, I was your age, perhaps older, about twenty- three, an old maid by society's standards. He looked dashing with a charming personality. Tall. Handsome. Rich. But much older than I. All the young women were after him. But for some reason he chose me. I am not going to say I was the most exceptional young woman there but I did look quite agreeable. Don't interrupt," she said to me as I was about to interject.

"I had my following of men, of course, younger blades and rich too. But foolishly I went for the more mature. Little did I know at that time that it wasn't up to me at all. It was all arranged with my father and a large dowry." She stopped a moment and sighed. "We married quickly because, Milton, that was his name, Milton. How I despise him now to even to mention that name!"

Cora and Milton Blackwell married at his father's estate. She told me. It was one of the richest in Cornwall. She was the happiest of people in England until their wedding night. When she first met him he seemed so proper and gentlemanly and so ambitious. He was a minor director in the Company because of his father's holdings, but he hoped for quick advancement if he transferred to India.

"Little did I know that his father made him go to stem gossip." But that first night that was supposed to be her happiest of all time, he asked her to perform the most outrageous acts. "It was horrible," she said. "I refused. He slapped my face and threw me out of the bedroom. There are more fish in the sea," he said without any feelings.

"I did not know what to do. It all happened so suddenly it was as if I married a totally different person. There was no one to confide in, after all, he was my husband. And who would believe me." A tear formed on her cheek.

"He had power and influence through his family." She continued after a few moments. "What could I say about his perversions. That night when he literary threw me out of the room he took our maid to bed. Would you believe it? He had her waiting outside the bedroom door. It appears that he had taken her many times before, willingly. She had been his mistress all along. I couldn't even discharge her. She just laughed at me in the morning daring me to say something. All the servants knew but of course, they could not say anything except perhaps feel sorrowful for me."

By the end of the week, they were on a ship to Calcutta. Cora, as a young wife could not protest. "The trip was agony. He even took the maid with him claiming she was my Lady's maid. What saved me was that my husband had the mal de mer from the beginning for the duration of the trip. By the time we disembarked, he was quite ill and still had to be in bed for many days after." She shook her head with a mild smile.

"Even as a minor official, we had a grand house because of his connections. By then I told him he could lead his life with the maid or anyone else but he must leave me alone or I will cause a scandal no matter the cost to me."

Cora stood and walked towards the rose garden. It appeared there was one flower with a broken stem. "I truly must tend to my garden. I have neglected it too long." She broke the stem and brought the dying rose and put it into a glass of water.

"As you know my dear, India has no deficiency of women, even white women who willingly will debase themselves for money or trinkets. And so I was left alone. Of course, when there were receptions I went with him as if nothing happened. That was our agreement. But I led a lonely life. Naturally, I had friends and lunches and soirées and teas but no manly company. It was, as you also know, a tight community. But I am certain everyone knew but was too polite to say."

"Then fate took a hand. Two weeks before the mutiny he was suddenly sent up north to Lucknow, on Company business. I, as his wife, was to follow with the baggage, as we were to stay for six months. A few days before the uprising I started up. I had an escort of ten company sepoys, a few carts, and a young English Captain in charge as he was being transferred to his new posting up north somewhere." Cora shook her hands as if it didn't matter.

"We had only traveled a day and a half when we heard rumors of what was happening in Meerut and other places. It was too late to return and we couldn't really go forward. We had to hide at a friendly Maharajah's fort. Our sepoys ran away with all the baggage and it was only me and the captain left."

"The news from the rebellion was bad. Very bad. I don't have to tell you. But we were safe. Two white people together, one a woman who has not seen love and a handsome captain looking for it. Must I go any further?" she asked me. "However it was not to last. His gentlemanly honor did not allow him, his regiment needed officers now. After a fortnight we parted. He went to find his regiment and he never returned. I heard later he was killed on the way. So useless…"

"I waited at the Maharajah's fort till it was over. Then I heard the news about my husband. He was also killed by one of his servants in revenge for the abuse of the servant's young wife."

I met Mr. Dunlop the next day. This time we were alone. I didn't care what gossip people will say. When I saw him ride up to me I felt goose flesh embrace my body. Could this really be love? Could it come so fast? When I was here as Henry, I felt something but it certainly didn't feel like this. Just because at this time I wore a dress, does that make that much of a difference?

"Is there someplace you would like to ride?" he asked again. "Is not Mrs. Blackstone to accompany us?" "No she is not but I am counting on you to behave like a gentleman," I said lightheartedly. Mr. Dunlop nodded and helped me mount my horse. "Where to then?" he asked.

The only place I thought of was that little bank by the stream. "Take me back to where we first met." Though I realized I meant when I met him as Henry, Mr. Dunlop didn't seem to notice. We rode there at a slow canter stealing secret glances at each other.

When we arrived we dismounted and let the horses have their way again. I went to that tree where I fell asleep the first time and sat down. Samuel sat down beside me. Thus we sat with our own thoughts watching the horses graze. By chance, Mr. Dunlop adjusted himself and his fingers touched mine. We looked at each other. He was hesitant. He seemed afraid to do something rash. We continued to stare into each other's eyes. "May I call you Samuel?" I asked. "And please call me Henrietta." "I would very much like for you to call me that. Henrietta," he whispered. "Samuel," I said hoarsely. "Kiss me..."

The next day I went back to London. "I cannot engage with this charade any longer," I told Cora. "This has gone too far. I cannot be two people anymore here or anywhere. I must decide what to do about my life." Cora said she thought she understood. "Take some time and think about what you want to do and please let me know. I wish you all the best my dear."

The train back to London was grim. I sat and thought about what happened when Samuel kissed me. It was a soft kiss as if a butterfly had landed and deposited the sweetest nectar on my lips. It was like nothing I ever tasted. And then he kissed me again, intensely. He hadn't meant to I suppose, but it just happened. We both felt embarrassed and mentioned not a word all the way back to Hampton Hall, I took my horse to the stables and told the groom to brush her gently.

Samuel walked me to the house and we just stared at each other again then I looked away not knowing what to say or do. "I shall see you again..." he said hesitantly. "Of course, you will..." I answered but somehow I knew it will not be so.

The first thing I did when I came back to London was go to see Alicia sing at the opera, then later I joined her for supper at Radcliff 's. Alicia always had a private table there so she could eat in peace with friends.

"You must tell me all about it, mon cher," she said to me after she drank a half glass of champagne. "What did he say to you as a woman. His eyes must have popped in his head when he saw you, you are so beautiful, no? Why are you back so soon?" I told her of my distress. "I felt so guilty about it at all times. I just could not continue and I don't know what to do. His kiss, you know, felt so wonderful but my guilt took all the pleasures away."

As wonderful as it seemed, I told her, "I do not wish to be tied down. I really desire to travel; I have always wanted that. I did not wish to marry or have children. I wanted to dance in palaces but of course, I could not travel alone. Who is going to chaperon me? But now, because you were so helpful to me, mon cher, I can travel, as a young man. That is what I shall do. Travel as a young man all over Europe and no one can tell me what to do.

"But, mon très cher ami, I have the most perfect solution for you. You know our contract is finished in two weeks and the opera must go to Vienna where we open next month.""I totally forgot," I said in despair. "What shall I do without you. You are my truest friend in London. I shall miss you very much," I said crestfallen.

"Ah, but I know what you shall do. You say you wish to see the World. Why not start with Vienna? Why not come with me. Vienna is tre magnifique. You will love it. I have an apartment for myself and my maid, it is very large. Why do you not come with me...? You have no other obligation here unless you wish to go back to your gentleman friend."

I sat there for a moment and thought what a marvelously brilliant idea that was. I certainly had no obligations here. Well, Samuel, but as I told myself before, I had no plans to tie myself down now. I needed to experience more of life. Samuel, though I had feelings for him, is my first. Maybe it is just puppy love, after all, a good kisser does not make for a life's companion. There was so much more to experience. "That is a wonderful idea my dearest friend you are so brilliant to have thought of it but are you certain I will not be interfering with your career?"

It was an easy decision to be made but also very difficult to explain to friends. Cora will probably feel good for me, she will miss me and understand. Then there was Flo, which I haven't seen much but still felt I needed to explain to her. I will write them all a letter explaining my reasons for leaving. Taking care of what to do with Henry, my imaginary brother, could be a dilemma but I devised a simple plan.

My brother felt guilty staying in comfortable London while his fellow officers were still fighting the rebels. It is like Cora's lover. He will return to his regiment with great haste. He will write a long letter to both Cora and Samuel explaining everything once he is established. This will give him at least a year to think about it.

But how to explain to Samuel my own leaving after what we did that afternoon near the stream. I was sure he will be heartbroken but he is also young he will meet someone else. I made myself believe that. And so, after packing my garments, including my 'brother's', I and Alicia and the opera company boarded a channel steamer to France with a stop in Paris, where we took a train to Vienna. It was the beginning of a new adventure.

Five months have passed. I enjoyed Vienna immensely. There was no end to what to do and because of young Alicia, who quite impressed the royal court the last time she sang there, we were invited everywhere. I met society and royalty. There were grand balls at fabulous houses. I met officers of the Royal Guards who danced me to exhaustion with waltzes. It was a grand time but for some reason, I could not get away from the memory of Samuel.

What was it about him that gnawed at my heart? I certainly met more dashing men there as Austria was an Empire that included so many nations your head could spin counting them. Austrians of course with their stiff Germanic ways and much heel-clicking. Handsome Hungarian hussars with their pelisses swinging as they danced the mazurka. Officers from the Balkans and from the East European provinces of the Empire, Russian Cossack Officers with their long tunics and cartridge loops on their chests, Polish Lancers, Italians Alpini with long feathers in their hats, really no end to young men who danced with me and sent me flowers and took me to cafés where there were the most wonderful pastries and coffees. All that without dressing in Henry's' garments.

Here in Vienna, I could go by myself almost everywhere and not worry about what society would think. But I was hardly ever alone. I made friends both male and female, nonetheless, for some reason, they all became Samuels in the end.

But all things had to come to a climax and now another contract was ending for Alicia and her opera. Their next appearance was to be in St. Petersburg in Russia. In spite of my travel fever, I started aching for home and London. I wanted to walk on the Strand, see the changing of the Guard, and hear English spoken in the streets.

Austria was the first, not that I have traveled so many other countries but it was the first I didn't speak the tongue. Oh, I learned some words to get by which Alicia taught me. 'Darf ich das Schnitzel mit Kartoffeln und Gemüse haben bitte', or 'Ein Kaffee mit einem Stück Schwarzwälder Kirschtorte, bitte' or 'Eine Dame ist küssen nicht ein Herr sie gerade erst kennengelernt.' The last more important than ordering food. They were quite romantic, these haughty officers of the Austrio-Hungarian Empire. But mostly I missed my friends Cora and Flo and, and to touch Samuel and have him kiss my lips. That's what I thought of the most. Poor Samuel, he had probably forgotten me as I hadn't even written to him since the goodbye letter those ages ago. And so, after a tearful farewell with Alicia I packed my garments again but this time I left my men's apparel in a church to be given to the poor. There will not be any more metamorphosis from me.

The trip back seemed even longer than the trip from Calcutta. The trains seem to crawl and the channel crossing seemed to sail backward. I had written to Cora about the date I will arrive in London and if I could once again impose on her to stay at her home. But as I will have to pass Redhill Station for London, I would stop at Hampton House to see Samuel for I could not wait a moment longer.

To my unexpected pleasure, Cora met me at the station herself. Oh, how I missed her so. We embraced and giggled for a long time. She asked me questions before we even settled in the carriage. Everyone at Hampton House received me most graciously. It was a grand welcoming but I thought at least that perhaps Samuel would be there to greet me and as soon as a chance provided some time I asked Cora about him. Cora apparently was waiting for this and took me aside and with a sullen face, she handed me a sealed letter. By Cora's look, I knew it wasn't good news. I took the letter and ran up to my room and tore it open.

"My dearest friend." No 'dearest love.' No 'dearest Henrietta,' but just 'friend.' A tear ran down my cheek and unto the letter smudging the word friend. I ran my eyes quickly to the end to see how it was signed. There was no love there either, just "your obedient servant, Samuel."

Obedient servant indeed... I didn't know if I could actually read this letter now. It was all over and it was my own fault. I went to the window and looked out. The sun had not yet set and in the distance, I could see the creek and the tree-line where we must have sat and where he kissed me. I brought my finger up to my lips and stroked at the spot. Tears were now gushing like that stream in the distance. I went to a chair and sat down, the letter still in my hand and started reading again.

My dearest friend,

The day you wrote me about your brother going back to serve his regiment I could not sleep. I wondered at his bravery and devotion to duty which is the greatest honor for a gentleman. I thought of my many wasted years sitting in my father's house doing nothing while the world around me was creating events. I thought myself a coward and I could not live with myself for that...

"Oh my God," I thought. "Samuel has done away with himself while I was waltzing with strangers" I was afraid of what was to follow...

... I could not live with myself for that and so I have decided to have my father purchase a commission in any regiment in India and hope to meet my dear friend, your brother, Henry, there, and we shall fight the foe till the end. I will take the first ship outbound to Calcutta and by the time you read this if, at all, I shall be serving Queen and Country.

Do not distress yourself about me, I shall be alright. If you still can find a good word for me please write a letter to HQ, Calcutta for I know not where I will be stationed. I shall never forget you and I shall always remember our last moment together

Your Obedient Servant,

Samuel Dunlop

I cried until there was a knock on the door and Cora asked if she might come in. "I must go to him…" I spurted out as soon as she entered. "But he's in India now. He wrote me too that he was going," Cora said.

"I know. Damn his eyes. How could he do that? What nonsense. Why didn't you stop him! I have no brother! Who even knows where the Devil he will be stationed. India is 100 times the largest than England! Why didn't you stop him!" I cried again.

Cora came closer and put her arm around me. "By the time I received the letter he was gone. There was nothing I could do. He was gone," and she also started to cry. "His parents are terribly upset" "What have I done?" I wept. "What have I done…" I went to my valise to start packing. "What are you doing?" asked Cora with great anxiously. "There is nothing to be done. How will you ever find him? We just have to wait and see. Perhaps he will write…"

"I am not waiting for a letter that might never arrive. I shall go to India myself and tell him this was all nonsense. It was all a lie. Why should he waste his life for nothing? There is no bravery or honor to be gotten there only death and destruction. I must find him myself and bring him home." Cora made me stay another day so at least we could plan the voyage.

One can't just take off and go to India at a moment's notice. Ships do not embark on a daily basis. She came with me to London to her house and we went to the shipping offices of the East India Company and through both, our influences received a cabin on a steam packet to Alexandria, Egypt. From there I must take a train to Suez where I would board another steam packet on to Calcutta. This time my voyage would be at least two months faster.

Of course, I needed to see my solicitor and banker. I needed bank notes and letters of introduction to the military so I can search for Samuel at the Company's Military Head Quarters and then wait for the packet's departure at the East London docks. So, another goodbye, again. It seems my life is meant for only goodbyes. It was sad for no matter what happens I would not see Cora for at least 2 years.

As the ship steamed off, I stood at the railing waving at her till she became a speck in the distance. I remember as I told myself many times I would never make a trip like that again and yet here I was. I still stood there till the smoke from the stack made my eyes burn. When I went down to my cabin I hardly even noticed that my cabin was so much better this time. I hardly noticed that it was cleaner with a finer mattress to sleep on, an actual little table, a mirror on the wall behind it, and a porthole that let in fresh air if the smoke from the stack didn't blow it in.

The trip was impossibly slow even though it was faster than the last. I couldn't sleep well nor eat much. By the time the ship anchored in Alexandria, I was quite disconsolate. From Alexandria, I was to take the train to Suez. At Suez, yet another steamer off to Calcutta. It seems my journey will never end, but it did, a little over a month later.

With my father's name and letters of recommendation from the Company Nabobs in London, I acquired accommodation in Calcutta for as long as I needed. After settling in I inquired at Military HQ about Samuel Dunlap. Yes, someone at the office by chance remembered the name because of his father, but not any particulars as HQ was still in the midst of the mutiny. It would take weeks to find him, the office wallah said.

I pulled the man aside and put 10 quid in his palm. "I want it in 2 days. Is that possible?" I asked. For that money he would guide the ma'am sahib to the Himalayas, he said. He will have it in two days. I then wanted my old friend Bazir Mughal found. Bazir had told me he would live in Dum Dum, a town north of Calcutta. I hired a messenger and promised him a bonus if he brings him to me in two or three days. I would spare no cost to find him. What use is all my fortune if I can't find happiness and happiness meant Samuel?

Then I purchased men's clothing for myself, not the English dandy style but native garb for the coming trip I knew was going to be hard. Mostly what the Northern tribes would wear with cloaks and blankets. I would let Bazir purchase rifles and I heard they sold the new Colt six-shot revolvers. They were expensive I was told but I did not care. This was not a time to pinch pennies.

When Bazir was found I knew he could find an escort for the trip. Also, horses and food needed to be procured. So many other things needed for a trip through rough country still probably filled with mutineers or bandits. Bazir was a veteran and knew what was to be done.

It took almost two weeks to make the arrangements. Bazir was found in three days to my delight. He did know men he could trust, good company pensioners who served the Raj and looking for adventure. Like him, swarthy cavalrymen who knew the frontier like the palms of their hands. He made them swear on their salt to obey my orders and if the job gets done an extra bonus will be paid to each man or his family if he is killed. It took the office wallah 4 days till he finally found Samuel's orders. He was to report to Skinner's Horse, a Company cavalry regiment defending Lucknow.

Once all was ready we departed early morning by horse on the Trunk Road heading north. We were all dressed in native garb and fully armed so that we looked like a collection of bad mashes to be reckoned with. The plan was to go to Allahabad by a horse about 500 miles up north from Calcutta, then by pulwars upriver towards Lucknow and see how things were. Though most of the mutineers were subdued by now, some areas still had them roaming the country as bandits.

On the first day we made over 40 miles, resting only when the horses were tired. We stopped at a small village by a stream. A fire was made and we took turns as guards. Even I took my turn. Before sunrise, we packed up and moved on. To me, every second was precious and so it went for 16 days when we reached Allahabad. The word there was that siege of Lucknow was broken at last. This was excellent news, however, there were still roaming bands in the region. Lucknow by the river was another 100 miles or so and then by horse about a 2-day ride.

It was a very slow trip upriver as the pulwars, we had three as we had many horses, 4 for supplies and 13 for us, depended on the wind but it was still safer than riding the countryside. Four days later we arrived at a wooden area about half a mile from the road leading to Lucknow. We disembarked at night and rode inland for an hour and rested.

All that time the countryside seemed normal, so far. There was much evidence of the mutiny with burned homes and empty villages. In the morning we started early but saw men marching towards us in the distance. We dismounted and hid in the tall grass as we saw the men marching and singing and dancing with packs on their backs and wagons pilled full of all sorts of furniture and boxes and whatnot. We even saw pots and pans.

"It is the 23rd Native Infantry, husoor, pie dog mutineers," said Bazir, "full of pillage to sell in the bazaars." He spits in their direction. "But no horses, bless the Prophet, we have no worry. Let us be off then, by tomorrow we shall drink tchei in Lucknow."

So we rode again following the road on our left. By late afternoon we heard shots in the distance near a rocky outcrop. It would be too much to bypass it as it spanned the road and the way we were going so we decided to take a closer look before we made up our mind. We were a strong little force, with new rifles loaded with the more accurate ammunition, and our new Colt six-shooters.

The sun was almost setting behind us when we arrived at the edge of the forest. We left the horses farther back and slowly crept up behind some trees and looked ahead toward the firing. I had a pair of field glasses with me and scanned the rocky outcrop. There I saw two groups firing at each other so I handed the glasses to Bazir to take a look. He climbed up a branch so he could look over the brush.

"By the Holy Prophet, I see British troops by the rocks, perhaps 4 or 5 firings and more lying on the ground perhaps dead. It is Skinner's Horsemen, I know. I also see the bad mashes around them, not too many perhaps 8 or 10 but the British cannot move from their position. They will be dead soon. Wait! There is a wounded man on the ground who cannot move. I think they are waiting for the others to try to rescue him and then they will kill them. There is no chance the British can escape the trap."

"Let me see," I said and climbed up beside him. "I can't really make anything of it but he seems like an English officer. We must try to save them. Can we do it?" "If you wish it ma'am sahib then it shall be done." We climbed down and he called his men around him and explained what they should do. Within five minutes the plan went into action. I and two of the men sneaked up closer to the mutineers as quietly as possible and waited for the signal, guns ready. The new Colt six-shot revolvers had given us an advantage at close range over the bandits or mutineers.

The other men with Bazir went around to the road and began to sing out loud some Hindi bawdy song as if they were mutineers themselves and headed towards the group surrounding the British. When they got close the mutineers stood up and thought they were getting more assistance which they didn't seem to be happy about.

At that moment everything happened at once. There was much firing and in the end, all mutineers were dead and one of Bazir's men was wounded. Immediately after, I ran towards the downed man. At the same moment, one of the British soldiers on the rocks stood and shot at me and I stumbled into darkness.

When I awoke I stared into Bazir's face. He smiled at me. "You will be alright Miss Henrietta bahadoor, you are a brave woman and all is well." I sat up and saw I was on an army cot surrounded by Company soldiers making camp and smiling dreamily at me was Samuel. "Oh, my dearest Henrietta, I thought when I saw you I was dreaming. I could not believe that you were here in the flesh. I couldn't imagine how in heaven's you came to be here, when your man, Bazir, told me all about it."

Of course, it was a miracle that I found him and a bigger miracle that Samuel was actually that wounded man Bazir and I saw being attacked by, as it turned out, by some of the men we saw the day before who stayed behind thinking it was an easy victory. Later when we all calmed down and had a light supper and I was introduced to his commanding officer, Samuel and I sat by the fire alone in each other's arms. We at first just murmured sweet nothings to each other. Then I asked him how he came to be here at this moment.

"It must start at the beginning," he said, "after we left each other that fateful day when you promised that we will see each other soon." "I did not..." I started to say but he interrupted me. "You shall be quiet and listen. When Cora told me you left for the continent. Where did you go, Vienna? Of all places. I felt you went away for good because I did something wrong... Oh, be still and don't interrupt.

I felt you decided I was a coward and to be honest I thought I was one too. Cora told me about Henry and how he went back to his regiment so his bravery gave me the motivation to do the same. After all, what have I done in life except gamble or sit on my arse? I have not even read a book in years. I was a wastrel. I said do not interrupt me and listen."

"I asked my father to purchase a commission for me in the army. He refused.""You are my only son, my heir, I shall not waste your life on a goose chase to India to get a Victoria Cross. I shall lock you up in the wine cellar first!" he screamed at me. "But I was determined to come and find Henry where ever he was and prove my bravery to him and to you."

I gave his arm a squeeze but said nothing. "Without my father's consent, I was going to sell one of my father's precious guns and borrow the rest from my mother, enough to purchase a chit on a packet to Calcutta..." "Oh my dearest, you stole from your..."

"I said not a word from you till I finish. No. I did not. I borrowed 500 quid from a friend, enough for the trip and extra for my equipment when I get there but I know that I can make it all back here." "Yes, if you steal it, you bloody fool. Have you no idea what..." If you do not let me finish I shall not say a word anymore," he said.

I let him finish. That friend of his was a gambler. 500 quid meant nothing to him. He was as rich as Crassus. He was banking Samuel would make a fortune in India, I suppose like my father and many other Company men who came back with pockets full of booty.

Anyway, Samuel got his trip and came the same way I did, through Suez. When he arrived he was practically lost at what to do. He looked for Henry as if he was around the corner waiting for him. When no one could find a Henry Ashwood he joined the East Indian Army. He was lucky here because he was a gentleman and so he was made an officer. Of course, he knew nothing of what an officer does but I found out that is not a detriment in the British army. I found that many so-called officers did not know from their left to their right. In the British Army, it was the sergeants that led the men.

And so Lieutenant, the former Mr. Dunlop, heir to the Dunlop peerage, was sent up north with twenty replacements. When he arrived at his post at Lucknow fortunately most of the mutineers have been trounced. But still, he was sent on patrols to the countryside as there might be bandits present taking advantage of the situation and to learn the trade of soldiering.

One might wonder how that was but in the English army there was a purchase system and it did not matter on experience but money. If one could buy any rank they wished. That is all I will say on this subject. After many untroubled patrols, he was finally ambushed by bandits and that was when my little band found him.

"So I was wounded and we all were almost overrun when your little troop came along. I think one of our men thought you were a bandit as you were actually dressed like one and he shot you. Fortunately, the man was a bad shot and just grazed your pretty head." He finished with a smile and kissed my forehead.

Soon after we rescued Samuel and his men, his own Captain arrived with reinforcements as Samuel's patrol had failed to show for many hours and bandaged us all up. After Samuels's fireside chat we all slept where we were and the next morning we rode back to the fort. That night we had a reception at the officer's mess and three cheers and a hooza for the lady.

Bazir and his men of course were not invited but I made certain they were entertained in their own way. I looked into Bazir's eyes and he understood the circumstance more than the smartest general in the British army. He and his men wanted to go back to their homes as their undertaking was over. I wrote out the documents they were to present to a solicitor I hired in Calcutta where they would get paid. I asked Bazir if he would come with me to England but he just shook my hand and I said in his profound way. "Oh no, ma'am sahib. I thank you very much. My country is India and one day it will be ours. Why should I go and live with foreigners?" We said goodbye as he rode off on the Trunk Road to Dum Dum and his family. "I shall see you again my friend," I told him.

Soon the mutiny was settled after much killing on both sides and much looting on our side, the British won, as predicted. Then one evening the question of Henry was settled during the victory celebration, again, at the officer's mess. Samuel took me out to the veranda and we sat down comfortably in one of the wicker chairs. It was a balmy cloudless evening, lit with sparkling stars above. A mild breeze embraced us, stirred by a punkah wallah lying inconspicuously below the veranda. We brought two glasses of iced punch with us and Samuel held my hand.

"What a wonderful evening it is Samuel. Finally, we have peace..." "It is my Dear, I only wished..." "Yes Darling, what would you wish for?" "Well, all this time we have not mentioned your brother Henry once. Have you heard from him? Do you know where he is?"

Oh my God, thought I. I had totally forgotten about that nonsense. What in the world am I to do. Lies have gotten us both here, I can't continue them any longer. But how to break this to poor Samuel now? "Oh Henry... Yes, we must see what happened to him."

"Do you know? For God's sake tell me if..." I put a finger to his lips so he doesn't continue. "Samuel, you must sit quietly and listen like I listened to you that evening and do not interrupt and I shall tell you all about Henry."

And I did. I told him of my trip on the Queen of Calcutta. How I met Cora. I said nothing of my father's fortune that was in my bank. This I will tell him at a later time when we arrive in London. Then I explained to him my thoughts about how I thought women were treated in society. How confined we were. How we must follow ridiculous conventions, unlike men who can do almost as they please. Oh, I went on for a while till I saw he was getting bored and counting stars I wouldn't wonder. Women's issues were not for him.

I told him that I wanted to live differently. I tried to make him understand that what I wanted to do was not to hurt anyone but unexpected things began to happen and at the time there was no way I could get out of it. Samuel wondered what any of this has to do with Henry but he promised not to say a word till I had finished so he sat patiently and waited till I must come to the point.

"It was all supposed to be a lark. I had no idea you even existed. I'm sure Cora at the time didn't know about you either so I decided to play act for fun. Samuel, my Darling... There is no Henry. There never was...""I don't understand," said Samuel finally. "Of course, there was a Henry, I met him, don't you know..."

"Samuel, listen to what I'm saying. I love you very much and I am ashamed of what I have done but there is no Henry..." I took a deep breath. "You see my darling. I am Henry. I impersonated him... I..." "What? I don't believe you!" He stood up and looked at me. "What about the hair the whiskers? And the clothes and the riding and... I don't believe you. If he's dead I can take it, You must be honest with me." He looked at me in confusion.

"Oh my darling, he's not dead nor was he ever alive. Sit," I explained again further and told him how everything happened. How I talked about it in fun with Cora on the boat. How I met Alicia, the opera singer, and the idea became a reality. How much fun I had on the train coming up to Hampton House. "Everything was just innocent fun till I met you and my reaction to you. My dearest."

"I think I fell in love with you the instant I saw you, you silly goose but I didn't know what to do about it. I thought by going away I would forget you with my infatuation, perhaps meet other young men and see the world. But no. It was you that was constantly on my mind and when I finally realized it and came back and you were gone. To India of all places."

"What a silly thing for you to have done for me. Did I care if you were a hero? I did not. Did I ever think of you as a coward? I did not! Could I live with you in a peaceful valley in the heart of England where there are no mutineers or badmashes, where there's no heat to boil a potato on a rock? I could."

I stopped and looked at those warm puppy eyes of Samuel and smiled. "It started just as a ridiculous jest and now it is over. Will you ever forgive me? Samuel just shook his head. "Really, no Henry?" "No. No Henry..." "He was such a fine fellow. I will miss him..." "I can always put on his clothes if you like " Samuel squeezed my hand and kissed me. "Don't ever think about that again!"

Part One: The End

All fairy tales turn out happily ever after. Well, not all. Unfortunately, ours didn't. Oh, it wasn't for the lack of trying. It wasn't that I didn't love Samuel. He was a tolerably charming boy. And that was the problem. It turned out that he was just a boy.

Part Two

After the mutiny was quelled, Samuel was transferred to Calcutta as his wound had not healed completely. There we decided to marry. It was a wonderful ceremony in the garden of the Governor's Palace. Since we had no family and in spite of the looks I received from the society ladies, Bazir gave me away dressed in the full regalia of a proud Bengal Lancer. Even the Governor finally stooped down and shook his hand. Probably for political reasons to show the natives have achieved equality.

And so we purchased, or rather I purchased, a small bungalow and set up home. I told Samuel I received a small inheritance from my father but not how much. Not that I didn't trust him, after all, he was my husband, it's just that it was perhaps for selfish reasons which I could not explain. Samuel was promoted to captain and took charge of a small company of native cavalry for ceremonial occasions. After all, he hadn't that much experience and the military tried to keep their experienced officers up north where they were needed more.

He left early and worked hard but Samuel never had the demeanor soldiers were made of. Oh, he was smart enough in his uniform. He knew his drills and the men respected him in a harmless sort of way. He was a good commander but he would never be a soldier like Skinner or Havelock who were heroes of the mutiny.

Not that I minded, you see, for I never wanted him to be a soldier. It was he who wanted to be the hero like my imaginary brother, Henry. I truly stifle a laugh when I think of it. So we lived a simple life or as simple as a rich person can have in India. Servants galore. Horse racing. Polo. Balls. Picnics. Etc. Etc. Etc.

I couldn't ignore society for there was nothing else to do. I wasn't going to be a pariah on purpose and till Samuel's contract with the army was up we had to do what is expected of us. I saw little of Samuel most of the day anyway because of his duties and he ate at the mess with his cronies most of the days, and like my mother, I settled in with knitting doilies for our divans and gossiping the time away. On occasion, Bazir came down with his wife and children and I dressed in a sari and we went out picnicking. I had the honor of being Godmother to the youngest, a girl, and performed the duties with the greatest of pleasures.

Finally, the year passed and when Samuel's duties were done, we were on our way home. We booked on a new steamer the company put into service and compared to what I had before, was in the lap of luxury. POSH was the word in use. A roomy stateroom, again with a porthole looking out unto the ocean.

The first few days we just relaxed and watched the waves pass us by, drinking exotic punches and cuddling under the stars. We didn't say much to each other, just enjoyed our company. This time there were some 30 passengers along but we kept to ourselves in the beginning as we finally had some free time which we hadn't had much chance to do so in Calcutta. I read some amusing books by Dickens and Samuel found some gentlemen who began to play cards in the wardroom. Well, what else is there to do on an ocean voyage.

We went to bed late sometimes without a word. Oh, we made love but the cabins were not conducive to energetic sighs as we soon found out with next-door neighbors so to speak. We thought if we can hear them, they certainly can hear us. Still, we tried doing it quietly. But then I remembered Alicia as she told me some of her passioned stories about her flings with her gentlemen callers. I was shocked but I listened to the tantalizing anecdotes while my cheeks glowed red and yet I would not let her stop. They weren't, may I say, bawdy, she wasn't that kind of lady, they were more, how shall I put it, romantic.

Now that we were with each other constantly in confined surroundings we or at least I found something lacking. Now that I had so much time on my hands I asked myself that even though I had been with Samuel for almost a year and married for about six months what did I actually know about my husband? In actuality, I knew very little.

I met him a few times at Cora's and he kissed me and then I ran away and then he ran away. Did I ever really fall in love?

Now, almost like Calcutta where he was away most of the day soldiering, now he was away most of the day playing cards. When we were together we really hadn't much to say to each other. Samuel really had no interest in much. He seemed almost like some of the men I met in London during the season. Empty heads with nothing to talk about except hunting, horse racing, shooting, his club, and cricket. They had come from the upper classes and of polite society. Pay his debts, drink port, and smoke cigars when ladies are not present.

Own land. Go to the proper public schools. All these virtues were attained without working a day in their lives. Yes, that was my laddie, Samuel. I recalled now that Bazir used to tell me about these stiff upper lip officers and now I knew why he looked at Samuel like he did and when I asked he just smiled and he said reminded him of some of his officers at his old regiment and wished me well though in retrospect now it was more in sarcasm. I suppose I was too much in love to notice then. Well, one can't fall in love like I did and then suddenly fall out of love. After all, I went all the way to India for him. Yes, I still loved him in a way and I was certain he loved me. In a way.

The days became longer and longer. Samuel became bored and spend most of his time playing cards with the other gentlemen passengers aboard. There were a few lady passengers but much younger than I and one who took care of her mother who was ill from seasickness. And two others who were widowed and stayed in their compartments in constant mourning. Once again on a long trip, I was lonely.

There was one passenger, a gentleman, who I perceived to be an American, who, at dinners gave me that "I wish to know you look." He was a tall man, well dressed and certainly moneyed. He wasn't the usual British stuffed shirt type, almost a happy-go-lucky fellow. He did not approach, I assumed because I was married and had a stout husband nearby and it was a small ship after all. Not that I wished him so because I felt uneasy at his look. He also did not play cards.

But one day, perhaps two weeks out at sea, I stood on deck taking in the breeze on the port bow, I thought I once heard a sailor say that, the wind suddenly shifted and blew some soot from the smokestack into my eye. It is not a pleasant feeling. It burned my eye and I believe I cried out. Suddenly this gentleman was at my elbow offering me his handkerchief.

"Stand still a moment and I shall help you out. I know the sensation as I have experienced it many times on these revolting steamers. I prefer to sail myself even though the passage is longer." All that while he fiddled with my eye till he took out the foreign object. "There you are. Pretty eyes like yours should not suffer such indignity," he said with that self-confident smile of his I noticed before. Oh God, let me not get involved in another love affair, I thought.

I thanked him for his quick response and tried to move on as we have not been properly introduced, and I told him so. "Well, now. Not to worry," as he stopped a passing sailor. "What is your name young man?" he asked him. "Why, it is seaman Thomas, Sir. Is there anything I can do for ye, Sir?" "Well seaman Thomas, as a matter of fact, there is. My name is Frank Walton from New York, USA, and you can introduce me properly to this here Lady if you don't mind." The seaman looked a little nonplussed at him at first. "Well, sir, er, Miss, may I introduce Mr, Walton, is it?" Mr. Walton shook his head in the affirmative. "Yes, oh, sorry Miss I don't know your name?" "It is Mrs," which I emphasized most emphatically. "Mrs. Dunlop." And so he introduced us and ran away. "Well, now we are properly introduced, perhaps we may be friends on this long voyage." "You realize Mr. Walton that I am a married woman and just because we have been..." "Mrs. Dunlop, I am not going to run away with you," as he pointed out the obvious that there really was nowhere to go, "I just wanted to talk. Most men just sit there playing cards, vint-et-un, what the devil is vint-et- un, and what's with the passing the port to the left business? Will there be a catastrophe if I passed it to the right? And I never hear so many My Lords in my life. What's with you British anyway?"

I had to laugh at him. "You Sir are obviously not informed of our customs." He smiled. "Honestly, I went through that in India, and where ever you people run a country." "May I ask where you are from Mr. Walton. I do detect an accent. I hope I am not tactless in asking. You are not a native American."

"You are very discerning Mrs. Dunlop, I congratulate you. Not many women in your country are so perceptive. No, I am not a native American. My family originally had come from Russia. We escaped after a massive pogrom..." "A pogrom? Mr. Walton, may I ask what that is? The word escapes me at the moment."

"Then you are fortunate that you have not heard or experienced it. It is something particular that originated in the Pale, a region in Western Russia mostly populated by Jewish people. Every few years or so they, the Russians, decided to teach us a lesson on our holidays and bring down the Cossacks on us. I do not wish to tell you horror stories Mrs. Dunlop but perhaps one might compare what the mutineers did to your fold and in turn what you did to them. Wipe out as many as you can.

"But that is horrendous Mr. Walton, why..." "Mrs. Dunlop, you, I see are an intelligent woman, am I to think you do not have any opinion about the Jews like your countrymen do?""Then you are of the Hebrew persuasion Mr. Walton? Your name Sir...?"

"Ah, my name Mrs. Dunlop? Yes, Walton certainly is not a name from Russia." He smirked. "Other than me, our family name was or still is Walenskovitz. I changed it when we came to America and I went to Harvard. Yes, even a democratic country has its demons."

I have never met a Jewish person before. Of course, I heard of them. There were many in England and Europe, some well-off I know, most of them in trade but very few in society. They seem not to be well thought off but I suppose that was the way we also thought of the Indian people and many times I thought that I would prefer to be with my Indian companion than some of my own up-in-the-air stuffed shirts.

And Mr. Walton, or whatever his name was, certainly seemed more like a gentleman than some I met in the streets of London. "Ah, I see your husband has come up for the sea air Mrs. Dunlop. It would be best if I am not seen entertaining you. Au Revoir. I hope we may talk again." And he left.

Samuel came up and kissed my cheek. "And who was that my Dear? "Oh, just one of the passengers. We just passed the time away from talking..." "Oh really?" he said in a snide way. "You know he's a Jew." "A

Jew you say. My goodness, Samuel, he had his hat on so I must have missed his horns. Do you know any Jews yourself, my Dear?"

"Yes, some trade's people I purchased some articles from. I still owe them money." "Ah, I see. It is their fault then, that you owe them money. Samuel, I thought better of you." I was tired and I headed toward our cabin. "Dearest, why are you upset about a Jew for Christ's sake?" he said following me down.

"Samuel, all you do is play cards and I am left alone with no one to talk to. This is my third voyage in one of these bloody ships and I have promised myself I would never be on one again. I shall go mad if I have no company."

Well, my dear husband isn't all fool. He stayed with me for a few weeks as we sailed towards the Arabian Sea and Suez but I could see his anxiety as he twiddled his fingers on the rail. I suppose he was going mad himself starring at the expanse of water with nothing to do but keep me company. He is not a conversationalist as I did learn. In a way, he has done nothing spectacular himself except join the Company's Army, and there all he had done was patrol the countryside with no action except the one where I and my little band saved his life. Perhaps he resented that.

And so I was a card-widow again. All that time I saw Mr. Walton, how could one not, we ate at the same table with the other passengers and on occasion passed each other while strolling on deck. At those times he doffed his hat to which Samuel just nodded and I gave him an economical smile. There were too, on occasion, that one of the older ladies came on deck and we talked about how long this trip was or the weather, which seemed unusually calm for this time of year.

Well, inevitably, Mr. Walton and I met at the rail. He was hatless, and in shirtsleeves, anathema to a well-bred English gentleman who would never go out without a frock and cravat and a top hat even with temperatures that would boil water. We were passing the tip of Somali Land heading into the Gulf of Suez. The landscape was totally barren of foliage with not a soul visible except an occasional Somali sitting on a camel staring at us as if we had come from the moon and no wonder as we were on a contraption with huge circles on each side which seemed to be turning around and in the middle a huge cylinder belching black smoke.

"Interesting isn't it…" Mr. Walton commented. "On what, Sir?" "How different many civilizations progressed. You English with your steam engines, where only centuries ago you painted your bodies blue and these people still riding the way their ancestors rode a thousand years ago." "You are a learned man Mr. Walton. Are all your people like that?"

"Well, we take education very seriously. All our boys at least, learn the Torah. Do you know what that is Mrs. Dunlop?" "I'm sorry to say I do not. Is it some sort of book?" "Well, you are close. It's a scroll. A very long scroll written thousands of years ago and has an answer to just about everything there is to know. At least that is what our Rabbis tell us."

"Rabbis?"

"Mrs. Dunlop. I see I will need much time to educate you about the Jews but it will take many a voyage longer than we have."

I smiled and shook my head. "I meant to ask you Mr. Walton, where actually are you from. You said something about the Pale is it?" "Yes, the

Pale. A little heaven on earth till the Tzar's people and his henchmen, the Cossacks, make it a living hell."

He told me that he and his family long ago had gone to America from a small village in the Pale which not even he remembers its name. It was after one of those 'pogroms' that he mentioned before, where half of his family were butchered that they decided once and for all to leave this wretched country. Many times, they have heard people talking about this land of milk and honey called America, where people lived free whoever they were and one could make riches if one worked hard.

It took them about two years to reach New York where they disembarked in such a tumult, he said. But it was mostly true. If you were smart enough you could make a home where you at least were not persecuted by the dreaded Cossacks. "My father worked hard selling drapery as he had been a draper in the old country. He was very good at it and soon had an established business.

"He did not want his son to do the same but had greater hope for me. 'You must go to school and learn.' He insisted. He made enough to send me to a prestigious University. Harvard. I suppose I would compare it to your Oxford or Cambridge. Believe me, there were not too many Jewish students there but I stuck it out and after graduation, my father and I expanded our business to an importing establishment. We import now from all over the world. That is why I was in India."

"I am what your class would call 'in trade' Mrs. Dunlop, perhaps your husband would not consider me a gentleman and probably not worthy to even speak to you. Are you not afraid that he..." "I, Mr. Walton, am not afraid of my husband I must tell you and I'm sure you do him an injustice, he..."

He laughed at me. "Mrs. Dunlop, please. If it weren't for you, he would not even look my way. A man in trade? I'm certain your husband had been spoon-fed all his life and eventually inherit his father's estate all without working a day in his life. I know the English. I have been in London before." There was no point in arguing.

"Never the less Mrs. Dunlop, I like you, you are made of different cloth if I may be so bold as make a comparison." What could I say? If there ever was a true gentleman I was looking straight at him.

A few days later we arrived at Suez and boarded the train to Alexandria with a stop in Cairo about 80 miles away. As we had to cross the desert with its high temperatures the train ran at night. To the shock of some of the ladies, I wore the Indian style of pajamas and sari for comfort. I do not think the gentlemen minded except for Samuel who was a bit miffed that his lady exposed herself to the world but I didn't care I was not to be confined to wools or cotton.

By morning we arrived in Cairo and were given a room at a hotel run by the East India Company. It would have been a shame to be in Cairo and not see it nor see the Great Pyramids of Giza as they were one of the wonders of the world.

My poor Samuel, however, was worn out. He had no interest in ancient objects. "They are just stones piled on each other, what benefit is it to me to see them." Of course, he and his gentlemen had plans for cards in the sumptuous drawing room of the hotel with their cool iced punches. Well, he might stay but I shall go as I did not think I would ever return to this country again. Ever!

The hotel provided excursion by carriage with an Arab guide who spoke reasonable English and off we went exploring the Great Pyramids that the Israelites build. Up till now, I haven't seen Mr. Walton as he didn't stay in our hotel but this thought reminded me of him and I wondered where he was.

It took a few hours to arrive there as we struggled through Cairo's narrow streets filled with people of ancient times and stalls that sold exotic wares and trinkets for the sightseer, it was of course almost like the bazaars in India. I made a note to myself to come and purchase something to remember this trip by.

Finally, we arrived at Giza. The carriage stopped in front of a monumental statue of a lion with a man's face. It was magnificent. It was the Sphinx. "See my Lady, how the face is full of holes? It was Napoleon's artillery that shot it away..." my interpreter said. I walked around it in wonder not even noticing the heat. How could Samuel have no interest in such a treasure to mankind?

Afterward, we came to the Great Pyramid which was close by. I have never seen anything so large. How could any man build this for a king, a Pharaoh? And then I saw Mr. Walton sitting on one of those huge stones that must have fallen from the top of the Pyramid.

He must have somehow felt me walking towards him and he stood and took off his hat. "Mrs. Dunlop, what an unexpected pleasure it is to see you here." "Certainly I could not miss a sight like this.." "It is, isn't it," he said almost in a spiritual voice. We both stood there and marveled at it for a moment.

"My people build it over a thousand years ago..." "Are you proud of that Mr. Walton?" "Can't say that I am. We were slaves after all but during the holiday of Passover we read that story, again and again, to remind us since the bible was written." "Oh yes, I believe I recall being told by the pastor about that. For some reason he made it sound so Christian."

"Ah, Mrs. Dunlop, much was stolen of our history in your New Testament almost as if we didn't even exist today." "Well, the paster accuses your people of killing our Lord..." "Ah, that rational again. Tell me, Mrs. Dunlop, if a strange man, say, arrived at the Vatican and said, or perhaps in your case, at Canterbury and told the Bishop he is the new Messiah, what do you think the Bishop or the Pope would do? Bow down and just accept him?"

"You know, the Israelites did not crucify people. It was the Romans. We probably would have stoned him. In any event, I think it was just politics." I did not know what to say as I never kept up my bible lessons. It was getting rather hot and standing on sand cooked by the sun was not pleasant. There was a teahouse nearby and we drove towards it and sat in a shady spot where we could see the whole majestic sight before us and ordered tea.

I must admit I was rather a trifle charmed by Mr. Walton. He seemed a well-mannered and traveled man and also well-spoken. Though not a gentleman in the true British upper-class manner, in some cases he was above all that. I rather liked him. He was tall, I noticed before, well built with a pleasant clean shaved face covered with a bountiful crop of black hair. His dark eyes shone bright topped off with bushy eyebrows. He wasn't as handsome as Samuel but he carried himself like a manly man. I was a little nervous sitting in close proximity to him not that I was frightened of what he would do to me but what I might imagine I would like to do to him. I was trying to remember a Mr. Dunlop when I first saw him so I had to tread very carefully.

"Are you married, Mr. Walton? I see a ring on your finger," I suddenly asked him without thinking. Mr. Walton looked down and turned the ring on his finger and without looking up he said. "I was Mrs. Dunlop. I am a widower. My wife died in childbirth a few years ago in New York. I was away on one of my purchasing trips and didn't know about it till I came back months after she was buried." He looked up with a wry smile.

"I am so sorry Mr. Walton, I..." "Thank you. God's will, people tell me." We stayed for a while longer and then we had to go back to our hotels or wherever Mr. Walton stayed. It would not have been tactful to ask. I did not see Mr. Walton again till after we sailed from Alexandria.

When I later arrived at the hotel Samuel was still at the gambling tables. As I came closer I saw he had a dejected look on his face. At first, I thought he might be angry at me for coming back late but he had not even seen me as he was staring at his cards intensely. He was playing a game I did not know but found later it was called Faro. By that dark look in his eyes, I knew he was losing. Not that he didn't lose before on the ship but at least it wasn't much, however, it was I, that must pay his debts.

I feigned sunstroke and broke off Samuels's participation. He took me to our room and we had a row. The loss to me monetarily wasn't that much but now it was the principal of it. He took advantage of my goodwill for gambling. I would have bought him anything, I certainly had the means, but not gambling. I will not allow that.

But suddenly he changed his demeanor and tried to get off the subject of his debt. "I see you've been out with that Jew," He spits out. "How dare you put me in this situation..." "And what my Dear, is this situation?" I asked. "You losing at cards or me being out with a gentleman..." "Gentleman you say. A tradesman, a Jew at that?" he hissed.

My face turned red. I did not recognize my Samuel suddenly. This isn't the man I married, that sad-eyed basset hound with the sandy mound of hair. The man who kissed me with butterfly wings, on my lips. I have never seen this before. Does losing at cards do that to a man? I could not understand. I went to bed but could not sleep. Samuel slept on the divan in the other room.

In the morning he apologized profusely. "I do not know what came over me." He said pleading. "I, I love you my Dearest, Dearest Henrietta." The sad eyes returned as I remembered and I accepted all he said. He was, after all, my husband and I believed I loved him. Samuel and I had made up as young couples do, with many murmurings of undying love and holding hands, and, other things. But somehow I felt that things will never be the same for us.

We were three days at sea in the Mediterranean when I saw Mr. Walton by the rail, staring at the horizon. "Ah, Mrs. Dunlop, so good to see you again. I have missed your company these past few days. Do you see that mountain there," he pointed towards a purple shape in the distance. "That is Malta and further on Corsica and Italy. Have you been to Italy Mrs. Dunlop?" he asked.

"I have not, but I always wanted to do so. Perhaps One day. For now, I have had enough traveling these past few years.""Well, when you are ready you must see Rome, The Eternal City. It is indescribable. Of course, it is of most ancient ruins and narrow streets but still magnificent." "I gather Sir, that you have been there and seen those ruins." "Yes, I have been fortunate and seen those..."

And I stood there as the ship sliced her way through the blue sea as he told me about Rome and its ruins. After about an hour he stopped and looked at me with those dark eyes and asked a subtle question. "Where is your husband Mrs. Dunlop, does he not share your interests in seeing the marvels of the world?" What could I say? My dearest husband's interest lay in little numbered cards thrown on green velvet. I looked away from him and stared at the horizon.

Mr. Walton also looked away and for a few moments, we both stared into the distance. "You know Mrs. Dunlop if I were your husband I would not at this time be in stuffy wardrooms playing cards." My cheeks turned red and I looked down at my hands. "And what Sir, would you be doing right now?" And then I looked directly into his face. He smiled and doffed his hat, "Good afternoon Mrs. Dunlop". And he turned and left me wondering.

In spite of our arguments, Samuel continued gambling and losing. He had always been an unlucky gambler even before I met him and his father was forced to pay his debts for the sake of the family's honor. Of course, I did not know that when I fell in love with him and his hair. Cora, hopefully, did not know of this either-or I should be extremely angry at her for not informing me. But I had faith in her that she did not know.

Since we left Calcutta Samuel gambled away almost £2,000. Which he himself did not have but I did, which, as Samuel says, under British law, he has rights to. I was afraid that within a few years unless he changes his ways, all of my father's fortune will go to pay his debts.

There was no point to fight him or use logic. It was a sickness without a cure. I could not legally do anything about it. When we arrive in London the debt will have to be paid or a scandal will ruin our lives. There is nothing worse in society than a reneged gambling debt.

By now we were within sight of Gibraltar. This was a coal station for our steamer and we were to stay at least two days to fill our bunkers. We took advantage to debark the ship and get our land legs a chance to recharge. I put on a light cotton dress rather than the sari that annoyed Samuel so much in Egypt and we went to the small town to see the sights. We were accompanied by some other passengers but not Mr. Walton. Again, I hadn't seen him since that talk we had when he pointed out Malta to me and I asked him that question.

The reader might ask why, on such a small vessel, we could miss each other but if one doesn't leave one's cabin one cannot be seen. There were other passengers that we didn't see too much off as they took their meals in their cabin not wishing to participate in the company. And so, Gibraltar, is rather a small place, mostly a naval port with some military stationed there to guard it.

Apparently, the military commander heard that a wounded veteran from the Sepoy Rebellion was on board, so we were invited to the officer's mess for dinner that evening. When we came back to the ship, Samuel dressed in his formal fig of Skinner's Horse. He especially looked fine with the long yellow tunic, gold lace, a blue turban on his head, sword, belt, and cross-belt with pouch, and the shiniest boots I have ever seen since our wedding. There were some other 'gentlemen' from our ship invited but not Mr. Walton of course being of Jewish descent could never fit at such a distinguished club, of snubs.

I truly felt abysmal as I saw him wave at us, or perhaps at me when we left the dock. We traveled by carriage to the mess and were greeted by the commanding officer General Sir Thomas Windworth K. C., K. C. B., And Rear Admiral, Sir George Cotton, K. C., G. C. B. They had more initials apparently than were letters in their name but I jest. These men deserve the honors bestowed upon them by the Queen.

As we entered the regimental headquarters and went up a steep stone staircase to the mess, all officers stood at attention and gave three, Hip! Hip! Huzzas! to Captain Samuel Dunlop, Indian Service Medal and Indian Mutiny Medal, pinned to his chest. I was quite proud then of my Samuel. He looked dashing even though I knew he really had done very little there but still he had shown himself able to lead men. Yes, my Samuel is growing up.

We were introduced to all officers who shook Samuels's hand and kissed mine. It was a superb affair. There was no shortage of food and wines on the table spread with sparkling regimental silver and much toasting with French champaign. Samuel was asked to recite some of his adventures and to my chagrin, he retold my stories from Bazir. There was a piper from the highland regiment who played regimental tunes, Scotland the Brave, Minstrel Boy, The Bear, and such. What with the officers being cramped on a rock of land off the coast of Spain or on a small steamer, like us, the lads were becoming a little boisterous.

Now, with the wine and the squealing of pipes my head began to explode. The officers were agreeable enough and gentlemanly, at least in the beginning but of course, most of them were young and full of military vigor and a little drunk. Samuel among them. Since I was the only woman there they all asked me to dance which I tried to oblige but it was beginning to wear on me. Thank the lord that the Admiral, a more mature man, appreciated my situation and offered to take me back to the ship. At least Samuel was understanding and I insisted he stay as long as he liked. It was a big mistake.

We left the next day with Samuel very badly hurt. After I left they became more riotous with wild dancing and drinking. When it was time to leave, I found out later, that Samuel tripped and fell down those steep stone steps and fractured his skull and probably his insides. All in all, there was much broken in him. Of course, I had no knowledge of this at that time. The regimental surgeon tried his best to patch him up but he was also inebriated and did not really know what he was doing he just wrapped a bandage on his head and body.

He was brought aboard ship in the morning on a stretcher and laid on our cabin bed in a state of unconsciousness. You may imagine my apprehension when I saw him with his bloodied head and chest all bandaged up like an Egyptian Mummy. There was an acting surgeon on our ship but he had no experience in such cases and when he looked at Samuel he just shook his head.

How I cursed him and the officers who came to express their regret. But of course, that did not resolve the situation. We must get him to a real surgeon as soon as possible. Fortunately, the coal was finished loading and we made as much steam as possible. There was nothing else to be done. What happened, happened and there was no going back. I have to take Samuel to England and procure the best surgeon and hope for the best. I did not wish to repeat my first journey with my father and have another burial at sea.

And so my Samuel, the man-boy I fell in love with so quickly, lay there on a bunk, still as a wooden plank. His breath was almost hesitant as if he knew he will not survive and all this waiting was a waste of time. I held his hand but knew he did not feel it, there was no moment of recognition in his eyes nor in his touch.

"Oh my Dearest, my Dearest, what have I done to you that you must pay such a high price for my actions. How could I ever have foreseen such a harmless joke could lead to this misfortune? Who will forgive me? Who will believe that I have done such a thing," I whispered to non-hearing ears. If only he never met me. If only I never met him. If only social customs were different. If only I could be what I wanted to be. How could this be God's will?

Two days later, my Samuel, the boy with the basset eyes and the bushy hair passed away owning the gambling gentleman on board almost £500. I did not want to go to the funeral service. One funeral service at sea was enough for a lifetime but of course, I could not stay in my cabin either. I put on a black dress I meant to wear to church on Sunday which I packed by chance on the top of my trunk almost as if I knew I would need to use it.

Mr. Walton was kind enough to help me up the ladder to the deck and stood by me for the ceremony. Last time it was Cora. This time I did not look like the body of my husband splashed into the sea nor stood by the rail watching where it fell and again no tears came to my eyes. I came to Gibraltar a married woman and left it a widow.

When the ceremony was over, the other passengers came to give their condolences and the captain sent his steward to bring me some brandy. Unlike last time I drank it quickly and asked for another. A chair was brought on the deck near one of those ventilators and I sat there looking blankly at nothing.

I saw one of the passengers, a man, wanting to come over to me but he stopped as I saw at the edge of my eye Mr. Walton wave him off. I was smart enough to think it was the gambler and found I was right when we landed later in port. Mr. Walton stood nearby in case I needed something I suppose, but right now I just wanted to be alone. I began to think of what I will do when we get back to England.

How am I going to explain everything to Cora and Samuel's parents? I do not even know what they thought about Samuel's leaving so abruptly to come and go chase a ghost of a brother that never existed. What will they even say to our marriage? I am certain they must have had someone more so from their class for him to marry. No matter how kind they were to me I doubt they would have accepted me as a bride for their son and they would never accept me as his widow.

After a while, Mr. Walton started to come my way then he seemed to change his mind and walk away. I thought to myself that now is not the right time for someone else to enter my life. I needed time but as he moved further away I could not stand it. I don't want to be alone now or ever. What harm is there to talk to a friend? I desperately needed a friend. I turned and asked him to come back. He sat across from me on a hatch and smiled slightly.

"Is there something I can do for you, Mrs. Dunlop?" "I suppose its widow Dunlop, Mr. Walton..." I started to say. "Oh my dear Mrs. Dunlop, you must not say such things. I know it is not painless for you and yes, you must mourn for a time but you are a young woman and there is another future for you..."

I changed the subject. I did not wish to dwell on this now, there will be a time when I go back to my cabin where I will truly be alone looking at our bed where Samuel... I could not bear to say the words even to myself. But now I wished to talk. Talk about anything else. "May I ask what your final destination is, Mr. Walton?"

Mr. Walton looked up and smiled again. "My destination Mrs. Dunlop is New York, but first I must stop in London to transfer my goods from this ship to another bound there. It will probably take a few days. I do not know the schedules to cross the Atlantic." "Oh, you have goods aboard this ship?"

"Yes. I have gone to India a year ago and bought silks and chintz, which is stored below." "So you will be staying in London then." "This is probably not the right time," he said as he stood and took out a card from his waist pocket and handed it to me. "But here, if you ever come to New York, you might say hello and I shall show you the sights."

I took the offered card and looked at it. Walton Department Store, it said. Union Square, New York, NY, Mr. David Walton, Purchasing Agent', all in engraved gold letters. I put the card in my sleeve and nodded. It was too early, I said to myself. I think he understood and again doffed his hat and turned towards the gangway. "Mrs. Dunlop, if you will excuse me I have to inspect my goods as it has been a while since I did so. If there is anything I can do please do not hesitate to call upon me." And he was gone below.

A week later we arrived in London. I had sent ahead a letter to Cora from Falmouth hoping she could meet me at the docks. I did not mention anything else. The voyage itself was uneventful except now I was a widow. It sounded so strange I could not believe that I, at 22, was ever married or in love or even twice in India. It seemed all like a bad dream but of course, it was not.

Mr. Walton kept my spirits up by promenading with me on the deck on occasion telling me of his adventures practically all over the world. He has been in Europe and Asia. Why, he has even been in Samarkand for carpets, of all the exotic places. He was where I always wanted to travel

Of course, I had to be careful as a widow to show some decorum and mingled with some of the other passengers and noted that the gambling man on an occasion regarded me in a queer way but did not approach. I decided to pay Samuel's debts when we arrive and get that over with. I did not need to have that over my head and cause an embarrassing confrontation later.

Just before the gangplank was put up I saw the gambler waiting to the side. I must seize the opportunity to end this business and walk over to him. "As you might know I am the widow of Mr. Dunlop and I believe he owed you a debt. May I know your name, Sir?" "It is Dick Taylor my Lady and may I..." I didn't let him finish. "Mr. Taylor, I know my husband owed you money, and I didn't want you to think I shall not honor it. I believe he told me it was around £500. Is that correct?"

"Yes, that it was..." "Then I shall send you a note if you be so kind as to give me your address and I shall send a messenger with it as soon as I get settled in..." "I don't understand Mrs. Dunlop, but the debt was paid in full. I have made an arrangement with Mr. Wa, er... It's all taken care of my Lady. The debt is all paid up. I am sorry but your husband insisted on playing and raised the Stakes... Forgive me I did not wish to talk of the..." "How was the debt paid, Sir my..." "It was paid my Lady that is all, I cannot say more..."That is what he said but he seemed to have a quick look at Mr. Walton but when I turned Mr. Walton looked away. "I see. Then have a pleasant day Mr. Taylor," I said and turned towards the gangplank deep in thought till I saw Cora on the dock seemingly crying and smiling at the

same time and waving a kerchief at me.

I cannot describe my true feeling at seeing my only friend in the world, that is if I told myself the truth this moment would include Mr. Walton. I was ashamed but could also not lie to myself. I liked the man and I was afraid, a little too much for I realized what had happened. He thought I was a penny less woman and paid off that man.

As I ran to Cora and we embraced for many minutes and just looked at each other and cried. Yes, my tears came now. Cora started to ask many questions but I asked for patience. First I must thank someone and say goodbye. I came over to Mr. Walton who was watching his cargo being lifted from the hold. He turned towards me and smiled. What can I say, I have done this before but it was not the same I told myself. I just want to thank the man for his thoughtfulness and give him back the money that he paid the gambler. That was all.

"Good day Mrs. Dunlop, so this is the end of our journey. You are home, at last, you must be relieved, and I see you had someone to meet you. A friend or relation?" "It is a dear friend, Mr. Walton. A very dear friend.

As I feel you are also." He smiled at that. "I hope I am, Mrs. Dunlop."

"Well, then there's the question of my husband's debt..." "Do you need some money to pay for it?" he asked. I can..." "I think you already had, Mr. Walton, which I am very grateful but it was not necessary." "I don't know what you mean Mrs..." I laid a hand on his sleeve. "I know. Nothing else will be said. I just wanted you to know I shall never forget you."

"Neither shall I forget you, Mrs. Dunlop. What shall you do now?" I told him I am staying with my friend, Mrs. Blackstone and, "She will take care of me till I am ready to face the world." There was no point in insulting the man for his good deed. It will be an excuse one day to repay it.

Eleven: Jackhammer

Ever since his wife passed away three years ago, Jack had no problem sleeping late. Even though he had a corner apartment on the second floor with traffic coming and going, the noise never bothered him till this day when he was awakened by a noise that sounded like a jackhammer. It came from the apartment next door which was recently bought.

He knew that the apartment needed some renovating and people had been working the past two weeks but up till now he has only heard some banging or scraping but nothing as loud as what woke him this morning. Well, there wasn't much Jack could do about that, he lived in a 30 story 2 building complex and anyone can have work done as long as it's from 9

A.M. to 5 P.M., so, after a quick breakfast of cereal, he picked up a book and went out to the garden between the two buildings to wait out the jackhammering or whatever made that horrendous noise.

Despite it being early November, the day was balmy with not a cloud in the sky. There were two tables that were still in sunlight, one being occupied by a woman unknown to Jack that looked like she was looking through a furniture catalog, and as he passed her table, she looked up and greeted him with a nod, Jack nodded back without paying much attention to her and sat down at the other table.

It had been quiet while Jack walked to the table but as soon as he sat down, the noise of the jackhammer exploded in his ear again. The apartment they were working in, happened to face the courtyard only a few yards away from where they were sitting. "It is rather loud, isn't it..." the woman unexpectedly said to Jack.

The woman, as Jack turned to her, seemed to be his age, perhaps a bit older than himself, probably around sixty something, certainly not much older. Jack himself was sixty-seven and retired. She was a handsome-looking woman, with eager eyes, styled silver hair, a slim body, and dressed expensively. He couldn't help but notice the Johnny Was flowery jacket she wore, Jack knew that not because he dressed in style or that he was a fashion guru, he was usually dressed in comfortable clothes, which consisted of an old sweatshirt over a faded polo shirt with an old pair of jeans and a pair of ragged tennis shoes.

The reason he knew styles was because he was married to a woman that was always stylish and took him to all those fancy stores that sold overstocked designer clothes which drove him crazy. Even in bed, she wore only high-end pajamas to his au natural look. And anyway, this woman had the exact same jacket which he gave away to one of those charity stores. Gad, he hoped this wasn't his wife's old jacket...

"Yes, it is loud, you should hear it next door where I live," said Jack with a lopsided grin. The woman raised an eyebrow in surprise. "You're my neighbor? Oh, I am truly sorry about that, but hopefully, it won't last long, maybe a day or two at the most, the contractor promised me." She said everything was going on time till she decided to change the floor tiles in the kitchen.

"Oi...!" Jack moaned playfully. "Another day, you say?" "Truly, I'm terribly sorry. I'm Alma, Alma Millner..." She extended her hand. Jack took it in his. It gave him a bit of a jolt as if he was struck with a memory of his wife. The same feel, the same size, and her favorite color of nail polish, taupe, or something like that. He held it for perhaps a moment longer.

"Jack... Jack Russell," he said, "and please, no jokes. Apparently, my father had a great sense of humor, though it was always a great conversation starter. That's how I met my wife..." "Oh, You must tell me about that one day. By the way, is she not bothered by that noise or is she just a good sleeper?"

"Not anymore..." Jack said dryly. "She passed away about three years ago, just as I retired and we were going to go and see the world." "Oh, I'm so terribly sorry."

"That's okay, I don't usually fling these facts on strangers... but as long as we're going to be neighbors..." He put his palms up. "Then you must tell me that story of how Jack Russel conquered with his name..."

"Okay, maybe on some dark and stormy wintery night... I'll tell you how we met..."

"Are you a writer? Mr. Russell?" Jack smiled; he liked that woman. "Sorry to disturb you, Mrs. Millner, could you come in for a moment? I need you to see something..." a man called out from her apartment window.

"Oh. Oh. I see a problem coming up," she said. "Glad to have met you, Jack Russel. I'm sure we'll see each other often..." As she got up her jacket opened and he could see the lining which, thank goodness was not like his wife's. Pheee... he breathed a sigh of relief. Yes, he liked his new neighbor, he said to himself.

By afternoon the hammering stopped and Jack was back in his apartment when the doorbell rang. As he opened the door there stood his new neighbor, Alma Millner, before him, her clothes all spotty and dusty and a large Coach handbag over her shoulder. "Hi. I'm sorry to bother you, Jack, but as you can see I got myself all dirtied up in there and I have no water right now. Do you mind if I use your shower to wash up... and change?"

This sounds like a beginning of a soap opera, thought Jack. "But of course... it's this way, I'll get you a fresh towel." When Alma came out, she was all cleaned up and dressed down to her jeans and a turtleneck sweater. No eyeliner, no lipstick, no other makeup and Jack thought she still looked pretty damn good. "How about a drink or something?" Jack asked.

"Oh, thanks, that would be nice. My throat is as dry as a bone, it's so dusty in there." Jack went to the fridge and poured her a flavored seltzer. "Is that okay?" "Wonderful! Just what I needed. You have a nice apartment here, Jack. It's bigger than mine, you have three bedrooms, right? Mine has only two but the kitchen is the same layout, I love your tiles. Maybe I'll bring my contractor in to see it if that's okay with you."

"Oh, sure. Anytime. Would you like to see the rest?" Jack asked. "My wife was an interior decorator. "It's lovely..." Alma said when they finished looking. "I see your wife had good taste..." she said that looking Jack from top to bottom. "I can hardly wait till I get mine in order," she said walking towards the door.

"Well, thanks for being so kind. I have to go and look for another place to stay while they get my place ready. They were supposed to be ready in two more days, but as you heard the jackhammering, I wanted a new tile floor in the kitchen. I'm sure your wife went through this a few times."

Oh, boy, did she ever, Jack remembered. Many, many times. "Anyway, my lease runs out in two days where I'm staying now. Nothing I can do; I signed a contract... they already signed up with another tenant." Alma said at the door. "I guess I'll see you around then... Thanks again."

"You mean they're kicking you out of your old apartment?" Jack asked. "By the way, where is your husband?"

"My husband? Oh, he's somewhere in Brazil or wherever with his floozy, I guess. Maybe he's canoeing on the Amazon River. I hope the piranhas eat him up..." She smiled. "That's why I sold our house and moved here..." she said and walked down the hall.

"Wait!" Jack called out just as she was getting into the elevator. "Come back please, I have a deal for you."

Surprised, Alma came back into Jack's apartment. Jack stood nervously at first, not quite knowing how to approach his crazy idea. He asked her to sit down on the couch and he sat down opposite her. Alma looked up at him expectantly. "What's up Jack Russel?" He really liked the way she pronounced his name.

With a wide grin, he made his offer. "Look, and please don't take offense." He stood up nervously. "OK, I'll lay it out fast before I get all frazzled up. This is the deal," he said. "Okay, look, I have a bedroom that just collects dust. To make it short, why don't you just use this till your apartment is ready. There's a lock on the door so you'll be safe," he paused for effect, "there's a TV, and there's the extra bathroom too."

He gave her a closed-lipped grin. "You can use the kitchen, of course, I hardly use it anyway, I can give you a spare key so you can come and go as you please. There's plenty of room in the fridge too. And you can keep a close eye on your contractor, right next door... What do you say? Alma... It's only for a few days anyway..."

Alma didn't know what to say. She just stared at Jack open-mouthed and stood up. Though it seemed rather unconventional, it sort of made sense to her. "I, I don't know what to say, Jack. It seems so outré that it might be the right thing to do," she said. "By the way, I'm a black belt Judo expert so no fears there." She looked him straight in the eye. Jack was a tall man, almost six feet, still in good shape, he exercised three times a week at the health club a block away, still with a full head of salt and pepper hair and a solid 170 pounds. Alma, now that he really looked at her, was about five- five and probably weighted about a pillow full of feathers, he thought. She probably couldn't even get close enough to him if he extended his arm. They both laughed nervously.

"Of course, if I do this, I'll pay my share. I'm paying at least $1,500 for that studio now; I certainly should pay you something. It's only fair..." "Okay, we can haggle about that later. Do you need help getting your stuff here, I can drive you. Of course, for that I should get an extra tip..." The corners of his mouth went up in an impish smile.

"Ha ha, Jack, you are a remarkable man!" she said. "Thanks, I can do it myself..." She came closer to him. "May I give you a hug?" She didn't wait but put her arms around his waist because she couldn't reach any higher. "Thanks, I only have a suitcase, I'll just pack up and grab a cab, it's not far away."

One week later, they had settled in. Alma did some cooking for both of them on occasion, but mostly Jack tried not to get in her way. He found out she was almost ten years older than him, though she didn't look it and was pining, he thought, with an old flame on Skype, in the bedroom, on a laptop. He could hear her laughing the first few evenings through her closed door. But after a couple of days, her talk seemed more serious and then a few nights ago, nothing. In the meantime, she checked on the contractor and they promised her, that they will be done by next week. Guaranteed.

By now, Thanksgiving was coming up in two days and neither had made plans. Jack's two daughters said they were sorry but decided to take their kids to Disneyland. Alma's friends were older than her and were mostly in senior homes or didn't feel up to it. "How about I take you out to dinner on Thanksgiving?" Alma proposed to Jack. "There's a nice restaurant nearby that serves turkey dinners."

He agreed. "Why not? Better than sitting home..."This evening, they both had some of yesterday's leftovers from a Chinese restaurant they shared then Alma said goodnight and went into her own room. There didn't seem to be any discussion on Skype tonight, thought Jack, but instead some reruns of a remodeling show on TV. After a while, he too went to his bedroom and tried to read.

Somehow neither could fall asleep. Later, Alma went to the kitchen for a drink, and on the way saw a light from under Jack's bedroom door. It was still on after she drank, so she knocked faintly on it. "Jack are you up?" she whispered. "Yup! You got insomnia too?" he responded. "Come in if you like..."

She came into the room wearing designer PJs, Jack could tell by now what designer they came from, in her case, it was a pair of Olivia Von Halle, silk or something like that and they were expensive. He gave his wife's away too.

He was lying in bed with an old peace sign T-shirt and a pair of red boxer shorts only because he had a guest. As she came closer he made room for her by pulling up the quilt so she could get into bed. Without much thinking about what she was doing, because she hadn't had a good night's sleep for days, Alma got on and sat back against the pillows. They lay there a few minutes till Jack asked her why she can't sleep.

"I don't know. Something seems to keep me awake. Maybe because it's getting close to my apartment being finished or..." "Okay, lie down, I'll douse the lights and we'll both try to get some sleep." They lay there in a fetal position, Alma with her back to Jack who was facing her.

Outside, the late November wind whistled like a hurricane. Alma pulled the quilt up to her chin, then somehow, both seem to be stealing towards each other as if drawn by a gravity, till finally, Alma wound up cupped onto Jack's lap like a teaspoon into a soup spoon.

Twelve: Debra's Dilemma

"Mother, I can't talk to you now," said Debra Curtain into her cell phone while shuffling documents on her desk.

Debra, a senior partner in an international law firm, sat behind a Louis XIV desk with New York City and the Hudson River in the background. Her office was divided by an all-glass wall looking at her secretary and into the main work area of the large office.

"Alright, for just a minute," she relented, "yes, I remember next Saturday's event for the Richardson's wedding at the Waldorf. Yes, I said I'd be there and I said I'd bring a date. No, you don't know him. Mother, I really have to go. Say hello to dad. What? No, I don't want you to get your friend's relative to take me" Debra shut off her phone and looked at all the paperwork she still had to do today.

Why did her mother have to call just now and bring up the subject of a date? She of course lied to her mother. She had no date. Debra doesn't even remember the last time she had a date. At her age to have become a senior partner wasn't easy in this mostly male firm but she did it by working hard and getting the big results.

Debra was an extremely intelligent woman with an IQ Einstein would be envious of. She had PhDs from Harvard and Oxford Universities in International Affairs. She spoke most European languages fluently and could practice law in three of them. She was five- six in flats but when she put on her five-inch heels she could match most men eye to eye.

She dressed smartly and probably could have been a model of what an accomplished attorney should look like.

Her problem was men. It's an old story. It wasn't that she couldn't get men, it's just that she just couldn't find the right one who could at least match her intelligence and not be envious of it. You just can't show up a man's ego and think he would take it easily. Certainly not with these self- assured lawyers. So now she told her mother she had a date for this coming Saturday's affair and it's already Wednesday and of course, she didn't, she didn't know what to do. She certainly wasn't going to take her mother's friend's relative, whoever that is.

There was no one in the office she could ask. Most of the partners were married and the ones that were single were old enough to be her father. She certainly couldn't ask the younger lawyers, it would look as if she was desperate to get a man for herself, and so weaseled someone from the office though she was sure any one of them would kill to be her escort. But time was getting short, she had to find someone even if it's that handsome security guard from downstairs.

"Martha called again, huh?" Her assistant, Alphonse, always called her mother by her first name. He had known her mother for years. Alphonse had started as her mother's assistant in this firm almost twenty years ago... Debra had thought of asking Alphonse once before, he was a rather handsome man and the right age too but he was gay and committed to his partner who was very jealous.

She was about to say something to him when she saw a man through her glass wall pass her office. She had never seen that man before and wondered who he was. He stopped at a desk further on to ask someone something, she guested. She asked Alphonse if he knew who that was. Alphonse turned. "Nice," he said. "But I don't know who he is, I'll check with reception.

"Never mind, I'll do it. Take these papers and mail them out for me please." When Alphonse left she dialed reception and asked about that man. Apparently, he was here to see one of the partners. George Higgs, the receptionist told her. However, the partner is finishing up with another client and the man is waiting for him in the small conference room next door to her.

Debra wasn't a crazed man hunter. She had gone out with plenty of handsome men before but for some reason, this one caught her eye. She stood up, took some papers in her hand, and walked towards the conference room. God, she suddenly felt silly. Just as she was about to open the door, the other partner, George Higgs, stepped out of his office, only a few feet away, and met her.

"Oh, hi Deb, I was just going to call you. You have a minute?" "Just a couple, I thought I left some papers in the conference room this morning." "Well come into my office first," he said. "I have a problem. An old friend of mine from the army just walked in and is waiting in the conference room here. We were going out to lunch but I just got a call from one of my clients in London and I need to speak with him right away. Would you take my friend out to lunch? I'm not going to ask one of the guys as he probably would rather go out with you and I'll try to meet you before lunch is over. You owe me one, from the Randolph case, remember?"

"George, I'm pretty busy myself..." "That's what I said then, but I did you the favor anyway..."

"David Bergman, I'd like you to meet one of our partners in the firm, Debra Curtain. I have to finish off with one of my clients overseas and if you don't mind she'll take you to lunch and I'll meet you a bit later. I'm sorry. In a law firm time is something we can't control. I hope you don't mind?" said George.

David Bergman stood up and shook Debra's hand. "I don't mind at all George.." he said. "It's a pleasure to meet you, Ms. Curtain..." It wasn't so much that David Bergman was good-looking, it was more the aura of the man. This man had a presence that you couldn't ignore. Debra thought that when he walked into a room all eyes would be upon him. It was one of the reasons she spotted him walking past.

"In that case, it's all settled. I made a reservation at The Bistro," said George. "So I'll see you there later?" They were still standing when George left and there was a pregnant pause as the two looked each over. Then Debra shook herself out of it. "Alright, give me five minutes to get ready and we shall go. Would you care for something while you wait? Coffee? Tea? A glass of water?"

"Thanks no, I'll just sit patiently right here Ms. Curtain, and await your presence..." David said with a smile. They arrived at The Bistro and were seated toward the back. The Bistro was where lawyers hung out when they wanted a quiet place to talk business or conspire against their competition. At least that was the joke around here. What this place was before only God knew.

It was set in a basement and if you didn't know about it you couldn't find it. But it was always pretty full. Debra thought of going to the lady's room to fix herself up before but changed her mind at the last minute. She would probably never see Bergman again and she didn't want to be seen taking any extra trouble about her appearance.

In a way, she wouldn't have come here anyway. She wasn't particularly fond of this place. It was mostly a man cave and the only women that would come here are the women the males wanted to show off though, why they would pick such a dark place only their minds could comprehend. She would have gone to an outdoor cafe where she could show off her handsome guy but sitting by a table with all the street smells and cars honking isn't much conducive to conversation either.

A waiter finally came and they ordered some white wine. "So how long have you known George?" Debra asked after a nervous silence. David Bergman played with his wine glass and looked up at Debra. David had not prepared to have lunch with a woman. He really wanted to talk to George Higgs about a problem he had and not discuss pleasantries with a female. Especially a pretty female.

"About twelve years I guess," he finally said. "He was a JAG officer in... I assume you know..." Debra interrupted him with a wave. "A

Judge Advocate General Officer, a military lawyer, I know..." David smiled. "Of course. Anyway, I'm not a lawyer but I once defended one of my men and won the case for him. It was nothing much. In any case, George and I went out for a drink after and we became friends. George then left the army and I suppose joined your firm. I only saw him once after that when I came to New York."

"I see. Well, you didn't have to take me out, I'm sorry George pushed me on you..." "Don't be silly, you're so much prettier..." and then he stopped. "I'm sorry. With all that PC going around I probably could be sued for saying that..." Debra laughed. "Well not by me. As long as you're not my boss you can say anything you want."

Each took another swallow. The waiter came over and asked if they were ready to order. They ordered one of the specials, neither was that hungry and each seemed to be flustered in the situation they were in. Debra grinned inwardly just thinking of what her mother would say if she brought this hunk of a man to the wedding this Saturday. Probably much better than what her friend had to offer. She would bet even the Bride would have a second look before she said yes to her Groom.

"Something amuses you?" David asked as she obviously hadn't hidden her smile well enough. "Sorry, I was just thinking something about my mother." "Oh, so you have a nagging mother too?" Debra almost choked on her drink. Is he reading her mind? "May I be honest with you David?" David moved his shoulders in a sort of acceptance.

"I have a wedding this Saturday and I need a date and my mother keeps nagging me about it and..." ".. you want to ask me to go with you?" asked David seriously.

This time, Debra's eyes almost popped out of her head. Is this going to be that easy? "Yes, just for a few hours if you have nothing better to do..." David twirled his glass and had a glum expression on his face.

"I think I'd like to, but unfortunately, I can't. I'm in New York till Tuesday. I just arrived last night. I wanted to take care of the business with George first and I certainly would have liked to take you, but

I too need to go to a wedding, and my mother's friend, I think her name is Martha or something, is making me take this woman..." "To the Waldorf...?" Debra interjected. "Yes, to the Waldorf... why are you laughing?"

Thirteen: Roses from Rose

Part One

I've decided to retire after 22 years in the Army, despite my fast track to getting my General's Star, I'm tired of working late hours and coming home to my BOQ alone. At age 40 I am beginning to miss some male companionship. I am at the point that if I date men above my rank, and that's only Flag Officers, generals or admirals, they are just too old or they're married. On the other hand, they can't date me either or shouldn't. Officers below my rank I can't touch due to strict military regulations. If you are interested, read AR 600-20, paragraph 4-14AR 600- 20, it's probably as dull as my private life.

When I was still a junior officer, a lieutenant, or captain, at least there were more candidates of equal rank around but they didn't have what I needed, and I'm not just talking about sex. Sure, I had some affairs but nothing serious enough to get involved in for life.

I'm not going to brag here, but I am quite educated. I hold a number of degrees and speak at least four languages that are vital to what the military is involved with today. I hold a few citations and awards like the Silver and Bronze Stars, and not the least, a Purple Heart, which kept me in a hospital for quite a while.

My birthday is coming up in four months, and I put in all the necessary paperwork to make me a civilian. I want to find a nice, well-educated man with at least one or two children. Hopefully a widower but I'll take a divorced man if he passes my requirements. He has to be self- reliant, doesn't need my money, taller than myself but not too much — a smart dresser. I don't want anyone with torn jeans. He has to know at least how to polish his shoes, walk straight — no pigeon-toed man for me and with reasonably good looks. I'm not looking for a movie star.

As far as my looks. Well, I won't stand on false modesty. I am five-seven, slim, an athlete's figure. I work out constantly. I have a nice face, and I look damn good in my uniform. You'll find I also have a good sense of humor. Though I commanded troops in combat, I stand out more as a staff officer. I know how to handle troops, their equipment and transport, and plan maneuvers. I excel at that.

I am getting out financially secure. I have invested very well, and with my pension, I won't have any financial worries. I might look for work. Perhaps teach history in a college, I've done that in advanced military schools, or do security work and I don't mean night watchman. I could run a security company with my hands tied behind my back and blindfolded. So, that's me in a nutshell.

Part Two

I have been out for four months now. I picked New York City as my home because I originally came from there before my parents were killed in a freak train accident on Amtrak. I'll leave out the details. I was 18 at that time with no other close relatives. I could have been a waitress or something, but I joined the Army instead to travel the world. I know the Navy takes credit for saying it but the Army does send you all over the world, and you don't have to worry about getting seasick.

Anyway, I lucked out with a great little apartment in the East Village, a two bedroom and two bath, try finding that in this town, overlooking a cute little park. It was found by the first agent I went to who happened to have served with me in Texas years ago. He was a reserve officer; a captain and I was a major then. I knew he had the hots for me and I also knew he was married, but I treated him fair after he screwed up on an assignment, I guess he remembered that so he proposed a deal for me.

He would drop any commission charges if I slept with him. Just like that. What chutzpah. I guess that's New York for you. The little twerp. I walked over to him with a smile, and before he knew it, I shot my arm into his throat with one of those oriental karate holds I learned from a special force's instructor, till he started to choke. I slowly whispered into his ear, either I get the apartment without the commission, or I go to his wife and introduce myself. Something like Vito Corleone did with that band leader. Well, the apartment is mine, and I saved myself two months' rent.

Sometimes, I am not so nice. Once I settle in with painting the walls, new curtains, and stuff, I'll look for a job and my man. No hurry. Though I have neighbors, I hardly see them. Guess that's life in the Big Apple too. Well, I'm pretty busy anyway so I don't care for now. I can be a friendly person; I'm sure I'll find someone.

As it happened, a week after I moved in, I ran into a neighbor, a cute young girl, well, woman, about my age with bags full of groceries trying to open the front door. A few cans of asparagus had flown out of one of her shopping bags, and I picked them up for her.

"Thanks. So, you're our new neighbor?" she said blowing her long brown hair away from her face. "I am," I said as she still tried to open the door. "Here, let me help you." I took one of her other bags loaded with vegetables, inwardly hoping she's not one of those veggie nuts.

If I forgot to mention, my building was a walk-up, which means no elevator. We both lived on the third floor, and the reason I haven't seen her was that she had to work pretty late this week. Her name was Susan Michaels, and she was divorced with two kids, an eight-year-old daughter and a ten-year-old son who are staying with her parents in New Jersey. I learned that while we walked up the stairs.

Her apartment was just opposite my door but faced the back. Her ex pays for it as a token of goodwill, she told me. "He really is a nice guy, it's just that he liked to fool around." She explained as if to satisfy my curiosity. In the days to come, she showed me around the neighborhood, and we became fast friends. She held a high position in a large investment firm as an assistant to the CEO. It was a tough job, she said, but she loved it even though she sometimes had to work late.

One evening we sat in a nearby coffee house sipping our lattes. It was a balmy evening late in July. For once Susan came home early, and we decided to take a break from my apartment decorating. She was a great help to me. I told her about my life in the army, and she said she could never live that kind of disciplined life herself. In retrospect, I wondered how I did it.

She told me some of her life, how she met her ex and about her kids, which she was sure I would like, and so on. Just girls talking. Finally, my apartment was ready. All painted and redecorated with little accents here and there, quite a different look than my old BOQ.

Now was the time to scout out the man folk and a job. The job was easier to find than a man. I didn't believe in this computer dating. I thought I'd rather scout the situation out myself. This, after all, was New York, with millions of men just waiting to be scooped up by me. Yeah. Sure. I was never a bar person either nor liked the noisy atmosphere of a dance club, so the only other place was a good restaurant or maybe a park where a man would come with his children or a dog.

The job I found was in an International Legal firm dealing with foreign clients on the phone or when they flew over, and it was face to face. Being multi-lingual was my asset. Of course, I had to be very careful, you know, European men and all that, but fortunately they were mostly professionals, and though they teased on occasion I told them in a friendly tone that I was engaged. I had my mother's engagement ring on just in case. With Italian men, it was touch and go sometimes, but in the end, they acted the gentlemen once I accidentally crushed a wine glass with my hand without a twinge, as blood ran down my arm. Actually, it was catchup that I always carried in small packages. Most men hate blood.

Anyway, I got nowhere really on my men hunting expeditions. Mostly I was just busy with work which I also enjoyed. Susan and I went out together many times to a show or dinner, and honestly, I had a lot of fun with her. She was two years younger than me and had a great sense of humor, like me. Why her husband left her I couldn't imagine unless she had some dark secret hidden in her closet.

Of course, men stared at us on many occasions but when I was with Susan I didn't want to get involved with them, and as far as she was concerned, one man was enough for her. Three weeks before school started, her parents brought her kids over. I fell in love with them immediately. I could have never imagined I would like children so much. They were well- mannered and quite smart, and they took to me. They made me feel like I knew them all their lives.

Part Three

All was going pretty well, except for meeting the right guy. But my work kept me pretty busy, and on weekends Susan and I did things together even when the kids came with us. Then one day I get called into the office of the president. I didn't think much of it. I was doing a good job, a great job actually. Everyone was as happy as can be. Our company only handled the cream of the business world. We weren't large, but we were effective. Clients came to town, and we had to show them a good time with dinners or Broadway shows and such. I took some of the clients out myself.

It was always professional. It was never one on one; usually, it was a small group, our people sometimes brought their wives along, and if there were some special wishes from some particular clients, well, I don't have to tell you the details, we had a special person assigned to that. What do I care? Men, after all, will be men and New York is a great town.

Anyway, the president told me to sit on the couch and joined me. He asked if I wanted coffee or one of his imported scotches. By then I thought this could be one of those special assignments and I was ready with my karate moves. "Have you heard of Sir Edward S. Brighten?" he asked. "The billionaire?"

"Yes, the billionaire. He owns more real estate all over the world than Hilton and Trump and many others put together. We want him as our client, and he wants to take you to dinner." He said it to me so strait-laced I just looked at him as if he was nuts. In our office, we had some super- looking girl receptionists that would fill pages in men's magazines. Why in heaven's name would this billionaire want take out a 40-year-old woman to dinner?"

When I told Susan about it later, she laughed. In a good way. "So he doesn't want some floozy but an intelligent woman, like you, to keep him company." She smirked.

"That's it?" I said. "He just wants to be seen in public with a mature woman who knows how to make good conversation?"

"I bet..." she retorted with a lop-sided smile.

"Well, he would be taking me out to Daniel's. We would discuss some business and then just small talk about the New York scene..."

"And you're buying that?"

I did buy that, after all, what can he do in a public place? It's just a business dinner. I've done a few of those but not with billionaires. Maybe it could lead to something else. Lady Rose? Silly me.

Part Four

The next day I took a long lunch and went shopping for a new dress and shoes. I hadn't bothered too much with party wear before as it was always in business attire. I think I had the concession in ladies' business suits before Clinton. During my army days, I had a dress uniform for any occasion. Bluejacket, long blue mess skirt and comfortable shoes. Miniature medals and bullion rank on my sleeves, white blouse. On a figure like mine, it's quite impressive.

Of course, that wouldn't do in this case, so I picked out a little black number with a proper length, not too short and not too long. Enough to show a good leg. I purchased shoes by Christian Louboutin with high heels I hoped won't make me taller than Sir Edward's head. Damn, did I look good in the mirror.

And so that afternoon I came home laden with a hand full of packages. I rang Susan's door to show her all my goodies when I was greeted by two smiling faces that were asking me all sorts of questions. "Okay, kids, let Miss Hudson through already," Susan's voice came from the kitchen. "Help her with those packages, William." Then she came over smiling and kissed me on both cheeks.

"Sooo, I see you've been shopping." I came home happy as can be. I bought, for the first time ever, a black cocktail dress and spend more money on shoes than maybe six months of food rations. Susan's adorable kids watched as I showed Susan the stuff I bought. I didn't think kids could be so nice. If only I could meet a man with kids like that. And tomorrow I might even meet one.

That night I hardly slept. I just lay in bed daydreaming of how life is changing me. All those years in the army I was awakened by bugle calls, and now I had pigeons cooing at my window each morning. Eventually, I did fall asleep, and when I awoke from those damn pigeons cooing, I had a glass of orange juice and went for a run. When I came back, Susan met me at the garbage disposal with a smile.

I gave her a sweaty hug. "How about I come with you to the hairdresser to make sure they do you up well," Susan said. "That would be great." Susan was indeed a good friend. By seven Saturday, again with Susan looking out for me and helping me get dressed I looked in the mirror and said WOW! to myself. Susan also made some wild comments. "You are stunning!" she declared and called in her kids to verify.

Sir Edward's chauffeur was waiting for me at 7 in a shining black Rolls as people on the sidewalk stared. We arrived at Daniel's exactly 5 minutes late. A majordomo or some flunky was standing there and when he saw me called out. "Miss Hudson?" "I was," I said. "Welcome, please follow me. His Lordship is waiting inside."

'His Lordship?' How much better can it get, I thought to myself. I recognized the dapper man immediately from pictures I saw on the Internet. He stood by the table, and when I came near, he took my hand and kissed it. Actually, he was a handsome man, tall, straight figure, well- groomed hair, a dark Savile Row suit. And a Clark Gable face with a guardsman mustache.

"I am glad you didn't change your mind. Please sit down; I've ordered some champaign."

A waiter stood and pulled the chair out for me and delicately pushed it back in under my derrière.

"You look C'est Magnifique," he said kissing his fingers and throwing it in my direction. I could feel stares from everyone around me. A glass flute with sparkling champagne was handed to me and His Lordship. I just loved that title...

"To you my dear. Health. Happiness and long life! Chin! Chin!" We clanked and drank. I was in a dream world for sure. In the Army, I have attended many balls at embassies and presidential palaces, but I have never been treated like this. He told me to call him Eddie. From His Lordship to Eddie. Can you imagine? What else can go right?

No menu was given to us. Eddie just told the waiter what he should bring. For an appetizer, he ordered a dish of Caviar. I found out later what it cost, and my hair stood on end. For dinner, he ordered Sturgeon which we ate slowly; there was no rush. Our glasses were always refilled. Eddie was a good conversationalist but did not hog the conversations. He knew, he said about me and my military career. How? I don't know, but when you have money like he seemed to have, you can find out anything. But he was very complimentary about it. He admired soldiering. In fact, he held a reserve commission in the Grenadier Guards.

He was only a Major, so he joked about how I outranked him. He was very sweet. After we finished the French-sounding fish dish, the table was cleared with a new table cloth because the maître d' found a breadcrumb on it. When we were alone again, Eddie reached into his breast pocket and brought out a long narrow black box and handed it to me.

"What is that, Eddie?" I asked. "It's certainly not my birthday," I joked.

"Open it." I opened the box and took a deep breath. The box held a string of pearls. "Eddie, why...?" He didn't let me finish. "It's just a small something for letting me take you to dinner."

"But Eddie, Lord whoever you are, I can't accept it. Why this must have..." He didn't let me finish again.

"Don't be concerned. To have met you is worth every penny. Especially if you let me put it on right now." And he stood up and took the string of pearls and snapped it around my neck before I could take a breath. People around us stared and smiled and yes, whispered.

Eddie sat down again. "It fits you like a princes," he said. I put my hand on the necklace and felt as my fingers caressed the pearls. I knew these were not something from the ninety-nine cents store. I was dumbfounded. I started to say something again, but he just put his finger to his lips and said. "Shh..."

"Would the lady care for some dessert?" The maître d's voice interrupted my thoughts. "Bring us some Tarte Citron Meringuee and some tea. Is that alright, Rose?" I was still in a stupor from the pearls and just shook my head in the affirmative. "In a way, it is also a farewell gift for a while. I have to go back to Jolly Old England. I would have left a few days ago, but when I saw you down the hall in your office, I wanted to meet you." "Eddie you are a flatterer," I said still playing with the pearls. The

Tarte Citron Meringuee arrived with the tea, and we munched on that for a while. Actually, neither of us ate more than a spoonful.

And then he threw the towel at me. "I have to leave for London on Monday. If I could, I would stay longer for us to get more acquainted, but duty calls. I'm building a hotel in Cairo, and I need to finalize the deal. I have a competitor, an upstart named Trump. Do you know of him?"

Part Five

"And then he asked me," I told Susan later that evening. .".. That he's throwing a party on his little yacht tomorrow at the Hudson River Pier and inviting his American staff to say goodbye. "I would very much like you to come. I will send my car for you, and I will not take no for an answer." "He told me." It was one of the most magical nights I have ever had. Then I showed her the necklace; she was astounded. What a catch, if only it weren't too good to be true. Did I see a ring? She asked was he married? I totally forgot to look, I said, maybe tomorrow...

The chauffeur was already waiting for me when I came down. I had no special clothes for a yacht, so Susan put something together from her closet. We were about the same size and seemingly had the same taste in clothes. Eddie was standing by the gangway when we arrived and opened the car door before the chauffeur had a chance to come around. When he said a small yacht, he probably meant a little smaller than the Queen Marry. He kissed my hand and took me up on deck where a small group had already gathered, and I could hear little murmurs. Introductions were made all around, and a young man dressed in a sailor suit asked everyone down to the stern for breakfast. I couldn't eat much, a pastry and some coffee. I really was too excited. We made some small talk and then when the sun rose above its zenith, most people found sun chairs and relaxed at the pool on the top deck.

Eddie took me to a secluded little area cast in shadow and sat me down. "Would you care for a drink or anything else?" he asked graciously. I guess here comes the big sell. Here's where he is going to propose to me or tell me he's married with six children. I have forgotten to look for a ring again and now he held his hands in his pockets — a nervous look on his face.

He was dressed in a white jacket and a black T-shirt with white slacks and white loafers and no socks, almost like a civilian admiral. He smiled at me, and I smiled back. "You are truly a beautiful woman, Rose," he said. Well, I can live with compliments like these.

Then I thought he would take me in his arms, but he just sat there admiring me. At least, that's what it looked like. I still forgot to look for his wedding ring. I could see he was still nervous as a cat. He tried to say something but stopped before the words came out.

He seemed to be struggling with words so I bent over and touched his hand. "Eddie, what is it?" I asked. "You're not planning to dump me overboard to the sharks. Are you?" I joked. He put his hand over mine. It was the first time he did that. It wasn't paradise but it felt warm and cozy. He smiled with his lips but his eyes were serious. By now I thought I knew what was coming. He's going to tell me he's married but wants a companion to keep him warm at night. Well, I wasn't interested in that. I was starting to say something myself, like, "Eddie it was nice knowing you..." and throw the damn necklace in his face.

Then suddenly he stood up. "Rose," he said, still struggling with his words. "Rose, I'm gay." I was frozen in time. "Gay?..." "Yes, I am gay. I am also married. I have six children spread in many countries that take care of the family business. My wife, and I'm sure some others know about me but not my associates. I made sure of that. My wife is a very understanding woman."

I bet, I thought. "She has whatever she wants." He continued. "I give her an allowance that a Saudi prince would be envious of. She can do whatever she wants including lovers as long as it's not in the public eye. In a way, we love and understand each other. I don't know if the children, my children, by the way, know, but if they do, they are keeping it to themselves." "I liked you the moment I saw you in the office. I knew I wanted you

to play the part of a woman I wanted..."

"Wait a minute my dear Lord Eddie," I started angrily, "you think I am that kind off..."

"Don't finish your words, Rose. It's the last thing in the world I think of you. I think you are the classiest lady I have met in a long time. You are truly wonderful, and I am terribly sorry..."

"... And then he said so much more," I told Susan later that afternoon as we strolled in the park. The gist of it all was that he just wanted to show people he was a manly man with a woman in every port. I was going to walk out, or give him one of my famous chokers holds, I thought to myself, "but he looked so sincere I just didn't have the heart to do it. After all, what did he really do? Buy me a nice dinner, give me a string of pearls? He hadn't touched me once except when he started to tell me about his choices."

"There really was no harm done. He didn't force me into some cave and. well he didn't. He acted like a gentleman every moment. He was

going to give me a pin. My God, you should have seen it. I should have taken a picture of it before I thanked him and returned it. I even wanted to return the necklace but he wouldn't hear of it."

"So he just needed you to show off a little the poor guy."

"I tell you it was so totally not expected. I thought he would say come home with me, and I'll divorce my wife. But gay? Never!"

"You're not one of those anti-gay people, are you Rose?" "What? Me? Of course not. Why would you even say that? We had many gays in the Army. Some you could tell; some you'd never know. I didn't care as long as they did their job."

"Did you ever make friends with any of them?"

"I guess, I must have. It never occurred to me to ask" I said looking at Susan's kids chasing each other around a tree. I loved them as if they were my own even though I only met them a few weeks ago. "If you had a friend, a good friend, who you didn't know was gay and then suddenly "

I stopped for a moment and looked straight at Susan. Now, I've been around the block a few times. I can tell when someone leads me on. Sure, it had come out of the blue, but I knew what Susan was leading to. I looked around and saw a free bench and took Susan by the arm and sat her down. "Tell me," I said.

Part Six

That night as I sat on my bed I reflected on what Susan told me. Of course, she was gay. It was the reason her husband left her. Not what she told me before that he was a womanizer. She didn't know her feelings when they got married but after her daughter, Cindy was born, something happened, and she didn't want her husband's affection anymore. Sure, they tried. They saw a shrink, a family social worker but words can't cure something like that. She didn't want to be cured of these feelings. She had never been with a woman before, nevertheless, those feeling were there and not going to disappear.

She told me that she would understand if I didn't want to see her again. Then she left crying telling the kids that some dirt got into her eyes. Those kids looked toward me and at her and understood something besides dirt in the eye happened. Kids nowadays are too smart. I was caught between a rock and a hard place. This morning I thought someone was going to ask me to marry him, and then I find out he was gay. Then my best friend, the only true friend I thought I had, confessed that she was gay.

How does anyone handle something like that? I had never thought about these things. I tried to remember who in my army unit was gay? Really gay. It just didn't come to me. Everyone was just a person to me. A soldier. Oh, except for Conner. Oh boy, poor Conner. For sure he was gay. Once, on parade, he wore lipstick and earrings. I thought he was just playing around and told him to report to my office after the parade.

I'll never forget this. He broke down crying at how unhappy he was. It turned out he wasn't really gay but trans-gender as it's known now. But then the Army frowned on things like that and wanted to give him a dishonorable discharge which I had changed to a medical discharge. It broke my heart. But what to do now? I didn't want to lose Susan as a friend. I didn't want to lose the kids. All of a sudden, a motherly instinct embraced me. I will not lose those kids if I could help it.

We got together again though the relationship was a bit strained. At work, I became more active. Eddie, Sir Edward, hired our company if I am involved. It was a multi-million dollar contract. There were a lot of international dealings with Cairo, and as I spoke Arabic, I handled all the communications.

And Susan needed to get the kids ready for school. New clothing had to be bought. Books, writing materials, pens, pencils, and the myriad of things kids need to further their education. So, during the week, we didn't see each other that much. We called it occupational fatigue.

A few weeks after, I met a middle-aged man by chance during lunch when we both reached for a muffin at the cafeteria and then shared it at a small table. He seemed like a nice person. Well-groomed. He had a pleasant face with a seemingly broken nose when he was young, but that didn't distract from his looks. It sort of added to his masculinity. He was divorced, with two girls, he told me, that he saw every other weekend. I didn't ask why he was divorced or who initiated it. At this time it wasn't my business. I was just hoping he wasn't gay.

He took me to dinner, not to Daniel's, but still a nice place, and for the second date, to a movie and a buggy ride in the park. I felt comfortable with him. We kissed a bit. It was nice. The sky didn't fall nor did fireworks explode above us but it was still early. We took walks holding hands. He lived further uptown, so he had to bus it to my place as there is plenty to do in the Village. We hung around mostly there.

I told Susan about it, and she was happy for me, but I noticed a lack of interest, however, I said nothing. On our fourth date, we went to an Off- Broadway play and afterward to a small restaurant on the west side for dessert. It wasn't crowded, and in the back, I saw two couples sitting and talking and laughing. The boys happen to be two Marines from a visiting navy ship with a couple of girls that looked of college age. They didn't do anything special; they didn't bother anyone. They seemed to be polite to the waitress that served them and just were happy to be where they were...

Suddenly my date, the man I was getting close to, made a remark about servicemen. It was a derogatory remark. He called them baby killers and in general, if it were up to him, he would totally disband the Armed Forces. "We could solve the whole problem by just getting together and..." "... Sing Kumbaya," I interrupted

This was like a slap in my face. At no time did I come across such visceral hatred from him. Where did this come from? Apparently, as he came out with, when he was a student he protested against the Viet Nam war and spat on a marine at the airport. The Marine deserved it he said for killing innocent people. The Marine gave him a black eye and a broken nose.

I looked at him as if for the first time. Am I going to get involved with a jerk like that? "I am a colonel in the Army. I served for twenty-two years. Proudly, I might add," I told him, getting up and taking my share of the bill out of my wallet, and left the restaurant. I walked home the almost forty blocks, angry as hell. I am not getting anywhere with men. In the long haul, I meditated on my future. Where am I actually going with my life? At work, there were a few unmarried men, but my excuse was I don't want to get involved in the workplace. I don't want to go online. I don't want to go to senior citizens' singles workshops. So where will I meet that perfect partner with two fine children?

Where? I couldn't think. My mind was a total blank. It occurred to me after a while that the only person I knew with kids and liked was Susan. But Susan was a woman. A lesbian. I wasn't a lesbian. It hadn't especially crossed my mind, but I always seemed happy to be around Susan and her two kids.

If only Susan was a man, but ifs don't cut it. Susan will never be a man, but, but, and I started laughing. First silently and then full-blown laughter as I thought to myself. "But could I be a lesbian?" By the time that hit me I was still laughing, and now I was in the village where there are always people around, and they must have thought I was high on something.

I finally stopped laughing and calmed down. I was a few blocks away from home. There are always little Korean convenience stores open 24 hours a day. Usually, they sell flowers. It took three stores to finally find one with the flowers I wanted. I bought as much as I could carry.

By now I was pretty tired too. It was a long day, but I made it to the third floor. I looked at my watch; it was 12:32. I knocked softly on Susan's door. Of course, she's most likely asleep and couldn't hear. Then I remembered that the kids had a sleepover with their friends a few blocks away. I rang the bell again and held it for a minute. Soon I hear a shuffling noise.

"Who is it?" Susan finally asked in a sleepy voice. "It's me; open the door," I said calmly. "Rose? What are you doing here this time of night? Are you all right?"

"Open the door, Susan," I said again quietly...

I heard the locks turning, and there stood Susan in an old housecoat rubbing her eyes like a small child. "What is it Rose, are you okay?" she asked me again in a worried tone. I gently pulled her inside handing her the flowers. I had no idea what I was doing or what the future holds but seeing her so vulnerable I just had to give her a hug. "Everything is going to be just fine now," I said closing the door behind me.

Fourteen: The Bashful General

Part One

General Mark Davidson loved his 10-year-old niece and his 8-year-old nephew very much, what The General wasn't especially fond of, was listening to them singing in school plays. But it wasn't often that he came for a weekend visit to their home in New York so he tolerated them as best he could. He had been invited for a weekend whenever he could get away, while stationed in Washington at the Pentagon. It just happened that this time, it came on a Saturday, at the end of the term, when the kids were performing in a charity musical at their school.

He would have rather had a root canal performed by a first-year dental student than hear the squealing voices, but everyone else seemed to look forward to this event, so he played along. The General had no children of his own as his marriage, at a very young age, didn't even last a year. Of course, it was army life that ruined it. Being away for many months at a time and the worry that comes from it, was just too much for his new wife and so she found a man with a nice steady job and divorced the young officer the same year. This had quite an adverse reaction on him, about women.

It wasn't so much that he disliked them it was more so that he ignored them. He would not have any women come close to him, especially if he was beginning to like them. Now at 37, he was a devout bachelor and reasonably happy. He was the youngest major general in the Army with a great career ahead of him. Finding a woman and getting married again was the last thing on his mind this Saturday afternoon, that is until he saw his nieces' music teacher. It wasn't that he thought she was the most beautiful woman in the world but there was something about her that just pierced his heart. He couldn't really tell her age as she stood on the stage introducing the children, but he thought perhaps she might be a few years younger than him.

This, however, wasn't the important thing he noticed about her. Oh, the first thing was a scar on her left cheek. It wasn't particularly prominent but he has seen too many scars on his soldiers, to know how they look. That scar did not take anything away from her looks in any case, but it was the dark eyes and the mouth and the nose and the shape of her face sitting on a perfectly formed neck and shoulders and torso and even her long legs, though he couldn't really see them for she wore cream-colored pants, just seemed so well put together. All that he saw in an instant, as he had a lot of experience in battlefield reconnaissance.

Well, there was nothing to do now except get the hell out of here and go back to Washington as quickly as possible. The General was not going to involve himself with this woman. This one would be trouble for him. But he, of course, couldn't just walk out right now, it wouldn't be polite and the musical numbers his niece was in, hadn't even started.

When the introductions were done and the teacher went backstage, his sister nudged him and whispered. "Isn't she something? I've invited her to our barbecue this afternoon." This seemingly innocent little sentence sent shivers up The General's spine. He knew his sister always tried to get him involved with one of her women friends and it took a lot of initiative to get out of these situations.

At this moment the music started as a group of eight-year-olds came on stage and began to screech their interpretation of 'Hello Dolly.' How to get out of this situation without hurting his sister's feelings was The General's immediate thought. By now he was certain his sister knew all his tricks, even the ingrown toenail. He needs a new excuse he had never used before, something simple but believable. His sister, who was sitting next to him noticed his fidgeting around nervously in his seat, so she jabbed him with her elbow and silently mouthed. "What?"

He put his finger to his lips and shushed her, to which she just shook her head in frustration. It took him a few minutes to find a good excuse as he heard some older man in the back speak Russian. 'Razve moya vnuchka ne talantliva? Isn't my granddaughter talented?' 'Da, Papa. Yes Papa…'

It was at that moment that he shaped an idea about how he can get out of here, at least after the play. He would blame it on the Russians. In any case, he couldn't leave now. His sister would be pissed so he stayed an agonizing hour and a half for the show to end. All this time he finalized his escape plan as if he was in some prisoner-of-war camp.

At the same time, he thought himself a foolish idiot the way he was acting. So what if he is suddenly going bonkers about this woman. He didn't even know her name. So he feels soppy about her, so what does that mean? She's probably married or engaged or going out with someone.

After all, a woman like that must have a line of men in front of her doorstep a mile long. So why would she want to be with a man that acts so idiotic sitting in the first row of a school auditorium? Finally, it was over. The music teacher came back on stage and asked the kids to bow again to great applause. When all quieted down and the kids left the stage, the teacher made an announcement to the audience.

The General could barely look at her, she was stunning. She had a great presence just standing there that one seldom sees in people. Perhaps he was exaggerating it to himself a bit but he couldn't help it. He had to stop himself from actually asking his sister for an introduction. So as the music teacher was still talking he took out his cell phone and nudged his sister indicating he has an important call and has to step out. Of course, there was no phone call. It was all a rouse. In the meantime, the teacher had told the audience that she must rush off to catch a plane as she was taking a week off now that her vacation had started.

The General had not heard this but told his sister that the Pentagon has called and there seemed to be some hubbub with the Russians and he must get back to Washington. His sister scoffed at him but there was nothing to be done. He has never used an excuse like that so perhaps it was true. She knew he had an important job there and if called, it was not for nothing. In passing, she told him that that were two people not coming to her party now, him and the teacher.

The General was surprised and now felt pretty guilty but he couldn't back out of his stupid plan even though he would now have liked to stay as there was no danger from that teacher. Damn it all. He certainly was acting like a child. Worse... So off they all went, back to their house to prepare for the other guests that were coming and The General to pack and go home to an empty apartment.

The General called the airline for the shuttle to Washington and was told he had just made the last seat. Sadly, he said goodbye to the disappointed family because they made the BBQ in his honor but stupidity won the day. The General insisted no one drive him, he would take a cab to the airport. He didn't want anyone to see the idiotic look on his face.

It was the normal New York traffic to La Guardia Airport, bumper to bumper with the usual honking of car horns and people cutting in. Finally, he made it just in time. He ran through airport security quickly as one of the guards once served under his command. He made it just as the gate was closing.

"You are very lucky Sir, you are the last passenger, I'll show you to your seat and please buckle your seatbelt as we are preparing for takeoff," the flight attendant said to him as she pointed out the window seat in the last row. He put his bag in the overhead compartment and then excused himself as he tried to step over the passenger in the aisle seat. He stopped dead as he looked down at the smiling passenger, for it was none other than the same teacher he had just run away from.

Part Two

"Excuse me, Sir, you'll have to sit down and put on your seat belt." The flight attendant insisted again. The General froze in mid-step and stood there straddling the teacher's legs he so admired only a while ago. His face turned red. "Sir, you have to sit down, please... The plane is moving." The General practically jumped over the teacher, sat, and tightened his belt.

"They're pretty bossy, the flight attendants, I mean," said the teacher with an upturned smile, as The General, red-faced, tried to get his seatbelt tightened and composure back. The plane ran down the taxiway for a minute and The General saw that the teacher's hands suddenly grabbed the armrests as if her life depended on it. She saw him looking at her and frowned.

"I get this way every time the plane takes off. I really hate flying." As the plane built up speed The General saw her fingers tighten so much that they turned white. Then he did something he never thought he would do. He put his right hand over her left and held it tight. The teacher gave him a wry smile and lifted her eyes to heaven.

After the plane finally lifted off, and made its turn toward Washington, The General had not as yet let go of her hand. "It's okay now," said the teacher, "it's just take-offs and landings I can't stand. Thanks for the support!" The General removed his hand quickly. "Sorry," he said.

The teacher smiled. "I'm Teresa Backer" She put her hand forward. The General took it and started to introduce himself but she cut him off.

"I know who you are. You're Brenda's brother, I saw you in the audience in my school not more than 2 hours ago... You're General Davidson." There went that smile again. "Do I have to call you General or do you have a simpler name?" To say the general was a bit taken aback was an understatement but being a general he snapped out of it quickly though his heart beat a little faster.

"Yes. My sister always teases me in French, Mon General, she calls me," why in blazes did he have to tell her that? "But my real name is Mark," he added.

"Hmm,"Teresa kind of looked him over, "I kind of like Mon General, it's sweet." His face turned almost pink but he liked the way she said it in that French accent. Mon General...

The flight attendant that scolded Mark before to sit down suddenly appeared with a tray of water bottles and asked him if he would like a drink then in a quiet voice she apologized for rushing him so, but hoped he understood as they were ready for take-off, then added. "You probably don't remember me, Sir, but I served in the same unit in Germany as you..."

"Of course, you worked in S3, battalion supply, let me see, Corporal Ramirez, right?" "Yes Sir! I'm surprised you remembered. Anything I can do just ring the bell, Sir" She said with an adoring smile and walked away just as Teresa tried to take a bottle for herself. "Well, I see who's a second- class passenger on this flight," she said following the disappearing bottles. Mark handed her his water bottle and just shrugged his shoulders.

"You get a lot of that, do you? How did you remember her after so long ago?" she asked. Teresa wasn't really thirsty and offered the bottle back but Mark wasn't thirsty either and shook his head so she put the bottle in the netting of the seat in front and looked at him sidelong.

"It's not difficult. Actually, I didn't remember her but I thought as long as I remembered her name it wouldn't make a difference if I didn't get the other stuff right."

"And you remembered her name?" Mark smiled. "Sorry, I didn't, but if you noticed she had her name tag on her chest..."

Teresa shook her head in absolute admiration. They sat silently for a while then both started to speak. "You first, go ahead..." Mark said. Teresa hesitated for a moment. "May I tell you something, Mon General, Mark?" She turned to him with a serious face. Mark wasn't sure how to answer that but he certainly couldn't say no.

"Of course..." he answered cautiously. "Oh, don't be such a milquetoast, I'm not going to berate you..." She smiled again like the cat who caught its mouse. "You know, your sister told me quite a lot about you since her kids took my class. Of course, she sort of hinted that you would be quite a catch for me... Let me finish Mark." As he was about to say something.

"She told me you were coming and invited me to this afternoon's barbecue. Obviously to meet you. To be honest, I wasn't interested." Mark just looked at her with a dry mouth. What could he say? He was just 'hoisted with his own petard.'

Teresa continued. "Please, Mon General," she said overdoing the French accent. "Please don't be upset. I know you felt the same way when I looked at you sitting so uncomfortably in the first row after you saw me. As a teacher, I'm familiar with seeing people feeling uncomfortable in my classes or at PTA meetings. It's that look one sees on their faces that say, wish I was anywhere else but here. Admit it, your sister probably told you about me and you suddenly had other plans on your mind though I couldn't help also seeing..."

"Okay, okay. You got me there, though at that time I didn't know you were coming officially but..." "But you suspected something, didn't you? Well so did I. Actually I like your sister and the kids and I kind of like you..."

The General just sat there a bit dumbfounded at the cheekiness of this woman and started to say something again. "Please, I'm not finished or offended,"Teresa continued smoothly, "as I said, I kind of like you Mark," she repeated, "but I'm not ready for a hookup. In fact, when your sister told me about the barbecue and that you were coming,

I made some quick reservations during the show to get out of town myself. Actually, I already made plans to go to Washington but I was supposed to leave tomorrow. You're gaping at me now."

The General did look a little flustered but he smiled inwardly. He had never met anyone like that, at least not a woman or someone below his rank and he started to like her more and more. But she still wasn't finished. "Yes. Amazing how our minds worked. But believe me, I never in a million years ever thought we would wind up on the same flight sitting next to each other." Then she just shook her head in disbelief.

She certainly has a great attitude thought Mark, but there was nothing to add to her story except to smile back and then laugh, and then she started to laugh and that's what they did while heads turned to stare at them. They ended with a giggle and just looked at each other and then away and at the same time reached for that water bottle.

"Please, you take it," said The General. "Oh no, Mon General, you take it, it was a gift from your admirer, she's not going to like it if I take it away from you. I think she's actually watching."

"Take it please..." Mark insisted.

"I don't mind sharing if you don't," she said taking a few swallows and handing the bottle back to him. The General was again taken aback at her forwardness. This could be more serious than he thought. If he drinks this, it's almost like making a blood bond. Should he do it? He thought with amusement.

Teresa was watching him with dark narrowed eyes. "Oh go on, Mon General, why, we were almost engaged," she quipped. Like a challenge, he reached for the bottle and put it to his mouth, took a few swallows, and gave it back. She took it without hesitation still staring at him and drinking the last bit, then looked towards the flight attendant who was watching them from the galley. Teresa smiled at her then turned to Mark.

"You know Mark, even though I like you, I don't want you to get the wrong idea." She put the empty bottle back into the netting and sat back. "So what do you do in that big Pentagon, if you can talk about it? I certainly don't want you to divulge any national secrets."

"Well, a lot of paper shuffling, to be honest. I also train a lot of men in many things."

And so time passed, each asking questions about the other. Teresa talked about his sister's children and how talented they are despite The General's aversion to the kids talents. And so, time passed. Forty-five minutes into the flight they hit a bump. The captain announced a weather front coming in from the Carolinas. He's going to try to get permission to fly around it. Ten minutes later he told the passengers that the front moved quicker than anyone thought and Washington is getting the worst of it and it was suggested by ATC (Air Traffic Control) that he land in Baltimore. "If there is anything worse that I hate besides take-offs and landings, is stormy weather," said Teresa nervously. The ride became bumpier and a child began to cry a few seats away. Teresa looked at the General with bravely closed lips, but it didn't fool him, she was pretty scared and her face started to lose color, the scar getting more prominent by the minute. The General took her hand and squeezed it. He had gone through worse on military flights. "The plane is pretty sturdy. Don't worry, nothing much can happen except for the bumpiness."

"That's what I'm afraid of. I should have taken the train." The pilot announced that it would get smoother once they drop down to a thousand feet and it should be a smooth landing in Baltimore. Only about ten minutes more. Teresa was turning white, but now Mark put his arms around her shoulders and held her tight. "A few more minutes. Just a few more minutes and all will be well," he whispered into her ear.

And so, they landed safely but Mark didn't let her go till they arrived at the gate. The plane parked just in time because as soon as the plane's doors opened, a thunderclap exploded overhead as they set foot into the terminal. Teresa was as white as a sheet by now. Mark took her into a bar and ordered a brandy which she drank with shaking hands.

"I'm not usually that frightened of storms but not when I'm in one, 30,000 feet up in the air. I'm sorry," she said still shaking. "Well, we're safe and sound now. We can wait it out and fly on..." "I am not getting into that plane again Mark. Can we rent a car or something? Maybe take the train or a bus to Washington, it's not that far away?" Mark didn't miss the word 'we' and wasn't quite sure what to make of it. "Sure, let the storm subside and I'll rent us a car"

But the storm didn't subside, the reports said that the storm will go on all night. "We'll get some rooms at the hotel here till morning. They say it should clear up by mid-day." Unfortunately, there was only one room available, what, with all the other passengers also stuck in the storm.

"That's okay, you'll take the room and I'll stay in the lobby," volunteered the General. "I've slept under worse conditions in my time..." "I couldn't let you do that, maybe we can get something in Baltimore,

it's even closer." "That's about an eight-mile drive. Take a look outside." Said, Mark. It was a downpour; one couldn't even see further than the tail light of the aircraft parked by the jet bridge.

"We are in a bit of a bind," said Teresa. "Look, we can't just sit here, let's take the room before someone else gets it and we both have to sleep in the terminal. We're both mature, we'll work something out. It's not like we're total strangers. Right? After all, we drank water from the same bottle."

They took the room; it overlooked a highway but you wouldn't know it. All one could see were ghostly lights of drivers who were mad enough to drive through this muck. The General just had an overnight bag and Teresa, had a small suitcase, her other still being on the plane, so there wasn't much to unpack. In any case, they would only stay overnight and hopefully rent a car tomorrow to drive to Washington, only an hour or so ride away. Nothing else to do. It must be some mischievous fate that had brought them together and they have to make the best of things.

Obviously, Teresa knew Mark wasn't some criminal so she wasn't afraid for her life and The General knew she wasn't some stranger out to rifle his wallet, but it certainly was a bizarre situation, and he has been in many of those with the army. By now it was late evening and they were hungry. The General suggested they go over to the restaurant and see what's on the menu.

Neither changed their clothes though Teresa refreshed her makeup and fixed her hair while The General watched the weather report on TV. It seemed like a rogue storm had hit this area and probably will be with them for at least another 24 hours. It wasn't the news he wanted to hear nevertheless there wasn't much he could do about it.

Well, there was plenty he could do, after all, he was a general with some influence in Washington and could certainly get himself a military ride out of here but then he would have to leave Teresa, and that, all of a sudden, he could not do. He somehow felt a responsibility to keep her safe. If nothing else, so his sister wouldn't kick him in the ass. But in reality, it was something else, but he wouldn't admit to himself what it was. The restaurant seemed very nice and crowded as expected. Again, as at La Guardia security and the flight attendant, one of the maître d's, a woman, recognized The General as she too served under him some years ago in the

U.S. Embassy in Paris. After a friendly greeting and this time a hug from the woman, which Teresa thought embarrassed The General, she found him a table right away.

Teresa followed marveling at yet another coincidence. "Is there anyone you don't know?" she asked teasingly as they sat down. The General once again shrugged his shoulders. A waitress came by within seconds with a menu and told them their specials. It appeared to be a Chesapeake Bay cuisine and so they ordered the specials. A minute later a complimentary bottle of white wine was brought to the table and poured into a glass for The General's approval.

"Very nice," he said. What else was there to say? It was complimentary after all. The dinner came pretty quickly too and Teresa looked at him and smiled. "Please don't tell me you also know the chef." It was more a statement than a question so The General just smiled and raised his eyebrows without commitment.

Teresa took a few swallows of the complimentary wine and shook her head in approval, the wine was good. "Would I be wrong if I said this was some conspiracy of yours just to get to know me? The accidental meeting on the plane. The sudden storm. The last room in the hotel. A quick table and the food practically prepared just waiting for you to bring me here..."

The General stabbed a piece of cod with his fork and put it into his mouth. After swallowing, he sipped the wine as if he had all the time in the world and looked at Teresa and shrugged his shoulders once more.

Part Three

After the meal, it was still too early to go up to the Room, to do what? Watch TV? Get into bed? So, they decided to go to one of the bars for a drink. In the back of her mind, she wondered if there too, lingered a complimentary cocktail and she had to chuckle inwardly. As impossible as the situation was becoming for her, she sort off began to like this General, she hoped she wasn't going to fall for all this illusion of contentment.

The storm outside was still in full swing and you could hear the howling wind even in the bar. They sat by a small table drinking another complimentary drink which made Teresa smile openly. "What?" The General asked. "So, tell me your connection to this maître d' that keeps sending us these drinks?" asked Teresa.

"Actually in her case, I remembered her." He said as Teresa's eyebrows turned upwards...

The General shook his head. "You seem to have a dirty mind, Ms. Backer. She was a young officer, that spoke French, and so she was sent to our embassy in France, perhaps a miracle of army efficiency, where I was a military attaché," he leaned forward, "and was one of many young officers there. I met her a few times as she brought me some documents and she was very efficient at her work so I gave her an excellent efficiency report. She was there a year and I suppose after her enlistment was up, went into civilian life. That's it. I haven't seen or heard from her till this evening."

Teresa stared at him for a few moments. "So that's it? No romantic interludes in Gay Paree? No walking down the Champs-Elysée arm in arm?" Now The General was quiet and looked into her eyes. "I know you're just joking and trying to tease me but to me, something like that is a very serious matter. I..."

She didn't let him finish. "I apologize profusely. You know I didn't mean anything by it so please let's not say more. That was a pretty stupid thing for me to say." Mark smiled and said, "Okay, no more of it." They each took a sip and looked back out the window. Nothing outside changed except it got darker.

There was a piano player in the bar by a small dance floor. He played old romantic songs from the 40s and 50s. Occasionally couples would get up and dance, many dressed in shorts as their baggage was still in the hold of the plane, but no one cared. Once in a while, the pianist would sing an old song, and those people that remembered sat quietly and listened. It was a time when one understood every word and the same lyrics weren't repeated every other line. Occasionally someone called out a name of a tune and the pianist would abide followed by a tip. What else was there to do on this starless stormy night.

"I love these old melodies, don't you?" Teresa said dreamily. "Would you like to hear a funny story of how I got this scar?" She asked Mark. Mark shook his head in assent... "Of course I wasn't always a music teacher. I wanted to be a singer. A singer on Broadway. That was my dream." She said in a melancholy voice.

"I had an old aunt that was in the theater in the 40s and she told me I had the voice for it. Well, to make a long story short I went for an audition for an upcoming Broadway musical. I thought I sang beautifully. I was standing center stage and the director with his entourage was sitting in the back rows of the orchestra seats, and I could see he wasn't really paying much attention to my singing. Somewhat like you this morning..." she said that with a grin.

"Anyway, I thought I was pretty good but it seemed he was ignoring me so I moved forward so that he could hear me better. I wasn't watching where I was going and fell into the orchestra pit right unto the trombone player." She moved her hand to her face, caressing her scar.

A beautiful face, Mark thought. "And whump. My face fell hard onto it and cut it. No more Broadway for me," she said. "But I still loved music and I loved children and so I wound up teaching it." At this moment the piano player started playing another old tune from the Big Band era. "Wow, this is one of my favorites. Do you know it Mark?"

"I do, its Glen Miller's Moonlight Serenade." "Do you dance Mon General?" The General stood up, clicked his heels like an Imperial Guardsman and took her to the dance floor then slowly moved her to the rhythm of the slow sentimental tune. After the tune stopped, The General paid the bill and they went up to their room with the single bed. The do not disturb sign on the doorknob lasted till Monday morning.

Fifteen: Mixing Green

Helen Green lost her husband two years ago in Ft Lauderdale. Both had retired there as teachers from New York schools. Her husband Robert, a history, teacher, and Helen, an art teacher. When Robert passed away they brought him to New York where they had reserved a cemetery plot years ago.

Their only child, a son, Harold, married to Carry, had two children and a dog, Max. After the funeral, the son asked his mother to stay with them for a while. The while turned into two weeks when Helen decided it was time to go. She knew her daughter-in-law was beginning to get antsy, after all, having your mother-in-law with you 24 hours a day can strain a lot of people.

During the next two years, the son and family came down and stayed with his mother during the winter holidays enjoying free food and a swimming pool, never inviting his mother to spend any time with him up north during the hot Florida summer months. Apparently, at some point, the daughter-in-law seemed to have gotten a guilt complex, so the mother thought, and invited her to spend this August with them in New York.

The mother wasn't particularly thrilled about this but all her close friends were leaving Ft Lauderdale to visit with their children in northern cities, so how would it look if she didn't do the same. Surprisingly Carry picked her up at the airport and actually seemed very friendly. "We are so glad you came; our house is fully air-conditioned and we have a great patio in the back and you'll have a great time," she said. "Max will be so glad to see you too. Every time he passes your picture he barks, when is grandma coming to visit."

She said that with such conviction that Helen actually smiled. When Helen arrived at their house, she wondered where the grandkids were. "Oh," said Carry, "didn't we tell you? They're away at camp for another two weeks."

To make things even worse, that evening they told the mother that it's their last chance to take a vacation this summer so they'll be leaving the day after but they'll go shopping so she can have plenty of food till they got back. To keep her company, they will leave Max so that she won't be alone. That Helen was upset would be an understatement but she held in her anger and wished them a bon voyage. She could have had a better time in her own condo without watching out for a hairy mutt. She thought of losing it somewhere just for spite but it wasn't the poor dog's fault.

The next day the son and daughter-in-law drove off to Vermont or somewhere, the mother couldn't have cared less at this point. The day after, it rained so there wasn't much to do except watch TV or read. She was too upset to concentrate on reading so she just watched what passed as entertainment on TV. Cooking shows and banal talking shows. After a while she just walked around the house checking for dust, going out of her mind.

Max didn't want to go out into the garden to do his business because of the rain, so he made on the covered porch. The mother left it for her dear daughter-in- law to clean up later. At some point, she found her son's wine cooler and drank a few glasses of his expensive French Chateau something or other wine, had a tuna salad for supper, and went to bed early shadowed by Max. This was no way to spend her time, she thought.

Helen was 66 years old. She still had the figure from when she was married, well, perhaps not on her waist, but still trim. She liked stylish clothes and her hair was always immaculate. All the ladies in her condo building watched their husbands when she came around even before she became a widow and now even more so. Helen wasn't particularly looking to steal anyone's husband; she was just a sociable person.

Fortunately the day after, the sun came out though it was still cloudy and hot but she wasn't going to stay indoors for another day. Where her son lived, there was a park a few blocks away and so she took Max for a walk along with a new book she bought at the airport. The park itself was about a block square surrounded by single-family houses from the early part of the 20th century. It had many trees and walkways, a central gazebo, and a children's playground.

During the week it was mostly occupied by young women and their little children playing on the swings and splashing under the water fountains. Helen went to the far end where their laughter was just an echo. Max had already done his business so she tied him up under a shady spot to the bench with a long leach and opened her book.

The book was a mystery novel but after the first horrific murder, Helen folded it and lazily looked around for some company. Apparently, people her age were settled in their air-conditioned rooms or at the sea shore. She read some more, till one of the detectives in the book, found a clue and the criminal committed another murder. Having enough bloodshed for the day she took Max for his walk home.

The next day she repeated the same walk again, it was better than just sitting in the house alone and found the same bench and started to read. This time the FBI was called in because the last murder was committed in another state. Now the main character appeared and the case was getting interesting.

She read for another hour while Max slept at her feet. At some point, she looked up and saw a man that must have come out before, unseen by her, and set up an easel and painted something in the park.

A plein air artist, Helen thought. She herself used to enjoy painting plein air when she and her husband vacationed in the country. It really brings out an artist's talent to paint the shadows and lights while the sun is moving across the sky. It takes a lot of concentration to get everything right.

Having been an art teacher she wondered if she should go over and see what this artist can do but she was a bit apprehensive about disturbing him so she watched for a few minutes and went back to her reading. By now the murder mystery was beginning to feel more like a horror story. Why she picked this book she couldn't understand. The next day she went back again to her bench and this time with another book, waiting for a while, wondering if the artist would come back out again. No artist so far, so she opened her book which began with two people meeting by chance in a London rail station before WWII.

After a while just as the couple had to say goodbye because her lover had to go to war, she took another breather when she saw that the artist was coming out of his house and set up his easel again. This time, she thought she would go over, after all, what's the worst that can happen. A grouchy man telling her to go away?

She gave him some time to set up and so she put her book down and untied Max and sort of ambled over nonchalantly. He smiled at her approach and she saw that he seemed friendly. "Hi," she said, "I couldn't help but notice you painting. Mind if I look?"

"Only if you promise to be gentle in your critique." He said with a grin. "I am a total amateur. It was my wife that was the painter before she passed last year and I was never really interested in painting myself but I was bored with my other hobbies so I decided to give this a try. What do you think? Not too good is it." Well, at least she now knew the lay of the land. Helen looked at the painting and saw the art of a predictable amateur. Typical flat colors, blue sky, green leaves, and brown trees. What can you say to that?

"Well, it has potential..." "Ha, potential, you say. My wife would have said. Awful, Marvin, go back to your other hobbies."

"She was that hard on you, was she?" Helen said looking at Marvin. He was tall. A little under six feet perhaps. Still a full head of salt and pepper hair. Clean- shaven. Nice teeth when he smiled. He wore a yellow polo shirt with an alligator on it, tan shorts, and sandals, but at least no black socks. He had a face that showed much character, he seemed perhaps in his late sixties or early seventies, at least that's what he looked like to her.

"So what do you think? Is there room for improvement? By the way, I'm Marvin Berg. I live here in that house..." He pointed to the house Helen saw him come out of.

"I'm Helen Green. Nice to meet you, Marvin. Well, there's always room for improvement. You have to interpret art the way you see it..."

"In other words, it sucks." He grinned. "Marvin, you have a way with words..." Helen said smiling back. The man had a sense of humor, she liked that. They both smiled for a moment. "I am willing to bet that you know something about art but don't want to hurt my feelings..." Marvin said. "Actually, I taught art in high school in the city till I retired..." "I can't believe they let anyone so young retire," Marvin interjected. 'Nice comeback Marvin,' she thought.

They kibitzed each other for a few minutes and then Helen gave him some pointers about color. The sky, if he pays attention, is not always the blue and white mixes he used here. On a day like this, mix in a bit of cadmium yellow to warm it up. The clouds aren't just white blobs, add a little blue or violet. Tree trunks aren't just flat brown. Add a little red or blue to raw sienna. More blue for shadows.

"Ah, now for the greens. There are many ways to make greens. Using viridian straight from the tube makes your leaves feel like it's winter. Make green with a bright yellow and burnt umber... May I?" she asked.

She took a spatula and started mixing some greens using quite unexpected colors while Marvin watched with interest. After about 10 minutes Helen realized she wasn't back in the classroom and stopped a bit embarrassed. "Sorry, I got a little carried away..." "No need; I enjoyed watching you. I wish my wife would have had the patience to show me."

With that remark out of the way, Helen had a choice to make. She could say the dog needs to be fed or she had a headache or it's August and she's been out in the sun too long. On the other hand, here's a good- looking man handing her an opening. She showed him how to mix a few other colors and later he invited her to sit in the shade on the porch for some lemonade.

Helen finally had someone to talk to, Marvin was a good talker and listener and before she left, Marvin asked if she would like to go for some ice cream later. All in all, it was a pleasant afternoon, Helen seemed delighted to have met someone interesting. She had not thought too much about men after Robert passed away.

But it's been two years now. It wasn't as if she and Robert had a perfect marriage but they understood each other. They had their own little worlds. She painted landscapes and he painted too, little military figures. He had at least a few thousand of them in an extra bedroom. His favorite interests were the Napoleonic wars. Now they just took up space and collected dust and she had no idea what to do with them. Neither her son nor grandson showed interest in that collection.

Later she fed Max, had a salad, walked Max around the block, and went to meet Marvin at a corner ice cream store. When she got there, he was already sitting by a small table and when he saw her, he waved. They shook hands and sat quietly looking at each other not being sure what to do next. It was a first date in a long time for both of them.

"So, what flavor would you like?" Marvin finally asked, pointing to the multitude of flavors on the wall menu. Marvin treated for the ice cream and they ate it silently. At first. It was good ice cream. Then the inevitable, how is your flavor and would you like to taste mine? Neither knew what to do next.

"So what did you do?" Helen finally asked to break the ice. "You mean in real life before I took up painting?" "Definitely before you took up painting," she I said in mock seriousness. "Well, I was a professor in Ancient history. I taught in the nearby college"

A sort of shiver ran up Helen's spine. This is some doppelgänger here. She was an art teacher. Marvin's wife was an art teacher. Her husband Robert was a history professor. Marvin was also a history professor. Are some strange forces working here? After they finished, Marvin took the cups and threw them in the garbage pail.

"Would you like to take a walk?" he asked. It was really the only option for people that have just met. This was one of the main shopping areas with many stores. Couples strolled everywhere. At first, they walked separately but then Marvin took a chance and took Helen's arm, she didn't seem to mind.

They walked up and down the long street looking at store windows killing time till sunset and with nothing else to do they sort of gravitated towards Helen's house. "Nice house," Marvin observed. She thought about inviting him in but checked herself. She has only just met him and it wasn't that she thought he might be a serial killer, God forbid, but it wasn't her house and so she decided against it. That's all she needs for the daughter- in-law to find clues of a strange man in her house. It was enough she'll find dog doodoo on the back porch.

"That was very nice Helen, I would like to see you again. Will you be taking Max for a walk in the park tomorrow? I could use some more lessons on mixing greens."

Helen went up to her guest bedroom with a contented smile on her face. This really turned out to be a pleasant day. Marvin seemed like a nice guy and she hoped nothing in the man would change that. How far this relationship could go she couldn't guess but was willing to give it a run. It certainly beats just saying, 'you're a good boy' to Max all day.

When they said goodnight, it was a bit awkward, neither knew if a kiss was required but eventually Helen took it upon herself and kissed his cheek. Marvin seemed to like it and left with a "hope to see you tomorrow." "Yes, Marvin, you will," she finally said to herself, drank another few glasses of the Chateau something or other before sleep took over.

Tomorrow came in with a heat wave. Even in the air-conditioned house, one could tell how hot it was out there. Poor Max didn't even want to go out in the back. Eventually, Helen threw a ball into the yard and Max's instinct took over before he knew it. Once out there he marked his little empire and barked when he was ready to come in. Helen ruffled his little head and gave him his breakfast. "You're a good boy, Maxie" she said laughing to herself.

She just had a bit of cereal and orange juice. It was still early; she was never a late sleeper even after she retired. What to do now. Still too early to go to the park. Later it would be ten times hotter and humid but she really wanted to see Marvin again, but she couldn't just walk up to his door and ring the bell.

Finally, at 11, she decided to go. If he's there, he's there, if not, well she'll try another day. To her happy surprise, Marvin was there, sitting on his stoop with an umbrella over his head lazily spraying his plants. "Hey, Helen," he cried out. "Miss Florida much?" he joked.

"Could use some snow right now..."

"Sure, would you like to come in for a cool drink? I see Max would love to." Helen walked into the cool house and was surprised how nice the inside was, all open concept as was now in style.

"It's all my wife's doing. Besides teaching, she liked to decorate. Move furniture around here and there. It's a wonder my back is still intact."

"Well, it is a beautiful home, Marvin."

"Thanks, it cost a bundle. Come into the kitchen we have an alcove by that window, it's nice and bright. I'll bring some drinks and some water for Max."

Helen looked out the window to a neat Japanese garden and complimented Marvin for that. "Ah, that's all mine. I was drafted and stationed in Japan with the army. I fell in love with their gardens." They sat for a while drinking their lemonade. Helen took a quick look at Marvin and thought he looked a bit uncertain.

"Is everything okay?" She asked a bit concerned. Marvin took a moment to answer." Oh yes, everything's fine. I... I just wanted to say something to you but am a bit apprehensive about it."

"Oh...?" She said.

"Oh, it's nothing frightful, and all that it's just..." Helen reached over and touched his hand." Marvin, if it's nothing, tell me."

"Actually, I wanted to show you something..." "Marvin?"

He smiled, "No, nothing like that either. Wait a minute." He walked into the living room and came back with what looked like an album and a composition book. He put the album in front of her and she gasped in surprise. It was a yearbook from her junior high graduation. "How... where did you ever get this and how did you know?" she asked in total surprise.

"First, let me tell you something..."

The day before they met, Marvin was taking photos of birds in the park across the street. One of his many hobbies. He had a Nikon 5200 with a 500-millimeter telephoto lens that could see a pimple on a person five blocks away. He had seen a red cardinal in a tree guarding its nest against a squirrel. What a shot that would be. By chance, his foot brushed the leg of the tripod that his camera was mounted on and it tilted down on one of the walkways where Helen happened to be walking. In that split second, Marvin thought he recognized her despite all the years gone by.

He wasn't certain till she came much closer and sat down on the bench, the red cardinal completely forgotten, and then he was almost 100% certain. This was Helen Friedman from junior high. He couldn't believe it. She was one of the most popular girls in school. "I didn't think I could just walk over and introduce myself. You'd have never remembered me anyway. I was just some guy and you were so popular," he said.

Still, he was too nervous to approach her but he thought of an idea. He knew she was an art teacher in the city because his wife once brought home an art magazine showing her work. He recognized her then but said nothing to his wife. There was no point. But to meet her now he would get his wife's old easel and paints and go outside hopeful that when she sees him she would approach him and have a look. The idea seemed good but didn't work. She had sat down on a bench, read, and left by the time he set up.

That was the first day. It worked on the second and now she was sitting in front of him listening to all this. "Marvin, you rascal you," she said." I'm sorry about me being such a prig then, but you know how kids are." Then pointing to the composition book she asked. "And what's that? Don't tell me you wrote a poem about me?"

Marvin opened the book and showed her. Inside was a sheet of paper with a drawing. "No, no poem." He said. It was a self-portrait of Helen that she drew herself from one of her art classes.

"How did you ever..."

He interrupted her. "I stole it from your desk when you went to lunch."

"I can't believe it. I looked everywhere for it."

"I'm sorry. I sort of had a crush on you but you wouldn't have given me the time of day then..."

"Marvin, you're not upset about what happened all these years ago?"
"Of course not," he smiled. I have forgotten about it till I saw you the

day before. No, I am not upset and besides, you are here now. How could I be upset?"

"You silly man. What we kids do when we are so young." She put her hand on his again.

"Helen, why don't you stay for dinner. I'm a pretty good cook though I hardly ever make anything for myself these days. Do you like Italian food?"

"Who doesn't. Sure, I'd love to. Is there anything I can do to help?"

"No, you just sit there, or if you like to see the rest of the house just feel free to walk around." "You don't mind?"

"No, please. I have to get some stuff together and when you come down we can talk about old times..."

One can't say that Helen wasn't a bit hesitant. She had not remembered Marvin at all. She had looked at his picture in the yearbook but still, nothing came to mind. He looked like someone nobody would ever remember but now he seemed mature, confident. A successful man living in an upper-middle-class neighborhood who did well for himself. She kind of liked him.

The house was beautifully decorated. Going up the steps she saw his wife's paintings hanging on the wall. She seemed pretty good and remembered some of her work also appearing in a few magazines. The upstairs was very neat. The three bedrooms were all decorated differently and in good taste. The master bedroom was large and it looked like no one has slept there in a long time.

Every bedroom had the bed neatly made and so she wondered where Marvin slept unless he was a very, very neat person... She came down as Marvin gathered his ingredients on the counter-top. "I'm making Fettuccine Alfredo, you'll love it," he said while grating some parmesan cheese.

Helen watched the magic take place. Marvin seemed to be a culinary expert. He put the pasta into a pot to cook it, stirring it with a wooden spoon. Everything was done with a panache only an expert can accomplish. He took the Parmesan and put it into the concoction with a flourish that put a smile on Helen's face.

While the dish was still cooking they sat in the alcove drinking red wine. They talked about themselves. Junior high wasn't even mentioned. Marvin talked about some of his amusing teaching experiences with the kids and so did Helen. At moments they said nothing with an occasional look at each other and taking a sip of wine. They talked a little about their spouses and how they met. About colleges, they attended, all in all, about their past life, till a bell rang. Dinner was ready.

Marvin put everything into a large bowl he said bought in Palermo years ago. Helen wanted to help with the salad but Marvin declined as she was the honored guest When everything was ready, Marvin set the dining room table with a beautiful table cloth and fine China dishes then helped Helen into a chair to the right of him. He poured another glass of wine and served the fettuccine. Garlic bread was not on the menu.

"Wow! Marvin, this is delicious. Where did you ever learn how to cook like that?" Helen asked after a few bites of the pasta. "How am I ever going to keep my figure if you feed me like that?" Marvin smiled. "Glad you like it. I'll tell you another time and I'll be more than happy to watch your figure for you." Helen smiled as he refilled the wine glasses and looked up at her.

"So what are your plans, Helen? How long are you staying with your son?" Marvin asked casually, twirling the fettuccine with his fork. Helen looked up. "I don't know. My plan was to leave the day they come home, probably next Sunday..."

Marvin looked down at his food. "Next Sunday? So soon?" he asked, still playing with the pasta.

"Well, that was my plan..."

"Is there someone waiting for you... In Fort Lauderdale?" he asked looking up.

"No, not really..." "Not really?"

"I meant no one..."

"So you're just going back to an empty apartment..."

"Well, it's furnished..." Helen tried to make a joke but Marvin hadn't cracked a smile.

They ate some more but now the air seemed a bit reserved. Marvin concentrated on his plate but didn't eat. Helen drank a little more wine and put her glass down and also looked at her plate. Finally, Marvin broke the silence. "Look, Helen, what's the point in going to an empty house. Even if it is furnished." He gave her a dry laugh.

"Look at this house, it's empty. Despite all this furniture. I certainly don't like it. I haven't slept in our bedroom since my wife died. Sometimes I just sleep on the couch or in one of the guest bedrooms. There are times I feel so lonely I could cry. I can't imagine going on like this. Can you? We're grown up, still young at heart, I think, but time is passing us by."

"What are you trying to say, Marvin? You don't want me to go? Then what would I do? Where would I stay? I certainly don't want to stay in my daughter-in- law's house..."

Marvin put his fork down neatly and leaned forwards. "I understand. But there is another way." He said looking straight at her. It was sudden and he was afraid she would laugh at him but what does he have to lose... "I want you to stay with me."There, finally, it came out. Helen looked at him as for the first time.

Are you proposing to me, Marvin?" she asked coyly.

"Yes. No. It doesn't matter. If you like we can get married, I wouldn't mind that, but we don't have to, we can just live together. Many people like us do it. In a small way, we already have a past." He smiled at that. "I think we could be good for each other." He added seriously after a quiet moment. Then his eyes twinkled. "And besides I do need a lot of help mixing those greens..."

Helen had to smile at that too, how life moves in those mysterious ways. In junior high, she hadn't even looked at him twice and now, so many years later, this man is putting forth a proposition she would have never contemplated. A piece of spaghetti had fallen from her fork onto the embroidered table cloth. It made a stain and she felt bad about that and tried to remove it with her napkin and some cold water. Marvin put a hand on hers.

"Please, Helen, I don't care about this stain, I have enough soap to wash everything in this house ten times over." Marvin stopped for a moment and sort of grinned at her. "I know I would be getting the better part of this deal so if you need a little time, I'll understand..."

Helen took another slow sip of wine. This guy surely had a lot of chutzpah, she thought. The history Marvin mentioned about them so lightly was of course laughable. Two days ago she didn't even know he existed.

She put down her glass taking that moment to think about what he just proposed. She stared at her half-eaten plate of fettuccine, its white creamy noodles almost sparkling in the afternoon sun. Then looked up at him as he stared into her eyes.

"Marvin, I don't have to think about it much. I can give you an answer right now   "

Sixteen: You're Just Too Smart

"You know what your problem is Bobby; you're just too smart." That was a comment from Debra Brown, Barbara's friend from college. Almost every other Saturday afternoon they met for lunch, either in Manhattan or where Debra lived, in Forest Hills, Queens. The topic of Bobby's single life seemed somehow always to pop up during dessert.

"Too smart, eh.," said Bobby. "So you want me to play dumb with every man I meet. 'Gee Fred why is the sky blue?' "Oh, don't be silly... I don't even know why the sky is blue. Look, you're a Ph. D., you teach a graduate class at NYU, you've met a lot of men..."

"Really Deb, not again, I don't.."

"Okay, when you talk to a man, can't you just dumb it down a bit? You don't have to know everything. Relax. Ask him a few questions and say, 'really, I didn't know that,' once in a while."

"I'm just not that type of a woman Deb. Anyway, let's drop it and order some dessert, I love their lemon meringue pie." After they ordered Debra came back to the subject. "Look, just because you found Fred cheating on you doesn't mean. "

On the opposite side of the street, a mother and her son also sat at an outdoor restaurant having lunch. That was a bimonthly affair as the son lived and worked in Manhattan. "Really David, it's time you met someone.

You can't keep taking your mother out to lunch or dinner all the time. You're almost forty, it's time you met a woman. Okay, Sylvia divorced you while you were away playing at being a soldier in Iraq or somewhere, doesn't mean you shouldn't find someone else. I want some grandchildren before I die." "Mother, First, you're too young to die. Second, I wasn't playing at

being a soldier; I was a soldier. Third, you look younger than me, and people always think you are my sister or, God forbid something else. I don't want to talk about this topic anymore, why do you always bring this up whenever we meet? And we seem to always sit outdoors as if you're parading me in front of all the passing women..."

"Oh, for heaven's sake, don't be so paranoid. I don't need to show you off here. I have plenty of names I can give you..." And so, as always, it's the same old story. When are you going to meet someone, marry and give me grandchildren?

After lunch, David walked his mother home; his father usually played golf with his cronies on Saturday, a sport David never acquired a taste for, and headed towards the boulevard taxi stand. It was only a few blocks away. Bobbie and Debra finished their lunch and promised to meet next time in the city. "No more talking about my man problems, Deb..."

"I promise.." said Debra as they kiss each other's cheeks and said goodbye. Bobbie walked up the block to the corner, towards the taxi stand. David was about the same distance from the taxi stand but on a parallel block. As they turned the corner both headed towards the only taxi now waiting by the subway stop. "Crap," each thought as they began reaching for the taxi door.

"Sorry," said David. "I guess ladies first," as he opened the door for her. Bobbie tried not to notice the man's features as she entered the cab, but she saw that he was good-looking though she ignored it and took her seat.

After her conversation with Debra, she wasn't going to fall for this trick. Obviously, a setup.

"Thank you," she said casually and sat back. "You're welcome," said David through the open window, "However, I need to go uptown on the West Side... how about we share the cab till 2nd Avenue over the bridge, I'll get another ride from there, and you can continue on?"

"Okay, I suppose," said Barbara tiredly. She'll play the game but it's not going to go anywhere. She moved over to the left to make room for him in the back. To her surprise he got into the front seat next to the driver and spoke to him quietly in some foreign language, then he turned towards her and explained what he said to the driver.

"I just told him to drop me off once we cross the 59th Street bridge." And before she could comment, he turned forward and opened his laptop and began punching at its keys. Barbara just shook her head in disbelief and tried to be calm. That's a new one for sure. What game is he playing? Hard to Get? Well, good luck to him!

The ride to Manhattan was quick. The late afternoon traffic to the city hadn't started yet. She usually would have taken the Midtown Tunnel which would have been closer to her home, but seemingly forgot all about it. Nevertheless, in twenty minutes the cab stopped on 59th Street by the curb, and the man got out. Outside he took out a fifty-dollar bill and handed it to her.

"That should cover my end with a tip. If we ever meet again, you can give me back the change." He smiled and was gone before she could get a word in. When she arrived home the first thing she did after throwing off her shoes, was call Debra. "Did you just set me up or something?" she asked angrily. "What?" Debra retorted. "What are you talking about?" Bobbie told her about the cab experience. "Well, you didn't look too smart did you and scare him off?" Barbara hung up the phone.

When David got out of the cab, he started walking towards 3rd Avenue where he would get an uptown ride, but when he passed a bar, he stopped and went inside. David hardly ever drank, but on occasion, he would succumb to a gin and tonic. He went over to an empty stool by the bar and ordered his drink and stared into the rack of bottles on the opposite mirrored wall.

He asked himself what had just happened. He couldn't believe it. Did his mother put this poor woman up to it, hoping he would think this was a chance meeting? Did his mother think he was born yesterday?

Nah, his mother wouldn't be so devilish as to make this lopsided plan. It had to be just a coincidence, he thought. Though the quick look he took of her in the rear seat, made his hair at the back of his neck tingle. She was a looker. Just the right age to be interesting. And what did he do about it? He sat himself in the front seat and started typing his silly book. Why didn't he sit with her in the back and start a conversation? Even if it was a setup he could have at least said hello to her. She probably thought of him as some backwoods yokel.

He finished his drink, paid the barkeep. and walked past a couple of admiring women at a table. "Not my type," he said to himself, then went into the street looking for a cab.

Soon time passed and the incident forgotten by both parties. Besides teaching, Barbara was working on her own project she hoped to interest large corporations and perhaps even the Department of Defense. It was taking much of her time in the evenings and weekends.

David also was busy. Even though he wasn't particularly fond of working in an office, the work was somewhat interesting. It had to do with the security of landlines and the Internet. He also was busy writing a book on military matters when at home — something about politics and war. Neither he nor Barbara went out much nor ever considered that they would ever meet.

And then as sometimes happens, stars line up and the moon is in the right quarter or whatever, a coincidence appears. David had just stepped out of his office at the other end of the floor when he thought he recognized that woman from the cab hurrying towards the elevator by the receptionist's desk, and as he tried to get there the doors closed and the elevator went down.

"Who was that woman?" he asked the receptionist. "You mean the lady that just went down.." "Yes..." "I'm not sure, Mr. Atkins brought her up with him..." David didn't want to know or ask Atkins about her if she's his woman then that's that! It wasn't that important anyway.

It was towards the end of summer on a balmy Saturday afternoon David, and his mother were out in the same restaurant having lunch once again, but this time David sat facing the street. His father was out playing golf again, and as David sees him almost every day at the office, it didn't matter. He truly loved his mother except when she pesters him to find someone so she could have those grandchildren which almost every friend of hers has.

But as promised, his mother did stop pestering him about women for now, and so they just talked about trivial things. There was to be a charity affair at the Metropolitan Museum of Art in two weeks, and she wanted David to attend as their company was a significant contributor.

David agreed but wasn't really paying attention at the moment because just across the street from him by some strange coincidence, there was that woman, sitting with a friend outdoors in the coffee shop. "Mother," he said to her." Are you playing some kind of game with me again?" "I'm sorry. What?" His mother looked so sincere that he thought maybe she was innocent and yet, this seemed too pat to be anything else but another setup. "There's a woman across the street in that coffee house, don't turn around, that I've seen before and by chance, we shared a cab together to the city..." "Really? So what happened?" "Nothing happened. But now I see her again over there.""Well, it's not any of my doing," his mother said just dying to turn around and see that woman. "I don't know. something strange is going on here..."

"Well, you think you like her?" his mother asked hopefully. "Do you know who she is? Does she live here?" "No, I think she lives in the Village..." "Oh, so you know where she lives?" "No, I heard her tell the cab driver to take her to the Village. Do you know where Atkins lives?" "Atkins? Do you mean George Atkins from the office? What does he have to do with anything?" "I, I don't know. Forget about it. So when's the Met party again?"

They talked about what kind of affair this was going to be. How much money they will contribute, and such. Everybody who was anybody in town will be there. They had to raise five million dollars to purchase a collection from a Western artist who passed away last summer, and every museum wanted it. David wasn't paying much attention as he was playing with his fork and watching that nameless woman across from him. He saw that they had just got their bill and he supposed they would be leaving the coffee shop.

"Mom, would you excuse me, something that I forgot to do at the office came to mind. I'm sorry, but I need to do it before Monday morning meeting?" His mother looked at him in a funny way but said okay, she'll take care of the bill. He kissed her cheek and told her he would call later then left trying not to bring any attention to himself. He walked quickly towards the taxi stand on the next corner and waited behind the Vitamin store for that woman to come for her cab if she even would.

This is really childish, he thought to himself just as she turned the corner and walked towards the first cab online. Then, as she opened the door, he ran towards it himself. "Hi, what a coincidence. We really have to stop meeting like this," he joked.

At first, Barbara didn't recognize him, but it wasn't too long before she did. "Well, hello yourself. You're not following me are you?" she asked, amused. For sure this must be Debra's doing, again. "Of course not, I was just having lunch with my mother, and now I'm going home." Before he knew it, he realized how stupid this remark was. "Oh God," thought Barbara, he's having lunch with his mother. That's all she needs, a mama's boy. But she's going to play along and then give Debra a good talking to later.

"So you're going into the city," Barbara said, "and we can share a ride again? Oh, by the way, I owe you eighteen dollars change from last time though honestly, I didn't expect to see you again, so I gave the money to charity."

David shook that off and this time sat next to her and told the driver where to go. "You didn't bring your laptop this time?" Barbara asked. "Ah, you remembered." "Yes. Too bad. I have never used a laptop. I am so not into electronics. You men can do so many things..." She thought, what the hell, maybe I should try the dumb routine. He looks like a nice guy. I'll have some fun with him.

"You never used a computer?" asked David. "What do you do then?" "I'm a buyer," she said using a routine she saw on TV once. "A buyer? You buy for large department stores?""Well, not exactly, I go to large department stores and buy things. Shoes. Dresses. Jewelry. Stuff like that." David had to smile. She liked the way he smiled.

"And what do you do Mr..?" "David. David Burns. I work for an electronics company." "Wow! That's interesting. I'm Barbara Hiller. Nice to meet you." This time the traffic on Queens Blvd seemed heavy, so David told the driver to take the Tunnel. "I guess, we'll drop you off first then. "Is that okay?" "Sure, that's fine. This time I'll give you the money, and you'll give me back the change if we ever see each other again." She had to rub that in.

What could he do? He smiled. David was dying to ask her about Atkins, but then he would have to give himself away. "Sooo, is there a Mr. Hiller?" He might as well get that out of the way. "Not anymore..."

They entered the Tunnel, and David thought he'd go for broke. He didn't know why but he liked this woman. Yes, she was attractive, but there was something else about her too. Okay, she never used a computer, but that doesn't make her backward. A lot of intelligent people don't like computers. But she certainly has pluck. Still, he would like to know the connection between her and Atkins. She could of course be his relative. He didn't know Atkins that well. He was the head of Human Resources, and David didn't have much to do with him.

"Boyfriends?" And so David went through a litany of men that she could be attached to. She laughed as they came out of the Tunnel now into the brightness of the street. "Look, David, if this is even your real name. I know what you're up to and you seem like a nice guy, but I'm not that easy to get. Is Debra paying you for this?" "Debra? Who's Debra? And why would she pay me for what?"

"Oh, come on. I know it's all a setup. Are you a friend of Debra's or some distant relative I haven't heard of?" She wouldn't pick a complete stranger thought Barbara to herself. David was perplexed. What is she talking about? "I'm sorry, what are you talking about?" The cab was now on 2nd Avenue and 23rd Street.

"Look, David. Are you really David? Anyway, I just left my friend Debra, and she said she wouldn't discuss my man problems with me, though I certainly didn't believe her. And now she put you up again. She must have called you when she went to the ladies' room before we left."

"Look, Barbara. I met you last time by sheer coincidence. I sat in the front like an idiot. I know. I gave you money as if you were some lackey. I was upset. When I got home, I felt like a fool. I don't know why I did it. Actually, now that I think about I did it because of my mother. I thought she set me up after she bugged me about why I haven't married so many years after my divorce."

All the while he was talking he went for his wallet. By now they passed 14th Street. The traffic was light. David took out his driver's license and handed it to her. "What's this?" asked Barbara. "You think I would go to all that trouble to fake a state driver's license just to please that woman. Debra? So I can meet you?"

"Anyway, as I was saying," David put his license back in the wallet. "Oh, I don't know what I was saying. This is ridiculous. I just happen to have lunch with my mother again just now, and by some chance, which

I thought my mother had something to do with it, I saw you across the street with your friend. Was that Debra by the way?"

Barbara nodded her head. "Anyway, I wanted to apologize for that time. And, I wanted to meet you." "Really? You're not fooling around?" "I don't speak with forked tongue." Barbara laughed. As the cab turned right on 3rd Street, David started to laugh too. By the time they stopped laughing, they were close to La Guardia Place.

"I get off around the corner next block," Barbara said when she stopped laughing. "We're here already? David looked around. They were in the Village. "Look, it's still early. How about a coffee somewhere?" The cab stopped facing Washington Square Park. David paid for the taxi, and they got out. Barbara pointed to the corner building. "This is where I live.""Nice." He commented. "My parents were teachers at the university and lived here since after the war, and when they moved to Florida a few years ago, I took it over from them. I teach... She stopped. She's not supposed to be too smart. Ah, what the hell, she's not going to play that stupid game anymore.

"I teach here too. I'm a professor of physics, the same as my parents. They met here." She pointed to NYU across the park. If he goes away at least, she nabbed it in the bud. "Physics? I'm impressed. My father was a physics teacher but went into the electronics business. So when you said you never used a computer you..." She interrupted. "I was just saying that because Debra told me I was too smart to catch a man, I should dumb down a bit..."

"Soo, you're not as dumb as you make out...? David grinned. He almost said as you look. "Very funny..." Barbara countered. "Sorry, so would you like to get a drink or some coffee?" She told him there was a place on 3rd Street two blocks away that she goes to sometimes after classes with a couple of professors if it was a rough day.

"This is becoming a rough day David." She said with a chuckle. David chuckled back. "Sure, I also could use a drink after this." A few minutes later a waitress that knew Barbara sat them at a small table in a corner and gave her a wink. "Pretty dark in here," David commented.

"Yes, a lot of clandestine affairs go on in this place..." "You know something, Professor Barbara. You are a wicked woman. I think my mother would like you." "Well, that's the best compliment I had in years. David." She mumbled to herself. "So who's George Atkins?" There, he spit it out. It's now or never. "I'm sorry? Why are you bringing up George Atkins? How do you know him?"

Now that David got himself into this mess, he wasn't sure how to get out of it. "Sorry, did I say George Atkins? I meant... "Don't give me that crap. How do you know I met Atkins? Are you from some other company tracing my moves?"

"What?"

"What, shmott. Now I'm beginning to understand. You're from some other firm trying to steal me away from WW Electronics.!" Now for sure, David was above his head. Steal her away from whom?

"What are we talking about? Let's calm down for a minute." "I can't calm down, I'm pissed, I..." "Look, Barbara. I'm not sure what is happening here but just give me a second to explain. I am not trying to steal you from anyone. I work for WW Electronics. In fact, my father owns WW Electronics. I didn't even know they offered you a job. I just saw you there once as you were going down the elevator..."

Trying to explain the whole story to Barbara from the beginning was like unraveling the Gordian Knot. He didn't even know what happened. "Really? You mean to tell me the whole thing just happened by some farcical coincidence?" "I swear on my Boy Scout honor." And he raised his right hand into a scout salute. "You realize I still don't believe you, but you certainly have a way with words." She guffawed. Just then the waitress came over. "You two ready to order or do you need some more time to argue?"

Seventeen: Mademoiselle Flash

As soon as I took a selfie with the Mona Lisa at the Louvre, I realized that I was in trouble, and it came almost instantly, in French." Que faites-vous? Êtes-vous fou!" In my excitement of seeing the most famous painting in the world, live, I totally forgot to make sure the flash on my phone camera was off. Startled, I turned around to see a dark shape of a museum guard pushing himself through the crowd of onlookers, fuming as hell, staring at me as if I had just painted a mustache under her nose.

"What? Sorry, Je ne parle français." I said, nervously, with the few French words I knew. "Ah, Américain, vous pensez pouvoir tout faire?" The guard shouted at me again, with a smug expression on his face, loud enough to be heard in Timbuktu. I understood Amereecain as he came menacingly closer, but I didn't think it was a complimentary remark. Shaken and embarrassed, I wasn't sure what to do or say as a horde of tourists gathered around me like snickering vultures.

Suddenly, out of nowhere, a young woman pushed her way through the crowd, and in a quieter, but very intimidating voice, stood a head taller than the guard and said. "Pourquoi criez-vous après la dame! Tu ne vois pas qu'elle ne comprend pas le français?"The guard looked startled that someone had the audacity to talk back to him, so he backed away while sputtering and pointing to a sign on the wall, this time in a little more civilized manner. "La femme idiote prend des photos flash, ne voit-elle pas les signes…"

The woman cut him off. "Évidemment, elle ne parle pas français, vous pourriez être plus polie. Connard!" Then she turned to me, took me by my elbow, and led me quickly towards an exit with a stupefied guard staring after us.

Once out of his view and hearing, she turned to me and in English, with a slight Brooklyn accent, which surprised me, said quietly. "You're lucky the guard didn't call the gendarmes. What were you thinking? The French are very sensitive about their art. But don't worry, let's just get out of here before it becomes an international crisis with this guy..."

This all happened so quickly that I was just bewildered. "Where are you taking me?" I asked anxiously as she continued, virtually dragging me out of that room. But once outside the museum, we stopped, her expression totally changed with a giggle. "Sorry about all this. You know you used your flash with your phone, which is not allowed..."

"I know," I said guiltily, "I was so excited to see the painting I totally forgot to turn it off.""Never mind, but you're lucky I just happen to be there or he'd probably lock you up in the dungeons below..." "You're kidding right..." I said. "Oh nooo, I am very serious, the last person that did this was sent to the guillotine..." she said grinning from ear to ear.

"Okay. Okay. I get it..." I shook my head and haha'd back. "Very funny." She reminded me of a good friend I had that moved to California and we lost touch, but she always pulled these pranks on me and I was always gullible to believe them. Of course, we were about seven years old then, but even now I fall for a gag, on occasion.

I didn't mind though. She seemed friendly, with a sense of humor, a few years older than me, and seemed like a person you would like to know. "So, you are from the States I gather, Americain?" She mimicked the guard.

"Qui," I said with another French word I just remembered. "New York..."

"Oh, so you do speak French..." she said kiddingly, "The City or the State?"

"The City, Queens, you know it? You sound like a New Yorker…" "Moi, You tink…?" She said, now making fun of her accent. "So, you

came here to make trouble or are you just a tourist?" I didn't know what to say, was she mocking me again? "By the way, I'm Roselyn, but my friends call me Renée. Sounds better in Française. I changed it when I came here from Roselyn Berger to Renée Bergère, makes life a bit easier. What's yours?"

"Sabrina Martin. My friends call me Brina…"

"Well, nice to meet you, Brina. Say, if you have time, how about we go for a coffee and some French pastry. I haven't seen anyone from home in a long time."

"Sure…" I thought that was very nice of her, besides, I had nothing else planned. Roselyn, or should I say Renée, seemed like she had a gregarious personality, unlike mine so introverted. It's very hard for me to make friends like her.

She took me to a small outdoor cafe and ordered us a café crème and for me a custard tart. "It's the best in Paris," she said. And for herself, an unpronounceable layered pastry. "It's called Mille feuilles," she pronounced it slowly after she saw me look at it when it was put on the table. "It looks like a Napoleon to me," I said.

"Yes, in the states that's what they call them, a Napoleon, here too sometimes, but it's not after Emperor Napoleon you know, it's named after the town of Naples, where these layered pastries come from. Go figure." She cut off a piece and let me taste it right from her fork. I felt as if we have been friends forever at that moment.

"Good isn't it? Anyway, so what brings you to our delightful city, Mademoiselle Flashé?" she asked taking herself a bite of the Mille feuilles?

"Mademoiselle Flashé?" I asked?

"Qui, in honor of the fracas you caused with the guard... Do you mind?" "Not the way you say it I guess..." I was getting a bit giddy from all that niceness.

We finished eating and there was some cream left on the tip of Renée's nose. "You've got some cream on the tip of your nose..." I said. She tried to lick it off with her tongue but couldn't reach it, so without even thinking, I reached over with my napkin and wiped it off.

I guess it took her by surprise but she said thanks. "My nose is too big, I know." Then she gave me a wink. No, her nose certainly wasn't too big. Maybe a little pointy. "So..." She leaned back and asked again. "So what does brings you to our delightful City? Museums? Looking for trouble?" "No." I shook my head. "Not for trouble. Yes, to the museums but actually to study art."

"Study art?" Renée leaned forward. " Really? Why, that's c'est magnifique! What a coincidence, I'm an artist. That's why I was at the Louvre this morning, not that I have my art hanging on those hallowed walls, but I was visiting a colleague who works there for some advice about art dealers. "Really? You're an artist? I mean you paint pictures on canvas..." She looked at me with furrowed eyebrows. "Yes, my dear. I paint pictures on canvas. And besides, I run a studio and a small boutique gallery on the Left Bank... "Really? You're not kidding me again, are you?" This time she smiled back and shook her head. "Yes really. Have you taken any courses in New York, Like the Art Students League or SVA?"

"Well, I did but only during the summers for a few years, the rest of the time I worked in my father's rare-book shop." As I talked, I watched Renée look at me, and shake her head with understanding. "Then about a week ago I decided I had enough of this. I'll be twenty- two in a few months and I don't want to waste my life getting my hands dry from old books. I want to paint!" We were quiet for a minute or two. I think Renée was contemplating as if she should tell me something. Then she leaned even closer to me and put her hand on mine.

"You won't believe this, Mademoiselle Flashé, but I'm from Kansas. Yes, no joke, Kansas. From a farm," she said quietly. "Something like that also happened to me. I ran away when I was eighteen. In high school my art teachers told me I had talent, I could draw and paint and I should continue by going to an art school maybe in Chicago or New York." She leaned back. "They said. But, just like your parents, they wanted me to work on their farm and marry, in my case, Kyle, our next-door neighbor's older son, so our properties would combine. He was ten years older than me, an asshole if you ever saw one."

We were interrupted by our waitress asking if there was anything else we wanted. We saw that there was now a line of people waiting for the cafe so we paid our bill, or rather Renée insisted it was on her, and walked towards a park across from the museum. There, she continued telling me how she ran away to Brooklyn rather than Manhattan because the rents were cheaper there, she said. "Hence my Brooklyn accent I guess. I stayed there a few years. We were a few girls renting an apartment and we all went to the Art Student League. I was good. In short, I sold many of my paintings, made money, and came here."

"There were other issues but I got myself together, had some money saved, like you, and with the help of my aunt, that also ran away many years before and became an actress, got myself a passport and came to Paris, again, almost the same as you." Her eyes met mine and I could almost see myself in them.

"When I heard an American voice in the museum, I had to do something. That guard, I know him, he likes to catch tourists for any infraction, especially Americans. I don't think he likes us." Both of us laughed.

"Maybe it's just fate that we came together. How about coming to my studio tomorrow around noon, we'll have lunch, talk awhile and maybe I can help you get started..." She gave me a card with her address which was on the Left Bank, we pecked our cheeks and I went back to my Pension Antoinette with a new mindset. Back in my room, I dropped onto my bed and looked up at the ceiling. Maybe I did the right thing coming here after all. I just wanted to paint! Then I thought of Renée. Was it just fate that I used the flash this morning? I mean, I did know better. Or was it Karma that made me do it?

The next day, I took a cab and we whizzed through the Parisian streets as if they were a maze, I don't think they have one street straight more than a couple of blocks and I wouldn't have figured out how to get there by Metro. The driver let me off at Rue Champollion No 26, I thought he got lost and just wanted me out. The street was so narrow I was afraid the cab would get stuck in it. But as I looked at the address on her card, I saw that this was it. There was a large wrought-iron entrance with a gate and behind it stood an elderly woman sweeping the cobble-stone entrance, as she looked up at me.

"Qui Mademoiselle," she stopped and asked, "Qu'est-ce que vous voulez?" I just showed her Renée's card. "Ah, Mademoiselle Renée qui?" "Qui..." I said. She pointed to the stairs and put up two fingers which I assumed was the third floor. She didn't give me the apartment number or maybe she did but I didn't understand so I just started walking up.

Unlike in the States, they count their floors differently. They don't count the first floor, their first floor is our second, and their second is our third. I forgot about that until I walked to their second floor and the steps stopped. Fortunately, there was only one door so I rang the bell.

"Hey, it's Mademoiselle Flashé, what a pleasant surprise. I was hoping you'd come, and here you are. Come in. Come in..." Renée said happily, as she propelled me through the door and kissed my cheeks. "Make yourself comfortable. I was just thinking about you. Are these flowers for me? Oh, you shouldn't have. They're beautiful. Have you eaten?" All without taking a breath.

I appreciated the invitation because I thought she might have changed her mind or forgotten about me, but she greeted me warmly and it was very nice of her. As I walked past the short hall into what seemed like a studio, I stopped because at the far end I saw a completely naked woman sitting on what looked like a fancy chair with a ball the size of a grapefruit in one hand and a short stick in the other. She must have been about sixty or so, with a nice face and an ample body, and when she saw me there was no embarrassment. Of course, I have seen many naked men and women at the Art Students League so it wasn't a big deal it's just that, I wasn't expecting it here now.

"Mademoiselle Flashé, this is Madame Picot, she's a neighbor from downstairs and a model. I just put her on canvas. "Nous avons terminé, Madame Picot, merci. Je te verrai jeudi. Tu peux t'habiller maintenant." "Merci, Renée." She said putting down her paraphernalia then turned to me, "Enchanté Mademoiselle Flashé." and went into a room to get dressed I supposed.

"Sorry," Renée said as she saw my astonished face. "She's been a model for many years and I pay her modeling fees after I sell her paintings. It works out well that way for both of us. Come take a look." What I saw was an almost life-sized canvas with a deep purple satin curtain in the background and sitting on, what Renée painted as a throne, was Madame Picot, in all her naked splendor holding the ball or what Renée painted as an orb and the stick as a scepter.

"It's an allegory of women's power. I see you can't understand why I paint portly women? Well, there's more character in them. Pinups you can get on any street corner here in Paris. In any case, there's a good market for my paintings." "Come on, I'll show you around and then we'll have some lunch and I see you brought something to show me too. Great!" That was my portfolio that I brought.

I was quite impressed by Renée's paintings. Her style was a mix of Monet's bright colors and lights like a Vermeer. I could see why she painted large canvases of her nudes; they looked as if they could jump off the canvas right into one's lap. I would give anything if I could paint half as well as she.

Her place was almost like a Village loft though smaller. She had large skylights above where her easel stood, with the drying painting of Madame Picott. On the right, the room was divided into a small kitchen overlooking a garden, and besides that, the bedroom, small but held two beds, one made up and one looking slept in, a small toilet from which Madame Picot made her entrée into the studio all dressed up, fixing her hair.

She waved us goodbye and left. There were dozens of canvases all over and one particular unfinished painting of a young nude whose face was breathless. I wouldn't have thought anyone like that could even exist except in some old Greek mythology we learned in our classic class about a woman with a face that could launch a thousand ships and her name was Helen. Ironically in love with a Trojan whose name was Paris. And here I was, in Paris.

I started to ask Renée about this painting but she just put it behind another. "Oh, it's nothing, I just made it up a long time ago." Then took me to a table all set up for lunch with fresh cheeses, still warm croissants, fruits, and more, plus a bottle of wine. The painting forgotten and I didn't ask again.

"My landlady, you must have met her downstairs, she's always sweeping the entrance, she's a great woman too, she went to the local market and got some fresh everything. You can't get all that fresh stuff in New York. Oh, and the croissants she made them this morning. Come, I'll pour some wine." "Do you eat like that every day?" I asked when we finished. It was one of the best lunches I've in a long time.

"Not really, most days I'll eat practically nothing, just look at me, I'm almost like a skeleton..." No, she wasn't. She was a little taller than I with a figure more like a Ruben's painting with jeans, but a little thinner and a moth-eaten paint- splattered, too large of a shirt.

"And sometimes, besides modeling, Madam Picot makes me a Soupe à l'oignon or a Bouillabaisse, and such, then she watches me till I finished eating, like a mother. And if she knew you were coming

God knows what she would have cooked." She smiled. "Anyway," she pointed to her spread, "I had her buy all this because I hoped you'd come for lunch."

It was a great feeling to be treated so nice, I don't remember the last time that was, even at home. After we cleared the table, Renée asked me to show her my portfolio. Nervously I unzipped the fake leather case in which, I thought, were photos of a dozen of my best work. When she finished looking, she leaned back on her chair and looked at me poker-faced then said with a wink. "You know, you're not too bad. Not bad at all."

I let go of my breath and practically jumped up and embraced her. "Thank you! Thank you! Thank you!" I said delighted with what she said. Renée embraced me too and momentarily we looked at each other when suddenly I got embarrassed and let go. My face must have turned red. "I'm sorry, I didn't mean..." I started to say. "No, that's okay. I can understand the excitement you feel. Your paintings are very imaginative and you have talent. Why didn't you continue your studies at the Art Students League?"

"Well, my father cut off the money," I said plainly. "I see, that's tough, so what is your plan? Do you still want to get into a school here? The well-known are very expensive..." she said. "That was my plan. I haven't had a chance to look for anything. I just got here and thought I'd sightsee before I try any schools. I don't speak French so I don't know how I'm going to do it?" "No plan, huh?"

I just spread my hands. What else could I have said. "I am crazy?" Renée took the leftover wine from lunch and poured us another two glasses. She looked at me, my face probably looked as despondent as someone facing the guillotine. "Look, tomorrow, if you want, pack your things and I'll pick you up from your Pension. You can stay here a while if you want to. I don't see many students from New York and I wouldn't mind having a hometown friend around. You can also come to my classes and paint and if you're good enough 'll put them into my gallery."

"Sounds great but how am I going to pay for those classes in the meantime?" I asked halfheartedly. "Oh, that's no problem, I won't charge you." "I'm sorry, what...?" "As I said. I won't charge you and when you're good enough we'll sell your paintings in my gallery and you can pay me back."

It sure sounded like a good idea, I thought, though I was a bit hesitant. After all, I just met her in a museum, nice as she seemed, could I just trust her enough to go live with her? Anyway, if she's after my money she's out of luck. She looked at my doubtful face and gave me a serious look. "I know what you're thinking, I'm someone you just met, and can you trust me. But nothing is going to happen and you can leave whenever you want. Though you're pretty enough to sell to some Eastern Prince," said Renée with half a smile.

"Trust me?" I thought. Famous last words in many a horror movie. But Renée seemed like a nice person, I wasn't worried she would sell me to some prince but the only thing about Renée, and I wasn't sure or feel comfortable about it, was that she was probably gay. I lived in New York so it won't really be a big deal. I assumed that the extra bed was for a woman she broke up with and then the beds were together. In any case, I had no other offers so I didn't care if I share an apartment with a lesbian, though I wonder what my parents would say. Which reminded me that I should call them.

Anyway, that's what I did. We hit it off like long-lost friends and I slept on her former, whoever's bed. Can't say I didn't wonder who slept on it before, but the sheets were clean and the bed was comfortable. And she did as promised. She brought me to her school, which had two large studios and about two dozen students. I wondered how she did it?

"I'm putting you into my other class because I don't want you to feel too obligated to me and the other instructor is Monsieur Renault, he's an old gentleman and a very good artist. You'll like him." And she was right. He told us stories while we painted of his life experiences which we laughingly thought were a bit over the top but made the time pass in a pleasant way.

Sometimes Madame Picot came by and posed for us, she and Monsieur Renault, were old friends, which we assumed were lovers at some point, with their fibbing at each other, and maybe they still were. Madame Picot still posed for Renée in her studio upstairs and I just watched the way Renée handled brush strokes. She was just amazing and I was learning a lot. On rainy days we slept late sometimes, had an Eggs en Cocotte, which Renée said she learned from Madame Picot, and sat on the floor and, at least I, practiced just charcoal drawings of whatever I saw. Renée had no TV so we had to entertain ourselves.

One evening on a rainy day, while Renée was painting a still life, I stopped my sketching and really looked at her. She was a good-looking woman with a happy face, and she told me she's going on 29, which I thought was two or three years ago, but who's counting. Right? She was never serious, always joking with her students, doing pranks on me, and always laughing about how we met. She was '29' going on 16. Life was never dull with her around. In the meantime, my work showed much improvement and I actually started to sell some of my pieces and contribute to our expenses. Some evenings, Renée took us to a Bistro visited by other artists and students from Renée's class, we talked art, sometimes till the morning hours. For me, these were some of the best times I ever had even though I couldn't understand much of what they said.

In the meantime, I kept absorbing more and more French and Renée showed me Paris on weekends. Sometimes she looked at me in a funny way, like just looking at me with a smile and when I caught her, she just winked and it was back to the canvas. I really didn't mind because I really liked her and I think she liked me too.

Weeks passed and so did months. I have never been so happy. I made new friends that were interested in the same things as I was. I also loved living with Renée, she was very smart and witty and constantly teased me about my flash experience when we went to museums. She also knew tidbits about the classic artists and explained how they lived, loved, and worked. We did come back to the Louvre but tried to stay away from the Mona Lisa exhibit. Madame Picot ever so often cooked for us and made us some great French dishes though I wasn't too keen on snails or frogs-legs. "It tastes just like chicken," Renée said with a grin. At first, I couldn't even watch as she ate about a half dozen of those but eventually she got me to try one and I began to like them too, but really, they did not taste like chicken but I never got used to snails even though they sounded better in French. Escargot? Ugh!

All those happy times disappeared one afternoon when we came home from class. First, the door wasn't locked, it didn't look like anyone broke in so it must be the landlady for some reason. But as we entered we didn't see anyone. Renée called out, Personne ici?

No answer. She tried again and this time a sleepy voice from the bedroom called out, Renée, c'est toi? I saw Renée freeze as if the voice came from a ghost. Michèle, c'est toi? She called out heading for the bedroom. Oui ma chérie je suis de retour ...

Renée stopped in her tracks and looked back at me. By now I had no idea what was happening. Maybe it's just a relative but before I could finish my thought, this Michèle, ran out from the bedroom practically naked jumping on Renée and starts kissing her like no relative would or should and as I took a glimpse into the bedroom I saw my bed disheveled.

Then, after the immediate surprise passed, they sat down on the old couch, with Michèle still hanging on to Renée like a leech. It was then that I realized who that floozy, with a face that could launch a thousand ships, and a body that could sell a million Playboy Magazines must be. It was the Greek Goddess, Helen of the unfinished painting I saw on my first day.

And I didn't like her. She must be Renée's old partner, lover, whoever, and now she's back, though I didn't see that same enthusiasm in Renée's face. I was just standing in the bedroom doorway when Renée looked at me with a grim expression on her face. She entwined herself from Michèle and came over to me as Helen of Troy watched with her perfect face and body.

"I'm sorry Sabrina..." Oh crap, now I'm Sabrina, I'm done here, I thought. "Michèle, doesn't speak English and she and I have to talk, it's nice out, can you give me some time with her, please." Then she took my hand and kissed me on my cheek. I didn't know what to make of that. I left disappointed. Is this person returning to my Renée? Yes, that's what I was thinking and if so what will I do? It's a selfish question, I admit, but I felt close to her, as a close friend and I didn't want to leave her, nor my classes, but mostly I really didn't want to leave Renée.

Why and from where did this Michèle suddenly appear? I began to hate her. So many thoughts came to my mind but none that made any sense. After all, what can I do? I certainly wouldn't be able to stay with Renée anymore even if she asked me to, but three in this case certainly would be a crowd. Compared to Michèle I looked like a provincial cousin. There is a park a few streets down and thought I'd go there and maybe something will come up. Surprisingly, I passed a McDonald's and a Burger King which reminded me of home and that calmed me down a little.

Well, after about an hour or so, I decided to come back. I saw Renée talking to the landlady and when she saw me, she walked over and smiled. "Hi!" She said as if we had just met by chance. So I said, 'Hi' and we both stared at each other for a moment till Renée took my hand. "Let's walk a bit, I need some fresh air," she said to me and took my arm. Here it comes I said to myself, I guess I'll need to start packing.

We walked a block and Renée stopped and turned to me. "I guess you probably want to know what this was all about?" I looked at her raising my eyebrows. "That was Michèle, by the way. I've known her from before, okay, we were together for a couple of years. She modeled for me and one thing led to another. We were a couple. I'm sure you remember that painting I wouldn't explain and by now you must have guessed my lifestyle. Anyway, we met when I first came to Paris. She modeled in one of my classes I took at the Sorbonne, she was, is, quite beautiful and who wouldn't want to be with her?"

I wanted to comment but kept my mouth shut. "She had her faults," Renée continued. "But I loved her, as simple as that.""Then, when I opened my gallery, I put in a life-sized painting of her in the nude. The one you saw was just a study. I put a high price on it because I really didn't want to sell it." "So what happened was that by chance, a French film star, who was at least twice her age, if not more, saw the painting and wanted desperately to buy it, no matter the price, on one condition, she wanted to meet the model herself," Renée told me.

"I couldn't refuse such a deal, I mean I can paint her again, so I brought Michèle to the gallery to meet the star. Well, if you haven't guessed it, Michèle and the star fell for each other right there and then, despite the difference in their ages, especially since the star promised her to live in a mansion on the Riviera and eventually a part in a movie. So she just packed up that evening and left me a note. I haven't heard from her since then," Renée said shaking her head.

We walked some more and an autumn leaf settled on my head. Renée brushed it off with her hand, then gave me a warm smile. "Anyway, she's gone again and this time she left her key. She just came to tell me or brag, how well off she was and she was sorry she left so quickly and all that bull. Can't say that I wasn't sorry, but I got over it quickly. In any case, there was no way I would have let you go." And then she put her hand around my waist and we went to the Burger King and got ourselves a milkshake.

We were walking back when suddenly she stopped near the house and looked at me. "Didn't you say your birthday was coming up next week...?" "Y... E... S..." I said wondering what she's up to. "Well, let's not wait, I feel like celebrating tonight? What do you say? There's a nice place on the other side of the river, a club, it's called Lea Mutinerie, I'll call some of my friends and we'll have a little party? Hmmm?"

"Sure, I'd like that." While my heart skipped a beat. We left around eleven, Renée said that that's when the place starts to hop. We took a taxi and got there pretty quick. There was a young crowd outside talking, smoking, and drinking, but not rowdy. Renée waved to a few people she recognized and we went inside where it was dark and noisy and crowded. "Follow me, I have a favorite spot where my friends hang out." We had to squeeze our way through the dancers, which I couldn't help but notice were all women. Well, thought I, Mademoiselle Flashé., this ain't Kansas anymore, then finally we entered into another room with bean bags scattered around a coffee table with candles and a small cake which Renée must have ordered before we came. It was just a large Mille Feuilles with a candle on it.

Introductions were made, Renée introduced me as Brina, AKA, Mademoiselle Flashé, and told them why, as we sat down, they all wished me a Joyeux Anniversaire, then someone handed me a glass of wine, and we had a good laugh about it. Renée looked at me and gave me one of those mischievous winks which gave me a warm feeling of acceptance.

They asked me where I was from and when I said New York they asked me about the Village and how that is compared to Paris' Left Bank. I still wasn't that good with my French but fortunately, most of her friends spoke English pretty well and sometimes spoke it much better than I. Not all were artists, some worked at embassies others were teachers, one was a banker, a pilot, they came from different professions, all women of all ages, well, not grandmothers I was sure, but we all had a great time.

Even if they spoke in French and I didn't understand everything, I still laughed with them. It was nice to be with friends that you liked and accepted you. They taught me to sing Happy Birthday in French, we had a small piece of pastry and then some couples went to the dance floor.

Renée asked me if I wanted to dance. I nodded my head silently and we went to the crowded floor. For most dancers, one wouldn't be able to pull a sheet of paper between them except for us. I wasn't sure what I should do? I have never danced with a woman before except when I was younger and danced with my mother at a relative's wedding.

But Renée didn't press it and I was beginning to feel guilty about that. Nevertheless, it was fun and then we went back to our corner with our friends. Everyone was happy. We talked some more but quietly this time. More wine was passed around and we just listened to some sad and melancholy music. Everyone just leaned against each other, smoked, drank, and listened.

At some point, someone put on Edith Piaf. I remembered her from when my mother used to play her records on an old Hi-Fi. Her most famous ones were La Vie En Rose and Padam. My mother used to cry when she heard them. When that song came on, there wasn't a dry eye in the room.

I looked at Renée as she turned to me and there was a tear running down her cheek too. A strand of hair had fallen over her eye, I reached over automatically and swept it behind her ear and wiped the tear off with my thumb. She smiled and put her arm around me. I put my head on her shoulder and we somehow connected right this moment more so than all the past time I spend with her.

Then something aroused in me, I wasn't sure what it was but I knew that Renée was my best friend, my intimate friend and I haven't really seen this till now. I turned to her again and she was looking straight into my eyes. I blinked a few times and came closer to her as she came closer to me. Our lips met and my life changed at that moment. We both stood up as if we had been lifted by the strings of a puppeteer and walked out the door silently through the crowd, holding hands. Once outdoors we hailed a cab and went home.

Eighteen: Authors Too

Sam Gottlieb sat in the shade on his porch with a cool gin and tonic next to him, writing his latest novel on his laptop. With 54 novels and eight feature films under his belt in more than forty years, he was in no hurry to finish his fifty-fifths.

He stopped a moment, took a drink of his gin and tonic, looked around for the thousand's time, and wondered at his success. As a young man from Brooklyn born of immigrants, he did quite well for himself. But life wasn't always so good to him. He had his tragedy which to this day influenced his life. His wife, after only ten years of marriage, has passed away from cancer leaving him without children. They were always too busy and by the time they were ready, it was too late. To get away from his city apartment, he purchased this house in South Hampton on a lonely stretch of road next to the beach with only one neighbor adjacent to him.

Sam valued his privacy, in fact, he wrote his books under a pen name so no one except his publisher knew who he was. At no time, despite his publisher's constant nagging, did he ever go to a book signing or any publicity event. Sam was a loner and saw very few people.

However, Sam didn't lock himself in the house and become a hermit. He went out to eat at local eateries and of course, did his shopping in local shops but no one knew who he really was. He had a cleaning woman once a week and a gardener for his little garden in memory of his wife. He was friendly with his neighbor, the Franklins, and some others in town and with his own family. He gave to causes though no one knew where this money came from. And so Sam lived this quiet life until today when he suddenly heard children's laughter coming from the Franklin house.

He knew the Franklins were away for the summer in Europe and that they told him they would have some distant relatives stay in their house till they come back but nothing was said about children. Not that Sam disliked children, his sister had three, which he saw on holidays and when they on occasion, stayed with him on weekends, it's just that he didn't expect any next door. He thought he would have a quiet summer for his writing. He didn't want to shut himself up in his office with the air conditioner humming in his ear just to escape a few boisterous kids.

But in a few minutes, things quieted down and Sam began to type again. He had already written almost ten thousand words and things were going well. He had seldom run into writer's block; it was almost as if he was born to write. Tap, tap, tap his fingers flew over the keyboard of his laptop, like a pianist playing a sonata, just as if he had words appear right in front of him as sheet music.

He stopped a moment to take another drink, dried his fingers from the condensation on the glass, and began his taping again when he saw movement from the backyard of the Franklins. "Excuse us, Mr. Gottlieb...?" Sam stopped pecking and looked up. There was a woman standing there with two children about twelve years old. In her hand, she had a paper bag that looked like it carried a bottle. She waved.

"We're sorry to interrupt you, I see you're working... we just came into the Franklins house and thought we'd introduce ourselves as we'll be neighbors for the next few weeks." She seemed a handsome woman, about 35 to forty years old or so Sam thought, due to the ages of the children. He stood up and greeted them hello.

She apologized again. "As a goodwill gesture, I come bearing gifts." She said that in an impish way. "The Franklins told me you like a good gin..." as she took out a bottle of Bombay Gin handing it to him. Sam didn't know what to say. He took the bottle offered and smiled back. "This certainly wasn't necessary Mrs..."

"It's Ellen Woods but please just call me Ellen and these two monsters are Scott and Anne. We won't keep you so you can get back to work." All of a sudden Sam remembered his manners. "Please, can I get you something? A cold drink perhaps?" "Thank you, perhaps another time, we just came in and need to unpack. I have to get these two ready for sleep- away camp tomorrow so we have to unpack and re-pack again," said Ellen. As Sam watched them go he thought he had seen this woman before.

He was certain he never met her personally but somehow she looked familiar. Anyway, he looked at the bottle of gin and marveled that the Franklins told this woman to get one for him. Perhaps a bribe for letting her bring her children.

Ellen went back to the house and started to unpack and repack the clothing the kids will take for camp. She was done in about an hour and just wanted to sit down and have a nice cup of tea. She send the kids away to play on the beach and got her laptop, thinking she would write down a few ideas she had while driving here from New York City. Ellen was a very popular children's book writer with millions of books sold all over the world. She was divorced now for over a year from a husband that couldn't appreciate her making more money than him, especially since he was a stockbroker. To make the divorce easier on him she gave up their summer home in the Berkshires and so she came to the Hamptons where the Franklins, who were cousins on her mother's side, offered, that she could stay while they were away. Fortunately, there was a camp nearby for the kids where they can sleep in during the week and come home on weekends. This gave her the time to write her latest book and also spend time with the children.

When she opened her laptop, the screen seemed dim and she saw that the battery was almost dead. It was then that she realized she forgot her charger, again. This is not the first time she did this because the charger was always plugged into a wall socket in her office at home and in the rush of packing, it stayed there. Each time she had promised herself she'd get a few spares and keep them in the laptop bag or in the car but she always forgot. What to do now? Where is she going to get a charger here?

It was pointless to get upset, it wouldn't help anyway. She made her cup of tea and sat herself down on the back patio with just a pad where she had made some notes the night before. She put on some music she had downloaded on her phone and sat sipping her tea and tried to expand some of her ideas while listening to Mozart.

Sam went back to writing but couldn't concentrate. It bothered him that he couldn't remember where he saw this woman before. He made himself another gin and tonic and stared at the screen. A sentence or two came to his mind and he pecked it out. It was then that Mozart came floating in the air. Sam liked Mozart but not when he was writing. He needed total silence to concentrate. He would have to have a talk with Ms. Woods.

Suddenly Ellen thought that Sam looked like he had the same type of laptop and therefore must have a charger. She would go over and ask if he could charge her computer's battery and tomorrow she would go to town and get a few chargers herself. She didn't think it was too much to ask. She hoped...

After a while, the music stopped and Sam could concentrate on his writing again but nothing came forth now that his concentration was broken. He took a sip and stared at the screen wondering how he knew this

Wood woman and why does he even care whether he recognized her or not. "Who cares..." he said out loud to himself.

He was about to type out another sentence that came to him when out there from the back yard the woman was coming over to him again, this time holding a laptop. "Hi, excuse me for interrupting, again," she said coyly, "I'm sorry, I see that you're still busy but I just need a small favor if you can do it…" .

Sam was a bit perturbed. He stopped in mid-stroke and looked up. They'll never let me go on, he thought to himself with a smile because Ellen was smiling too and then it hit him. By chance he saw her on TV just the other day being interviewed, though he flipped the channel so fast, he didn't get her name or why she was being interviewed. A politician? No. He would have known about her because he was a political junky. Well, he's sure to find out soon.

"What can I do for you?" he asked in a friendly tone. "It's my laptop, my battery is almost dead and I forgot to bring my charger. I'll go tomorrow and try to get one in an electronic store. In the meantime, may I…" "Of course, I have one in the office. Come up, we'll plug it in."

As they walked to his office Sam said that he believed he saw her on TV a couple of days ago. "I just caught the last few seconds so I didn't catch who you were." "Oh, that," Ellen said. "I guess that must have been on the TV morning show. It was about the publication of my new children's book." "You write children's books?" asked Sam puzzled.

"Yes. Well, I'm sure a children's book author wouldn't have interested you. I write for young adults." "Oh," said Sam. He almost blurted out about his publications but caught himself in time. There was no reason to give himself away just because she was an author too. Instead, he took her laptop and plugged it into the charger. "This should take a couple of hours or so." Then he remembered his hospitality again. "Would you like to wait and have a drink…"

It was the first time he actually invited a woman for anything after his wife passed away. "Well, I… Okay, if you don't think I'm keeping you from your work, I see you're doing some writing on your laptop." "It's nothing, I'm retired and I just scribble sometimes just to keep my mind busy?"

"Anything interesting? I don't mean to pry." "Not yet…"

As they were walking out of the office, Ellen saw a collection of Patricia Hemings' books on a shelf. "I see you are a big fan of Patricia Hemings," she said. Patricia Hemings is one of the most popular romance and suspense writers in the world. "Actually, I'm a fan myself."

"Really? I thought they just look good on the shelf. It's my sister's collection for when she comes for a visit." He lied though he felt a little guilty for it.

"Well, I read them on long trips for book signings. They take away the boredom in airports and on long flights to the West Coast or Europe." "I suppose…" Sam answered as if he didn't care. They went outside and Sam motioned her to sit in one of the chairs while he got her a drink, she just wanted some ice water. "So what do you do Sam… Uh, may I call you Sam?"

"Of course, Well, I'm retired so I don't do much. I'm trying to write something about my parents' life before they came to America. They came from Poland and escaped the Germans to Russia. It's a miracle how they survived there." Actually, while he was saying it he was wondering why he never thought about writing about that before. Maybe because his parents never talked about it. In any case, he hated lying to Ellen but he wasn't about to tell her the truth about what he actually wrote.

"That sounds very interesting," Ellen said. "My parents also survived the war in Europe. Now that you mention it, I wonder why that idea didn't come to me as well. Maybe I could write something like that for a children's book." And so they spent some time on that subject while Sam began to have a guilty feeling for his lie.

"Mom! Mom! Where are you!" Ellen stood up and called out. "I'm here on Mr. Gottlieb's porch, I'll be right over." She turned to Sam. "Can I just leave the laptop here till it gets all charged up? I'll pick it up a bit later."

"Of course, no problem," said Sam as Ellen walked out to her kids.

Sam watched her go and wondered how old she really was, probably not more than her mid-thirties. So what was he doing suddenly having carnal thoughts about her? 'Idiot,' he thought to himself, 'you're old enough to be her father, for crying out loud.' He turned back to his laptop. Ellen returned to her house as her kids looked at her questionably.

"How come you were over there?" Anne asked. She made nothing of it and explained about her laptop battery dying and Mr. Gottlieb was kind enough to charge it for her. "So you had fun at the beach?" She asked, changing the subject. "So what's for dinner?" asked Scott.

'Hmm, maybe we'll make a barbecue, I brought some hamburger meat and hot dogs, some corn, and I think we have some baked beans and salad. What do you say?" Scott was all for it but Anne made a smirky face. Even at twelve, she was watching her skinny figure. "What about some veggies?"

"For you, I brought some special veggie burgers hand-made in the deli." "Okay! I'm going to take a shower." And she ran upstairs to her room. Ellen winked at Scott who winked back. "Girls!" "Go wash up..." his mother said.

An hour later Ellen was preparing the food and the barbecue when Anne came down. "Honey, do me a favor and go to Mr. Gottlieb and bring back my laptop. It should be all charged up by now and thank him for it. Also maybe let's ask him to come for dinner, it's the least I can do for letting him charge up my battery. Okay?"

"You want to invite a stranger for dinner, Mom?" "Oh, he's not a stranger, he's our neighbor, he's OK. He's really a very nice man once you get to know him." At least she hoped so. "Come on you be nice too..." "Okay," she grumbled. "And tell him he doesn't need to bring anything! Dinner will be ready in about half an hour or so."

Anne went a bit reluctantly to Mr. Gottlieb's backyard and saw him sitting by his laptop staring at the screen. "Hi," she said. "I'm Anne from next door." Sam looked up and smiled. Another interruption. Anne was a gangly young girl but pretty in the face. Oh well... "Hi yourself." He said smilingly. "I guess your mother sent you over for her laptop. I'll see if it's ready. Come on up. Would you like a drink or something? A beer or wine?" he said jokingly.

"Uh, no thanks. I'm okay." Sam came back and handed her the laptop. "I was just kidding about the beer and wine you know." He handed her the laptop smiling. "Be careful it's a bit heavy." "Oh, okay. Oh," she said again. "I almost forgot. Mom said you should come over for dinner in about half an hour."

Forty-five minutes later, Sam walked over next door with a bottle of wine. He couldn't find anything in the house for the kids. "Didn't Anne tell you that you didn't have to bring anything?" said Ellen looking at her daughter. Anne looked down embarrassed. "Um, I'm sorry, I forgot." "It's okay. I'll just take it back then" retorted Sam with a grin. Everything was laid out under a tent gazebo. Ellen pointed to a seat for Sam. "You need any help?" he asked.

"Nope, been doing this for years while the menfolk went a-huntin' for victuals in Western Massachusetts." The food was good. Apparently, Ellen was a good cook. Sam never ate much anyway; he just had a burger and a frank with beans and drank Ellen's beer. She made him promise to take his bottle back. During the meal, he told them about the Hamptons as this really was their first trip here having spent their summers in the Berkshires.

Then out of the blue Anne asked Sam what he did. "Anne, it's not polite to ask Mr. Gottlieb such a question." Sam felt guilty about that too, he liked the kids. In fact, it was probably the first time he had ever spent more than ten minutes with kids around except his sister's children. He wasn't going to tell them the truth of course but being a fast thinker he would tell them something. Another lie...

"I'll tell you but you must keep it a secret." They both answered that they would. Sam looked at Ellen questionably. "Oh, sure. Cross my heart and so forth." She quipped. Sam bent over conspiratorially and whispered out loud. "I worked for the CIA; my code name was

DANGER. I can't talk about any specific missions but they took me all over the world."

You mean like James Bond?" asked Scott in wonder. "Yup. Just like him except for real..." Sam looked at Ellen and winked at her. Ellen looked at Sam as if to challenge him. "Maybe you could tell us at least one old story of a mission from a long time ago..." Sam saw the challenge in her face. Well, he'll show her.

He took his time as if trying to decide if he really should. "OK, but this is for your ears only. No one must ever know. Come closer," he said as he leaned over conspiratorially. "I don't want anyone else to overhear this. They might even be watching me now." He looked around making sure no one else was within earshot. The kids moved closer and after he looked at Ellen again, she rolled her eyes and moved closer.

"It was many years ago, I was sent to Russia to save a famous scientist, whose name I still can't divulge but let's call him Boris Yeltsin..." Ellen had to stifle a laugh. It took Sam about 25 minutes to tell this made-up story which had the kids in total concentration. Even Ellen at times was totally intrigued, though she assumed it was a made-up fairy tale for the kids. Sam was brilliant and she wondered how he made up a story so quickly and what does he really do or did. Maybe he really was a spy...?

After dinner, the kids went into the house to watch TV and he and Ellen sat and talked some more about their parents. Though what Sam said about his parents certainly sounded true, Ellen wondered how much of it she should believe. Sam certainly was a good storyteller as he proved by telling that made-up story about being a spy. Or maybe that was true too. How can anyone make up a story so quickly with all those details?

Then suddenly Sam changed the subject. "By the way where is your husband?" That is what he really wanted to ask her for hours. Ellen gave a lopsided grin. Maybe she should make up some story about him being a prince from some small European principality and suddenly because of his father's death having to go back and take over the reign of the kingdom. But of course, she wasn't as fast as she thought Sam was and the truth is always the best way not to trip up on a story.

"Ah, my husband?" she finally said as she turned to him and took a swallow from her bottle. "My husband is probably spending his nights with his new wife. His ex-secretary. We're divorced for about a year and a half now. He divorced me because I made more money than him and he felt emasculated. He wanted to get himself a Ferrari probably to show off he's a big shot but he didn't make enough to layout almost $350,000 and I wouldn't agree to give him anything towards it because he was past fifty and we didn't need a car like that. I'd rather spend the money on our children's education. So he left me and the kids."

"So, leaving you didn't much help him get that car anyway. I'd rather not say what I think of him." Ellen shook her head and smiled. "No. He got it all right. He sold our summer house in the Berkshires and bought the car. He didn't realize how much it would cost to keep it up, especially the insurance, and where in the city would you drive it. He probably couldn't get it out of first gear on a city street much less speed about at 175 MPH, and so he had to sell it after a few months."

"Idiot," Sam murmured. "So tell me Sam, were you really a spy?" Sam smiled and shook his head but didn't answer. "Well, as long as you're not wanted by the FBI, we can be friends." After 10 they said goodnight. Ellen and the kids had to get up early for camp.

Ellen went up to bed and wondered about Sam Gottlieb herself. For some reason, the man intrigued her. Just the tale he made up about being a spy or even about his parents was fascinating enough for a movie. He must be a writer or something but she knew no one by the name that was even close to being known in publishing. With these thoughts, she fell asleep. Tomorrow they all have to get up early for the camp bus. She had set her alarm for six-thirty.

The next morning Sam thought of an idea. He would go to an electronic store in Riverhead and get her a charger. After a run on the beach and a quick breakfast, he put on his street clothes, grabbed his car keys, and walked out the door just as Ellen walked out of her house towards her car. "Good morning," she greeted him. "And a good morning to you?

Where are you off to so early?" he asked. "Well, I don't want to impose on you again to charge me up, so I'm off to get my own." There goes his idea about him buying her a charger but he wasn't a million bookseller for nothing.

"I was heading to buy some batteries for my flashlight, why don't I give you a ride, I know this area like the back of my hand." "You sure you have nothing better to do? I mean I could get some batteries for you." "Come get in. Anything that I have to do, can wait and it gets me out of the house."

Ellen got in and strapped herself into the seat. It was an older Cadillac convertible but looked brand new. For some reason, she thought that perhaps Sam might even have a Ferrari hidden in his garage. With her luck, he could have bought her husband's.

"What? No Ferrari?" she joked. "I only buy American," quipped Sam. It was a pleasant morning in the Hamptons, for a change, the humidity dropped into the 40s. Sam drove like an expert through Southampton's spidery streets without a GPS telling him where to make a turn. Neither spoke for a while. Ellen's long hair blew from the wind like a wave in the ocean.

"There's a scarf in the glove compartment if you like." Ellen opened the compartment and withdrew a long colorful scarf and wrapped it around her hair wondering how many women wore this when Sam took them for a ride. "It's for my sister when she comes for an occasional visit. It's brand new."

It seemed to Ellen that this guy has an answer for everything. In any case, it's none of her business though she was glad no one wore it before. "The kids got the bus okay?" Sam asked. "With seconds to spare," said Ellen. "They still talked about your heroic acts from your last night's story. "Right? Well, every word was true. They will keep it a secret as they promised." Ellen laughed. "Of course." "You don't believe me?" "No."

"I write fiction, I sold many books under a pen mane that I don't want to divulge right now. I'm sorry. It's important to me not to be a celebrity. I just don't like it and I don't want people to follow me around and I don't want TV interviewers or paparazzi outside my house. I have nothing to be ashamed of in my life I just don't want publicity."

Ellen looked at him but said nothing. She was almost the opposite. She sold millions of books too but she's been interviewed many times on TV and in magazines but the paparazzi don't follow her around much, a children's book writer isn't worth their effort but she understands people like Sam. If even that was true? "There's a large store in Riverhead; I'll take you there."

"I truly hope I'm not taking you out of your way," she said again. "I'm tired of sitting in the house all day looking at a screen. I'm glad to have an excuse to get out." They were on Sunrise Highway close to Hampton Bay. "Have you had breakfast yet?" asked Sam suddenly. "Breakfast? No, not really I made something for the kids but only had some orange juice myself." "Good! Let's stop at the Canal Cafe in Hampton Bays and have something." "Is it far?" "Not far." In a few minutes, Sam pulled into the parking lot of the cafe he sometimes eats in just to get away from the house.

A waitress who knows him showed them a booth overlooking the harbor and left some menus.

Ellen looked out the window. "Pretty little harbor here. I lived in New York all my life but never came here. Isn't that sad?" "In a way, I'm glad that I am the first to show it to you..." "Are you ready to order?" The waitress interrupted their thoughts. Sam looked at Ellen. "Hmm, everything looks so good," she said, "maybe just some scrambled eggs with cheese, whole- wheat toast, no potatoes, and a decaf."

"Okay." The waitress looked at Sam. "I'll have the same with an extra order of your blueberry pancakes. They make the best around here, and we'll just share." The waitress repeated the order and left.

Both watched the little boats swaying in the marina in quiet meditation. Sam was fighting his nerves not really knowing his sudden feelings towards this woman and Ellen wasn't sure what she is doing here with this man, especially on her first day in the Hamptons. She hoped he was not taking this, relationship, or whatever, seriously, though she suspected that Sam might be. You'd have to be blind not to notice. Sure, she liked Sam too but she knew him, what? Twenty-four hours? Even less.

Food came with extra plates to share the pancakes. It was good country food, fresh from the farms around there. When they finished eating Sam took her around and showed her the harbor and the locks and explained some of the historical sights. Ellen was impressed by his knowledge of minutia. It was as if she was following a tour guide.

"I hope I'm not boring you too much," he said. "Actually there might be a good story here for a children's book. That's why I brought you here." He said trying to explain himself. "Plenty of pictures of boats and old houses. They used to go whaling from here. I know it's not a politically correct subject now but the men used to go out for a two-year journey from here and some never came back. Sailing in those days was a very dangerous occupation. I also looked you up online and saw your artwork. You're a very good illustrator."

"You actually looked me up, Sam?" "Well, I had to. You think I believe everything anyone tells me?" Ellen shook her head and laughed. "Okay, let's move on to the chargers. Onward to Riverhead." "Is it far, the store?" "No, about fifteen more minutes. You in a hurry?" "No. I'm not but I'm afraid I'm taking up much of your time. You probably could have gotten batteries in any store in the village." "I probably could but I don't like the owner of the store," Sam lied.

They rode quietly again. In another fifteen minutes, Sam pulled into the parking lot of a popular electronic store and they walked in and looked where the chargers could be found. Ellen bought two just in case and they left. It was only a few minutes into the drive home that Ellen realized Sam hadn't bought any batteries, but she kept it quiet.

The road back seemed longer but she took in the sights with an occasional comment from Sam of a famous landmark. When they got home, Ellen thanked Sam again and they each went into their own house with a 'see you later.

Sam went inside, grabbed a beer, and laid down on the couch. He had such a simple life only twenty-four hours ago. He was a bachelor all those years and it hasn't fazed him a bit. Now this woman is changing his life and he hardly knows her. She could be a bitch and that's why her husband left her as far as he knew. How is he going to get out of this? Does he want to get out of this? He couldn't understand how someone he hardly knew could get so under his skin.

Ellen walked into her house a little confused. She put the chargers on the table and took out a bottle of white wine and poured herself a full glass even though it was still early in the day and went upstairs to her bedroom. The house was as quiet as in the Berkshires. The only sounds were the waves beating on the shore and a fly buzzing somewhere in the room. She was used to loud noises in her East-side townhouse. Horns blaring. People shouting. All that went over her head without notice but this quiet was suddenly driving her crazy and that will last till her kids come home Friday afternoon.

In the meantime, she wasn't in the mood to start to write anything, not that she had any ideas anyway. Whaling of all things. She could just see her publisher looking at her in shock. She laid down on the bed and watched the blades of the ceiling fan turn hypnotically above her. What is going on in her head? She was so happy till she got here. She couldn't believe that this man could suddenly beguile her so.

He suggested that he was a writer but how does she really know that? She has never read anything of his though he certainly told fantastic tales. She sat up, swallowed the whole glass of wine in one gulp, and laid down again. As she watched the fan turn, she fell asleep.

Sam had also fallen asleep without even realizing it. A half-spilled bottle laying on the floor beside him. He cleaned it up quickly before the room smelled of beer. He looked at the clock and realized that it was almost seven in the evening. He hardly ever did that, sleeping during the day. He went to the fridge and saw what was there to eat. He saw a dish from a few days ago that his wife taught him to make. A Stir-fried Beef with Eggplant. About as appetizing as a rubber sole. He had no appetite anyway. He went to his laptop and opened a new document. He would write the story of his parents even though he didn't have all the facts. He knew enough of those times to write it almost blindfolded but as fiction.

At eight o'clock, Ellen woke up with a headache. She grabbed a couple of Tylenol and went down to the fridge. She hadn't had lunch and she certainly skipped dinner but looking in she found nothing appetizing. Leftovers from last night she wasn't in the mood. She'll wait till her headache dissipates maybe she'll make herself a salad and tuna sandwich or some eggs.

She went out on the patio and took in the cool air coming from the ocean. On the far end of the yard, there was a hammock tied between two trees. She took a glass of water with her and laid down on it. She thought she felt better already. Though the sky above was blocked by branches she could still see the glimmer of the stars. She'd lay till her head cleared. She looked at her watch, it was past nine-thirty.

The total quietness disturbed her. She was never alone in the Berkshires. Her husband or her kids were always there. She didn't think twice about it. But here it was nerve-racking for a city person. Only the crickets were in full chorus with an occasional bark from a dog somewhere. Otherwise, it was graveyard stillness.

What in the heavens is she going to do? Going into the quiet house was anathema to her now. Every step she took inside, a board squeaked. Eire sounds came from everywhere. A crack here. A squeak there. She thought of maybe going to one of the motels in town but that was ridiculous and there probably wasn't an empty room anyway. She would swallow her pride and ask Sam if she could stay in one of his empty bedrooms. It was of course silly but she just couldn't stay in that silent house alone.

She took a toothbrush and some night accessories in a small bag and walked over to the hedge that separated the properties. She saw a light coming from the back porch and also saw Sam pecking at his laptop. Does she dare? What could he say? No? Go away? Or worse still, laugh at her.

But she didn't think Sam was that kind of person though this certainly is a strange arrangement and she didn't know how Sam would take it. But she didn't want to go back to that squeaky house. She took her chance and walked out into his backyard.

"Ellen?" Sam called out. "Is that you?" "Hi Sam, I'm sorry for disturbing you. May I come over?" "Of course, come on up. What are you doing there in the dark, is everything all right? There is no problem with the kids?" How remarkable that Sam even thought of the kids, Ellen reflected.

"The kids are fine. I just need a favor." "Oh no, don't tell me you lost the chargers again," he said jokingly. Ellen had to laugh. "No Sam, they're fine." Sam came down from the patio and walked her up to the porch and to an Adirondack chair. He seemed happy to see her thought Ellen, so that's a good sign. "Can I get you anything?" "No, thanks but I need to ask you something and if you're not comfortable with it please just say so and I'll understand." Sam looked at Ellen seriously as he sat down opposite her and waited.

Ellen explained that it's probably a silly thing but all of a sudden, she's a bit uneasy being in that quiet empty house by herself. Last night with the kids there, she didn't even think about it but being all alone with only the sound of an insect or a dog barking in the distance just seemed kind of eerie. Could she stay in one of his empty rooms at least for a night?

"Is that all?" Sam asked. "I thought, well I didn't know what to think. Of course, you can stay. Stay as long as you like. It would be nice to have a guest for a change. I'm so used to the quiet that when I go to New York for a few days to see my publisher, the noises drive me crazy. Let me get you some fresh sheets and blankets and pillows and whatever else you need. You have a toothbrush?"

In fifteen minutes, a fresh bed was made up. It was still too early to go to bed so Sam sat her down again and brought her a cup of tea. It was then that her stomach grumbled. "Sorry, I haven't eaten anything since breakfast," she said. "I have some food in the fridge I can get..."

"Don't be silly, I'll make us a grilled cheese sandwich that is out of this world." After eating and drinking they sat again and like Ellen did before, they stared at the sky. "A marvelous sight isn't it. I wonder if there is another civilization like us up there somewhere." Ellen quipped. "God, I hope not like us. I hope they have better brains not to cause themselves all the problems we have in this world." "You certainly know the right thing to say, Sam."

Sam laughed. He had a deep basso laugh which she thought was very nice. "I saw you on your machine. Did you finally start your story?" "Yes, about my parents." Ellen smiled. "Really?" "I'll let you read it tomorrow" "I would like that," said Ellen. "Sam, may I ask you a serious question first. No jokes. Do you mind?" She asked pensively. "Shoot..."

"Are you really an author or are you just pulling my leg? Please, I don't mean to imply you're not but perhaps you're a reporter or some technical writer or scientific writer or something else. I mean, I write children's books, that doesn't mean that anything else is..."

Sam looked at her closely as if he was deciding what to do. After a minute of making his mind up, he stood up. "Okay, okay. Come with me. I want to show you something." Sam took her hand and walked her to his office putting on the light. "Now, as before, I need to trust you on this. No one must know. This is no joke" Ellen shook her head as she stared at his serious look. She was going to raise her hand and swear but thought it might be overdone.

Sam pointed to the volumes of Patricia Hemings' collection on the shelf plus a box set of eight films. "I am Patricia Hemings," he said looking straight into her eyes. Ellen put her hand towards her mouth. "What?" Sam didn't repeat himself, just kept looking at her then went to a drawer and pulled out computer disks all marked with the name of his stories.

"These are my files. I kept all the revisions and saved them on these disks. I also have duplicates in my vault at the bank." "You are Patricia Hemings? The Patricia Hemings? The Patricia Hemings the world would pay anything to find out?" Sam smiled, "Is there any other? Hard to believe an old Jewish man from Queens wrote all these..." he said grinning like a man that just explained the meaning of life. "So yes. I am a writer, author, whatever. Perhaps not a Shakespeare or a Hemingway, but still one of those." "I... I don't know what to say. No wonder you don't want the world

to know. You're a man..." "Last time I looked, yes," he said. "Sam, do you have something hard. I really need a stiff one." When that came out Ellen turned red in the face. "I meant something like brandy or whiskey or..." "I know what you meant, I'm not a dirty old man. Yet." He laughed.

Sam went to a small bar and poured off some Napoleon brandy into a sniffer and handed it to her. "Do you mind if I sit down? I just don't know what to say. I..." She drank it down in three gulps. Sam took the glass back and poured a bit more into it and handed it back. Ellen's face was still flushed. If she was a reporter and wrote about this, her paper would be sold out in five minutes. Everybody would like to know who Patricia Hemings was. Her, his books sold in millions. It would be headline news. Sam leaned against the bookshelf with hands clasped across his chest.

"WOW!" Is all Ellen had to say. "It's okay, you don't have to make a big deal about it. Even I wonder myself sometimes how I did it." "Sam, you are a WONDER!" When they came back out on the porch, Sam explained why he chose to write as a woman. "Can you imagine selling romance novels as Sam Gottlieb... Anyway, it's getting late would you like to go up? You must be exhausted."

"Maybe I should, it's been a long day..." "Not another word. Go up, have a good rest, and pleasant dreams. I'll lock up down here." Ellen brushed her teeth and got ready for bed. This is going to be a long night. She noticed Sam had put a few bottles of water and a glass on the bedside table and she smiled to herself. Sam certainly was a thoughtful person.

There was actually one of his books on the night table, perhaps as he said from his sister's visit. As tired as she was she picked it up and got into bed. It was one of his first publications which she read a million years ago but started up again. She remembered it was a really good book about a young woman who lost her lover that was wounded during the civil war and she went out to search for him.

It was sad and poignant and sold over two million copies and made into a movie. How this man could write like that from a woman's point of view was beyond her understanding. In about half an hour she closed the book and shut the light. The night sky shone through the window and she didn't need a night light.

Another hour or so must have passed and she still couldn't fall asleep thinking about Sam as the author of these books. Or maybe it was a strange bed or that the man she hardly knew was sleeping behind the wall or that she just found out a secret that everyone would have liked to know. She just couldn't sleep. She got out of bed and then noticed a door that seemed to go to a balcony. As she opened the French doors a cool breeze embraced her and from there she could see the ocean with a quarter moon reflecting on the surface. Almost a romantic sight.

She took a quilt that covered a sofa and wrapped herself up stepping outside when a voice from the dark startled her. "Couldn't sleep either?" It was Sam, of course, sitting on his side of the balcony. "Hope I didn't startle you." "A little I guess. I just can't fall asleep," she said. "Me too. Come sit down, it's nice out here. Let me pour you a glass of wine."

Ellen sat down across from him and took the offered glass and drank what she thought was a Rosé. Somehow she didn't think Sam would be a Rosé drinker but it was a good vintage. She loved Rosé. It was sweet and tangy. She liked it better than the dry wines. Then she wondered why Sam would have a second glass with him. Was he really expecting her? Would he really know she liked Rosé?

"I love this time of night during the summer. Look how brightly the stars shine here. Can't get that view in the City," Sam said pointing at the stars. "No you can't," Ellen said hoarsely. What is she doing out here with this man? "You know, you are so lucky to have those two children, they are so nice. I never had kids. Now I'm a bit sorry I guess," said Sam wistfully.

Ellen was surprised that Sam brought up the kids at a time like this. Nevertheless. "Thank you, Sam, they are nice kids. May I ask you if you were ever married?" Sam told her his story while looking up at the night sky. For some reason, it wasn't as hard as he thought it might be.

"We wanted kids but couldn't so we decided to adopt. We filled out a ton of papers and waited and waited and then we got the news that a child was available. A woman was in her 2nd Trimester and her man left her so she wanted her baby to be adopted. It was great news and then, my wife got ill. It was so sudden that we couldn't do anything about it. She died the day the baby was born."

Of course, he couldn't take the child now, and besides, he was beside himself with grief. When he finished he looked at Ellen with a wry smile. "That was so many years ago and yet I remember it as if it was yesterday."

"Oh, Sam, I am so sorry and you never thought of remarrying?" Sam felt a lump in his throat. "I guess I just didn't find anyone interesting enough." And then you came along, he thought silently to himself, but you're so young.

They sat quietly for another few minutes. "What about you, you planning to get married again? You're certainly too young to be alone the rest of your life," Sam said to Ellen. "I don't know. Haven't thought about it much. Been busy with the kids and thinking about my latest book I guess. I suppose the kids would like a man around the house..."

"You know Ellen if I was only thirty years younger..." Sam said out of the blue. Ellen was getting warm despite the cool breeze blowing in the night. Perhaps it was the Rosé though she doubted it. "Thirty years?" she asked. "Why, how old are you Sam? I'd guess in the fifties. No?" "Ha! Now that's a compliment. A little older," he said. "Well, how old do you think I am then?"

Sam took a swallow before he answered. Telling a woman's age can get you in a lot of trouble. Better chance on the younger side, but in any case, he had her pegged mid-thirties, maybe a year or two more. Certainly not past forty. "I know I'm getting myself into trouble so forgive me but I thought, because of the kids, you're about in your thirties, about mid-thirties I'd guess." Ellen burst out laughing spilling some of her Rosé on the quilt. "Sam you are a winner for sure. But it's very kind of you..." "You mean you're younger?" He laughed himself. "Next January 17th, I'll be forty-nine..." she said with a serious face.

"Forty-nine? " Sam didn't believe how he could have mistaken her age so, she certainly looked younger to him. "But your kids are about eleven or twelve..," he said. "Sam, as you know, a woman can have children past middle age. But I couldn't in any case. My story is almost the same as your wife's. My two children were adopted. I couldn't have any myself. That's another reason my husband gave me such an easy divorce. He didn't want children; he wanted a Ferrari. But I was a children's book writer. How could I write children's books if I didn't have children of my own to please? Scott is 10 and Anne is twelve. We were lucky to get them both at the same time. A boy and a girl. They're wonderful kids. I love them as if they were my own. They are my own!"

For the first time probably, Sam was at a loss for words. He leaned over and took Ellen's hands in his. "In many ways, we have so much in common. We are both writers. We both couldn't have children. At least you adopted. We both are a bunch of old farts, at least you fooled me at first but now as I look closer you do look a bit wrinkled," he said jokingly and squeezed her hand, "but the moment I saw you, something clicked inside of me which I have only felt once before."

"It was the same with my wife. I saw her come down an escalator at Macy's as I was going up. I quickly turned around and ran after her. We married ten days later. It was the happiest time of my life. She died almost to the day we met almost as if it was written somewhere in the stars." "Actually, see that star?" Sam pointed to a star in the Little Dipper. "It's the brightest star that forms the bowl. It was named Kochab by Arab astronomers but I renamed it for her. Edith. I know, it sounds comical but I guess not as funny as Kochab."

Ellen smiled. Always the funny man even in misfortune. She saw which way Sam was heading. She'll bet her Pulitzer he's going to ask to marry her. What is she going to say? Twenty-four hours is not a long time to know a person but as he said it sometimes happens. Especially in many of the romantic novels he wrote. Does she feel that way about him? Their age gulf at this stage doesn't make much difference. What're fifteen years? He does seem to like her children though, that would be an important thing. His looks? Well, he's not a bad-looking man. He's tall. Seems in good shape. A good head of hair, gray, but then so is hers if she didn't color it every few months. Well, maybe she's just jumping the gun. Maybe he just wants her to jump into bed with him. Not that she'd mind at this stage.

After all, it has been a long time...

With that though, Ellen started to giggle to herself. "Kochab is that funny?" he asked. "No. I wasn't laughing about Kochab. I was just thinking of something else. "Okay, then let me ask you something else. Are there any men in your life? Men of interest or a fiancé or anything like that?" "Of hand, I don't think so but I'm pretty tired. I'll check in the morning to be sure..."

"We're not even engaged and you're giving me a hard time.""Oh Sam, you're sweet. No, I don't have anyone special. Why are you asking? You're interested? "I was till you started to give me a pain in the ass," Sam whispered quietly with a smile.

Ellen smiled back. "Sam- today is only Tuesday. Give a lady at least another day to make up her mind." "Okay, it's late, let's hit the sack. Is your bed comfortable?" he asked. They both went to their rooms content but deep in thought. Ellen was worn out and fell into a deep sleep right away. When she got up late in the morning she smelled coffee downstairs.

Nineteen: The Old Photograph

It was to be a plum assignment and I approached it with the knowledge that this would be the crowning achievement before my retirement. I was asked to put together a retrospective on the work of the world- renowned photo- journalist Robert Whitmore. In two years, he would approach his eightieth birthday and he thought it fitting to ask my firm to publish his photographs for that occasion. Robert Whitmore was to arrive in New York and meet with me for the initial conference in a few days.

Although I was a great admirer of his, I had never met him in person, therefore I was not surprised that he stared at me for a long moment when he entered my office, for I have a rather peculiar scar on my face, a souvenir from the Battle of the Bulge in 1944. "You must forgive me old chap," he said in his upper-class British public-school accent I heard him use so many times on TV interviews. "You have a face that would be hard to forget, eh?" Before I could reply he waved me off. "I have seen you someplace before, I never forget a face, although for the moment it escapes me where.

Never mind, it shall come to me." He said to the point as always, and with that, we sat down at the conference table to discuss his book.

Whitmore was a prolific photographer; he had been everywhere and seen everything important since the Spanish Civil War in 1935 and through our involvement in Vietnam. But when he left he didn't forget

277

to remind me that he'll look through his archives as he was certain he had a picture of me somewhere, though how or when he took it, I couldn't imagine.

Some weeks passed and, in the meantime,, my mind was preoccupied with other things and I had forgotten all about it. Then, one Saturday at a party my wife and I were giving for our granddaughter's 16th birthday, a special delivery came in the mail in the form of an eight by ten manila envelope postmarked from London. It was from Whitmore. I took the envelope towards the kitchen where I was mixing drinks for our family and friends who were outside in the garden.

I was anxious to know what the contents were because his work always arrived at my office in the city rather than this time at my home, so I put the drinks aside and opened the envelope. There were two photographs clipped together, with a handwritten note torn from an old memo pad. The note, written in the undisguised scribble of an old man read. "Reims, France, April 18, 1945. That is you in the picture, isn't it old boy? And I wonder," it continued," if what's in the other photograph is what you were looking at?"

As I looked at the top picture, now yellowed with age, a smile broke over my face, for there I was, a somber young officer, sitting at an old cafe a month or so before the war ended. My brand new scar sharply etched on my left cheek. I appeared to be looking at something across the street. My God, this was more than forty years ago.

And then I turned to the next photograph and the blood drained from my face. It was an unassuming black and white picture of two young women by a doorway looking out towards the street. My eyes looked up through my kitchen window and the scene framed itself in front of me. It was April of 1945. It was only two days before that, that I had been released from a military hospital in Paris from serious wounds I received in an artillery barrage a few months before.

I was attached to the 4th Armored Division then, in Patton's Third Army. We were racing to relieve part of the 101st Airborne surrounded in Bastogne, an unknown village then, in the middle of Belgium. I had been in command of a reconnaissance platoon of half-tracks with a mission of finding the enemy as soon as possible and report them back to HQ.

The weather was brutally cold that winter, with snowdrifts up to three feet or more and the temperature falling mostly below freezing. Dark snow- laden clouds constantly pressed down on us like a limitless dirty blanket. We had not seen the sun in over a week. My platoon had advanced for over 36 hours without any rest or even time out for a hot meal when we spotted a smoldering farmhouse silhouetted against the gray horizon.

It appeared unoccupied by the enemy so I thought we would take advantage of this opportunity and rest for a moment before pushing further north where we thought the Germans were. This would also give my men a chance to cook themselves a well-earned hot meal. I dispersed part of my platoon to stand guard while the rest would take turns eating in the kitchen, which surprisingly still had its roof and one of its windows intact.

My own crew and I were the last to take our turn, when, as I sat down to have my first sip of steaming hot coffee in days, I heard an explosion outside. I leaned back and turned to the window on my left to see what was happening. In that instant, another explosion, directly in front of that window blew all that glass right into the left side of my face and the concussion knocked me onto the floor.

When I awoke I was still in a daze from all the morphine that the medic had filled me with. I was being driven in an ambulance to the field hospital towards the rear of our battle lines. The left side of my face and upper torso were completely bandaged, the medical orderly informing me that it had looked like hamburger meat. The only consolation to me was that I was the only casualty at the time and with that in mind, I slowly succumbed to the morphine.

As it turned out, I sustained other major injuries, but I was back on my feet within 4 months. Everything was back to normal except for my face which was to receive plastic surgery when I returned to the States. The surgeons there, I was told by the army doctors, could perform miracles with skin grafts.

The war, however, was ending, and I insisted that I be allowed to return to my men, who I had been commanding for the past year. Although the army doctors advised against this, in the end, they agreed that my scars would not interfere with my military duties. I took a supply truck that went as far as the French town of Reims where I had to get another ride to my unit. While waiting, I saw this cafe and thought I'd take a breather.

So now I found myself sitting at this café, contemplating life and drinking vintage French Champaign in this ancient French town with its old history of conquests and defeats. Reims is an old place, known for its medieval architecture. Its cathedral dates back to the 6th century, where in later years Joan of Arc led her king to be crowned on its steps. Among other things, it's also the capital of the Champaign industry. Its tree-lined boulevards, now crowded with military uniforms mixed in with the potpourri of war-worn civilian garments, all celebrated the certainty that the war was ending soon.

It was a warm, bright and lazy day, allowing me to enjoy this moment without feeling sorry about myself. My gaze wandered to the far end of the boulevard towards the cathedral to admire its ancient charm. With the afternoon sun striking its spires, it reminded me of that Charles Laughton film, 'The Hunchback of Notre Dame,' which coincidentally, was also the name of this cathedral, without the hunchback of course. I bemused that probably every other cathedral in France has inherited that same name.

Closer down the street, a typically European marquee already displayed American Western films glued over the old German military proclamations, was being scrutinized by eager young boys. There were a number of shops open, though the only goods sold were either cheap souvenirs or black-market items. The smell of freshly baked bread from a nearby bakery permeated the air, trying to compete with the noxious gases of military vehicles passing on their way to the front.

I glanced lazily towards my left, and saw, sitting there, a few tables down from me, what appeared to be a war corresponded. He was busily snapping photographs of the surrounding scene with his 35mm camera. I assumed now, that it must have been Whitmore and that was when he took the picture that I was holding in front of me right now.

I didn't give him much thought then, for at that moment my eyes suddenly caught a glimpse of two young women across the street, framed in a doorway. One was leaning against the door jamb gazing at the crowded sidewalk filled with milling pedestrians. The other, however, sitting on a stool in front, had, I thought one of the most striking profiles I had ever seen. She was perhaps between the ages of 18 and 22, it was hard to tell from across the street where I was sitting, my gaze constantly being interrupted by the flow of traffic

But what was interesting though, was that whenever I looked at her, all I ever saw was her right profile. And whenever she turned my way traffic always obscured my vision of her full face, and as soon as it was clear, she again turned to her left. Turning to see what could possibly hold her interest there, I saw nothing unusual, unless, of course, she was waiting for someone. I continued to watch her. And perhaps it was wishful thinking, but I thought I saw her occasionally when she thought I hadn't looked, gaze at me with a bemused smile on her face. How I wished for her to look in my direction a bit longer so that I could admire what I imagined was a beautiful face but I kept seeing it only from her right side.

Also, I imagined that perhaps she was flirting with me. For many months the only women I've seen were the nurses at the hospital. I thought perhaps I could meet her and we could both share some champagne while I waited, but what right did I have to approach her with that raw face of mine? The scar, still so fresh, still reddened by lack of time to heal. I couldn't face such a beautiful girl in spite of the craving in me.

But I finally decided that I had to do something, I had to satisfy my own curiosity. I couldn't, however, just walk up to her and stare. I had to take a more wily approach. So I finally decided to walk to the end of the corner, making believe that I was fascinated by the architectural views before me. I then crossed the boulevard and began my nonchalant return on her side of the street. As I got closer, apparently, she must have guessed what I was about and put on a scarf that covered the left side of her face. At that time, I wondered why.

Finally, when I stood in front of her, I took off my forage cap and knotted it nervously in my hands, trying somehow to say something in my broken high school French, with sweat forming on my forehead as I faced her. Before I could open my mouth she suddenly removed her scarf and gazed at me with an unsettling look.

At first, all I could see was the reflections of sunlight glistening off her tears as they flowed down her cheeks. But as our eyes met the blood froze in my veins. I have seen many disturbing sights in my years of combat, from men torn apart by explosions or felled down by gun fire with horrible wounds. Things I really could not imagine ever experiencing in my lifetime. The view before me was almost one of those. It was a picture of a young woman that must have been dazzling beyond words but now amazingly disfigured on her face in the same way as I was. She was looking at me with a knowing smile that radiated from her scared face. She had an almost identically burned scar on her left side, it was a virtual mirror image of my wounds.

I couldn't control my emotions. I fell to my knees in front of her and tried to voice my feelings, but nothing came out. My throat was as dry as the desert. I couldn't offer her any solace. All I could do was let my own tears run down my scared face. What possessed me to put my arms around her I couldn't say, but to this day I can still feel the warmth of her hand stroking my face.

"Dad, dad." My daughter coming from the doorway returned me to the present. The vision of yesteryear dissolving in front of me. "We're all waiting for those drinks dad... Didn't you finish making them yet?" My daughter's voice registered in my mind, but my eyes continued staring out that window as I saw the real face, not a vision, turning her head in my direction.

My stomach still knotting as that disarming smile that sustained me all those years since I first saw it across the street from the cafe in Reims, radiated at me. Her scars of course are all gone by now, due to those miracles the plastic surgeons performed in the years after the war. But not all the scars have gone, the internal ones had taken longer to heal, and as far as my own scars, well, at that time we could only afford one scary face, and I guess, by the time we could afford mine, I didn't want to bother with it anymore. "Come on dad, it's Becky's birthday, you're not going to daydream it away, are you?" No, I thought to myself. Not with that woman in front of me. I put the old faded photographs with my dusty memories away in a kitchen drawer. I must remember to write a thank you card to Whitmore; I was certainly impressed by his memory. Picking up the drinks, I walked happily with my daughter towards the laughter in the yard.